Bello:
hidden talent rediscovered

Bello is a digital only imprint of Pan Macmillan, established to breathe new life into previously published, classic books.

At Bello we believe in the timeless power of the imagination, of good story, narrative and entertainment and we want to use digital technology to ensure that many more readers can enjoy these books into the future.

We publish in ebook and Print on Demand formats to bring these wonderful books to new audiences.

About Bello:

www.panmacmillan.com/bello

Sign up to our newsletter to hear about new releases, events and competitions:

www.panmacmillan.com/bellonews

B E L L O

John Prebble

John Prebble was a journalist, novelist, documentarian and historian. He was born in England but his family moved to Canada following WWI, later returning to England where Prebble was educated at Latymer School.

Prebble began his writing life as a journalist in 1934, and drew on his experiences as an artilleryman in WWII when he wrote his first novel, *Where the Sea Breaks*, published in 1944. He joined the Communist Party of Great Britain, but abandoned it after World War II. His Canadian prairie experience also influenced his work: *The Buffalo Soldier* is a historical novel about the American West.

Scottish history formed the subject of many of Prebble's subsequent novels. His Fire and Sword Trilogy, focused on the fall of the clan system in 17th Century Scotland. *Culloden* was the first book, chronicling the defeat of the clans in one pivotal battle. The second book of the trilogy, *The Highland Clearances* (1963), remains one of Prebble's best known works because the subject matter is still one of great historical debate. *Glencoe* (1966), the final book, was a study of the causes and effects of the Glencoe massacre of 1692. His later works, *Mutiny* (1975) and *The King's Jaunt* (1988) extended the theme.

Prebble also co-wrote the screenplay of the film *Zulu*, as well as radio dramas and documentaries. He was awarded an OBE in 1998, just three years before his death.

John Prebble

THE EDGE OF DARKNESS

BELLO

First published in 1947 by Secker & Warburg

This edition published 2012 by Bello
an imprint of Pan Macmillan, a division of Macmillan Publishers Limited
Pan Macmillan, 20 New Wharf Road, London N1 9RR
Basingstoke and Oxford
Associated companies throughout the world

www.panmacmillan.com/imprints/bello
www.curtisbrown.co.uk

ISBN 978-1-4472-3370-1 EPUB
ISBN 978-1-4472-3395-5 POD

Copyright © John Prebble, 1947

The right of John Prebble to be identified as the
author of this work has been asserted in accordance
with the Copyright, Designs and Patents Act 1988.

Every effort has been made to contact the copyright holders of the material
reproduced in this book. If any have been inadvertently overlooked, the publisher
will be pleased to make restitution at the earliest opportunity.

You may not copy, store, distribute, transmit, reproduce or otherwise
make available this publication (or any part of it) in any form, or by any means
(electronic, digital, optical, mechanical, photocopying, recording or otherwise),
without the prior written permission of the publisher. Any person who does
any unauthorized act in relation to this publication may be liable to
criminal prosecution and civil claims for damages.

The Macmillan Group has no responsibility for the information provided by
any author websites whose address you obtain from this book ('author websites').
The inclusion of author website addresses in this book does not constitute
an endorsement by or association with us of such sites or the content,
products, advertising or other materials presented on such sites.

This book remains true to the original in every way. Some aspects may appear
out-of-date to modern-day readers. Bello makes no apology for this, as to retrospectively
change any content would be anachronistic and undermine the authenticity of the original.
Bello has no responsibility for the content of the material in this book. The opinions
expressed are those of the author and do not constitute an endorsement by,
or association with, us of the characterization and content.

A CIP catalogue record for this book is available from the British Library.

Visit **www.panmacmillan.com** to read more about all our books
and to buy them. You will also find features, author interviews and
news of any author events, and you can sign up for e-newsletters
so that you're always first to hear about our new releases.

To My Wife and My Sons

Of all things it will be the roads we shall remember best. They formed the circumference of our lives in a world that was as yet indeterminate, as much in process of destruction as liberation. Where the broad face of it was changing vividly beneath the emotions of battle and weather we were assured and comforted by the firm confidence of the roads.

They were strange roads for the most part, and in our memories they will transport our anecdotes from point to point along their routes. Some were cut by the bulldozers from the yellow earth of Normandy or the black mud of Holland. Some were old and ran for miles between long lines of friendly beeches. They were roads that carried us forward, and in our affection we swore at them and remembered them as friends by names or numbers that were our own inventions. We made them part of our lives at the climax of our lives.

They were roads that went forward, always forward. That was a great encouragement to us although we knew that there was an end to them somewhere on the dark edge of the world where the infantry crawled forward and took the earth from the darkness. We began to understand something of the great and simple significance of a road, for upon it we relied for the least and greatest of essentials. The planes in the sky, fresh from England where dreams were maturing, seemed less of a reality to us than the roads beneath our wheels; and without a road that went forward there was nothing.

In historical perspective all those roads will be fused into one.

If we had thought of them longer than to curse them for their craters or their ice-broken surfaces we might have been proud of them. They were not good roads as a Sunday motorist might understand them. But it was something to push a road forward against the edge of darkness. They were to us solid and certain, the basis of things to come after us, even where they climbed the rubble of broken towns, their slender width held by the white tape that kept us from the mines. The road was always there because we were making it, and, whatever lay ahead in the wilderness yet to be cleared, the road itself was there, going forward, pushing back the darkness.

Perhaps, later on, all that may be said of the six years we gave to the task will be that we made a road, and that the labour was hard.

Part One: 1944

1. Jones

The mongrel came out of the darkness into the yellow circle of light from the incandescent lamp. It ran down the muddy roadway between the stables, ran with a ludicrous, side-stepping trot, skirting the wide puddles that reflected the moon and the full-bellied rain clouds that were moving across the sky.

The dog had smelt food, and the hot, sweet odour of the men who were crowded beneath the broken beams of the stable roofs.

In the press, the steaming sweat of their bodies and the wrench of equipment at their shoulders, not many men noticed the dog. Only a few of them snapped their fingers at it, and it ran from one group to another, quickly swallowing the scraps of biscuit held out to it, licking the salty perspiration from the hands that fondled its muzzle. It had never known such affection. It wagged its hind-quarters furiously, its ears lying back along its neck, a pink tongue lolling over its yellow teeth. Its flanks were matted with wet mud and hair, its ribs formed ranges and hollows down the narrow barrel of its wretched body. It had never eaten so much before, but it went on eating, trotting from one dark-faced group to another, gorging the food that was thrown to it. The light of the moon, when it showed its face from behind the rain, shone in the animal's limpid eyes.

In their boredom more and more men began to notice the dog. Something in the poverty of its happiness and the wet wretchedness of its body reflected their own feelings. The dog expressed their excitement vicariously with every quick movement of its wet rump and nervous flutter of its tongue.

A blow in its ribs shook it from its pleasure. It leaped to one side with a yelp of pain as the wooden shoe swung towards it again, and it loped off into the darkness with its head hung low and its nose tracing the whirling currents in the manure and mud. It was as used to kicks as it was unused to generosity, but it quickly forgot both.

'Leave it alone, you little bastard!'

The voice came from behind the glow of a cigarette. The man did not move as he spoke, only the tip of his cigarette flickered up and down with his words. The French boy who had kicked the dog from his path did not understand the words, but he sensed the rebuke. From the doorway of his home in the town, where the smell of cabbage soup filtered out into the rain, he had heard the singing of the soldiers down in the stables. He had buttoned up his jacket to the throat, pulled down his cap to his eyes and slipped off into the darkness expectantly. With his hands in his pockets, thrusting down his trousers until the ends of them curled under his heels, he had shuffled up to the thick, wet, masculine crowd that sheltered there from the rain. He kicked the dog from his path with derisive contempt for an inferior rival. His eyes wide with curiosity, he looked at the man who had rebuked him, and said:

'Cigarette for poppa? *Chocolat?*'

The soldier laughed shortly and spat out his cigarette at the feet of the boy, who picked it up, quickly nipped out the end and stored it away in his pocket. His dirty fingers groped quickly for the chocolate and cigarettes that were occasionally thrust at him. Time was short. He was as yet the only civilian there among the Englishmen, but soon the men would come up from the town, just as he had come, and they would drive him away just as he had driven the dog. He smiled at all who spoke to him, whether he understood them or not, occasionally giving a quick and cunning nod of confirmation. The soldiers called after him jocularly.

'Hey, Charlie! Ten cigarettes, how much?' A pause and then 'Combien Charlie?'

'Dix francs!'

'You've had it! Hey, Charlie, you got a sister? Madamozelle, jig-a-jig, yes?'

The men flung the questions at the boy as idly as they might have skimmed pebbles across a pond. They had been waiting for two hours in the rain. Two hours ago the trucks had brought them from the Reinforcement Unit to the siding, and left them there without explanation. They had not expected any more explanation than that things should continue to happen. But nothing more had happened, and now they waited there without expectation. At dusk it had begun to rain and they had grouped themselves under the stable roofs, five hundred of them, leaving their packs and rifles against the wall, or sitting on them with complete and utter resignation. Earlier there had been officers walking up and down along the muddy roadway between the stables. The rain had gleamed on their white mackintoshes, and those who carried short, leather-covered canes smacked the skirts of their coats sharply, or pointed with them into the darkness of the stables.

They at least had looked as if they knew what was going to happen, and the resentment the soldiers felt was softened somewhat by the respect they held for this knowledge. But no officers had been seen for an hour now. At first the soldiers had not cared, they were glad to be left alone. They grouped themselves under the broken rafters and sang sentimentally. There was an unusual absence of obscenity in their songs. They felt strangely happy in the enjoyment of a vague unconditional freedom from responsibility. Things would happen without their volition and they rejoiced in the animal liberty of slaves. But as the rain drenched through their clothes it was as if it found and gave life to the seed of their self-respect. This flowered truculently. Their tempers grew shorter. They shouted violently into the darkness and called upon their officers with great gusts of obscene derision. Now and then a burst of sardonic laughter would roll down the stables like a wave curling itself lazily on a shingle beach. And they began to sing again, to the melody of 'Adeste Fidelis', a song that had four words only, 'Why are we waiting?' and they sang as soldiers always sing it, with rising volume and feeling.

But it made no difference, and they did not expect that it would. It was merely a medium, an outlet for their frustrated feelings. In the signalman's cabin the officers huddled closer together and fed the fire with boards torn from a ration box. They had laced their tea with rum. When they heard the song they looked up at each other and smiled knowingly.

Beneath the yellow lamp in the stables there was a table with three great urns of tea and a pile of white-papered field biscuits resting upon it. Up to the table trailed a long, wet queue of men with enamel mugs in their hands. The light of the lamp picked out the coloured flashes on their sleeves, the wet cheeks, and the glow of cap-badges. With mud on their white gaiters and belts Military Police splashed up and down the queue, pushing and swearing, angered by the sarcastic catcalling that taunted them from the darkness. Of its own accord the shouting died away and the voices rose again into the warm sentimentality of 'Nellie Dean'.

The men from the village had joined the boy and the dog. The noise, the singing, the shrill shouting, had brought them tardy warning of the liberality that was to hand. They kicked the dog from their path and swore resentfully at the boy. They paid for cigarettes with a quick, calculating efficiency and handfuls of greasy notes that the soldiers looked at curiously. They hovered on the outskirts of the stables, hands in their trousers, and when a soldier looked towards them they would step forward quickly to ask for food, for cigarettes. Colourless shadows, they seemed to be a part of the rain until a flash of their white faces showed suddenly. And the soldiers stared back, slightly shocked by the different aliases that Liberation could assume.

Ted Jones sat down on his pack and lit the stub of a cigarette for the third time. His mouth was dry from smoking and his stomach sick with tea. There was a strong taste of soap in the biscuits and he had given away his last bar of chocolate.

'What time is it now?' he asked listlessly.

'Quarter past eleven.' The voice came impersonally from the darkness behind him, and then, as an amused afterthought, 'It'll be Lights Out soon.'

Jones gulped at his tea again and spun his cigarette-end into the rain. A dark shape from the group of Frenchmen bent over the cigarette quickly, nipped its end into a shower of sparks. Jones stared dispassionately and he drank some of the tea again. It was sugarless and weak, but it was also hot, and the warmth of it flowed through his body, giving it some comfort. He lit another cigarette and looked out into the rain. The queue was still shuffling past the tea-urns, and the Red-caps, with Sten-guns hanging muzzle-downward from their shoulders, were pushing at it, shouting and splashing.

'Are they going to leave us here all night?'

'You've heard all about forgotten armies, haven't you Slash?' said a voice behind Jones. 'This is how they get lost. Someone makes a mistake and puts five hundred of us into trucks and says take these men away and lose them. It's easier overseas. They don't even tell the War Office. Where do you *think* the officers have gone? To get on with the war nice and tidy like without us.'

No one laughed. It seemed a plausible enough explanation. They spat at the mud and waited, and soon the singing ebbed up from the depths of their boredom. They sang about the wicked Old Monk and the Great Wheel, and the obscenity of it was moral intoxication, a medicinal brandy succouring their spirits. The unanimity of their feelings, their disgust, anger, amusement, welded them into one great complex feeling so that a man at one end of the crowd could have defined with accuracy what a man at the other end was thinking, feeling, or saying. Their clothes, their thoughts, and their problematical future seemed uniform.

The man behind Jones said again: 'I suppose when they've finished their char and wad and the rain stops they'll come back to see if we're still here?'

'Will we be?'

'You got anywhere to go, china?'

'Where's that bleeding train?' said Jones.

'What train, are we waiting for a train then? Where are we going?'

'Brussels.'

'My mob went into Brussels with the Guards Armoured. That's

what I call liberation. If I hadn't got wounded on the beaches I'd 'ave been with them.'

'We know all about your wound, Corker.'

'Oh Christ! Why doesn't this rain stop?'

'What rain? You want jam on it too, you do Corker.'

'Aw, get some foreign service in!'

'Bless 'em all, bless 'em all, Nobby. All the dear little sergeants and captains and majors. I do hope their boots don't let water. Where are the little dears, I'd like to thank 'em for the holiday.'

'What are you belly-aching about? It was worse than this at Dunkirk.'

'*Reload!* Hand me my steel helmet.'

'All right, extract the urine if you like, but you should have been at Dunkirk, if you think this is bad.'

'I should've been home in bed with the old woman, and that's where I was. You and the Dunkirk Harriers!'

'You ought to've had a couple of years in the desert, mate.'

'Put some sand down, Corker, I thought we'd get to Alamein eventually.'

The conversation, which had flared up with the suddenness of a match, spent itself as quickly. The group about Jones was quiet again, he could hear their heavy breathing, the press of their thighs on his shoulders as he sat there below them. For him now it seemed as if this period of waiting would stretch out into an eternity, that he would sit there for ever, living on luke-warm tea and the acrid stimulus of cigarettes. The whole of the world, its movement and violence, had retracted into this one wretched, rain-swept spot where he sat. And he marvelled that he did not care.

Over by the tea-queue the orderlies in their shirt-sleeves were shouting and slamming down packets of biscuits on the wet table. They're all right, he thought, they know what's going to happen to them. They'll have their feet under some French table tonight when they get rid of us, if they ever get rid of us. He enjoyed the unreasonability of his own jealousy.

The lamp spluttered and wavered in the rain. As it swayed, dipping down into the darkness like the bow of a ship into a wave, it gave unusual and eerie movement to the splintered supports of the roof, and threw an umbrella of sickly light over the soldiers. Behind the orderlies, in the only part of the stables that did not leak with rain, two large 'sawyers' of water steamed and boiled. The scarlet glow of the fire beneath them spread an entirely fictitious warmth over anybody who stared towards them. But most of the men leaned against each other in the dark, closed their eyes and tried to sleep.

Jones strapped his mug to his pack, thrust his chin into his hands and sought sleep himself. It was as if a fire were burning inside his head, sending little hot streams of memory before his eyes. It was a few days now since the landing-craft had left Newhaven, and ploughed out into the grey Channel where the waves rose up in welcome and carried it to the broken beaches at Arromanches. The days that followed had one by one shed his past and left him there in a dirty, rain-dripped stable to the north of Amiens, with nothing to make him a man of substance and property but the fifty-six pounds of soaking equipment, a rifle, and the battledress that clung damply to his waist and buttocks. His brain was tired, but aware at the same time of a great freedom. The knowledge that someone would feed him, would push him forward or hold him back without even asking his opinion, gave to his mind a delicious sense of emancipation. Things would happen independently of his own actions. He was in the war, and even that hadn't found him yet. The tide of it had washed him into this stable and left him stranded.

The long war-years in England, the monotony, the disillusion, the bitterness they had bred had dropped from his shoulders. None of it seemed real any more. The dog scratching itself in a puddle was more of a reality, and now that it had stopped the reality there was already lost. Life had just begun and was just ending. The war had just begun, and perhaps that too had ended. One would never know the war. The war was rain, the smell of manure in this stable, the dryness of his throat after so much tea, a Frenchman picking a cigarette-end from a puddle, and the man called Corker patiently telling how he had been wounded on D-day.

'There was the beaches, see, and my mob comes off bright and happy-like slap-bang in the middle of a minefield. The OC said it wasn't fair, they could've cleared them, they'd had the time, but no, they left them there just to spite him. And I was driving a 15-cwt up to the top when bang it goes and I only wakes up in Worcestershire with a beautiful tart saying "Drink this"...'

It had been easy to fit the war into a neatly-ordered pattern so long as you saw it only in maps and speeches. There weren't things like this stable to obscure the picture. You could take the broad view, but the reality of war, when you saw it, was a smell, the itch of dirty clothes, the longing for a woman, or the desperate hunger for sleep.

He had volunteered for an overseas draft, two months after the first landings. Everybody assumed he had done that because of Mary, but that conclusion had been only a half truth. The other he could not define, even wordlessly to himself. Well, I asked for it. Me, Driver Ted Jones, Royal Regiment of Artillery, one-time estate agent's clerk from Stockwell. The war had begun. Look out Hitler, here comes Ted Jones. Oh Christ, could even Hitler be worse than rain that never stopped?

He opened his eyes to grope for a cigarette, and was surprised to find that the rain *had* stopped. He was disturbed by the appearance of the sky. The black, high-piled masonry of clouds towered in colonnade and pediment behind which the diaphanous moon moved quickly. A fretted light fell over the stables and the men therein, and they looked up at it with childish surprise. It was as if someone had just turned up a feeble flame, and the men found themselves among strangers. They looked at each other curiously, into eyes dragged from sleep, faces scored by frowns. Jones, in his surprise, found himself remembering the days when, as a boy, he would often stand at his bedroom window on a summer's evening, his bare toes curling away from the linoleum, and his eyes staring rapturously at the late sunset, making sandbanks and islands from the clouds, and a glorious sea from the rich, red flow of the sinking sun. His father had thrashed him often for getting out of bed to let such sights play upon his imagination. He remembered that now as he stood there and looked at the moon and the deep-night blue, and he wondered if his father, in the old war, had ever been impressed so and yet had forgotten so quickly as to punish a child for reaching towards such happiness.

'Nice night,' he said, and offered a cigarette to the man behind him.

'Nice night be ...! Thanks.'

Down at the end of the stable a shower of sparks burst suddenly and floated up into the sky, each one dying with a last wink above the soldiers' heads. It left behind it a thick, sulphurous odour. There was an impatient cough of a heavy locomotive, the high protest of metal on metal.

'The train!'

'Don't you believe it, mate, it's a mirage. You get like this after a while. That's just the OC Troops lighting his cigar. "Will you have another magnum, Forsythe?" "Thank you major, don't mind if I do. I wonder how the chaps are getting along?" "Oh don't worry about them, old boy, this'll do 'em good."'

Jones grinned. 'They're probably as wet as us, and as browned off.'

The train was shunting. The clatter of buffer against buffer and the shrill whine of wheels as they slipped on the metals, comforted the soldiers. Some of them began to swing their heavy packs on to their shoulders. At least there was a train. They began to sing again.

> 'Oh dear, what can the matter be?
> Three old ladies locked in a lavatory.
> They've been there from Monday to Saturday
> Nobody knew they were there!'

Jones shouted out the chorus, and found Tomsett whistling at his elbow. A sudden glow of matches ran down the dark, eddying outlines of the crowd as cigarettes were relit. It could be a matter of minutes only now. For all the rain, the weariness, the filthy stench of the stables, Jones was aware that he was excited. He had been like this, disturbed by the tenseness of unusual excitement, ever since he had stepped aboard the landing-craft in England. The war had come to life. The dullness of years past dropped from his mind and his nerves tingled with the newness of experiences unknown, even heavy, physical weariness. He had been like a child, as excited as a child on the long tramp from the beaches, past the prisoner-of-war camp crowded with a grey mass of singing, shouting Germans. Everything had excited him because for years as long as he could remember there had been only the drab streets of Stockwell and Brixton, the two annual weeks at Brighton or Hove. He had stared at the great Norman farms, set in the bastions of their thick walls. He had choked over the heady taste of Calvados in a fly-strewn café below the cathedral at Bayeux, and he had sat by the lonely grave of a Highland Light Infantryman on the edge of the orchard near Ryes and placed a little wall of dried cider-apples about its length.

Then the cattle-trucks had brought him with the others from Bayeux, through the torn and desolate fields outside Caen, and through the sight of the great ruins that had hit him like a blow in the stomach.

The French people had flooded to the train at every stop, catching the cigarettes and chocolate flung to them, throwing back rough little apples and holding up chipped mugs of sharp-tasting coffee. With the wind playing in his hair he had sat by the open door of the truck, staring at the bonneted Clydesider who leant out to chalk 'Good old Joe!' and 'Scotland for ever!' on the red woodwork.

The excitement had not faded, it had deepened with expectancy. He had written about it all enthusiastically to Mary. And then he had remembered and torn up the letter.

Ahead of them in the darkness lay Brussels, the Dutch border and Arnhem. Tomsett had been talking about the Airborne all day. Somehow he had got news and he had sworn about the tragedy of it.

Jones noticed suddenly that he was shivering, and as he ran his hands over his face they came away covered with chilling sweat. His body ached. 'Flu, that's a joke. Mary would see the joke. As he thought of her his excitement wavered and he felt slightly deflated. The stable and the rain, the mud and the weariness became what they were in reality, sickening and unpleasant.

He had forgotten and was ashamed of himself for forgetting. He had not come over for the excitement, but to get one of them at least. That was it, he, Ted Jones ('Well we have a nice little semi-detached to offer on a forty years' lease just off Brixton High Road, madam.') had come over on business.

'Can you hear it, Ted?'

He could hear nothing but the pounding of blood in his own temples, and Tomsett's question irritated him without reason. He looked up. Tomsett stood in front of him, against the moon and the clouds, against the lamp and the tea-queue that was etched in fine outline inside the other stable. Tomsett had his head cocked sideways, beret on the back of his thick hair, and the light of the moon shining on his cap-badge. His mouth was open slightly and a cigarette was stuck to a full, lower lip. He was listening carefully.

'Listen!'

Jones could hear nothing, for the Frenchmen had begun to run about in the muddy lane, shouting and waving their hands and pointing up into the sky. There was a proprietorial air about their gesticulations, as if here, in contrast to the sense of inferiority which this mass of armed soldiers imposed on them, was something of their own, something which they knew well. Jones could not understand them but there was no mistaking that something up there in the angry magnificence of the sky was causing all this excitement. The soldiers were walking out into the open and looking up, squinting and wiping the rain from their faces. Then Jones heard it, the chugging, ludicrous and purposeful throb of a flying-bomb. He got off his pack and slithered into the mud. Behind him someone fell over his kit, toppled forward and struck Jones sharply on the shoulder with the butt of a rifle.

'Sorry, mate, some sod left his kit there.'

'It's mine.'

'Stupid place to leave it!'

'I'll get my batman to move it.'

'*There it is!*'

Against the clouds, a red-tongued flame for its tail, a little black dart flew towards the north-west. Jones looked at it with a peculiar sense of intimacy.

The bomb flew on and was lost in the rain, but the Frenchmen still ran up and down, shouting. Perhaps they had helped to make the bombs. Jones remembered the factory at Flixecourt where the bombs had been made. He remembered the yellow warheads which had been used as swill-bins. He remembered the château where the Gestapo had had their headquarters, and the well at the back with the bloodstains on its sill. There was too much to remember.

Tomsett stood at his elbow. 'Wonder where that'll fall, Ted. You're a Londoner, what're they like when they come down?'

Jones turned away without answering. He did not want to say. He did not know what they were like when they came down, and yet he knew better than most what it was like to have one fall.

'*We're off!*'

Down towards the end of the stable men were stumbling out into the rain and moving in a disorganized rabble towards the railway track. They slipped and cursed in the mud. Suddenly the lamp over the tea-urns spluttered and went out.

'That's it!' shouted a voice, wrenched from the heart of the crowd. 'Now take the ground away and we'll fly there. Oh, mother sell the pig and buy me out!'

In ten minutes five hundred men were shambling and stumbling into the darkness. The clouds had joined hands and covered the face of the moon with the great mass of their bodies, as if to shield from it a sight which revealed so ludicrously the humiliation of patient humanity. None of the men had any idea where he was being led. Those in front followed the white gaiters and cross-belt of a Military Policeman, and behind them, dragging equipment and rifles, the rest pushed and staggered in ignorance.

Something in their own blind, animal disorganization touched their sense of humour. They began to baa like sheep.

Seeing no officers they shouted for them furiously, to come and leave the women alone. The Red-cap led them into the cobbled streets of Picquigny. He ignored the men who were calling upon him to bark. He accepted the common dislike of his job as readily as he accepted its responsibility. The streets were deserted except for the flood of wet khaki that eddied and whirled towards the station. No man was conscious of the past or the future, only the miserable wretchedness of the present, bounded by the jostling shoulders of the men on either side of him, the sting of rain in his face and the tug of his equipment. Jones felt his face burning with fever, his body trembling at every step, but he baaed and shouted with the men about him. The crowd would stumble forward a few steps and then be brought to a halt, and at every stop the men threw their packs and rifles on the ground and swore that they would go no further. Once the wide window of a shop split and broke as a crowd of men swirled against it. The sharp, encouraging noise of destruction epitomized the men's feelings and they cheered ironically.

Above the shop a window opened and a woman thrust out her head, but the stridency of her voice was drowned by whistles and cries which greeted her. 'Jig-a-jig, ma'amzelle?'

Yard by yard Jones felt himself carried forward in the dark. His rifle butt trailed and bumped over the cobbles, and before he knew it he was stumbling along a narrow track beside a line of cattle-trucks. The air was full of shouts and curses of the soldiers, their broad, ironic baaing. Now and then a man would stumble and slide in resignation down from the track into the darkness below. There would be further swearing, a splashing of water and a roar of laughter from the bank.

Tomsett was at Jones's elbow, keeping up a monotonous train of obscenities.

'This'll do!' he said finally. 'I've gone far enough. In we go, Ted!' He threw his kit through an empty door of a truck, climbed in himself, and dragged Jones after him. The following men began to throw their kit through the door, and pull themselves up on their bellies to the floor that was an inch deep in lime and dung. 'Beautiful smell!' said Jones from the floor.

'What do you want for your money?'

Tomsett pulled him over into a corner and Jones lay there with his face resting on his pack. He was so tired he felt like crying, he wanted to be left alone, he wanted to go to sleep, but it was as if someone were beating a great drum in his ear. He felt himself being pulled up by his shoulders and pushed against the wall of the truck. He knew that the truck was in complete darkness, but bright sparks of red, blue, and yellow light were flashing before his eyes, and each flash was a sharp pain. Tomsett was tugging at his overcoat, flinging it over his body. 'You'd better go sick in the morning,' he said ironically. 'A nice clean bed with sheets and a smashing VAD tart to look after you. How would you like that, mate?'

'I'll take the bed,' Jones heard his own voice floating towards him from a distance.

'Some Second Front this!' said Tomsett, and he began to shout at the men who were still crowding through the door, striking matches and falling over the bodies and kit that lay on the floor. 'How many more of you third-class people coming in here? There's a sleeper up front.'

'Whoever said that can't fight either.'

'Mooo!' The noise and the burst of laughter that followed it whipped the spume of anger away. Jones could feel his feet burning, but he could feel nothing else between them and his forehead. 'Drink this!' he heard Tomsett shouting in his ear, and the splintered spout of a water-bottle jarred against his teeth. "*Kinell!*" he spluttered, 'What's that?'

'Whiskey, rum, and cognac. It'll do you good, mate.'

Jones felt the spirits burn their malicious way through his body. His head seemed suddenly to take wings and he noticed that the train was strangely quiet. 'What's up?' he asked weakly.

'It's another of 'em,' said Tomsett, 'Listen!'

Jones could hear his head throbbing, but he could also hear the steady noise of another bomb.

'Proper bomb-alley this,' said Tomsett, 'Wonder where it'll drop. You're from London...'

'Oh, shut up!' Anger boiled up inside Jones unreasonably. The fumes of the spirits carried him off into an odd, insubstantial dream.

His body seemed to lose its firmness and became wavering and fluting like the stem of a stick seen below the disturbed face of a pool. The fire burnt furiously inside his head. He felt Tomsett's body pressing close to his own as the man eased himself down against the wall of the truck. The air was full of scuffling, of curses, anger, and laughter. Most of the men had dropped to the floor where they were, but some still stood up, striking matches futilely, wrestling with their equipment. Their voices beat in frustration against the darkness. To each of them there came only one thought, to make this filth-littered perimeter in which they had been crowded as habitable and comfortable as possible.

'Oh Christ who started all this?'

'There will be no war this year, nor next year!'

'My brother-in-law's in an ordnance factory. He told my old man he'd be proud to change places with me.'

'He's had it. There ain't enough glory for all of 'em.'

The darkness grew thicker with cigarette smoke, but some-how it subdued the smell of the lime and dung. Beside Jones a body moved restlessly and a voice grumbled irritably. 'What the hell are you doing, Corker?'

'I'm trying to get my Tommy-cooker so's we can have a brew-up.'

'Well, that's my pack, and where do you think you can brew tea in this pigsty. Go to sleep!'

'I can't sleep in a strange bed.'

Jones heard the bright London accents faintly. He listened to them as if they were miles away. He believed that the sound of them would remain in his memory always.

'The cook down at that last mob said the radio says the Russians are about to launch the death-blow on Germany.'

'Then what the effinell did they bring me over for? They won't get me out of my shop when this lot's over.'

'You haven't got a shop.'

'I will 'ave. Stationer's. You know, kids' comics, betting slips, and rubber goods.'

'Go to sleep Corker!' There was a long, stretching yawn that seemed to speak for the whole, crowded truck, and then, 'Corker, 'ave you been to see if the officers are all right?'

'I've sent 'em their hot water bottles, what more do they want?'

The darkness seemed almost tangible to Jones when he opened his eyes and looked into it, as if he could stretch out his fingers and feel its substance, somehow oily and resistant. From its repugnant thickness came the smells, the heavy breathing, the muttering, cursing of the fifty men crowded there on the floor. The voices of the Cockneys cut the darkness sharply, and now and then the flare of a match lit the dirty space with scarlet and caught the wide black shadows of a snoring mouth, the heavy, expressionless eyes of a man who could not sleep but sat there motionless with his back against the wall and his knees drawn up to his chin.

Jones felt Tomsett move uneasily as the Midlander struggled to get at his water bottle. There was a gurgle of the liquid, a satisfactory smack of Tomsett's lips, and the smell of the spirits slipped past Jones's face in tantalizing invitation.

'Smells like a four-ale bar in here,' said a sleepy voice.

'Ever known a pub to keep pigs?'

'I've known some pigs who kept pubs.'

'How's the 'flu?' said Tomsett in Jones's ear, 'Want another spot of this gravy?'

'All right. Thanks.'

'Pull my groundsheet and overcoat over you if you like,' said Tomsett gently, 'It'll be a bastard in here during the night. You lost someone in the flying-bombs, Ted?'

'My wife,' said Jones without emotion, 'She was killed by that big one in Lewisham. Remember?'

He did not hear Tomsett's answer. The rich, heavy sleepiness of the spirits welled up at him from his feet, and the wash snatched at his flimsy consciousness and carried him on and out of the darkness towards Mary's face.

No more matches were struck in the truck, and one by one the cigarettes died, to be stubbed out in the dung by the men's thighs. Told long ago, by training sergeants of traditional stamp, that a soldier's best friend was his rifle they had soon learnt that such a philosophy was a deep lie against all inherent weakness in humanity. There was only one friend, the soft forgetfulness of sleep. Sleep to a soldier is a woman whose power of seduction never loses its excitement. It comes nightly to take the man from himself, the slave from his master. Its solace was a prize to be contested whenever possible. It was the only liberty left to them and they cherished it. To it they paid the grateful plaudits of their thick breathing, the deep sensual intake and exhalation of the foul air in the crowded truck. In sleep all soldiers find brief demobilization.

Down the line the thin wail of the engine pricked needle-sharp through the rain, and a lurching, sudden jolt shook the carriage and flung each man against his neighbour. A rifle slipped from the wall and someone cursed as it struck him. The train began to move.

2. Waithman

The Troop Commander studied the map he had stretched on the table before him. He had weighted one corner of it with an enamel mug of tea which his batman had brought him an hour before. Ignored, the tea had grown cold and the surface of it was congealed with a thick scum of tinned milk and cigarette ash. The greasy print of the batman's thumb, like the skeleton of a beech leaf, scarred the surface of the mug near the handle. An impatient movement of Captain Robert Waithman's body had slopped the tea over the chipped edge of the mug and spilled it on to the map, where it lay in a rich brown stain across one corner of the Reichswald.

Waithman chewed his short moustache and glanced at the stain now and then, his restless mind playing with the idea that the tea was in truth a vast area of brown flood water that had spread across that corner of the Siegfried Line. He rubbed at his upper lip with one long forefinger and grinned to think of the Boche struggling in an ocean of syrupy Army tea. He tapped his chinagraph pencil on the table and composed slogans in support of the idea. Long ago, almost in his schooldays it seemed to him now, he had been an advertisement copy-writer. He had been proud of himself and would sit in the corner of the train that took him to his home in Redhill watching his fellow-passengers as they read the advertisements he had written. Conscious of the fundamental hypocrisy of the words there, the grand, unashamed deception of them, he would feel flattered by human credulity which could still be swayed by such artificial eulogies.

He scribbled idly on the back of his wife's last letter, glad to take his mind from the exacting dialectics of the map. 'The tea that Monty used!' (He wondered if the Chief's ascetic tastes permitted tea) . . . 'Everything stopped for tea' . . . 'When the Germans tea-ed up!'

A sudden disgust with the puerility of the pastime filled him, and he scored out the words heavily. He rested his elbows on the map again and with a big fist below each ear he frowned at the opposite wall. His civilian life had been full of such childishness, and he felt a sneaking gratitude, of which he was half-ashamed, for the war which had taken him away from it. The war had offered him the risk of death, but in payment it had offered him responsibility, relative importance, and social eminence within a narrow sphere, a state of affairs he had never believed would come his way. He could not remember his civilian identity, so completely had the war absorbed and obsessed him. He had never been adventurous, but having had adventure unavoidably thrust at him without the drawback of economic risk, he felt as grateful as a child given its first house-key.

Now, with a hundred men under his command he had an authority and an importance which fifty years of civilian life would never offer. He lit himself a cigarette and stared at the map. In its convolutions and neat characters he found an immense and satisfying fascination. It was the same with all his work. He was tireless because he was enthusiastic, he was cheerful because he was never bored. If he had any fear it was that one day he must go back to his typewriter, to his copy-writing, to the six-eighteen to Redhill.

It was a great comfort to know that most of his men liked him, and while he had no ideas one way or the other, he did not understand why some of them were so obviously dissatisfied with Army life.

He picked up his chinagraph pencil again. Along the two-mile stretch of the River Maas, which curved in a half-moon from the right-hand corner of the map, he had marked a series of eight blue circles, and from each he had drawn yellow lines that converged across the green mass of the Reichswald Forest. Against each circle he had pencilled a few figures and letters, and a time. He stared at them for a long time and then began to whistle to himself with satisfaction. He knew that each blue circle represented a searchlight, the yellow lines its beam lying across the front, the Germans in the forest. Along the eight-mile strip of the Maas Sector where his Troop was stationed lay a band of still, artificial moonlight.

He whistled a tune to which he and his wife had danced in the days before he left for Normandy, and the careless nature of his married life, the respect of his wife, and the unruffled, if conventional tenor of their relationship, increased his self-satisfaction. There was nothing so damning to a man enthusiastically preoccupied with his job as to have personal domestic trouble. He was grateful to Maureen for saving him that inconvenience. He looked at her photograph, in WVS uniform, leaning against his map-case, and he winked at her cheerfully.

On the shelf above his head the railway clock chimed out nine precise notes. The Troop Commander looked at it, spat out his cigarette and lit another one quickly, glancing at the cigarette-lighter before he replaced it in his pocket. A going-away present from Maureen. Nice of her.

He looked across the floor of the booking-office to where his sergeant-major lay stretched out on his blankets. The warrant-officer, a thin, ascetic-looking man with a wisp of a moustache and no hair at all on the crown of his head, had fallen asleep. His mouth was open and he sucked in the thick air of the little room in strangled gasps. Beside his body was a mug of tea, resting awkwardly on a half-eaten corned-beef sandwich. His thin hands were crossed on his chest, and his fingers were loosely gripping the covers of a book. Waithman twisted his head to see the title. It was *War and Peace*. He felt a little discomforted by it. He recalled that almost the only serious quarrel he had had with Maureen had been when she discovered that he had never read it. He wondered whether it was really more than that. He wondered whether the Army had changed him, whether he had become more tolerant, less stiff-necked and opinionated. In those days he had been young, anxious to succeed, and ready to practise any trivial deception so long as he did not lose ground.

But now at thirty-three he was older. The Army had brought

him conditional success, and his wife, at thirty-six, was less inclined to prejudice a position already in jeopardy, from her superior age. They compromised admirably, he thought. Thorough in his intentions now, he decided to borrow the book.

He looked at the map again. The village of Guderijn, three-quarters of a mile from the Maas, was shaped like an arm, raising a clenched fist. The main part of the village was the fist itself, and the houses straggled along the forearm, turned right at the church to the weak biceps which was another group of houses about the station. It was in the station itself that Waithman had made his headquarters five days before, and spread out his detachments along the river as he had been requested by the Infantry Brigade.

He reflected that he had picked the best billet since they had landed, not excepting the pill-box on the Orne. When they had come into Guderijn, except for isolated American paratroopers marauding in the empty houses, the town had been deserted. Not long before, a German tank had turned in its retreat and come back down the road. Waithman had been alone in his Jeep, a mile ahead of his own convoy, and when he saw the tank he had wheeled quickly and confidently into a garden and waited there, with the scent of flowers, crushed by the wheels of his Jeep, rising up and almost intoxicating him with their headiness. He had not been afraid, but pleasantly excited, and extraordinarily curious.

Inhumanly, for it did not seem to have any relationship with the men who must have been hard at work within its mechanical carcass, the tank had moved slowly down the street, placing its shells methodically through the bright orange walls of the houses, its machine-gun chattering occasional approval. Waithman had watched it with a ghoulish intensity and a queer fascination for its thoroughness, almost forgetting that sooner or later it must inevitably discover him. Then, from somewhere behind him, an anti-tank gun had fired a single round and the tank stopped in a bonfire of mauve and orange flame.

The rain that had fallen during the following days had rusted the ugly metal and washed the embers of clothing from the body of the German who lay half in and half out of the turret. Waithman always felt a little sick as he drove past the tank, and each time he made a mental note to send a burial party down to get rid of the German. But he had never given the order, and he knew that the corpse had become the subject of monotonous humour for his dispatch riders as they drove by it. They called it 'Sunny Jim'.

There was one other reason why Waithman left it there, one which perhaps he did not really know himself. The sight of the decaying German body gave him a deeper appreciation of his own confident and vital ability.

The station was indeed a good billet. It was on a branch line from Nijmegen. Five miles to the west, on the way to Nijmegen itself, a bomb had collapsed the embankment over the line and blocked it. And half a mile to the east the railway met the Maas. There the bridge of gaunt green girders slipped brokenly into the blue river. There was a spearheaded bridgehead across the river and the pontoon that led to it was shrouded at each end by the waving fronds of camouflage netting.

Waithman was satisfied with the billet although he knew what the rest of the troop did not, that less than a mile away in the village of Groesbeek was a regiment of German infantry, and between them and his headquarters was only half a company of British. He was not afraid, it never occurred to him that he was in danger of becoming a deathly caricature like the German tankman. He was still too naïvely obsessed by the surprise that he should be in such a vital position to reckon its less pleasant side. In Normandy his own lack of fear had sometimes worried him. He was intelligent enough to think that perhaps it might be due to the fact that he had no imagination, but he reassured himself with the memory that his imagination had been fertile enough to compose some of the most pungent of advertising slogans that ever sold patent foods. These days the thought of fear rarely concerned him, he was enjoying himself far too much.

The station was well-masked by a high sandbank of gorse and young pine, and although at night enemy mortar shells wound an eerie path over its head, none had as yet fallen on it. Waithman reflected that he had a flair for such things.

He got to his feet and yawned, blew a smoke ring expertly, went to the door and opened it. Down towards the river he could see the motionless beams of his searchlights pointing across the river. He counted them slowly, eight was correct. They lay across the horizon and pointed resolutely into the German forest and because of them the night was made luminous with a beautiful lilac mist. It was very quiet, and Waithman knew that out there, lying close to the earth in silence, German and British infantrymen were looking at the pale moonlight from his projectors. A light breeze touched his face with a promise of rain and he drew back his shoulders and breathed it in gratefully. He closed the door and went back to the table. He loosened his belt and revolver and dropped them on the floor beside the sergeant-major's head.

The warrant-officer did not move. He opened his eyes and stared up at Waithman with a blue wateriness that showed no feeling.

'Damn it!' he said, 'If you can't sleep, sir, I can.'

'You get all the sleep you need,' said Waithman cheerfully. 'What about a hand of crib?'

Thompson sighed obviously. 'You're the OC,' he said and got up, scratching himself thoroughly from groin to armpits. 'When the hell are we going to have a bath-parade?'

'That's your department. By the look of THQ every manjack of them hasn't had a bath for weeks. Not since we left Brussels, anyway.'

Thompson scuffled into his boots and shuffled across to the table, passing his hand over his head with a quick nervousness. 'Why did we leave Brussels, anyway?'

'What do you care? You wouldn't get any medals down there.'

'You know damn well you get the same medals wherever you are in this war, if medals is all you want.'

Waithman grinned. 'You're afraid Sarn't-major. No one gets killed in this Troop.'

Thompson looked up at him quickly. The sharp, inquisitive thrust of his nose made him look like a querulous hen. 'No,' he said, 'Not when you pick the sites. But you don't always pick them.'

Waithman flushed. 'Nijmegen was in the run of the war. Mr Smith can't be blamed for it.'

Thompson snorted. 'Tell that to the marines, or rather tell it to the rest of the Troop!'

'Let's play cards,' said Waithman stiffly.

They played in silence, flipping the greasy cards between their fingers and smoking incessantly. Waithman smoked in short snatches, holding the cigarette between his stained fingers most of the time, but Thompson kept his in the corner of his mouth, drawing past it long whistling inhalations, until the glow of its tip was almost lost in his moustache. The guns began at half-past nine and the anger of them shook the plaster from the roof and scattered the table with it. Thompson brushed it irritably from his shirt.

'Half an hour of this,' he said, 'And Jerry will have a go. Aren't you glad you're not in guns?'

Waithman flushed again, he suspected all the time that Thompson was trying to discomfort him with such bald innuendos. 'I didn't ask to be put into searchlights. Three-sevens are my mark.'

'A good gun,' Thompson admitted, 'I was a bombardier on three-sevens at Plymouth. But for a bleeding, perishing, thankless job you can have searchlights. And no glamour.' He spat out the words past his cigarette with evident distaste.

'There's glamour enough here,' said Waithman. He wanted to say it jokingly, but found that he almost believed it.

'Glamour?' said Thompson, 'I was counting up the other day. Since we left Normandy we lived in fifteen pigsties. Or at least the men have, you and I generally get the house, *Captain* Waithman. One windmill, fourteen slit trenches, a monastery, a railway station and fifteen pigsties. We've been shelled eight times at headquarters alone, and we were sniped at Nijmegen, and that's not all...'

'I know,' said Waithman irritably, 'we lost four men at Nijmegen, across the bridge.'

'Mr Smith can count himself lucky he didn't lose the whole lot.'

'It wasn't his fault, I told you,' said Waithman, raising his voice and putting his cards face downward on the table, 'Men do get killed in wars. Did you write to their next of kin?'

Thompson pursed up his mouth and splitting a match with his thumb-nail, he began to pick his teeth. 'It's not my pigeon. I told Mr Smith he should. I suppose he did. I went down with the burial party myself. Hopkins was a good lad,' he chewed his lips. 'He came up with me. It was a pity he got killed.'

Waithman did not answer but moved his cards one by one with his little finger. He could not remember Hopkins' face. It was as if death gave an unpleasant anonymity to its recruits.

'Has Corporal Michaels come in?' said Thompson.

'I didn't hear the truck. Where's he gone?'

'He went back to Belgium to pick up two reinforcements. A driver for your Jeep was one.'

'If I know them they'll send me a driver who's never driven anything but bulldozers.' Waithman pushed back his chair and stretched out his long legs to the fire.

'I don't like being pessimistic like that,' said Thompson, 'I didn't used to be, ever. Before the war I had a nice little job in Enfield.' He rubbed the top of his head. 'I had all my hair then, too.'

'It doesn't notice with your cap on,' grinned Waithman.

Thompson grunted. 'The men can see through my cap. Do you know what they call me?'

'Baldy.'

'Who told you?' said Thompson suspiciously, 'Michaels I suppose?'

'What do you expect them to call you? Battery sergeant-major Thompson?'

'It's my right. Anyway, do you know what they call you?'

'Claude. It's my second name. I rather like it. Comradeship and all that.'

'Get out!' said Thompson, 'If I catch 'em using those names I'll run them so fast their feet won't touch the ground.'

'You're not the type. Whoever heard of a sergeant-major reading *War and Peace?* You're too intellectual. You ought to be more like the cartoons.'

'It's a good book.'

'Never read it,' said Waithman, 'Your game. How much do I owe you?'

'Fifteen guilders. That makes forty in all.'

'I'll pay you sometime,' said Waithman easily.

'You won't, you never do.'

'Why should I. Officers aren't supposed to gamble with OR's.'

Thompson scratched his head. 'You've got no conscience like I have. It's always been a trouble. That's why I don't like this business at Nijmegen.'

There was a pause. Waithman stared at his warrant-officer. He thrust out his lower lip rather like a petulant child and Thompson returned the stare defensively. Suddenly the officer picked up the cards, shuffled them nervously and pushed them into a drawer. 'We won't play any more tonight,' he said, 'Get some sleep in, sarn't-major.'

The warrant-officer went over to his blankets. He slipped his braces over his shoulders and stepped out of his trousers. Waithman grinned suddenly to see the long, thin legs, and the underpants that ended halfway above Thompson's hairy ankles.

'You're no pin-up, Baldy,' he said amiably.

Thompson grinned back. 'Good night, Claude!' he answered and pulled the blankets over his head.

Waithman sat down at the table and looked at the map again. He did not feel like sleep. His eyes followed the course of the railway to the edge of the map. From then on he knew its trace by heart, how it curved and entered Nijmegen from the south. He remembered the town with its beautiful gardens, its clean streets, and brightly-painted houses, and the dust of exploding shells settling over the marigolds and hanging in the air like outsize, purple umbrellas. The noise of their passage was as the ruffling of a stiff, linen sheet.

He thought of Smith too with a queer, irritated uneasiness.

The Troop had gone into Nijmegen in the late afternoon. Across the river and a few miles to the north was Arnhem. He had stood and looked across the steel framework of the bridge to the purple smoke that lay on the horizon and the red brushstrokes of the guns that punctured it. The guns were speaking all day and in Nijmegen, in some of the houses and amid the trees, there were German snipers still. Waithman had driven in at the head of his convoy, and although he had felt an uneasiness, an odd, sustained excitement, he had joked with bravado. When the long convoy had pulled up in the centre of the town the Dutch had come out of their houses and swarmed over the vehicles with cups of dry, acrid coffee, and bows of orange crepe paper to tie to the radiators.

Smoking a cigarette by his Jeep Waithman had looked back and smiled to see how suddenly each of his dusty, weary trucks had blossomed with the bright happy colour of liberation. His men had climbed down with red-rimmed eyes and, caught immediately by the flaring enthusiasm of the Dutch, had begun to dance in the streets, even while the sharp, cautionary rattle of rifle-fire reiterated down by the river. A few vehicles back Hapgood, the Troop dispatch rider, had stood by his machine, his legs wide apart and a steel helmet pushed back from his forehead. He had thrown handfuls of cigarettes high into the air and shouted:

'A present from Uncle Happy! Next week we'll want money for 'em! Alles is good! Mof aweg!' And around his sturdy legs half a dozen children had linked hands and danced, their mouths wide open in song and their cheeks smeared with chocolate.

And then, like a wave, the shells had come nearer, and Dutch and soldiers broke up and ran for safety. Waithman had stood up, his head high with an indignant bravery until he heard a harsh, sarcastic voice, which he suspected was Hap-good's, condemning his own idiocy. He had lain under his jeep with a little frightened boy of six, and had found himself giggling unrestrainedly.

They had slept in basements that night, mixed up with Dutch families where the children were alternately crying and singing, and as Waithman dozed he was awakened now and then by rifle-fire. Beside him, with earphones strapped over his head, his wireless operator brewed tea and cursed quietly and incessantly, brooding resentfully on his home in Oldham.

And then Waithman had had to send Smith's section across the river. Although there were other searchlight batteries across there, and being shelled, he had had to send a detachment. He could not leave Nijmegen himself to find a site so he had sent Smith. 'Tojo' Smith, a fat, short officer with swarthy black hair, who appeared to have no consciousness of his weaknesses, who was hated by his section and yet strived with a pathetic earnestness to acquire moderate popularity. Waithman had sent him across the bridge with four lights to shine down the road leading to Arnhem.

Smith had put the section in full view of the enemy artillery across the Leek. He had been lucky to escape with only four killed. It would have been something if Smith had stayed with the section, but when the shelling began and the radio went dead, Waithman had gone out with Corporal Michaels in the Jeep and found Smith on the south side of the bridge. His motorcycle was in the ditch and his face was pale. There was earth and sand down the front of his battledress and he said that he had had a spill. It was Michaels who had said what was in Waithman's mind.

'Lucky you got spilled in the ditch when the shelling started, wasn't it, sir?'

Smith had flushed, a deepening of the sallow colour in his cheeks, and he had looked at the Corporal and then at Waithman. There was such a look of pathetic incredulity on his face that Waithman said gently, 'Get in, John. We're going over to the section, don't you know what's happened?'

The infantry had been running across the bridge and the bodies of German snipers still hung grotesquely from the girders. Waithman had found Smith's section in slit trenches. They were badly shaken. Hopkins and three others were laid out under the bushes with blankets over them, and the sergeant of the section was standing on the lip of a slit trench, swearing. When he saw Smith he started to run across the rough ground towards him, shouting and waving his arms. He was saying something about Hopkins and Waithman noticed with surprise that he was crying. It had been Michaels who stepped between the officer and dragged the sergeant away.

Waithman dropped the cigarette on the floor of the booking office and ground it out with his heel. He brushed the ash from the map. It would have been something at least if Smith had admitted that he had sited the projectors badly, but he had rubbed his hands up and down his disgusting paunch and put all the blame on the Germans. Perhaps it had not been Smith's fault, Waithman would not be certain, but it was a fact, as Thompson said, that the men had no doubts about the matter. Poor Smith!

Outside in the yard of the station he heard a truck change gear, and as the engine roared before it died he knew that Michaels was back. He heard voices and footsteps on the wooden platform, someone was cursing the lack of light, and then he heard Michaels whistling 'Swinging on a star'. There was a casual knock at the door.

'Come on in, Michaels,' said Waithman cheerfully.

The Corporal came in first, a big man with his cap on the back of his head, his leather jerkin belted with a Wehrmacht belt and a splash of yellow colour from a silk scarf about his throat. 'Two blokes from Brussels, sir,' he said. Behind him stood Jones and Tomsett.

'Well, come in,' said Waithman, 'there's a black-out here too, you know.'

Michaels grinned and stepped aside to let the two men pass. They came in wearily, their packs hanging from one shoulder and their rifles slung across the other. Waithman stared at them curiously. He saw in their faces an age-old expression, half truculence, half despair, and yet overall indifference, the indifference of men completely at the mercy of greater forces than themselves and yet preserving, by the tilt of a cap, the slope of shoulders, and the unconscious stance of their bodies, a stubborn independence which refused to be uniformed.

'Put your kit on the floor,' he said genially, 'and let's have a look at you.' The words were traditional, and because of that the sense of examining livestock was merely superficial.

'*Kinell!*' said Tomsett under his breath, 'An 'undred miles in a truck and now a beauty parade.' As he said it he looked down into the watery eyes of Thompson.

'If you've anything to say, my lad,' said the sergeant-major, 'let's hear it!'

'What are your names?' said Waithman. They told him and he bit the end of the pencil and stared at them. Jones was an ordinary-looking man, young, not very outstanding except that he looked cleaner than Tomsett and his eyes were intelligent enough. He had loosened the buttons of his collar and looked pale and tired. He stared back at Waithman without really noticing him, and the Troop Commander was frankly aware that he must appear as just one more of the many officers who had passed into this man's life and out of it, directing, ordering, and controlling it, but never discovering the man beneath. Jones was obviously dead-tired. There was a diamond of black crepe on his arm and he held his rifle lifelessly.

'Can you drive a jeep?' asked Waithman. 'Right, then you'll be my driver here. And you, what did you say your name was?'

'Harry Tomsett, sir.'

'Tomsett will do, we aren't all that intimate here.' Tomsett scowled back at the sarcasm. 'You'll be going out to a detachment tomorrow.'

'Can't I stay with my mate, sir?'

'You'll go where you're told my lad!' said Thompson. 'We aren't running a Friendly Society. If you don't *mind* Mr Tomsett?'

Tomsett looked at the warrant-officer's bald head and thin shanks, and he grinned back happily. 'Just as you say, sir.'

Thompson pulled on his trousers and told Michaels to take the newcomers away. 'Just a minute, Jones,' said Waithman, 'All right, Michaels, I'll send him in later.'

The Troop Commander looked closely at Jones after the others had gone. 'My name's Waithman,' he said at last, 'Since you're going to drive me I think we'd better get to know each other. The job may be a bit dangerous sometimes. If you don't want it, say so now.'

'I'll do it, sir.' Jones seemed disinterested in the warning.

'Where're you from. London? Married?'

'I was sir.'

Waithman's eyes flickered over the black crepe and he rubbed his moustache with the pencil. 'I see.' He pulled in his breath. 'Well, it's a dirty life this, but I think you'll find the other chaps OK, and I shan't bother you much if you do your job well. There's not much bullshine this side of the water, you know. And my Jeep runs like a bird.' He noticed that Jones seemed bored with the conversation. 'What was your civvy job?'

'I was an estate agent's clerk.'

'Well, you'll find this a change. They're mostly knocking houses down over here. That's all, Jones. Go down the platform to where all the light's coming from and you'll find the rest of the chaps. Good night.'

'Good night, sir,' Jones fumbled a salute and pushed himself through the door where the fresh air, after the thickness of the booking-office, made him feel strangely light-headed. The door banged behind him and as he stood there he heard the sergeant-major saying:

'Surly sort of bloke.'

'He'll do. What do you make of the other one.'

'I'll give him *Harry Tomsett!*'

'You can't discipline anybody in your winter woollies, Baldy.'

'Damn my winter woollies!' Waithman laughed, a queer, booming laugh of confidence that made Jones start with embarrassment. Dragging his rifle and pack he moved down the platform to the waiting-room where the light streamed through the gaps in an inadequately-pinned blanket and flooded over the platform. Jones looked down the line, where the rails were drawn taut to the horizon like fine strands of shining wire, and at the end of their silvered trace the long, mauve bars of the searchlights lay across the horizon. To the north the skyline flickered uneasily with gunflashes, where some giant hand was impatiently thumbing a cigarette-lighter. But there was no sound, the silence was less sinister than exhausted.

Jones had an odd, inescapable feeling that he had come to the edge of the world. If he went on, followed the railway lines, he would drop into darkness, in a fall that would never end. If he went back, however, he knew that he would move closer to the source of light, to the sanity of half-forgotten things, to the physical presence of Mary, to the sound of her voice and the whine of the trams running down Stockwell Road. But there would never again be any going back.

3. Jones

The waiting-room was small. Within its damp, torn walls it had a furtive look of shame beneath the light of a single bulb that hung from an ornate rose in the ceiling. On one wall a splash of poster colour flowed with the spires and curving eaves of a street in Rotterdam, but the name of the city itself had been scored out, and a crude hand had pencilled 'St-Leonard's-on-Sea' instead. Beneath it, hanging from a bayonet driven into the plaster, was a steel helmet and a battledress blouse. From about the little, fireless stove all the debris and paraphernalia of a soldier's kit washed in an untidy wave to the far wall where it broke in a froth of ammunition boxes, rifles, overcoats, and equipment. The bodies of sixteen men littered the floor with the grotesque sprawl of their half-naked figures and the twisted turmoil of their blankets. The room was a lazy, sensual orgy of untidiness that is a soldier's unconscious protest against the customary neatness expected of him.

The air was filled with the stench of sweat and smoke, a thick, blue atmosphere that gripped the throat and cut sharply across the eyes. Through it the sound of a radio trickled to Jones as he opened the door and pushed aside the blankets.

> 'I'll be seeing you in all the old familiar places
> That this heart of mine embraces ...'

He looked about him uncertainly. One or two of the men stared back, shaggy heads raised slightly from the floor, and from beneath

Jones' feet one of them dragged a mess-tin of corned beef and dry, crusted potatoes.

'Shut the door, Slasher, there's a good bloke!' said a voice.

He pulled the door to and looked about him for his friend. Tomsett had found a clear space behind the stove, where he was sitting on his pack and drinking tea, holding the mug in both hands and dipping his rough face into it like a dog. He waved a hand to Jones through the smoke. 'There's room for two of us here, Ted.'

Jones climbed over the legs and sat down beside Tomsett. 'Got a cigarette, Harry?' he said, 'I can't get at mine. This is a queer sort of place, isn't it?'

Tomsett gave him a Woodbine. 'All the comforts of home except the missus, and there's replacements for that, they say. Don't like the look of these Dutch women though.'

Jones eased his equipment from his shoulders and let it fall to the floor. Beneath it something yelped sharply. As a dirty-white puppy, with flopping black ears and a rose-pink mouth cowered away, Jones bent down and picked it up. 'Hullo, you little devil!' he said and he rubbed its ears furiously only because he wanted something on which to expend his emotions. The puppy snapped and snarled happily, and, settling down into the crook of his arm, began to breathe itself heavily into sleep. Jones smiled at it and fondled its ears gently. He drank some of the tea Tomsett handed him and sat there smoking. His face, which always held a look of reserve, almost to the point of surliness, made most of the men ignore him resentfully. He listened to Tomsett as the man bragged with cheerful unconcern, and from the floor the men boasted amiably of their cowardice and bravery and they swore deeply at the black mud and sparseness of Holland, recalling, almost with regret, the days in Normandy that had now become memories seen through a distorting mirror. Their imaginations caught flame, and, as all soldiers will on first meeting, they matched experience against experience and scored anecdotal successes without shameful regard for truth. Jones hardly heard them, he closed his eyes and let his thoughts wander back to an England he hardly believed existed. He felt himself falling asleep.

He opened his eyes suddenly to find Michaels standing before him. The Corporal had taken off his coat and rolled up his sleeves to the elbow. He was smoking a short, black briar with an amber stem, and its pretentiousness was heightened by the inexperience with which he smoked. He still wore the yellow scarf of silk about his brown throat and that at least, thought Jones, seemed to suit him. Michaels looked friendly, at ease, a master of the situation and slightly bored by that mastery. Somehow he looked too clean to Jones whose body was itching with grime and sour with sweat. Michaels' hair was parted and neatly combed, the curls falling smoothly into place. He took the pipe from his mouth and held it with the golden stem pointing at Jones.

'All right, Slash?' he asked, 'I put some blankets there for you.'

'All right, Corp, I shall be glad to kip down.'

Michaels looked at him steadily, so obviously summing him up, and then he nodded. 'You don't get much sleep in this hellhole, though. Not before midnight when Happy's still awake.' He jerked the pipe-stem over his shoulder.

Naked to the waist, his chest superbly muscled, a little man with close-cropped hair and a sharp, shrewd face was standing in the centre of the room. His body had the unconscious stance of a man who, although no professional boxer, was ready enough to fight. There was an arrogant challenge and a swagger in the set of his shoulders, and on the brown dirty skin of one forearm the carmine body of a tattooed snake coiled about a rose-bud. On the other two blue hearts were almost obscured by wiry black hair. Resting on his thigh, above oil-stained breeches and black riding boots, was one huge fist, on the little finger of which was a great ring in the shape of a skull. Red stones gleamed from its eye-sockets. His breeches were held up by a Wehrmacht belt similar to Michaels' and against his left buttock there flapped the short length of an American bayonet.

He ran his hand through his hair and pursed out his lower lip. 'Where is the little bugger?' he said, 'Dempsey! Where are you? I'll do you when I find you!'

'It's the pup he wants,' said Michaels, 'He got it from a slit trench near Rouen, the filthy little brute. Here it is, Happy. The new bloke's got it.'

The dispatch rider stepped over to the stove and held out his hands. 'Shit over my blankets again,' he said resentfully, 'He's got no more manners than the rest of you, have you Dempsey? Give him to me mate.'

Jones handed up the dirty animal. It whined and nuzzled its nose in the hair of Hapgood's chest. The man looked up and grinned, and then down at the dog. 'I'll do you,' he said brutally, and then he rubbed his cheek gently against the animal's fur. 'How do you like it here, Tosh?' he said suddenly to Jones.

'What?' said Jones who had not caught the question.

''Ot?' said Hapgood, 'I'll say it's 'ot!' And he climbed over the sprawling figures and back to his bed. Jones frowned, but Michaels grinned and stuck the pipe into his teeth. 'Happy's all right,' he said, 'You should see him ride a bike, like a beautiful dream. If you want anything let me know.'

Jones pulled his blankets into a bed, spilled his small pack over the floor and scooped it together to make a pillow. He lay back and stretched his legs gratefully. The drive from Belgium up into the narrow corridor had been quick and it did not seem hours since he had been lying in the black stables north of Amiens. He had ridden beside Michaels most of the way into Holland, while Tomsett snored comfortably in the back of the truck. Jones had been fascinated by the drive, staring at the road with grave eyes. Throughout most of the journey Michaels had sung happily, steering his truck dexterously down the broken roads and past the burnt-out vehicles on the verges. Something of his easy nature touched Jones, and when Michaels said that the line ran on either side of them, less than seven miles away, it was hard to believe, for the countryside was quiet and glowing with the rich pastels of autumn. The huge red, white, and blue sails of the windmills turned slowly against the sky, and the children ran out of the houses to wave orange bows at the truck as it passed. But darkness had brought a queer uneasiness to it all. From nowhere, it seemed, had come vehicles to choke the roads, to prick the blackness with their masked headlights. Michaels slackened speed and drove with his lower lip gripped between his teeth. Then suddenly, to the north, ran a rippling shudder of orange flame.

'Arnhem,' said Michaels briefly. 'They're shelling Nijmegen again.'

Long after the flash the noise of the guns had come to tug at the muscles of Jones' chest and turn to fluid the pit of his stomach. Once they passed a long line of tanks going westward, ugly black beasts with the shining teeth of their tracks biting at the darkness and the faces of the men in the turrets white splashes against the sky. Jones caught glimpses of their mask-like eyes, the downward thrust of their black berets, and the hard, cursing note of their voices as Michaels' truck loomed before them suddenly in the dusk. Michaels had laughed, and swung his truck over to the right and let them pass.

And then had come Guderijn, the black, smelling mystery of it, the edge of the world with nothing beyond. A little, dimly-lit box crowded with men and outside nothing but the darkness.

The blanket at the doorway was swung aside violently and Thompson came in. He carried a cardboard box beneath his arm and he was wearing no jacket over his braces. 'You might as well have these now,' he said, 'Five cigars each, free issue. They're Jerry cigars.'

'What, no paper hats?' said Hapgood and the puppy yelped as he pushed it in laughter at his own joke.

Thompson flung the cigars to each man in turn. 'There isn't one of you man enough to smoke them,' he said with morose contempt. 'So you might as well flog them to the Wogs.' He looked distastefully at the room and eased his braces on his shoulders. 'Get this room cleared out by morning. Headquarters shouldn't look like a pigsty.'

Somebody snorted like a pig and Thompson looked sadly at Hapgood. 'You keeping pigs as well as dogs now, Hapgood?'

'Not on my pay, sir!'

'Unless that dog of yours behaves better we'll leave it behind. It messed up the OC's blankets last time.'

'It ain't Dempsey that smells,' said Hapgood with an engaging quirk of his lips that caused Jones to feel a sudden affection for him, 'but Corporal Michael's socks.'

Thompson brushed his moustache irritably and pushed aside the blanket. Hapgood laughed shrilly, stuck one of the long cigars in his mouth and began to dance up and down the congested room. Somebody turned the radio louder and with the cigar between his stumpy fingers Hapgood began to sing, a nasal, sardonic burlesque:

> 'Long ago and far away
> I dreamed a dream one day ...
> And now that dream is here beside me!'

'Pipe down, Happy, and let's get some sleep!' The voice had a patient note of despair in it. In the corner a man sat up in his blankets wearily. He rested his arms along his blankets and Jones saw the bombardier's stripes sewn neatly in white on the faded shirt. He was a little man, with a square, young face and small eyes. About him was an untidy sea of clothes, weapons, greasy tools, and half-eaten food. He frowned back as Hapgood swore at him cheerfully.

'It's all right for you, Happy, but some of us want to sleep.'

'Oh fly a kite!' said Hapgood.

'*Eh?*' The bombardier turned his head sharply.

'Hooray?' said Hapgood, 'There's nothing to cheer about, you know.'

A shell keened over the roof of the station and fell in the rear with a sickening explosion. The plaster snowed from the ceiling and the blanket blew in from the window and flapped its joyous approval. The stove-pipe slipped wearily to one side. 'Oh Christ, the bastards!' said a voice quickly as the light went out.

'That's the fourth time this week the light's been cut,' said Michaels easily from the darkness. 'Considering the power station's on Jerry's side you'd think he'd just switch it off without sending us presents.'

Jones pressed himself against the wall and wondered if he were afraid. It had happened so quickly and unexpectedly that he did not know what to feel. He was afraid that his nerves might make him sick. About him in the dark the men were complaining irritably. To Jones it seemed as if his life was always to be spent in angry, frustrated darknesses. Snatches of daylight would be but excited dreams.

'Light a candle, Busty Jordan!' said Michaels.

'Why don't you go to sleep now that you've got the chance?' asked the bombardier.

'Because I want a shave, you tight old twister. Light a candle.'

Another shell sighed over with an impatient rustle. The waiting-room shook with the explosion and Jones felt the plaster drift across his face. He brushed at it and found his hand wet with perspiration. Beside him Tomsett stirred uncomfortably.

'Go to sleep, Joe, can't you?' said Jordan, 'I don't like this any more than . . .' A third shell passed and fell without explosion.

'Good old Czechs, one for his nob!' said Michaels, 'Maybe you can sleep in this perishing row, Busty, but I want to shave.'

A match flared in the corner. The bombardier was sitting up in bed again, holding the match before his face. His eyes were screwed into a knot of wrinkles and he was staring down the room towards Michaels. 'Haven't *you* got any candles?'

'You know damn well we haven't! Light yours. Don't you scrounge them all, you hard-neck? Oh God, here's another!' The stomach-kicking explosion flung Jones against the wall. His head hit the plaster sharply and he began to giggle foolishly. The match went out.

'Who the effinell's that laughing?' said Hapgood out of the oily darkness, 'Dempsey, come and die with Uncle Happy.'

'It's all right,' said Michaels from the window. Jones could see the outline of Michaels' figure silhouetted against the window where he had pulled back the curtain. The head was held confidently on the broad shoulders, but there was nothing indifferent about it, rather a deliberate contempt. 'It's all right, they're after the counter-battery. They've hit something though.' The sky was suffused with dull crimson.

Jones began to pray that the candle would be lit soon; he felt foolish and trapped in the darkness, waiting for the next shell.

'It's all right. I'm psychic. We're all right.'

'To hell, Jack!' said Michaels shortly, 'I want to shave.' A second match flared in his hands. In its fluttering glow the room saw Jordan's naked buttocks of white against his shirt tail as he scuffled in his pack for a candle.

'Never mind the exhibition, Busty,' said Michaels, 'find a candle.'

Another shell that fell was so near, and its blast so immediate, that the sickening pull of it seemed to suck the life out of Jones. There was sudden silence in the little waiting-room. The candle fluttered in Jordan's hands. Jones looked about him. The white, livid faces stood out against the mud-coloured blankets. All eyes were open, staring blankly at the ceiling, or the window where the blanket was twisted by the blast into some demoniac convulsion. It was as if each man were holding his breath. Only the puppy whined slightly and buried its nose in Hapgood's hand. And then Hapgood sprang suddenly to the middle of the room and began to dance, kicking his legs forward, leaning back to rest on one heel, and hunching his shoulders in rhythm with the ludicrous music that still blared from the radio. The white figure of Christ that hung on the crimson rosary about his throat, swung among the hairs of his chest. 'One, two, three, *hup*!' he chanted.

'Sit down, Happy, and stop rocking the boat!'

Two more shells rushed over the station and expended their velocity in a belly-clutching explosion that forced the bile sharply into Jones' mouth. Hapgood froze in his dance, his body contorted, his head raised and his lower lip thrust out as he stared at the thin roof. 'Lucky we're under cover!' he said.

But most of the forced humour of the situation was gone, and Jones realized something he had not seen before, that the men were desperately tired of this sort of thing. Now that the candle was alight and fixed by its own grease to the dusty-floor-boards at the foot of Jordan's blankets, the flame flung gross caricatures to the ceiling and fluttered the emotions from the features of the men. Hapgood went back to his blankets and sat there quietly, one dirty, long-nailed finger exploring his ear, the other hand fondling the whimpering dog. There was nothing about which the men could talk that would take their attention from the relentless, flailing Death in the air outside. In silence they waited and listened. They heard the soft plop of the gun far off beyond Groesbeek, and then the eldritch scream of it coming nearer until it raced over them and expended itself violently among the counter-battery.

The walls shook and the splinters rattled outside. Michaels stood up slowly and pulled his shirt over his head. He stood there flexing his fingers across the muscles of his chest, so conscious of the cleanliness and youth of his body that Jones stared at him, half in admiration and half in amusement. He watched the broad wall of Michaels' shoulders as the Corporal leant over and dipped his shaving brush into a bowl of water. For all the arrogance of the action, the obvious pride Michaels had in his own healthy body, he looked admirable and Jones found his admiration tinged with jealousy. He wondered why, in spite of this, there was something about Michaels that he did not like.

Across the Maas four guns began to fire salvoes. 'Oh Christ, eighty-eights,' said a voice. Jones, watching Michaels, saw the Corporal pause, the shaving brush resting on his cheek, and then he went on indifferently. He did not stop lathering even when the shells burst. Jones did not know whether to laugh or clap such obvious posing.

The door banged and a sentry pushed aside the blanket and stood just inside the room, his bayonet catching the folds and draping them about his steel helmet like a burnous. "*Kinell!*' he said briefly, and held up his cuff. A strip of cloth had been torn from it by a splinter.

'Well, don't show everybody,' said Hapgood, 'or they'll all want one.'

The sentry stood there, rubbing his hands nervously. He wanted to talk about his little experience, but the rest of the men were listening and waiting for the next salvo. After a while the tension relaxed and the sentry lit a cigarette and went outside again. Someone changed the radio programme. The rich, bubbling good humour of the voice that slipped from its speaker flowed easily into the room. The odd impersonality of the shelling struck Jones queerly. He had a sudden, crazy desire to reach out with his hands and pull the walls and ceiling about him, to make their spurious protection more exclusive and certain.

The shells came over regularly and as the station remained unhit, shaken only by the blast, the persistent tug of noise, the men grew used to it. It was not, they said, as bad as the Orne. Jones pulled off his boots and gaiters, rubbed his toes sensually and scraped the dirt from between them hoping his actions were not betraying his inexperience. He looked up to find Michaels watching him above the razor. The Corporal smiled confidently and pulled the blade down his cheek in a broad, sure sweep. Jones returned the smile dubiously, but he found the action reassuring. He lay back and stared about him.

Across the room he saw a man with long, lank hair and a red nose that sniffed monotonously and querulously. He was writing on a letter-pad perched on his knee. He wrote evenly and without hurry, his body inclined a little to catch the light from the candle. When the shells screamed their high protest he would pause, the point of his pencil resting on the paper, his head bent over it and his eyes slewed round to the window. When the noise of the explosion subsided he would turn his eyes back to his letter and continue writing. Pinned to the wall behind him were half a dozen nudes and a creased newspaper portrait of a full-breasted woman in a bathing-suit. Below them all was a faded photograph of a nondescript woman who might have been his wife.

Jones watched him sleepily. Beside him he heard Tomsett breathing deeply, his head below the blankets and a battledress blouse over his feet. But Jones knew that Tomsett was not asleep, that he was listening carefully just like them all in that room.

The shelling died away slowly to sudden but infrequent rushes of noise like shaken linen, and the intervals between the explosions grew longer. Then suddenly, just below the windows of the station, it seemed, one after another, the twenty-five pounders of the counter-battery began to fire. They had a deep-throated clap of indignant protest.

'Oh Gordon Childe!' said the bombardier and sat up in bed, his shirt open and the greasy string of his identification discs swinging across it.

'Go on Charlie, have a go!' shouted Hapgood, leaping excitedly from his blankets.

The noise of the guns beat about the little room and the candle fluttered and trembled in the blast, the radio spluttered to survive. The man opposite Jones finished his letter slowly and with careful deliberation scored a line or two of crosses across the bottom. He folded it and addressed an envelope. Jones watched him as he ran the flap of the envelope along his tongue, pressing the letter between his hands and placing it above his head on his pack. From where Jones lay he could see only the words 'On Active Service' standing out clearly against the white paper, and below it a tangled, scribbled address. The writer sighed and eased himself down into his blankets. He put a cigarette end in his mouth, lit it between cupped hands, and blew a mouthful of smoke about the papered nudities on the wall.

Jones closed his eyes and tried to sleep, but the smoke and dust beneath his eyelids smarted and made them water when they were closed. The noise of the guns made his body tremble, an unconscious reaction because his brain was heavy and tired. How long he sat there, staring at the oily shadows fading and reappearing on the far wall, he did not know, but eventually the electric light bulb flashed into life. Almost immediately the firing stopped.

'That'll teach 'em to cut our light off,' said Michaels sleepily.

The sudden silence was almost more unbearable than the noise. Jones felt his ears singing, felt too that the trembling of his body must be obvious to others in the room. But each man lay on his blankets with his eyes closed, alone with his thoughts in that rich moment of solitude that comes to a soldier before the oblivion of sleep, the darkness that brings transient, intangible satiation of his desires. They snatched at the freedom jealously, and Jones watched their faces, the expressionless masks which approaching sleep drew over the bone structure, the hollowed eyes, the dirty skin, and drooping mouths. Crowded in the room with sixteen men he felt desperately lonely. He groped in his pack and dragged out a crumpled letter-pad which he smoothed between his palms. He began to write quickly and expertly on his knees:

Dear Mary: I've arrived at last in the front. I suppose that is what you'd call it although it isn't anything like 'All Quiet on the Western Front'. It's strange. In the daytime you can't believe there's a war on, the chaps say, and at night nothing up here seems real. I don't know where I am because it's so dark outside, and anyway I couldn't tell you. I seem to be on the edge of the world almost stuffed into a little room with sixteen men and a dog called Dempsey. I know one of them called Michaels, and he's interesting although somehow I can't like him yet. He doesn't seem real. There's a war going on outside because just now we were shelled, it seems funny to write that, makes me feel as if I am showing off. Harry Tomsett is here with me, remember I told you about him in my last letter. I won't write any more tonight, except to little Mary, because I want to get some sleep. I am so tired. But before I go to sleep I wanted to wish you good night and say I love you so very much. Do go to the shelter when the warning goes, dear. All my love, Ted.

He folded the letter and placed it beside him. Then, on another sheet, he wrote shortly:

Dear little Mary: This is just to tell you that your Daddy's all right and getting along fine. I've gone to a new place with some strange men. You mustn't worry about Daddy because he's quite all right. This morning I saw some little Dutch girls wearing clogs just like the pictures in the book Mummy gave you last Christmas. I shall write to you again. Look after yourself and give my regards to Grandma. With love from Daddy.

He scored some crosses at the bottom of the second letter, sealed it and addressed the envelope. He stuffed it into the pocket of his blouse. Then he picked up the first letter and read it through slowly, correcting the punctuation and adding crosses to that too. He stared at it for a while, smiling gently, and pulling at his lower lip and the lobe of one ear. Then he screwed the letter into a little ball and dropped it on the floor beside the stove. He looked at it and frowned. He struck a match and held it to the ball of paper, watching the fire consume it with bright orange jets of flame and spurts of blue smoke. The flames died out and the letter collapsed into a drifting ball of black ashes on which a hundred sparks glowed and winked out of existence.

Jones looked up to find Michaels staring at him curiously. The rest of the room was already asleep, or clutching at sleep with open-mouthed gasps, fists and eyelids closed in determined concentration. Michaels grinned, and flicked his fingers in friendly acknowledgement.

'That's how I feel about my letters,' he said, 'There isn't much worth writing about from over here. You're writing to people who haven't a clue to what goes on anyway. What's your name, Slash?'

'Ted, or Jonesey.'

'OK Ted, most people call me Joe. Good night.'

'Good night!' said Jones, and he watched the Corporal pull the blankets over his naked shoulders, stretch out his long arms with a straining yawn. Jones looked from the figure of Michaels to the ashes of the letter. Beside him Tomsett moved jerkily and the draught of the movement caught up the ashes and scattered them in the centre of the room. They flicked across the nose of Dempsey who was sighing dreamily on Hapgood's feet. The animal sneezed twice and began to scratch itself. Hapgood kicked out a foot and the puppy rolled in the dust with a yelp, scratched itself again thoroughly and crawled up over Jones' blankets to his shoulder. He stretched out an arm, gathered the animal into the blankets, where it wagged its rump delightedly and began to snuffle at Jones' shirt.

He sat back and closed his eyes. No one had turned out the light. It swung there gently above them, as if disturbed by the heavy breathing. Once more Jones was surprised by the oppressiveness of the silence outside, broken, almost inaudibly, by the thin, fluting whistle of the bored sentry on the vehicle park.

4. Michaels

Joe Michaels was twenty-five, but he had a firm and easy assurance of manner that made him seem thirty at least. He wore his clothes lazily and carried his well-proportioned body with a grace that made others treat him with unconscious respect whatever their rank. Devoid of spite he was amused by their respect and thoughtlessly exploited it. At the wheel of his truck he drove with a competent nonchalance and a deep, happy satisfaction. Had he analysed his feelings he would have decided that he was more or less happy all the time. He accepted the filth and changing excitement without resentment or introspection. He accepted the Army too with more condescension than resignation. He fitted its incidents into their relative importance, relative to his aim in life which was a self-satisfaction without antagonism. He knew that people liked him and he was amused by it. With those he disliked he maintained an owlish gravity that ill concealed his contempt.

For reasons which he hardly understood himself, except that he was aware of a deep and personal embarrassment, he hated physical defects in others, and yet he appreciated the self-satisfaction they inspired in his own easy health and vigour. To Michaels a cripple was unfortunate, but also a lingering challenge to his own perfection.

He lay on his back in the wretched little room and thought of Jones. There was something in the new man's surly features that irritated Michaels. He liked others to reflect his own good humour, and he felt strangely ill-at-ease with anybody whose thoughts seemed indifferent to contact with Michaels' superficial amiability. He stared at the electric light bulb, at the flyblown ceiling, at the poster of

Rotterdam fluttering lazily on the wall, and he wondered if Jones was married.

Michaels did not think of his own wife very often, at times he found it hard to believe that he was married, particularly since he left England, and he was secretly pleased when anybody expressed surprise that he should be married. It was an unspoken compliment to the indivisibility of his character. He had met his wife on a mixed gun site in Sussex, late in the Battle of Britain when the bombers had weaved a lace network across the ceiling of England. She was an ATS plotter and between them they had shared the weekly dances and drinking in a public-house where the landlord marked off the fallen bombers with chalk-strokes on the wall. Marriage had come upon them both before each seemed to realize it. And then D-day which, for him, had all the characteristics of divorce. The weeks that had followed had been so clear-cut and uncompromising in their reality that most of what had gone before seemed unreal. He wrote to her now and then, and she to him from stations in England, of the dances she was going to, and he reflected with more objectivity than bitterness that she did not really miss him, any more than he missed her. He remembered her animal vitality gratefully enough, but what prospect it held for the future he did not know.

He lit his pipe and wished that he could sleep. The drive down from Brussels had unsettled him, keyed up his body to action and left it without complete satisfaction. He wished that he could have stayed in Brussels for more than the one night before he picked up Jones and Tomsett; to have stayed just to get drunk, to hear some music, to dance, to buy some cognac, to talk to another woman. He remembered the woman with whom he had spent that night with a gratified feeling of realized experience. But then the war had pulled him back into the darkness of its orbit.

Outside the air was quiet. He could hear the sentry stamping his feet and whistling 'Lili Marlene'. The nostalgic melody broke through the surface of his brash cynicism and left him embarrassingly sentimental. Next door in the booking office he heard Thompson coughing and Waithman's voice on the field telephone, the click of its bell as he hung up. He dozed and dreamt hazily that he was playing football again with the club in Bristol. The banging of the door opened his eyes and he saw Waithman standing above him. 'You awake, Michaels?'

He sat up and grinned a welcome. 'Yes sir?'

'Nothing's coming over the R Toe from Jig Three. Go out and have a look will you? I don't know where the shelling landed. Take my Jeep.'

They looked at each other and smiled. There was a deeper understanding between them than either realized. Michaels said, 'Have you tried telling them to close down? It usually works.'

'No, it's genuine enough, I think.' Waithman rubbed his hands. 'Haven't you any tea in this stinking hole? I feel like a brass monkey.'

'No tea here sir. Happy gave the last to Dempsey. Any chance of ruin before I go out?'

'I'll give you a shot, yes. Come in and see me. You'd better take Pearce with you, you know.' He pushed aside the blanket and Michaels heard him stumbling down the platform. Michaels rubbed his knees with pleasure. He wanted to go out. During these days he regarded even sleep as a theft of his consciousness. As he leant over and shook the shoulder of the man beside him Pearce rolled back and stretched out his arms, yawning. 'All right,' he said, 'I heard, but I thought you'd have the common to let me sleep on. Aren't Jig Three in that village where the stoves are? The cook was asking for one.'

'We aren't going looking for stoves in the dark, Slash. Keep your looting till daylight. Those houses are full of mines.'

They dressed quickly, belting their leather jerkins about them and slinging their Sten-guns. Michaels picked up his tool box and as they stepped outside the night air hit them with a sharp reminder that behind the mellow colours and warm days of autumn there hung the breath of winter. Michael tightened the yellow scarf with a flourish. They shivered and looked up to where there was no moon and the sky hung like a broad, ultramarine cupola in which the stars winked. The night was so very quiet except for the soft throb of an engine miles away. Even the front was quiet, and to the east the searchlights fretted the horizon and caught the sharp relief of the trees against the sky. Behind the station the red-brick pillar of the church thrust up the finger of its spire. By a burnt-out railway coach three white crosses gleamed translucently.

'At home,' said Michaels, 'they'll read in the papers tomorrow that things were quiet over here tonight. It's queer I've never known a night to be so quiet as it can be here, just where you'd think there always ought to be noise.'

Pearce grunted. 'A good job too,' he said, 'I'll get the Tom Thumb.' He came back with Waithman's mug in his hand, his soft brown eyes smiling at Michaels affectionately, his body swaying with self-satisfaction. The oily, amber liquid sent jets of fire down their throats and Michaels wiped his lips with the back of his hand.

Pearce grunted, thrust up his chin and strapped his cyclist's helmet tight on his head. He grinned at Michaels who smiled back easily. These two men matched each other in the simple pleasure they took in experiencing the same emotions, in their superficial cynicism. Pearce dropped into the Jeep with one gaitered leg hanging over the side. His Sten clattered against the metal-work and Michaels saw his white teeth again in a grin. 'Let's get cracking Joe, and get back and have some kip.'

They drove through Guderijn. The darkness submerged the houses in a black, watery mystery, above which the orange gables jutted and caught the pale light of the searchlights. By the church the evening air seemed to have brought out the strong obnoxiousness of the rotting German in the turret. Michaels spat over the side of the Jeep in disgust.

'Sunny Jim smells nice tonight,' said Pearce.

'Poor bloke,' said Michaels, 'I suppose he had a mother.'

'Don't you read the papers? No Jerry ever had a mother.'

'Waithman saw him killed,' said Michaels.

'And Happy's after his ring. Have you seen it? Big thing with a swastika on it.'

Michaels tensed over the wheel as he drove. The road was lined with tall poplars, grey and upright in the night like the aged pillars of a cathedral nave. The road between them was black and treacherous. Four or five times Michaels drove off it into the verges and bumped back on to the camber. Now and then Pearce would shout '*Anchors, Joe!*' and Michaels would brake hard in front of a crater, circle round it and drive on. Neither of them was sure of the way and they groped for it in the dark, feeling the strain fraying their nerves. They talked little, the night, its blackness and sinister mystery seemed to absorb their attention. But each felt comforted by the presence of the other.

They drove for three miles by the river and branched off where the road dipped into a castellation of elms and oaks. From the centre of the copse the broad column of a searchlight thrust itself up to the sky and filled the night with a bold illumination that picked out the grotesque and submerged what sympathy the soft trees and fallow land might otherwise have offered.

The trees masked a village that had died suddenly under one furious bombardment. German and British artillery, as if turning on some neutral, depersonalized object, had exhausted their futile anger on its cluster of little houses and stump of a church. The red-slated roofs had been devoured by fire and great streaks of smoke had splashed the white walls with ugly shadows. The Jeep drove down the streets carefully, for they were littered with bricks and stones. But in the light of the searchlight Michaels could see that the gardens were aflame with orange flowers and the sight of them left him with a shadowy sense of depression. In his nostrils he felt the acrid sting of cordite.

'There's been shelling here all right,' he said and slowed down the Jeep by the gate of a farm. The sentry challenged them from the post against which he was leaning, and then came out into the roadway with his rifle slung across his shoulder and the light of the beam gleaming on its burnished bayonet tip like a bead of water. His head, deep in a great balaclava, was tilted in mild curiosity. Pearce leaned over the side of the Jeep and shouted as it bumped forward into the farmyard, but the man's reply was lost as Michaels switched off his engine. The sentry stumbled up to the Jeep unhappily.

'Everything nice and safe at Headquarters?' he asked sarcastically.

'Now tell us you've been shelled to muck!' said Pearce and swung himself out of the Jeep.

'Go and have a look!' said the sentry and stumbled back to the gate unhappily.

Pearce followed Michaels into the farm. He switched on a torch and they wandered through the rooms by the light of it. Furniture and furnishings were strewn about the floor, and the light of the torch spun in sharp sparkles from the glass and the cartridge cases that were scattered on the boards. The drawers of the cupboards had been torn out and emptied on the floor. Crockery crunched beneath their heavy boots as they walked through. Pearce picked up a wax poppy, blew the dust from its scarlet petals and stuck it in his jerkin. 'They've made a mess of this,' he said, 'Where the hell are they?'

'Through here most likely. Can you smell it?'

'Yeh,' said Pearce, 'Bacon and eggs. Trust Nobby.'

Michaels pushed open the door of the kitchen and went through into the stable. 'Any tea, Nobby?' he said cheerfully.

In the stable half a dozen men were grouped about the kitchen stove which had been brought out there and placed between the pigsties. The glow of its red surface lit their faces and made black apertures of their eyes and mouths. They held mugs of tea between their fingers and crouched over their knees with a surly indifference. About them the darkness was diluted by the red light into an oily, brown stain. They did not move as Pearce and Michaels came in, but turned their heads slowly on their shoulders and sat there staring. One or two were wearing steel helmets and the wide, ugly bowls dropped a veil of shadow across their eyes and thick mouths. Beside the fire, skilfully flicking fat in a frying-pan of eggs, was a bald man in his shirt sleeves, sweat on his forehead and the ash of a cigarette floating over the pan with every breath he took.

'Look out,' he said, 'watch your kits. Michaels is here.'

'Come off it, Nobby!' said Michaels cheerfully. 'Where's the tea?'

'In the dixie, Joe, over there.' Michaels scooped himself a cup of tea and sat down on the edge of the pigsty, warming his hands on the enamel mug. The corner of the stable roof was broken, and straw, mud, and wood dropped in an untidy waterfall of rubbish to the slimy cobbles. A ground sheet had been draped loosely over the hole. Michaels noticed that two men were sleeping on the floor, curled in their blankets and overcoats, black, shapeless stains against the mud. It seemed as if there were only two colours in that crowded little space; the dark, crouching figures of the detachment and the warm, hospitable glow of the fire, the oily crimson of the lantern on the table. The men ate sandwiches of bacon and eggs hungrily, thrusting the food into their mouths and drinking tea in satisfied gulps, as if the food interfered with the desultory conversation that ebbed and flowed from them dispassionately. The cook leant on his ladle by the fire and watched them with contented complacency.

'I've cooked in some places . . .' he said, and gave a sharp studied hiss between his teeth, looking about him as if in demonstration of his point. The firelight and the lantern caught moist reflection from the soft eyes of a cow that watched the men quietly from a stall, and on the perch above its head five white chickens stared with beady impertinence, jerking their heads irritably and executing a nervous, side-stepping dance up and down the pole.

'Aren't you my beauties?' said the cook and pushed the ladle up at their dirty feathers. 'You're coming with us when we move, but you'd better lay else we'll screw your neck and boil you.'

'I like 'em roasted,' said a man by the fire, staring into its hot coals as if to draw nostalgic inspiration from them.

'You'd eat anything that was 'eated,' said the cook with contempt, 'Seen the pigs, Jack?'

'I've smelt 'em,' said Pearce and he looked over the sty. 'There's six of 'em here, Slash,' he said to Michaels, and then, 'Have you killed any yet, Nobby?'

'Naow!' said the cook, 'We've got plenty of rations.'

'You'd better not let Happy in here with his hammer,' said Michaels, 'He hasn't killed a pig since Normandy.'

'He shot a pig when we were stationed near Wolverhampton,' said the cook in disgust, 'and we had to run the thing over with a truck to make it look like an accident. It wasn't worth cooking then.' He carefully made himself a sandwich laying the egg on the white bread and covering it with two slices of bacon. 'I wouldn't mind this life,' he said, 'if it wasn't for the smell.'

'Corporal Michaels!'

The men by the fire halted their idle conversation, turned their heads slowly and stared down towards the end of the stable. Michaels slid off the pigsty and looked with them. Sitting on the edge of a camp-bed, half-obscured by the darkness, was a grossly fat man in a lieutenant's uniform. His hair was cut close to the nape of his neck but strayed in disorder over the crown of his head. His round hands rested on his knees and his chin was drawn back into his collar. He frowned irritably at Michaels.

'Why didn't you report to me when you came in, Michaels?'

'Sorry, sir. Didn't recognize you down there in the pigsty.'

Someone sniggered and the officer's frowning eyes slipped nervously over the crowd. He picked up his steel helmet and then, struck by the pointlessness of the action, dropped it to the stones. 'The radio's out of action. I presume you didn't come down here for tea and a chat?'

'Just warming up sir, that's all. What happened?'

Lieutenant Smith got off his bed and came into the circle of resentful silence. He knew that the men had forgotten he was there, and now that they had been reminded of his presence they retired behind the defences of a surly silence that always alarmed as much as irritated him. All except Michaels with his impertinent self-confidence. He felt Michaels' disgust and dislike stinging him as if he had plunged his body into a bank of nettles. He rubbed his hands uneasily on his paunch and forced the tone of his voice into casualness. 'There isn't much you can do. It was completely destroyed. Fortunately O'Neill wasn't there at the time, although,' and a querulous note of impatience crept into his voice, 'I don't know why, he should have been.'

The cook spat on the fire suddenly. The hiss of steam sounded extraordinarily loud in the silence, and Smith, looking anxiously at the staring faces, felt his spirits collapse. He was always saying stupid things like that.

'Lucky he wasn't sir,' said Michaels cheerfully. 'A man doesn't look very nice when he's been hit by a shell, does he?' He said it with an easy nonchalance but a hardness in his eyes, and Smith's hands rested motionless on his stomach, staring curiously at Michaels.

'I know,' he said a little tartly, 'Perhaps a little better than you, Corporal.'

Michaels turned to Pearce. 'Coming Jack? It's a bit close in here.'

'Not while there's still some tea,' said Pearce, 'I can stand the atmosphere for a while. Bit tight on cigarettes aren't you, Nobby?'

The cook gave him a Woodbine. 'Don't you ever smoke your own?'

'I've only got Churchman's.'

Listening to the idle conversation Smith felt that each word was a barb deliberately aimed at him. Even the sudden way in which they seemed to have forgotten his presence was itself an insult. He supposed, resignedly, that it was what the Army called 'dumb insolence', but what could he do about it? He went back listlessly to his bed and sat on it, glad of the darkness that could swallow him up so hospitably.

Michaels went out into the yard, feeling his contempt for Smith lying angrily in his chest. It was not only the man's incompetence, nor his reputation for cowardice, which Michaels believed to be exaggerated, but his disgusting caricature of a body. The way the yellow flesh hung about Smith's neck in a thick roll was something that stirred Michaels's impatient disgust. No man had any right to look like that, least of all here. He was a creature for cartoons, for nightmares, for cruel and bitter jest.

The mud and the broken stones beneath Michaels' feet were bathed in the silvery water of the searchlight. Over by the black hump of the projector, dimly illuminated by the pilot-lamps of its instrument panel, three shadows were pricked by the red glow of cigarettes. As always the sight of soldiers at night, hunched into the shapelessness of overcoats and steel helmets, gave Michaels an impression of brooding solitude, even though they had lost all the conventional signs of personality which daylight could expose. The cigarettes glowed with each inhalation of breath and revealed the tip of a nose, the point of a chin, the thin reflection of spectacle frames.

The projector had been sited in the stubble of a field of maize, about a hundred yards from the farmhouse, and two or three crude slit trenches were dug by it. Michaels stumbled over the husks of corn and whistled cheerfully. A sergeant came up to meet him.

'Hello, Joe,' he said, 'I thought it was you. There's nothing you can do except bring us another wireless set.'

'Everything else all right?' asked Michaels, 'Claude's a bit worried.'

'Yes, most of them landed down in the village. Right in the middle of the stonking the cow broke loose and walked into Nobby's tea.'

Michaels laughed. 'I didn't know "Tojo" Smith was here.'

The sergeant swore. 'He stuck in there during the shelling. But perhaps he's well out of the way, Joe. I can put up with him now. If you hadn't stopped me up at Nijmegen I should have killed him that day little Hopkins was killed.'

Michaels stared at the sergeant's face. It was white in the light of the beams and curiously earnest. Michaels realized how tired the man must be feeling. 'I don't think it was Tojo's fault,' he said tolerantly, 'Anyway a man can't help being frightened.'

'We're all bloody frightened,' said the sergeant angrily, 'but an officer should never show it.'

'A man who looks like that should never go overseas,' said Michaels.

'Who should?' asked the sergeant cynically. He spat out his cigarette and walked over to the projector. 'You'd better change carbons, Alf!' and he pulled up the knife switch. The beam of the searchlight collapsed on to the field, and in the sudden darkness it seemed to Michaels that he had been deserted. He did not like loneliness. He stuck his hands through the arm-holes of his jerkin and looked to the east. The other beams were still laying their eerie, artificial glow across the line. Not far away, he thought, are the Germans. He told himself that again and again, but it was hard to believe. Between the two armies lay a band of silence that was almost tangible, and on either side of the river men lay alone with themselves in the damp earth and dry leaves. Each, in his own thoughts, German and British contributed a buttress to the lonely wall of silence that followed the green and curling banks of the river.

Michaels rarely felt lonely, only the darkness could make him feel so weak and uncomfortable. He shook the feeling from himself roughly. To his right he heard the soft whispering of footsteps by the fieldside, the muted clattering of equipment, and he started as the sergeant spoke at his elbow.

'It's an infantry patrol going up, Joe. Every night this time. Who'd be in the infantry? OK Alf, *expose!*'

The long beam sprang into the air as if joyously released by the dull green barrel from which it had leapt. It hesitated and then burnt steadily. At once the wide world of darkness changed to a little ball of incandescence about the projector, and on its perimeter, walking slowly towards the river, Michaels saw the infantrymen. They were walking in single file by the ditch, little men dwarfed by the breadth of their helmets beneath the camouflage netting of which the shell-dressings stood out in grotesque swellings. They turned white, expressionless faces to the men about the searchlight, but they did not stop. One man was carrying an armful of loaves and the incongruity of the sight made Michaels smile.

'Good night!' he called to them, and then softly, 'And good luck!'

'It's all right,' said the sergeant. 'It's quiet up there. It's all right.'

'It's never all right for the infantry,' said Michaels, 'How long's Tojo going to stay with you?'

'I don't know. I suppose he thought it was safer here than at Section HQ, but tonight shook him.'

'I don't like him,' said Michaels, 'but I feel sorry for him sometimes. It's a bit pathetic when a bloke knows he's no good and unpopular, but won't admit it.'

The sergeant swore slowly. 'You know, Joe, he wouldn't write to Hopkins' people. I had to. I didn't know what to say, said what a good little bugger Hopkins had been, but what can you say? Wanted to tell them where we had buried him but Tojo censored it. I suppose little Hopkins is a military secret now. When's this war going to end, Joe?'

'You tell me,' said Michaels, 'What do you care, three square meals a day and two pairs of boots thrown in. I'll get back. We're moving shortly, down the corridor.'

'Hell! I was beginning to like it here.'

Michaels walked slowly to the Jeep. Pearce was sitting inside and he grinned happily at Michaels and swung a leg lazily over the side of the vehicle. On his knee was a large blue enamel washing-bowl. 'I've been wanting one of these for a long time,' he said.

'Corporal *Michaels*!'

Michaels turned slowly, swinging his Sten-gun back over his hip. He could see Smith standing by the door of the farmhouse, his battledress blouse open and his hands resting on his stomach. Michaels swore gently and went over to the officer. Smith rubbed his hands nervously on his trousers and then thrust them into his pockets with a jerk. 'I'd like to apologize, Michaels,' he said, 'We've had a bit of a time here and I spoke perhaps a little too sharply.'

'Did you sir?' said Michaels non-committally.

Smith fidgeted his feet in the mud. It was cold and he wished he had put on his jerkin before coming out, because his chin was trembling. 'I think we understand each other, Michaels. You're a cut above the average. You appreciate how things happen.'

Michaels felt disgusted. The man's obesity seemed unclean and repulsive in this repentant pose. 'Do I sir?' he said gravely. He could not see very plainly but he felt that Smith's face must be turning that customary brick-red of embarrassment. The round outline of the officer's figure jerked suddenly with the next words.

'An officer's life is sometimes a lonely one, Michaels. Men are apt to forget that and believe the worst of us.'

'Yes, I suppose that's natural,' said Michaels conversationally. He felt moved by sudden malice. 'Pearce had a letter from Hopkins' father the other day. Did you know, sir?'

He heard the sharp intake of Smith's breath. The fat little hands rested like white fish on the round stomach. 'Good night, Michaels!' said Smith tonelessly.

Michaels went off whistling. Somehow, by the crude malice of his words he felt that he had punished Smith, not for his nature, but for the greater crime of his misshapen body. The rounded notes of the melody Michaels was whistling seemed to strike the lieutenant in the face. He stood there listlessly, and when he put his hand to the back of his neck to wipe away the perspiration, he noticed that his fingers were trembling. He heard the Jeep's engine cough suddenly into life, and the red eye of its tail-light swayed gently as the vehicle climbed over the rubble at the gate and turned into the road.

Lieutenant Smith went back into the stable, half-frightened by the thought of the thick, accusatory silence that would drop over the men about the fire as soon as he rejoined them.

In the Jeep, Pearce shifted the bowl from his knees and said curiously, 'What did Tojo want?' But Michaels did not reply, he pressed his foot harder on the accelerator, and with the action Pearce's full, uninhibited laugh rose knowingly above the noise.

5. Hapgood

During that October the mornings were fine and brittle with an extravagant sheen like cheap jewellery. From the dawn until midday the sky held its golden mellowness and warmed the seared leaves of the trees, bringing a flush of colour to the flat features of the land. There was an invitation in its warmth and a breath of promise in its golden light, both of them hollow and faithless, for the winter lay behind them. The soldiers looked up at the sun from the roadside and smiled incredulously that it could so shine on a battle.

Above, in skies of a clear, washed blue, the Fortresses going across the river to Germany spun a weft of vapour trails and sewed the fine weave of it to the linen sky. The men of the Troop lay on the platform of the station, resting their backs against the splintered wood and counting the planes. The machines flew in an unwavering phalanx to the east. High above the filmy golden mist they caught the full strength and passion of the sun and reflected it in bright stars from their fuselage. Up to meet them as they flew puffed the ugly, pear-shaped explosions of gunfire. The ground shook with the fall of the bombs, and now and then one of the bombers would turn wearily on its side and slide down to the earth at the end of a long, black-scarlet column of smoke and flame, staining the sky with oily blots.

And yet there was a sunlit complacency about it all, and the burning planes were so remote as to seem mere colourful metal and no more, and the sun glinted pleasantly on the swinging parabola of the parachutes as they floated down.

On the ground the armies stopped their obscene preoccupation with destruction to stare up at the sky, and hold their breath as they watched the eerie, ugly beauty of the bombers. When the planes and the noise of their engines had gone there were only the widening, artificial clouds of their wash, laying beams of cotton wool across the roof of the world.

Or sometimes, out from the sky above Groesbeek, across the green sea of the Reichswald would come the black shadows of German bombers, and the ground and sky about the station shook with the sharp fury of angry gunfire. Then it was that Pearce leaped between the platforms and fired the Browning, with sweat stinging his excited eyes and a curious exhilaration lighting his surly face with magnificence. He and Michaels worked at the gun in joyous animal spirits. Michaels would come back with the muscles of his shoulder aching and his mind peculiarly intoxicated.

The German bombers dropped bombs that fell lazily to the sand and the gorse and the tortured houses, and the idle chattering of machine-guns gossiped fretfully in the sky.

But it was the sun and the beauty of those October days that pointed the longest finger of derision at the stupid business in which Man found himself engaged. Except when night thrust its darkness upon the men there they could not believe that they lay within the dangerous perimeter of Death. The sun was more than a spectator, it was a warning that the warmth and life it still had to offer would soon be withdrawn. Man, civilian and soldier, must prepare for winter. Back to the village came little caravans of civilians, riding in their high wooden carts, with a cow or two ambling behind the buck-board and curious, doll-like children with fair hair and blue eyes riding atop the mattresses and bedding that filled the cart. The faces of children flowered incongruously against the green dust of the camouflaged vehicles.

Hapgood rode off the road to the verge and stopped his motorcycle to let one of these homecoming caravans pass. He sat in the saddle with an unconscious swagger and picked his teeth reflectively as he watched the convoy move slowly past him.

A policeman came first, in his dark blue shako and a white, braided lanyard looped across his chest. He was wheeling a bicycle to which was strapped a great cavalry sword, and walking beside him was an old man who did not lift his eyes from his shuffling clogs. Behind them both was the farm-cart, drawn by a heavy-bowed shire horse, kicking the grey dust about its swinging head. The cart was piled with scarlet mattresses, folded blankets, a chair or two, and a child's chamber-pot slashed with painted roses. A man held the animal's bridle, looking back anxiously over his shoulder to a girl sitting high on the blankets. She was young and fresh and Hapgood clicked his lips as he noticed the press of her young figure against her white blouse, but she stared back at him without recognizing the compliment, or resenting the insult. Then, as the cart drew abreast of him, she took her hand from her lap and threw him a scarlet-coated apple which he caught deftly. She smiled in a slow, beautiful manner and he grinned back and flipped his hand in the air.

The cart swayed past him, and after it walked a woman, wheeling another bike. A ridiculous, feathered hat was set on her hair and her round irritated face was red with sweat and exertion. She looked at Hapgood apathetically and did not answer as he took a large bite from the apple and mumbled 'Morgen, Ma!'

He kicked the starter of his machine and nodded gravely as it roared with life. He rode through Guderijn with an easy grace and by the church he stopped again, took the apple from his pocket and gave it to a grave-faced child sitting by the roadside. She took it from his hand and said 'Thank you, Tommy,' with a careful precision that delighted him. He took her up gently and sat her astride his petrol tank, playing with her flaxen hair and talking to her in a sharp, self-conscious voice that she did not understand, and laughing now and then with a hard, ironic guffaw. But, although she did not follow his words, the expression, the grimaces of his coarse face were readily understandable, and she smiled back, pulled at his silken scarlet scarf and explained to him that she wanted a ride.

His right foot kicked quickly at the starter and he swung the machine on to the road. Three times he rode down the avenue of trees, and the scarf blew out from his neck and the girl's soft hair dusted his face. She leant with her back stiff against his chest and her little hands gripping his breeches. He laughed with her and she screamed her excitement with the rush and sway of the cycle. He rode like a fine horseman, and to make her laugh and enjoy the exciting intoxication of fear he took his feet from the rests and pedalled them in the air comically, as if he were riding a push-bike. In the streets the Dutch, paddling their hands ineffectually among the ruins of their houses, stood upright to watch him and grin their approval. There was nothing Hapgood could do so well as ride a bike. It seemed to him in a dim sense that all of his life had been but a preparation for moments of exhilarating happiness like this. The doubts, the self-consciousness, the brooding hatred of a world that seemed confidently organized against him, flowed away in the broad stream of joy he felt when the bike was between his knees.

He stopped at last, took the little girl from the tank, sat her on his sloping shoulder and carried her into her garden where he sat her on the doorstep, and left her with a crushed and dirty packet of chewing-gum. He picked a marigold and threaded it through his jerkin where it glowed like an orange coal against the oily leather. The child screamed again to him, and waved as he throttled his engine and drove with a wide sweep on to the road. The delight of the child filled him with great gratitude. He felt that he could give her anything for such uncritical appreciation, for such frank and ready affection, even Dempsey. He rode back through Guderijn with the sun percolating through the dirt and thickness of his Tyneside skin and warming his soul.

By the church he caught the sweetness of the dead German in the turret of the tank. He slowed his machine to a halt, wiped the sweat from his neck and sat there with his feet resting either side of the machine and his narrow eyes staring at the ugly carcass of the metal animal. The German, black and horrible in the sunlight, lay half out of the turret with his long, claw-like fingers hanging down to the tracks.

Hapgood stared at the body curiously. He lit a cigarette and watched the tank closely, as if expecting it to move at any moment, or the grotesque caricature in its turret to straighten into life. The sunlight caught a glint from the German's right hand and Hapgood remembered the ring. He thrust his cycle over to its rest and strolled to the tank with a rolling, swaggering gait that the wide breeches and tilt of his helmet exaggerated to the point of clowning.

By the side of the tank he wrinkled up his nose in disgust and swore under his breath, but his eyes still stared at the man's hand. On the scaling forefinger was the black, swastika-embossed ring. Hapgood whistled in delight. Quickly he glanced up and down the street and then carefully picked up the dead man's hand. He pulled at the ring and it slipped off smoothly into his palm. He stared at it with satisfaction, wiped it carefully on his breeches and then pushed it on to his own finger. It settled there beside the skull of his other ring.

He climbed up to the tank and stared cautiously into its blackened belly. There was only evil-smelling darkness and he jumped quickly from the turret, surprised to find his stomach fluttering, his back weak. But he would have despised himself had he not taken the ring, or climbed the side of the dead animal. He looked down the street and saw a brown-robed monk staring at him from the church-gate. Hapgood stared back insolently and his lips moved with his defensive, arrogant thoughts. He hitched up his breeches with one hand and walked over to his bike. As he started up his engine he looked over his shoulder again; the monk had gone.

He rode, and the rush of the wind, the bright warmth of the sun encouraged him to sing. He opened his mouth and sang sentimentally in a tone which to anybody who did not know him would have sounded like a crude parody. Now and then he looked down to the broad, brown hand gripping the handlebars, to the two rings shining there. His breast warmed with a peculiar satisfaction.

He was a picture of easy competence and nonchalance. The day was beautiful. To his right the front spat now and then with the veiled venom of a machine-gun burst, but on the road there before Hapgood the birds sang and the dust placed a white shroud over the mutilated soil of Holland, the green flatness of the meadows peppered with craters, the silver stain of flood-water. Over them all the sun shone its warm tolerance, asking absolution for the winter that was to follow it.

Where the road branched and led to Jig Three Hapgood met the Troop Jeep. Jones was at the wheel and beside him, with his yellow scarf marking the tan of his face, was Michaels. They grinned at Hapgood as he flung his machine into a wide circle of exaggerated skill and pulled it up neatly by the Jeep.

'Look what I got, Joe,' and he held up his hand, 'off Sunny Jim.'

'You liberating twister!' said Jones, 'Going to Jig Three?'

'Can't catch me!' shouted Hapgood and he drove off, his feet pedalling the air as he bumped over the soil. Jones and Michaels looked at each other and grinned.

Hapgood was waiting for them at the gate of the farmhouse. He was waving his arms excitedly. As Jones pulled into the yard Michaels noticed that the detachment was running out of the building, some men were lying down behind the lorry, others were dodging backwards and forwards behind the doors of the barn. By the lorry stood Smith, in his shirt-sleeves with his revolver in his hand and his fat, white face slewed round over his shoulders to watch the Jeep as it turned through the gate.

'What the hell's going on?' said Michaels incredulously. He caught Hapgood by the arm, but the dispatch rider shook himself free and began to push a magazine on to his Sten-gun. 'There's a couple of Jerries in a slit trench down the field,' he said, 'Have a go, Joe?'

'Are the perishers armed? What's Tojo doing?'

Hapgood spat expressively and pointed his gun down to the farmhouse. Smith was still staring at the Jeep and his revolver was thrust out from his body as if he were afraid of the weapon. Michaels leapt out of his seat and ran across.

'It's all right, it's all right, Corporal!' said Smith half-defensively, 'Everything's under control!'

Michaels looked at him and went out into the field. By the projector the cook was placing a Bren on the ground, dropping beside it and pushing a magazine into its breech. Michaels grasped him by the shoulder. 'All right, Nobby, take it easy, what goes on?'

The cook shook his shoulder free, thrust his cheek against the butt of the gun, screwed up his lower lip and pressed the trigger. The Bren jumped busily into life, and following the bright line of the tracers Michaels saw the bullets kicking up the earth and turf at the end of the field. The cook stopped firing and looked up at Michaels with a triumphant grin. The sweat had gathered on his forehead in dirty beads, his mouth was open and his eyes held a mild eagerness. 'They're in a hole down there, Joe,' he said, 'Three of 'em.'

The Bren jumped in his hands again and the red fire of it darted at the corner of the field. In the lull between bursts Michaels thought he saw a white hand waving against the black earth. 'Cut it out, you bomb-happy grub-spoiler!' he shouted and dragged the man away from the gun.

The cook rolled over on his back and stared up at Michaels. His face was livid with excitement and sweat, and he looked queerly drunken, but he did not touch the gun again. About him and Michaels the others gathered slowly; they stared at the Bren, or down the field, and were strangely silent. Michaels felt Smith at his elbow.

'It's all right, sir,' he said, 'I think they want to surrender.'

Smith bit his lips and looked down the field. 'Yes, of course. That's it. We . . .' and he looked at Michaels.

'All right!' said Michaels, 'I'll go.' He slung his Sten down. 'Come on Ted!'

Smith began to run after them with a peculiar, ludicrous stagger. Hapgood sniggered, ran past the officer and caught up Michaels and Jones. 'What's the hurry, Joe? Do you want all the watches and rings?'

'Turn it up, Happy,' said Michaels, 'This Troop haven't got their nappies dry yet.'

'Before you came up Michaels!' said Hapgood cheerfully.

To Jones it seemed as if the walk from the projector took an hour. Beside him Michaels was walking with one hand in his pocket, his yellow scarf falling across his shoulder, his lips pursed in a silent whistle. Behind them Jones heard the panting of the lieutenant, the slither of his feet on the muddy ground. There was something ridiculously melodramatic about it all. In the group about the projector someone shouted derisively, 'Double up there, that man at the back!'

Before they reached the corner of the field they noticed the slit trench, the lip of it scored by the driving thrust of the bullets. In the trench itself they saw the humped backs of three men. Michaels swung his gun down like a stick, ran the last four or five yards to the trench and stood there with one hand still in his pocket and his feet wide apart. Jones saw his handsome face broaden with a grin.

'OK!' said Michaels to the men below him, 'Let's be having you!'

Hapgood whooped, ran up and pulled back the bolt of his Sten. Michaels turned on him angrily. 'Unload that damn thing, Happy!' But Hapgood did not notice him, he stared down at the crouching Germans and shouted, 'Wakey-wakey. Out o' that wanking pit you supermen!'

Smith, painfully conscious that of all that ridiculous situation he must look the most ludicrous, looked down into the trench reflectively. Staring up at him were three young men. Their uniforms were wet and their faces were streaked with mud where they had pressed their cheeks against the walls of the trench. They returned Smith's stare with blank eyes and their lower jaws drooping. A chance lurch of his body as he slipped on the mud brought forward his right arm and the revolver swung across his body. The Germans stood up unsteadily. One of them raised the tips of his fingers to the crown of his head.

The Englishmen looked at them, Jones could not think that any one of them was older than twenty. Their fair, straight hair was long and pushed straight back from their foreheads without partings, and the chins of two of them were blotched with ugly sores. The red, white, and black ribbon of the Iron Cross was tucked into a button-hole of the tallest.

'Missed the last train to Berlin?' queried Hapgood conversationally.

Smith frowned again and his mind struggled for action. 'Tell them to get out, Michaels,' he said weakly, 'This is silly.'

'*Raus!*' said Michaels, and swung the barrel of his gun across his body. The three men pulled themselves over the lip of the trench and the last, the most exhausted, lay there and gasped for breath. Hapgood caught him by the shoulder and pulled him on to the ground. 'Shake yourself, cocker!' he said cheerfully. The German pulled himself on to his knees like an animal and then, without warning, vomited on the ground in deep, agonized retching.

'*Oh Lord!*' said Smith in sympathy, but the other Germans stared at their comrade with irritation. Hapgood dropped his Sten over his shoulder, grasped the sick man's head and jerked it up and down between his knees. 'What did you do that for?' he asked, 'It's all right for you. You're out of this war. Five cigarettes a day and an English tart to warm your feet from now on.'

'Turn out their pockets, Hapgood!' said Smith sharply and pushed his revolver back into his holster hoping that none would notice the action. Hapgood whooped in delight, 'Here we come gathering watches and rings!' He ran his hands expertly through the German's pockets and found a bone-handled knife, a ring, two wrist-watches and no papers. One of the watches he slipped into his pocket with a broad, triumphant wink at Smith's back.

Smith pushed his hands against his stomach. 'Can you take them into Troop, Michaels?' he said, almost pleadingly. 'We've been warned about this. They come over to do a bit of sabotage. Give them some tea first.'

'*Tea?*' It was Jones. 'Why should we?'

Smith turned slowly to him. He did not know Jones, but he saw the scarlet face, flushed with excitement and incipient anger. 'Yes, tea!' he said with a little asperity. 'They're half dead, and as human as you or I.'

'Hope I'm a bit more human than a Jerry, anyway.'

Smith's face went a little red. 'Nonsense! Take them down, Michaels.'

The cook had taken the Bren back into his cookhouse. It leaned against the stable wall and the cartridges of a spare magazine spewed a bright yellow stream about its butt. Michaels shouldered the Germans into the foetid atmosphere and pushed them to a bench where they sat silently, hands between their knees and their faces expressionless. 'Give 'em some tea, Nobby, will you? You might as well. You just tried to kill them.'

'I'd kill the whole lot if I had my way,' said the cook happily. 'Castrate every male German after this war and ship the women to Uncle Joe. The Red Army will go through them like a dose of salts.' He dipped a mug into the dixie and thrust it at the tallest of the three prisoners.

'Thank you very much,' said the German politely. 'It is very welcome for we have not eaten for three days and the Maas was cold to swim.'

There was a strained silence, and then Michaels laughed. 'That shook you, Nobby!'

'Well if that ain't a typical Jerry trick!' said the cook. 'Don't you half-inch that mug or I'll do you!'

The tall prisoner with the medal ribbon dropped his head sharply in acknowledgement and passed the mug to his friend. Then he looked up at Hapgood and said courteously. 'You have my watch?' The men laughed and Hapgood grinned back. 'That's right, Slash!'

The German nodded and began to tear at the seam of his jacket and pulled from the hole a small signet ring. He held it up between his fingers and thumb. 'For cigarettes?' he asked.

'Let's have a butcher's hook!' said Hapgood and deftly snatched the ring. He nodded appreciatively, transferred it to his left hand and slipped it on the third finger. He leant back, stared the German coolly in the face and began to whistle.

'Give him the fags!' said Michaels.

'Go and get. . .!' said Hapgood.

'The Jerry probably got it the same way, Joe,' said Jones, and he turned to the German. 'You loot this from France?' But the German did not reply. He held out his hand to Hapgood and smiled, 'Cigarettes?'

'Take a running jump, Jerry!' said Hapgood not changing position.

'Give the fags, Happy!' said Michaels, raising his voice. Hapgood shrugged his shoulders and grinned, flinging the man a packet. The German snatched it open hungrily, thrust one into his mouth and gave one each to his friends. He lit his from Michaels' cigarette and lent back, inhaling luxuriously.

'I'll give you twenty for Berlin,' said Hapgood.

The German blew the ash from his cigarette calmly. 'The war is nearly over,' he said, 'You will see, and perhaps then you will give me ten cigarettes for what is left of London.'

'You can have it,' said Hapgood, 'but you won't get Tyneside.'

The German looked up and frowned, and Jones burst out angrily. 'Suppose we give 'em the best bed and a week's compassionate leave!'

'What do you want to do, Ted,' said Michaels, 'beat 'em up?'

'What do you suppose they do with their prisoners?'

'Rob them I suppose, like Happy's done.'

'Anyone'd think this war was a football match!' Jones almost spat out the words.

'Your pardon,' said the German gently, 'You do not like the Germans?'

'I love 'em,' said Jones. 'That's right, isn't it. We're all Aryan brothers?' His face was red and he was conscious that he was shouting.

'You are very young,' said the German, 'And not a very good soldier, I think.'

'I don't want to be a soldier!' shouted Jones and as the rest of the men laughed he turned pleadingly to Michaels, 'Get 'em out of here Joe, before I hit this bloke.'

The German looked up at Jones and smiled slowly. He pinched out his cigarette, put it carefully in his pocket, and stood up, pulling at the edges of his tunic. 'We are ready for your concentration camps,' he said slyly, 'It will be a short rest for us.'

Hapgood rode back to the railway station ahead of the Jeep. He felt that it had been a good day, with the memory of the soft hair of the little Dutch girl blowing about his face, the fierce excitement of opening the throttle along the smooth road when he came to it, and the two new rings that gripped his fingers. When leave came, if it ever came, he would take the watch home to his brother.

He thought of Jones, and the sudden, sentimental affection he felt for him clouded his face. He knew that Jones' wife had been killed by a flying-bomb and he thought that if he had been Jones he would have hit that German. As he thought of it he began to believe that he should have hit the man anyway, not only for Jones but for himself. The mixed, tangled knot of his emotions lay in his throat and he knew that he could only untangle it by the animal sensuality of fighting. The more he thought of the German's calmly confident face, the slight calculated sneer in his voice, and the arrogance that lay behind his eyes, the more Hapgood wished that he had crashed his fist on the thin, supercilious bridge of the German's nose.

He swore heavily. His blood was charged with a peculiar excitement, and he opened the throttle and thrust the dusty bulk of his machine faster down the road. Behind him he heard Jones sounding his horn sharply, but he would not slacken speed. The rush of wind about his face cooled his temper and he rode as if he were being pursued. Somehow all he wanted was to get back to the station, to pick up the dirty body of Dempsey and rub the puppy's soft fur against his own harsh cheeks.

6. The Troop

The war did not end that autumn. The impetus that had carried the Army through France and Belgium and would, it was supposed, carry the war on into Germany and the neatness of a negotiated peace, ended amid the dykes of Holland as if thin hands reached up from the stagnant marsh waters to grasp at the wheels and pull at dragging feet. The black earth claimed the soldiers as its winter tenants and drew warmth from the bodies of the infantrymen as they lay belly to belly with it. They watched winter come towards them, fingering their breath and holding it in the air in soft, white clouds. They watched it frosting the fields in the mornings before the sun was warm, and although at midday that sun shone bravely they knew that night already belonged to winter and that the war would never end. It was a conclusion they accepted indifferently rather than in despair. It was yet another curiosity in a land where curiosities were already commonplace.

The men of the Troop came to know Holland with a peculiar mixture of affection and distaste. They detested it for its flat fields and the winds and sleet that could pass so mercilessly, turning the ground to iron beneath the entrenching spades. They detested it for the mines that had been sown in the fields, in the farmyards and cupboards. They would pull into a farm behind the infantry and sleep in the trucks until dawn so that they might not in the darkness and their weariness set spring to the sharp irony of death.

Winter washed forward in icy rainstorms. It gripped the vehicles as they bogged down in the mud. Tea was cold before it was sipped. The soldiers hunched their bodies about their souls and grew irritable. They stood over their petrol fires as the wind dragged out the flames like the long petals of bronze chrysanthemums, but the soldiers were less conscious of the beauty than they were of the warmth. The mud oozed up from the soil when it thawed at midday, ugly, oily mud. It rose in high fountains from the wheels of convoys. The soldiers swore at the rain. They were black with it.

It was a narrow strip of Holland that the Troop helped to hold. The names of the towns through which the convoy passed were recalled only for the variance in the shelter they offered. Broken farmhouses and pigsties, a tent of ground sheets beneath a lorry. The winter came on fast as if it were frightened that the soldiers would have too little time to appreciate its full strength and bitterness. In the depths of the Troop's swill bins strange figures ferreted. The children were pale and their cheeks a scurf of sores. They had little to eat that winter and the soldiers fed some of them from their own stoves and were warmed a little by the flowering of the children's cheeks and the strange incongruity of their laughter.

The hardest days were when the mail did not arrive. Then the soldiers knew that, if only for hours, they had lost contact with that other world which they still believed existed.

They moved on, always they were moving on and leaving promises to write, to return. Moving on to a windmill, to a butter factory, to a slit trench, to the winter grip of night again.

Night was the time for warfare. Every tree became a shell-burst. Distances were compressed into dangerous proximities. Contacts with familiar things were lost. The soldiers started at their own shadows. The adders' tongues of gun-flashes flickered wickedly. The war was sincere at night; at night each man knew that the war would never end.

7. Waithman

Waithman leant back in his chair and stretched his tired body with pleasure. He looked at Smith and wondered why, since he disliked his Section Officer so much, he could feel sorry for him. He had known Smith for two years, from the day when Smith had come to the battery at the time it was being mobilized for overseas service. Until Smith had been posted to his Troop Waithman had paid little attention to the man. He had joked in the mess about Smith's gross figure and evident incompetence, laughed sycophantically at the Colonel's sly digs. It was regarded as inevitable that Smith would be drafted out of the battery long before it left for overseas.

But he had been made Waithman's Section Officer. Six months had taught Waithman that somewhere there was a canker eating at Smith's self-respect. It successfully blocked any real amity between them. Yet they lived in an atmosphere of friendship, calling each other by their Christian names and exchanging as much personal information about themselves and their families as decency demanded. There was little of the frank intimacy of common soldiers in this relationship, each was conscious of a position to be maintained, of inhibitions to be preserved. Where their conversation advanced beyond conventional depths they skirted essentials and guarded their thoughts jealously. Neither liked the other, but circumstances made them cherish the spurious friendship that existed between them.

Waithman played with the buckle of his belt and watched Smith as the lieutenant sat at the table and ate hungrily. Waithman did not like Smith's manners although there was nothing vulgar in them, the vulgarity seemed to exist mainly in the fact that a man of such obesity could still find the desire to eat more. He did not look at Waithman as he ate, nor did he speak, but kept his head over his plate, eating without pause and drinking regularly from the china cup at his side.

Smith did not billet with Waithman. He lived alone with his section, and Waithman, who could make life tolerable by jocular familiarity and political argument with his men, knew what torture isolation must be to Smith. Even his batman did not indulge in that familiar insolence which Waithman humorously encouraged in his own, but served his officer with a taciturn surliness that ill-concealed his resentment and contempt. Long ago Smith had asked permission to look after himself, explaining that shortages of men did not permit the wastage of one as a batman, but Waithman, always jealous of the privileges of commissioned rank, had curtly refused.

Every week Smith came to Troop Headquarters to spend a night with Waithman, to discuss the week's work, to arrange for re-siting his projectors, and to cling to the shred of comradeship maintained by games of cards. They sat this night in the amply-furnished room of the little Dutch farmhouse in which Waithman had decided to make his headquarters for Christmas. The men were next door in the cold loft of a butter factory, choked with smoke and awaking each morning to find their blankets thick and stiff with frost. Smith could hear them now, singing, and the noise of their ribald shouting came to him as he ate the last of his rice and stewed fruit.

He pushed back the plate, wiped his mouth with a handkerchief and looked up at Waithman. 'You've got a jolly good cook here, Bob.'

Waithman nodded. His eyes were fixed on a grain of rice that clung to Smith's right cheek. He had hardly heard the praise, he was wondering whether it was worth-while to comment on the rice-grain just in order to see the look of pain in Smith's eyes, or the furtive manner in which he would wipe it away with that ridiculously small handkerchief. But the rice fell on Smith's battledress as he leaned forward.

'How long are we going to be here, Bob?'

There was something pathetic in the question and Waithman shrugged his shoulders. 'We might move tomorrow, we might be here until spring when Monty moves us into Germany.'

'That'll be nice,' said Smith with a simplicity that made Waithman want to guffaw. Smith, he thought, was the type of man born to be hurt by others.

'How long have you been an officer, John?' said Waithman.

'Longer than you, Bob, I think. Over four years. Why?' Almost with every sentence each used the other's Christian name, as if to disprove the obvious fact that there was little friendship between them.

'I was just asking. What made you take a commission?'

'I don't know,' said Smith, spreading his hands on the table and looking down at them. 'I felt I wasn't able to do my best in the ranks, you know. And Ivy kept saying I should take a commission.' He smiled a gentle disagreement with his wife. 'She said it wasn't right that a man of my age, and a qualified accountant too, should be what she called "an ordinary soldier".'

'You're forty, aren't you, John?'

'Thirty-nine, Bob. I suppose I wouldn't have been called up if I hadn't been in the Terriers.'

'You'd've made a better air raid warden, perhaps. Are you happy?'

Smith looked at Waithman quickly, this unusual catechism made him apprehensive. 'Happiness isn't important these days, is it? If you mean about my work, I think I do it all right, you know.'

'Shall we have a hand of crib?' asked Waithman, inconsequentially.

Smith hated cards but he always seized at the opportunity to escape Waithman's slighting mockery and unspoken criticism, and tonight with the danger of it being spoken he readily accepted the suggestion. But Waithman, as he stared at his cards and ran his forefinger backwards and forwards across his moustache, seemed perversely malicious. He placed a card on the table and said casually:

'You know, John, your section thinks you're a coward. That's as it may be, but you're certainly the most unpopular officer I've ever met.'

There was a silence. Against the wall the clock quietly clicked out the seconds and in the big-bellied stove behind Waithman the peat fell with a burst of sparks and spurts of smoke that filled the room with fine, sharp perfume. The silence was broken as Smith slapped his cards on the table and pushed back his chair. 'You've no right. . .!'

'I've every right, John!' Waithman looked up sharply as he said it. Opposition always irritated him and he least expected it from Smith. The Section Officer's face had turned dark and in his eyes was a furious, helpless look of anger. Waithman was disgusted to notice that Smith's thick lower lip had drooped open and, shockingly, he looked as if he were about to cry. 'Oh stop being a fool!' said Waithman irritably, 'Consider the thing intelligently.'

Smith did not answer. Into his mind crowded sentence after sentence but none of them seemed adequate. He had hoped that Waithman would never bring this matter out into the open, but at every meeting he had been frightened that it would happen. His fingers played nervously with the cards he had placed face upwards on the table-cloth.

'I can see your cards,' said Waithman easily.

Smith turned them over, one by one, looking down at them and then up at Waithman frankly. 'Do you think I don't know you're right, Bob? I don't want to be an officer, I don't want this life. I'm a physical coward I know, there are hundreds of us, but someone's got to do this job.'

'Why didn't you stay in England and serve char in a canteen then?' said Waithman brutally, 'Look here, John,' and he leaned across the table, 'I don't care a hoot about you, but I do about my Troop, and so long as you're Section Officer, I'm not having the lads going round saying you aren't fit to shovel you-know-what.'

'They obey my orders!'

Waithman laughed sardonically. 'And they can't forget Nijmegen.' Half-believing the taunt he said it only to hurt.

Smith pushed back his chair. 'You said you'd never mention that again!'

'How can I help it when little Hopkins' face pops into every man's mind directly he sees yours. Oh, I believe your story, John, not that it matters. But that doesn't excuse your bloody foolishness!'

'Send me back then,' said Smith miserably, 'If I don't have your confidence there isn't much I can do.'

'Oh, don't be such a blasted fool!' They sat with the table between them but it was more than that which separated them, a difference in years, in experience, in self-confidence and morality. 'Look here, John. You've got to do something, anything, but get yourself rehabilitated. Pull your socks up.'

Smith looked up. He felt suddenly calm and surprised Waithman by the evenness of his voice. 'You don't understand, Bob. You're like a lot of people. You subscribe to the conventional hatred of war, decide that it is indecent and inhuman, and yet when you come across a man whose stomach can't take it all, you condemn him out of hand, not realizing that you really like all this. You like the excitement, the disjointed values, the transient importance which wartime gives people like you. I may not be well-liked by the chaps, but I think I know the real reason why. It's because I'm an officer, it's because I get the plums of living just because I'm an officer and never have to earn them. If you weren't such a fool you'd see that they resent you too for the same reason. The more we assert our authority the more we weld them together. There's something fine and reassuring in their unconscious solidarity, but I wish it weren't so uncompromising.'

'Oh, be damned to your politics,' said Waithman, disconcerted, 'What the hell are you talking about?'

'There's another thing,' Smith's voice rose to a tense squeak, 'But for the war I don't suppose I would have known what it is really like to be unhappy. I had confidence in myself. I was an extremely good accountant, you know Bob! I was doing well, and I had a good home, two children, and a good wife. Even after I joined the Army I still had my self-respect. But this. . .'

'Do you know what you're talking about?'

'I know,' said Smith quietly, 'I mean that since I came over here it has been as if someone has pulled back the curtain I've lived behind for years. It isn't just that other people see that I don't fit, but I've discovered weaknesses, real weaknesses of spirit and character that make my early life seem very paltry indeed. You'll see these things about yourself eventually.'

Waithman felt embarrassed. He shrugged his shoulders and turned to kick open the door of the stove. The flames leaped out in a smoke-ringed, orange bound. The gust of hot air and the aromatic sparks glowed across the table and caught the livid roundness of Smith's face.

'I wish to God I'd never come over,' said Smith. 'If I'd stayed in England I'd never have met myself, but I don't know why, I've got to go on, and you won't stop me. Why is this sort of dirty business the only test of man?'

Waithman grinned, stuck out his boot again and tapped the stove door with his toe. 'Haven't you heard? This is a war against Fascism, war for the liberation of the world.'

'That's true too,' said Smith, 'It is to me, and to most of the chaps down there,' he thrust his thumb in the direction of the butter factory, 'Except their idea of freedom is a material thing, not the abstract entity of people of our class, and they'll surprise us when this business is over. But you, Bob, you're here for the fun of it. You could get the same satisfaction on the other side.'

'I say, you're laying it on, aren't you?' said Waithman, alarmed. He had never expected this reaction to his badgering.

'You don't understand, do you?' said Smith, feeling strangely calm.

'I'm not in the box!' Waithman looked up sharply.

'And I don't have to be!' retorted Smith.

'Now look here, John,' said Waithman in conciliation, 'I don't care about all this moralizing. I'm not a trick cyclist. I'm as much interested in getting the best out of you as I am any other lad in this Troop.' He brushed away his discomfort by exaggerated firmness. 'And by God, I'm going to get it!'

'You know, Bob,' said Smith with a grin, 'for all your self-satisfaction I'd hate to be you after this war. I heard two of the blokes saying they expected to see you selling cars in Great Portland Street.'

Waithman concealed his anger. 'OK John, but let's try to put our backs into it, shall we?' He sat up suddenly, 'We've had enough of this talk. Here's what I want you to do, and I'm making no bones about it. Do something to get your section's respect, anything, but do something.' He looked up into Smith's eyes with a peculiar harshness, and Smith felt his nebulous superiority dissipating before it. His thick flesh hung on him like a spiritual weight.

'I understand you,' he said, 'At least *one* of us understands the other.'

'Oh be damned to your self-pity!' said Waithman irritably, 'What would you have done if you'd been an infantry officer?'

'I suppose I would have been killed long before this.'

'Naturally,' said Waithman brutally, and then with a gentle inclination of his head, 'I'm sorry about all this, John. We've all got to pull together. You know that, we can't afford to be weak. Sure you wouldn't like to go down for a rest?'

'No, I'll stay,' said Smith flatly.

'Good! Now do you want to kip down in the corner, old boy? I'd like some sleep myself.'

'If you don't mind, Bob,' said Smith slowly, 'I'd rather go back to the section. I want to be up early to check over the new site.'

'As you wish,' said Waithman without emotion. 'But get your chaps to go over that yard with bayonets. It hasn't been cleared by the Engineers.'

Smith pulled on his jerkin and overcoat, wrapped a scarf about his throat and said good night quietly. Waithman did not even answer from the side of the stove, but clattered open its door with his foot again. Smith accepted the rudeness indifferently. He was glad to get out into the night air. It was snowing again, slowly, the thin, crystal-patterned flakes drifting through the air. They rested on his cheeks and stung them sharply. He thrust his hands into his gauntlets and looked up to the sky. It was so clear of clouds, so deep a blue that he wondered at the snowfall. Around him the flat fields were still and white, stained by the black humps of occasional farmhouses. To his right the black ruin of the butter factory was slashed with thin strokes of light at the windows from which there rolled a song.

    'Sing hi, sing ho, wherever you go,
    Artillery buggers they never say no!'

As Smith walked by he heard the sentry whistling the refrain softly, and he called 'Good night!' into the darkness. He was surprised to hear Michaels' voice answer and he turned and went back. 'Hullo Michaels, doing your turn?'

Michaels nodded the shadow of his head casually. He beat his gloved hands on his arms and made no attempt at conversation.

'Pretty quiet so far, eh?' said Smith, 'No shelling?'

'Oh, no,' said Michaels, 'We're all safe, you know.'

Smith turned sharply on his heel without saying good night again, and he walked on down the road to his billet. It was a mile away and his little feet and ungainly body staggered down the slippery road. It was bitterly cold but he felt his cheeks burning with emotion. He was still surprised by his own temerity in talking to Waithman as he had. He beat his hands against his thighs and trotted down the road in a curious, ludicrous jog which he hoped would warm his feet. As he passed the headquarters of the infantry battalion two sentries called after him ribaldly, 'Pick your feet up Shorty and roll along!' He knew that had he been Waithman he would have charged the men, forward area or no forward area, but he knew too that Waithman was not cursed with a tragi-comic figure that invited derision.

He had stationed his section in a half-ruined house, in one undamaged room of which his batman had placed his bed. In the field beyond two searchlights burnt steadily as if their beams had been frozen into incandescent ice, and down through the pale, cream light the snow drifted in dark shadows.

His bed was unmade, but he could not blame his batman whose voice he could hear in obscene argument next door. He dropped on the bed, wrapped in his overcoat and fought stoically for sleep.

8. Smith

He was aroused in the morning by his batman who stood resentfully by his bed with two enamel mugs in his hand, one of deep brown tea and the other of tepid water. Looking at them, at the steam rising from the tea, Smith wondered whether he could ever bring himself to the point of shaving in tea, since it was always hotter than the water. But he was recalled from such thoughts by his batman who said with evident dissatisfaction, 'I thought you weren't coming back last night!' And he put the mugs down and left the room without waiting for an answer. Smith sighed and pulled himself from the bed.

The section moved at nine, in an ugly, untidy convoy of four lorries and three trucks. Smith rode at the head of the convoy, in the first truck, and his driver drove silently, with one hand on the wheel and the other clasping a mug of tea. On his lap was a dry bacon sandwich. The chains, wrapped about the wheels, flapped irritably on the snow-frozen surface of the road, and the cars moved like black animals, slowly and cautiously across the whiteness. Smith's driver drank his tea with deep, satisfying gulps, smacking his lips and licking them in calculated appreciation. He wore his scrubby beard like a defiant favour, but he drove the truck with a skill that Smith secretly admired and envied. The man missed nothing to emphasize his nonchalance, even to the contemptuous spitting over the door into the roadside when the truck skidded on the ice.

The new billet was a mile and a half down the road, screened from observation by a group of trees hard-hit by shell-fire and honoured by a distinctive sign that declared laconically, 'If you're going on, get out and WALK!' The leafless heads of the trees drooped over it and almost obscured it, the torn bark stripped in yellow scars from the trunks. At the gate Smith's batman was sitting morosely on his motorcycle, his white breath hanging above his head. He was slapping his hands together and when the lorries drew up he shouted a greeting, 'Get out and walk, you scroungers!'

The men jumped from the vehicles and began to run towards the house. Smith hastily scrambled out of his seat and waved his arms urgently, 'Come out of there!' he shouted, 'Sergeant, get those men out of there, that yard hasn't been cleared!'

His section-sergeant, a taciturn man from Wolverhampton, with an abrupt and violent manner, called the men back from the gate with unequivocal references to their progenitors. They came back grinning and stood by the vehicles, so many hunched and misshapen figures in leather jerkins and overcoats, jumping up and down in the cold, banging their hands together or pummelling one another's backs. Smith went over to them, breathing a little heavily and hooking his thumbs through his belt. He hated addressing groups of men, hated seeing, their eyes and the profound, cynical disbelief that was only too evident there.

'Now I'm afraid we'll have to clear this yard ourselves,' he said briefly, 'Get hold of your bayonets, the sooner it's done the better.'

'*Kinell!*' said a voice of patient resignation from the group, but Smith ignored it. 'Get them on to it sergeant!' he said.

Grumbling, shivering their shoulders, the men pulled the bayonets from their belts and, with the gate opened, knelt on the snow-covered ground. One of them began to wail unhappily, beating his hands on the earth in supplication, and the others, sniggering at him, began to prod the ground before them with short, jabbing strokes, moving forward inch by inch. The angry, discontented murmur of their voices came back to Smith as he stood uncertainly by the truck. He felt his driver's eyes staring at him from the cab, and in a sudden moment of bitter anger he turned on him. 'What are you doing there? Go and help!' he said quickly.

The driver got out of his cab slowly, pulling down his jerkin with exaggerated slowness and strolling over to the group to stand behind them jeering, before he dropped on his knees too. 'This is a fine time to say your prayers! Half of you have had compassionate leave to Hell already!'

Alone there by the empty vehicle Smith stared at the humped figures of the men, like strange, prehistoric animals bobbing and stabbing their way foward into the unbroken snow of the farmyard. He was jealous of their community of spirit, the mutual tolerance beneath the veneer of abuse, and he longed to be taken into the circle of their unassailable comradeship.

'You can smoke!' he called to the men and then noticed with confusion that they were already doing so. One or two of them glanced back over their shoulders, with expressions of amusement, and he realized what a strange, lonely, and amusing figure he must look as he stood there. He lit a cigarette and walked up and down the road to keep warm.

He smacked his hands together and then threw his cigarette away in disgust, half-smoked. He turned back to look at the farmyard. The men were straggling, some far in advance of the others, and he walked over to them irritably. 'Get back, get back!' he shouted angrily, 'Don't be such damned fools! You've got to keep in line.' The men in front sat up and waited, and as Smith walked away he heard one of them mimicking him with dry humour.

Something in the white rectangle of the yard fascinated Smith. It seemed unbelievable that beneath its clean surface were round, neat objects which at a touch could erupt into ugly black and crimson death. The house was empty, a shell had struck its roof and torn off a great area of its slated skin and left the grey rafters bare, and through the gap the snow had drifted to form a soft, deep bank against the other wall. A checkered blue and white curtain, half torn from its railing, waved out of the windows of the kitchen like a banner. Smith reflected unhappily that in this weather the pump would be frozen and probably it would be hard to thaw it, even with boiling water.

The stables had been burnt and lay in unbroken piles of black embers, crowned comically with the white caps of snow. There was an atmosphere of deathly desertion and unhappy solitude about the place that he did not like, but his spirit, already paralysed by such sights as this, watched it all dispassionately.

Only the yard itself fascinated him still. No mines had yet been discovered, and the men were becoming impatient. Some of them were sitting back on their heels, looking at the ground with disgusted suspicion and blowing on their fingers. Smith wondered whether it was his imagination or their indifference that struck the greatest comparison between them.

He thought of Waithman and of the conversation the night before, and as he remembered it and stared at the bobbing, moving line of men he was struck by the deep significance of Waithman's order.

As an idea took shape in his own mind with the growing importance of it, the excitement he felt burnt his cheeks and made his eyes feel weak and clouded. He walked up to the men quickly and looked at the yard and the house, and then as quickly he turned away and walked back to the truck. As he glanced again at the house he felt that its open doors and the cheerful, flaunting scrap of blue and white curtain were a challenge.

He pushed back his narrow shoulders and walked resolutely to the men again, but when he reached them his driver sat back and looked up with such an expression of disgust that Smith wavered. He turned to the sergeant.

'All right?' he said, 'Nothing yet?'

'Nothing yet, sir,' said the NCO briefly, 'Shall we keep on?'

'Yes, yes!' said Smith quickly. He was afraid that the opportunity would pass. 'Keep at it, lads!' The pathetic cheerfulness of the words sounded more banal to him than to the men who had hardly heard them. He went back to the truck, around to the side out of view of the men and there he fought a battle with his own fears. He placed his shoulders against the stiff, frozen tarpaulin and pushed his body backwards as if he were straining away from some physical object. His lips moved quickly, and he thrust his hand nervously into his hip pocket and pulled out the little silver flask which Ivy had given him before he left for Normandy. 'You can put something in it,' she had said, 'just in case you get 'flu, darling.'

He pulled off his gauntlet with his teeth and unscrewed the cap of the flask. The strong, warm smell of the brandy floated up to him and he took the glove from his mouth, raised the flask to his lips, and tilted his head. The spirit shot through his body with a sudden burst of fire and he spluttered and wiped the tears from his eyes. His hand fumbled as he pushed the flask back into his pocket and it fell to the ground with a sharp clatter on the ice. He dared not bend down immediately to recover it, lest the men should turn at a noise which sounded extraordinarily loud in the silence. He leant against the tarpaulin again with his forehead sweating. At last he bent quickly, picked up the flask and thrust it into the map-pocket on his thigh.

He stood away from the truck and lit another cigarette, left it hanging from the corner of his mouth and put his hands into his pockets to stop their trembling. The men did not hear him coming as he walked towards them, and he was glad they did not, for he did not want them to see his face. They would wonder why it was sweating in that cold. He walked up to them quickly in his short, ridiculous way, and stepped through them as they bent over the snow. As he walked through he heard a sharp exclamation of pain and he knew that he had trodden on someone's hand, and his quick intelligence realized how such a trivial accident as that made the whole of his actions seem momentarily paltry. But he dared not look back.

He did not know whether he would reach the house alive, and as he slipped and staggered on he realized that perhaps he should have told the men to stand back out of danger.

He suddenly recognized the stupidity of his action. Behind him the men were standing to their feet in amazement and they were not discreet in voicing their opinions of what he was doing. He tried not to think of its silly aspect, of what matter it would be if he won their belated respect by blowing himself to death in the most ridiculous action of his life. He knew how comical he must look, his hands still in his pockets and his fat body slipping and swaying on the icy ground. The cigarette dropped from his loose lips and hissed itself into extinction in the snow.

When he reached the door he wanted to turn about, to grin cheerfully at the men and to tell them to come on, as Waithman would have done. But he could not summon up the words of jovial, half-jeering exhortation. There was still the house, the possibility that its half-open door, its snow-drifted tiles might themselves be mined, and they beckoned his foolhardiness. He stood at the step for a moment, caught his breath, and placing one hand on the door he pushed it open. It creaked and swung back innocently as he walked through.

The passageway was dark, and smelt mustily of an empty house, the heavy stench of damp clothing and peeling paper. He walked up and down the tiles slowly, pushing at the doors of the rooms like a cautious child. The rooms were deserted, except one bedroom where a dog lay dead on the bed, its body frozen into a rigid caricature and its tongue gripped tightly between its bared teeth. A few drops of blood had dripped from its mouth and they clung in bright, frozen beads of scarlet to the white sheet. Smith closed the door and leant against the post. He felt as if his spine had been snapped in the small of his back.

Outside in the yard he heard the men coming, their voices raised excitedly with a tension suddenly broken. He started, walked quickly down the passageway, into the kitchen where the sickly odour of decaying food stung his nostrils, and through into the cow-byre. There he saw what he wanted, the crude wooden lavatory between the pigsties. He walked over to it, stumbling on the frozen mire on the floor as he went inside. He slipped the bolt and sat down on the seat, thinking that his head would burst, but thinking, with inconsequential humour, that the Germans might have mined this too.

He heard the voices of his men floating over the house in a series of incoherent, noisy waves. To the frozen bones of the deserted home they brought a new and violent life. He heard them coming down into the byre, and the door was kicked open as three men stepped in. He heard his driver speaking, a bored, slightly disappointed voice.

'Nothing in here. Not even a pig by the look of it. This is a bastard place to come to, I'm not kidding. Bet this is where he'll make us sleep while he has that big bed up there.'

'Bed's no good without a woman in it, might as well sleep with the cows.'

'You never sleep with anything else. Where is Tojo anyway?'

'Somewhere. That was a daft thing to do, wasn't it?'

'Made us look a lot of twits.'

'But I always thought he had no guts.'

Smith felt the blood quickening at his temples and he held his breath.

'What do you think?' asked his driver casually, 'He knew the yard was all right. Even if there is mines there the ground's frozen stiff. You couldn't set them off by standing on it. He was trying it on.'

The noises crowded through the door of the stable and back into the passageway. Smith leant against the cobwebs and filth of the wall. With a sudden, queer giggle he realized that his driver had been right. The ground was frozen so hard that even his lorries might not explode the mines as they drove over it. If there were any mines there. He sat in the lavatory for a long time before he came out to find his sergeant, to find the cook and drink a mug of tea which the man had already brewed.

The men of the detachment were standing about the dixie, leaning over the steam as it arose from their mugs. They were laughing and quarrelling good-humouredly. Smith did not notice that they treated him with any marked difference of manner.

9. The Three

Between Jones, Michaels, and Hapgood there had grown a close and superficially opposite friendship. The friendships of soldiers develop from insignificant accidents, from a chance that flings them together to share an incident of momentary importance, so that men bracket their names together when speaking of it. These accidents, mere physical juxtaposition at given moments, are the cement of a soldier's friendship; the bricks are tolerance, generosity, and humour. From such beginnings, a guard shared, mutual victimization by superiors, or common origin in a provincial town, come the keys that unlock many doors to the recesses of intimacy, moving ever closer towards the centre but never reaching it, for a soldier, bereft of name, liberty, and the pursuit of his own interpretation of happiness, defensively preserves something within himself that is solitary and his own, be it grief, cynicism, lust, hatred, or fear.

When the three brought back the Germans to the station at Guderijn they discovered that just such a chance had touched them, and, accepting it, they casually developed the incident into friendship.

There was little in common between them emotionally, except a quick and impulsive reaction to the occasional excitement of their lives, and the longer monotony of its boredom. They shared also a love for the dirty puppy, Dempsey, and a protective guardianship of a little Dutch girl Nelly van Huyk, whose home lay a few yards from the butter factory. They shared their meals with her, gave her their chocolate, and inveigled food for her from Johnny the cook.

What they knew of each other was little, and hardly relevant to the life they led. They built their own common experiences and shared mutual memories that did not extend beyond that fine September day when Michaels had brought Jones to Guderijn.

Of Hapgood the other two knew that he came from Tyneside, that he had worked there in a factory or a foundry, in a mine, or along the docks. But his anecdotes were not of work but of his wife and the public houses in which he had drunk and fought. He spoke of his wife with a peculiar mixture of brutality and affection and wherever the Troop moved Hapgood found in the round-limbed, red-faced Dutch farm-girls carnal gratification for the passions which memories of his wife could not satisfy. The Troop argued humorously that Hapgood, during his brief months in Holland, had done much to replenish the gaps in its ranks which German slave-labour had made. He got drunk when he could wheedle whiskey or gin from the sergeants, and when drunk he skinned his knuckles on somebody's jaw or on the walls where he spent a furious, inarticulate passion by beating the bricks in shame. In the end he would cry, weeping unashamedly in front of Jones and Michaels, stumbling out his bitter hatred of others. He was always sorry when he hit another man because, whatever his size, 'he's only a little bugger'.

Michaels was no enigma to Jones or Hapgood, though their opinions differed. Hapgood worshipped the Corporal for his ease of manner, his open contempt of the officers and NCOs whom Hapgood hated and feared. Hapgood loved Michaels' skilful driving, his ready conceit, his indifference and knowledge of women which was far more theoretical than Hapgood's experiences. Both he and Jones knew that Michaels was married, and Hapgood envied him for the absence of the doubts and fears that plagued Hapgood in his own married life. Michaels spoke once of his wife, and told them how he had met her, leaning back against his truck and smiling the while, as if to impress upon them that there was really nothing in it and there was no need for them to worry because it had not laid sap to his independence or self-confidence.

Unconsciously they knew that theirs was a transient friendship. The end of the war would destroy it and would pull them all back into another life. Unreservedly they took what comfort the friendship had to offer and believed themselves the stronger for it.

And as the weeks drew on, one into the other, each like its predecessors was cold, wet, full of movement and dirt, and the presence of an obscene death that lay like a sardonic leer behind the slipping crosses of the roadside graves. But death was always something that called on the next man. It could not be otherwise.

Jones realized dimly that he was changing, that a peculiar hardness was creeping over his feelings although they remained hot and intense beneath their new skin. He drove as nonchalantly as Michaels now, swore as explosively as Hapgood, and although his eyes still saw the dereliction and mute suffering imprint of war in every face and wretched village, between that sight and his emotions he placed a defensive wall. There was no cynicism in his attitude or in that of the others, but no man can live within such a perimeter and be part of the instrument of destruction itself, without hardening the surface of his soul.

In a queer, tortured manner which he could not easily translate to his mind Jones found that his own grief had been submerged in the wave of bereavement that washed over Holland during the weeks of liberation and struggle. Every broken house, whether it had been crushed by German or British artillery, every scabeous infant face and thin adult cheek were to him mounting evidence of a great crime, his indignation at which he could only personalize in a hatred of the enemy that lay in the darkness and uncertainty ahead of him.

He avoided subjectivism by plunging into the roughness and rude experiences of his friends. He affected their manner of dress and wore about his throat a scarf of red flannel that the little Dutch child had given him, and embroidered on it in blue silk was her name, 'Petronella van Huyk'. He practised shooting with Pearce when the days were quiet, and between them they manned the Browning at night when the sky became tense with the presence of German bombers. He liked Pearce for the simple, engaging interest the man had in the weapon he had dragged from a crashed

Fortress in Normandy. Jones liked him for his complete lack of affectation, his generous good-humour and simple faith in himself.

And all the time Jones wanted things to happen, to keep on happening.

During those winter months the Army lived on the land. Cynically backs were turned to orders against looting, as cynically as they were turned to pious General Staff prohibitions on the brothels of Belgium. The capital of that country itself was now known as 'Brothels'. The forward area was in the hard grip of ice and snow and the farms were empty, gaping open with the precious intimacy of their entrails tumbled out into the snow, and amid the ruins wandered half-starved, half-frozen live-stock that died in the frosts, or were killed by the soldiers before they had time to die. Among the soldiers there was a hunger for fresh meat. But half understood by them there was also a hunger for the excitement of stalking and killing it, a blunt, uncompromising belief in the fact that they had the right to take what they found. There was no law except the old one of all armies, that the men who captured the earth had first right to its fruits.

From the butter factory the one road ran through marshes to the line that lay less than a mile ahead, a road strangely peaceful within an area which the rest of the world, looking at its newspapers over breakfast cups, or in its air-raid shelters, believed to be thick with battle. This road was quiet, and on either side of it were stacks of peat cut the season before and now piled up like the Giants' Causeway. It was quiet, so quiet that the snow, crunched underfoot, sounded like the breaking of so many dry sticks, and the infantry as they moved along it in file to the slit trenches and the silent night watches by the river, seemed small and insignificant against the snow. It was along this road, and in the deserted, ruined farms that lay back from it, that cows and pigs were stalked and slaughtered.

At Troop Headquarters every morning Sergeant-major Thompson held a parade outside on the hard, dry snow, and he walked up and down the two ranks with his arms straight at his sides, pulling at the cuffs of his blouse with nervous fingers. He inspected the men closely, the length of their hair, whether they had shaved or washed, and he pretended not to notice the ribald derision of the infantry as they passed in file.

One morning Thompson came out of the operations-room with a piece of paper in his hand. 'It's about looting,' he said, pulling at his sleeves, 'Now you know, and I know, and Captain Waithman knows, there's looting *and* looting. There's pretty exceptional circumstances here, but some of you people have got to realize that you're in a country you're liberating, not paralysing.' He cleared his throat and spat behind him. 'The Wogs have got to come back and live here, and they'd like to know the British Army left them something to live on.'

Michaels stuck his hands in his belt, 'How about pigs?'

Thompson frowned. 'A lot of you have got the idea that it's on the cards to kill pigs, but, to my way of thinking, it's still looting. Oh, I know, I've eaten the ones Hapgood's had a do-lally at. But you're not supposed to be a lot of ruddy Jerries.' He looked embarrassed and rubbed the back of his head. 'Now, any more questions?' He looked at them with a querulous forward thrust of his features and grimaced as Michaels nodded his head. 'Always got something to say, eh Michaels?'

'That's right, sir. The OC said it was OK to go down the marsh road and get one of those pigs. There were five the other day, but the infantry and the frost have probably got a couple since.'

Thompson sighed. 'What's the good of me saying one thing, if the OC says another?' He asked the question with a sideways twist of his head as if he really expected it to be answered by one of the mute, indifferent men who stood before him. Jones flashed a glance at Michaels and they both grinned. Thompson walked up and down and then shouted indignantly. 'OK, OK! If Captain Waithman OK's it. But don't get caught, and some of you stand closer to the razor tomorrow morning. I'll have this detachment clean, wherever it is. Fall out!'

He walked quickly into the operations-room, into the musty office of the butter factory, banging his hands together and blowing his pursed lips in disgust. Behind him Hapgood burst out of the ranks, doubling up his body and kicking out his legs, singing 'Here we come gathering pigs and 'ens, pigs an 'ens!' He danced round Michaels. 'When are we going, Joe?'

'Might as well go now,' said Michaels, 'Waithman says it's OK but you have to tell Baldy to stop him feeling hurt. We'll go in the blood-wagon. Coming, Ted?'

Jones tightened his scarf about his throat and grinned. 'Of course!'

They drove down the marsh road, with a head-wind blowing from the river and flapping the canvas covers of the truck. The ventilation flap was open at Jones' feet and the warm air of the engine rushed up into the cab. Hapgood sat on the battery-box between the others, a huge sledge-hammer on his knees and his curious, high voice singing raucously.

'Shut up, Happy, for Christ's sake!' said Michaels.

'Seems a pity they can't collect all this livestock and take it back down the line for the Dutch,' said Jones.

Michaels grinned with a sidelong glance. 'What, and leave none for us? Here we are!' He swung the vehicle off the road into the yard of a farmhouse. The frost had frozen the deep ruts of the lane into great crystalled valleys and plateaux. The Bedford leaned over and came to a stop. 'For God's sake Happy be careful where you put those plates of meat of yours. The place is probably thick with mines, see that?'

He pointed through the yard to the far end where beneath the gnarled apple trees stood a small American tank, the lid of its round turret open and one of the rusty tracks torn off and coiled in a violent paroxysm about the trunk of a tree. 'Mines,' said Michaels, 'There's a dead Yank on the other side of it and he's not very pretty.'

Hapgood whistled. 'Anything in the house?' he asked.

Michaels grinned. 'You heard what Baldy said? Anyway the infantry and the Yanks and the Jerries have been through it like a dose of salts, unless you want some women's underclothes, Dutch peasant style. You could put all your kit in one leg. Still, you know all about these things, don't you?'

They climbed out of the cab and stood there in the farmyard, and suddenly, without any of them being aware of the reason, they looked at each other with silent embarrassment. Behind them the farmhouse was gaunt and destroyed, as if some giant hand had struck away one end of it and idle fingers had gouged out its furniture and furnishings and left them strewn carelessly among the frozen manure and snow. The wind had blown the snow into the opened rooms and washed it in delicate ripples along the floor.

'Pity, isn't it?' said Jones.

'Yeh!' said Hapgood, but Michaels added with his accustomed hardness, 'It's war. What do you expect, a garden suburb with half-hourly buses?' He pulled his Sten from the cab. 'Let's have a look at the tank, the infantry may have left the radio in it.'

'Mind the mines, Joe!' said Hapgood in sudden alarm.

'Tread in my footsteps boldly!' said Michaels and they walked down the deep ruts which the tank had made in the yard, and halted about its silent carcass. The ground was littered with American razor-blades and sticks of chewing-gum wrapped in scarlet papers. Hapgood bent down and picked one up, turned it over in his hands thoughtfully and began to unwrap it. 'Put it down, Happy!' said Michaels disgustedly. 'Do you want typhoid?'

Hapgood flicked the stick of chewing-gum into the air. It spun up above the tank and dropped neatly into the open turret. He grinned in simple satisfaction. 'Couldn't do that again if I tried,' he said, 'Pity the blades are all rusty.'

'A six-inch file's good enough for your face,' said Jones. They walked round the tank slowly, keeping their feet in the marks of its tracks, until they saw the dead tankman lying by the vehicle. He was a young boy, his body twisted round grotesquely so that while he lay with his face and breast pressed into the frozen earth his buttocks were resting on the ground, his knees bent and pointing into the air. His face was burnt black and his trousers had been half-torn from his body. Jones bit his lips deeply and stared. *'Jeesus!'* said Hapgood.

To Jones it did not seem as if the boy had ever been a human being, and there was something cold in his curiosity after the initial shock had past. He looked at the black profile, the singed line of eyebrows, and on the wrist that was out-stretched to grip the earth, was a silver identification disc. Half against his will Jones bent down towards it.

'Leave it alone, Ted!' said Michaels sharply.

Jones looked up in anger. 'We can't leave him here!' he protested, 'At least we can find his name and bury him decently.'

The sound of their voices was sharp and uncannily loud in the still air. Michaels shifted his Sten easily on his shoulder.

'I heard of a bloke in Normandy, remember Happy? Tried to do the same thing. The Jerries had mined the body.'

Jones did not believe the story but he stood up and said simply, 'OK'. They walked back to the house along the ruts, the radio forgotten, and slowly they circuited the house. Shreds of curtain fluttered from the windows and the sharp, spearheaded spikes of broken glass were frosted with delicate patterns. As they looked into the dark rooms they noticed that the house had been already looted. The drawers had been torn from the cupboards and emptied on the floor, the tables and chairs overturned. There was a pile of children's school books on the table, an algebra book with a green pencil lying across it and a pile of German rifle cartridges flowing in a glittering yellow stream over one corner. A bible lay open on the floor and its pages were stained pink; where the edges had been rain-wet the dye had run indiscriminately across the small type. On the wall of the kitchen hung a large engraving of the Last Supper, with a gaping tear where once had been the central figure of Christ. There was a horrible smell at every window, and beneath their feet as the three men walked was a persistent crunch of broken glass. It was a sound which Jones now believed to be inseparable from European houses. The door of the barn had been blown from its hinges and lay fifty yards away against a tree. They could see the stalls and the blown-up carcasses of the animals lying there, like great footballs. Hapgood picked up a brick and, throwing it at the bodies, he watched it bounce off against the wall. 'I thought they might burst,' he said in disappointment. 'They should, you know.'

In the front of the house, Jones and Hapgood looked through

the main window curiously. Looking back at them from the tangled mass of filthy blankets on a huge, brass-knobbed bed, were the soft, terrified eyes of a large and emaciated rabbit. Hapgood stared at it and guffawed. 'What?' he said incredulously, 'Look at the pretty bunny!' He swung himself lithely over the sill on to the broken glass, the torn books and paper. He stood there for a moment without moving while the rabbit, crouching on the stained blankets, stared back stupidly. Then suddenly he flung himself upon it, caught it by its ears and held it up while it kicked weakly.

'Don't kill it, Happy!' said Jones.

Hapgood looked up and showed his yellow teeth. 'Kill it?' he said, 'I'm not going to kill it, I'm going to take it back with me.' He tore open the buttons of his blouse and thrust the animal against his chest, where it stayed without any movement but the nervous twitching of its nose. Hapgood buttoned his blouse about it and looked at the room. 'The bastards!' he said softly. The dereliction of the room, its utter misery, suddenly seemed to appal him. 'The bastards! Look at it Ted, all because some people want more land, eh . . .?'

He was still murmuring that as he climbed out of the window and went round the barn with Jones. Michaels was already there, parting the straw from a dung-heap with the butt of his Sten. They went over to him and saw that at his feet lay the pink, frozen bodies of five young sucklings. 'There's a pig here, all right,' said Michaels, 'What the hell have you got there, Happy?'

Hapgood pushed the rabbit's ears back into his blouse. He looked embarrassed. 'Couldn't leave the poor bugger to starve, could we?' he said.

'I should've thought Dempsey was enough to handle.'

Hapgood looked hurt. 'Dempsey's sick,' he said, 'I think it's distemper. Somebody gave it to him. Why don't they leave 'im alone?' He turned to Jones. 'Eh, Ted, Baldy wants me to shoot him.'

'He won't like your bringing a rabbit back then.'

Hapgood put his hand into his blouse and fondled the rabbit's head. 'When I was a young tyke,' he said, 'I always wanted a rabbit, but my old man wouldn't have it.'

'Well, you've got your rabbit,' said Michaels shortly, 'Let's get on before you adopt a horse.' His feet kicked the bodies of the sucklings and they rebounded from his heavy-toed boot like pieces of rubber. Jones looked at Michaels' face and was struck by the hardness of it, the thin lips that were normally so full and humorous. 'I'm browned off with hanging about here,' said Michaels.

Jones stood where he was while the others moved cautiously into the barn. The house fascinated him. What seemed to emphasize the tragedy of its wounds was the fact that the destruction was not complete. A house gutted by fire took with it all memory of its occupants and left only uncompromising cinders and blackened stone. But where a house still held remembrance of past warmth, mute evidence of human tenancy in an old hat, a child's books, the tragedy was fine-edged. It hurt Jones far beyond his understanding. He was frightened by the fact that a few short minutes of furious bombardment could sweep away man's precarious tenure and make ridiculous nonsense of a lifetime's endeavours.

The metallic winter light struck new colours from the desolation about him and he was impressed by them, but his emotions sabotaged such appreciation and turned to bitterness an excitement he could not suppress. He felt that retribution could not make the criminals replace what they had destroyed, that retribution made further destruction obligatory. Here were things stronger and more terrible than man, and his faith was being tempered in their fierce, uncompromising heat.

A sudden shiver at the extreme cold trembled down his spine and he shook it off as he shook off his thoughts. He followed Michaels and Hapgood. Within him, deep down in those recesses which he revealed to no one but himself he felt no pity, no hatred or love, only a furious and inexplicable desire to find some occupation for his hands.

He heard the others shouting to him from the barn. They were standing by a ditch with their feet resting on the broken spokes of a cartwheel. Their necks were craned forward and they were looking over the top of the cart itself. Out of Hapgood's blouse poked the long, incredulous ears of the rabbit, as it if too were sharing their curiosity.

'It's here, Ted!' called Michaels.

Jones ran over to them, pulled himself up the side of the cart and looked down into the narrow space between it and the wall of the barn. Below him he saw the long, bristled back of the pig, filthy with mud and manure. As it turned a wet, pink snout up to Jones and snorted, its ears flopped over its grimed eyes. It was ugly and primitive, meant for death.

'Chase it out, Ted, there's a good lad!'

Jones reached down with his rifle and thumped on the animal's back. It gave a grunt of anger and pushed itself under the cart. Hapgood watched its head appearing and he sucked in his lower lip apprehensively, rubbing his hands together and picking up the sledge-hammer with both of them. 'What a beautiful face you've got,' he said, 'C'm'ere!'

Lying on top of the cart Jones saw the black head of the hammer swing easily through the air, and the sound of it whistled smoothly. It fell with all its weight on the pig's head. There was an indignant squeal of pain and anger and the animal rushed forward at Hapgood's legs, burst through them and ran with a peculiar, drunken stagger across the yard. Michaels and Hapgood laughed. 'Like the Palais Glide!' said Michaels.

'For Christ's sake!' said Jones and he slid off the cart. The pig was running about the yard comically, crossing its legs in stupefaction and squealing in agony. In the odd silence of the icy day its cries seemed the louder and more human. Jones unslung his rifle and dropped on his knee.

'Don't shoot it, Slash,' said Hapgood in alarm, 'Pigs should be bled to death.'

'Shut up, Happy!' said Jones and pulled the trigger. Hit behind the ear the pig fell over on its side and kicked its puny legs futilely. A pink bubble of air and blood welled up behind the flopping ear and as Jones looked at it he felt a little sick. Still kneeling on the snow he saw Michaels walk over to the struggling animal, place his Sten against its skull and fire a round through its brain.

'Here we come gathering pigs and 'ens, pigs and 'ens . . .' Hapgood began to dance about the farmyard, swinging his bandy legs across his body.

'Turn it up, Happy, and let's get the brute back,' said Michaels.

They dragged the bleeding animal through the mire and frosted straw to the truck. They were not sure that it was dead; occasionally it gave a convulsive jerk of its body that almost tore its legs from their grasp, and the bubble of blood gurgled throatily. When they had swung up the back-board and locked the pig in the truck, they noticed a black-red stream of blood dripping down over the hinges. Hapgood wiped it away with a handful of straw. 'Drive fast past the Red-caps, Joe,' he said.

'That's not blood,' said Michaels easily, 'it's paint.'

Hapgood opened his blouse and stroked the frightened rabbit. 'Don't you worry,' he said to it, 'nobody's going to do for you.' And he pulled up the silken ears and rubbed them gently against his cheek, looking up at the others with an almost defensive spark in his watery blue eyes. 'I like animals,' he said.

Michaels laughed. 'I can see that by the way you stroke 'em with seven-pound hammers.'

Hapgood pushed the rabbit back. 'I do really, Joe, I'm not kidding. But did you see the way Ted shot that big one? You're the kiddie, Ted!'

They drove back to the factory silently, with Hapgood sitting between the others, his blouse open and his crooked hands stroking the soft coat of the terrified rabbit. At the crossroad Jones said suddenly, 'The Dutch could do with this pig.'

'To hell with the Dutch!' said Hapgood and pushed the rabbit's ears against his cheek.

'Unless they want to pay for it,' said Michaels.

As they approached Troop Headquarters it occurred once more to Jones how lonely and miserable was the butter factory, insignificantly small, like a black stain against the snow, with the green and yellow scars of the Troop's vehicles grouped about it.

From one window there rose the rusty chimney of the cook's stove, and from it poured a steady up-thrust of white smoke.

'Dinner's up,' said Hapgood cheerfully.

And yet, thought Jones, once inside the factory, while you're there it seems to be all the world, with no reality outside its walls.

'There's Nelly,' said Michaels, 'And she's got Dempsey with her.'

'What?' said Hapgood, and he pushed the rabbit back into his blouse.

Standing by the factory, close to the roadside, with the feathering smoke of the cookhouse chimney spouting above her, was a little girl. From that distance the customary pathos of her appearance seemed emphasized by her insignificance. Her thin, black-stockinged legs rose uncertainly from her heavy clogs and disappeared into the narrowness of a short coat which she had long since outgrown. Her head was wrapped with an old scarf against which her white face gleamed in a peculiar vividness. Only a bow of bright orange paper flamed against her forehead where she had tied back her hair. Michaels did not take his eyes from her as he drew closer and leant over to change gear. 'She's crying!' he said.

'Eh?' said Hapgood and he sat forward and stared at the motionless black and white body of the puppy which the girl was clasping to her breast. 'It ain't Dempsey, d'you think?'

'Take it easy, Happy,' said Jones, 'We'll find out.'

Michaels switched off his engine and dropped from the cab beside the girl. 'Hallo kleine vriendchen,' he said kindly, 'Was is los mit Dempsey?'

The girl looked up at him, her brown eyes were wide above mauve bruises. A slight smile drew back the corners of her mouth at the sound of Michaels' careless German, but the tears that came suddenly to her eyes washed away the smile. Struck by the peculiar wax-like pallor of her cheeks, Jones dropped on his knee and put his arms about her shoulders. It always gave him a shock to feel the sharp angles of her bones beneath her skin. He put his cheek against hers and kissed her. 'Don't worry, Nelly,' said he, 'What's the matter.'

The girl turned to him and smiled again. 'Dempsey sick,' she said, and held out the dog to Hapgood. He took the puppy's body in his hands and looked at it. A frown cut a deep and angry cleft between his eyes. 'Who's been muckin' about with him?' he said, 'I'll do the bloke that touched him.' He held the puppy's body close to his face and looked up at Michaels in bewilderment. 'Joe, he's hot!'

Michaels placed a hand over the dog's muzzle. Saliva had dried its harsh fur into stiff spikes, its eyes were closed and the lids trembling. 'Happy,' said Michaels firmly, 'it *is* sick. Why don't you let it be killed? We can't keep a pup in a life like this.'

'No one's killing Dempsey,' said Hapgood stubbornly, 'Nobody would look after him when we found him, nobody's gonna kill him.'

Michaels looked down to where Jones still knelt with his arm about the crying girl. 'Nix cry Nelly,' he said, 'Uncle Happy will look after Dempsey. You want some dinner. Essen, yes?'

The girl nodded sadly and they took her hands and led her into the cookhouse. They sat her by the fire and gave her a plate and a spoon and the cook grimaced comically and filled the plate with rice pudding and prunes. She looked at them and smiled. 'Good!' she said happily.

Hapgood sat on the other side of the fire, pouring milk into the puppy's unresponsive mouth with a spoon. 'Happy,' said Michaels, 'it's no good, Baldy'll make you get rid of it.'

'He can go take a jump at himself,' said Hapgood doggedly. He looked up at the girl suddenly. 'Look!' he said, and from one pocket of his blouse he pulled a bar of chocolate and pushed it into her hands.

'There goes five eggs!' said Michaels with a grin.

'And this!' said Hapgood and slowly he opened his blouse. The twitching nose and long ears of the rabbit suddenly flickered into life beside his naked, dirty skin. The girl dropped the spoon to her plate and clasped her hands together ecstatically, her mouth making a round oval of surprise. Jones bit his lip to see the girl's eyes cloud again with tears behind her smile.

Hapgood screwed up his nose and curled a forefinger about it expressively. Then, pulling the rabbit from his blouse by its ears, he put it down on the floor at the girl's feet. 'You take that home,' he said, 'But mind, it ain't to be eaten.'

'Oh, dank you well,' cried the girl, pushed her plate aside and clasped the animal to her.

'A rabbit,' said the cook in disgust, 'And I thought you went for a pig.'

'It's in the blood-wagon, Johnny,' said Jones.

They sat watching the girl, enjoying the sight of her simple happiness as she pushed the rice into her mouth hungrily, or stroked the rabbit's brown fur with long hands that were almost all bone. When she had finished the pudding Jones stood up.

'Come on, Nelly,' he said, 'we'll go home, shall we?' and he held out his hand. She grasped it and he picked up the trembling rabbit and put it under his jerkin. 'Keep something hot for me, Johnny, will you?' He leant over the table and picked up half a loaf. 'You didn't see me take this did you?'

'Take what?' said the cook and he began to pick his teeth with a fork.

Jones led the girl to the door and was about to leave when the cook shouted. 'Eh, Ted! Catch!' He threw a tin of corned beef into Jones' hands. 'You dropped that just now,' he said, and he winked broadly at the girl.

10. Jones

The soldier and the Dutch child walked slowly down the road to her home. Jones liked to feel the firm, trusting grasp of her bony little hand in his. He liked the way she would occasionally turn up her face to his and say, 'My beste vriendchen!' He did not know why she preferred him to the others. Hapgood gave her all his chocolate and let her play with Dempsey. Michaels was able to play with her and catch her childish emotions by the bold parade of his confident arrogance. All Jones was able to do was to smile at her, to talk to her about his dead wife and his own daughter, to sit with her on the running board of Michaels's truck, to give her food from the cookhouse, and once he had cut up one of his bootlaces for her tiny shoes. Her gratitude for such insignificant favours left him peculiarly embarrassed. She wore his cap-badge on her coat and carried a photograph of his wife and daughter in a thin cotton bag.

There was something about her nondescript appearance that attracted him, and the beauty of her full name, Petronella, charmed him. Her fierce hatred of the Germans, and the incongruous manner in which she drew her thin finger across her throat whenever she spoke of them alarmed him. Her body seemed too light for such intensity of passion.

Three years of malnutrition had wilted her tiny frame, and left her a grim and sickly spectacle. A pale light gleamed behind the yellowness of her cheeks and the slightest of exertions left her panting fiercely for breath. She took a particularly hateful medicine, a black powder from a piece of paper which she showed proudly to the British soldiers as if the illness itself were a decoration, for the medicine had been given to her by the British medical officer. She did not believe that the British could do wrong, and Jones found in that innocent faith a greater indictment of his growing hardness than he could discover in his own conscience.

As he walked down the road he talked to her. He told her that his own daughter, Mary, had written to him and sent her love to Nelly. He pulled the letter from his breast-pocket, smoothed out its creases and showed it to her while the rabbit moved restlessly under his arm, and she did not know whether to smile at the jerking animal or look up to him in tearful gratitude. He had found that he could talk of his wife without embarrassment to this child, and she listened with a peculiar gravity that made him feel as if he were the child and not she. In all that crude obscenity of life and the licence given to sensuality, he found that his friendship with the Dutch girl was restful. It was while he was with her that he felt able to think again, to attempt some co-ordination of his feelings.

She skipped along beside him, chattering with a peculiar intensity in the language he did not understand, and as he walked with her his mind began again its desultory attempts to grapple with his thoughts. He could find no answer to the paradox that contradictions within human society should find their reflection in human beings, that kindness qualified cruelty and hardship bred tolerance as much as licence. There in the bleakness of a battle area, the rain, the shell-bursts, the long nights of doubt and despair, the nostalgia, and the prodding fingers of material expediency, there seemed no values to be distilled from rationalization. Jones sometimes felt the suffering about him as if it were something tangible although he never betrayed it. At night when he went out with Waithman, beyond the beams of light to the flame-ridged edge of the world, he wanted to cry when he saw the ambulances coming back, but his tears fell only behind a hard-eyed casualness.

He felt that it was good to have friends, never had it been better. It was good to come out of the factory in the morning from the straw where men were lying like bundles of clothing amid the stench of their bodies, to find the roads frozen and touched with the pink warmth of the rising sun. It was good to ride at night with Michaels as the rain beat at the windscreen and to hear Michaels singing to himself. To have Michaels light him a cigarette and place it between his lips as he drove with both hands on the wheel. Friendship seemed an enormous structure of many chambers, whose doors were locked against one but opened to another, yet the whole was built on flimsy, changing foundations.

He wrote of these things, the incongruity and complexity of the problems they raised in his curious mind, to Mary, and now he would carry the letter in his pockets for two or three days before he finally decided to destroy it and write another.

He wondered if the whole world was cursed with such inarticulateness, that somehow humanity was like himself, never able to express either its gratitude or hatred; that the deepest of feelings could only be intimated by a proffered cigarette, a smile across the wheel of a car, an upthrust thumb when agreement was reached on some trivial matter.

Yet he knew that no matter how deep the friendship seemed, no matter how real its character and how necessary its existence, its permanence was slight. They would outlive their friendship as times changed. Separation and loss of mutual purpose would amputate it like a knife. He had hardly seen Tomsett since they came to the Troop, and when he did visit the detachment where Tomsett worked their greetings were limited to a grin, a casual word. But, thought Jones, the shortness of friendship was not important, its existence and the depth and sincerity of it, was all that mattered.

He looked down at Nelly, and on sudden generous impulse, bent down and kissed her, smiling as he rubbed his hand gently over her head.

'My best vriendchen, kleine Nelly,' he said haltingly.

He grinned, with a sudden wry twist of his lips. He had always imagined Dutch children as little rosy-cheeked bundles of colour in clogs, clasping bunches of tulips beneath placid windmills. And he looked down again at the grim, black and white skeleton of the child. 'Thanks to you, Hitler!' he said aloud.

'Hitler nix good,' said the girl seriously.

'No, Nelly,' he said, 'Hitler nix good. Here we are.'

The house was a rambling puzzle of rooms, each seeming in argument with its neighbour and turning their backs to make communication more difficult. Most of the windows were glassless and boarded-up with cardboard taken from British Army ration boxes. But the woodwork of the house was picked out by broad lines of peeling orange paint, and at those windows where the panes remained there hung coloured glass effigies of unhappy saints. The house was dirty and it had a sexless, unimpassioned air about it.

The girl led Jones to the door and opened it, taking him down the tiled passageway that smelt damply of cabbage soup. The clatter of her clogs on the red tiles brought her mother from the kitchen, wiping her hands on her apron and smiling in welcome. In a bursting spate of words that sounded odd on her lips (it always surprised Jones to hear children speaking any language but English) she told her mother about Dempsey and the woman pursed her lower lip in sympathy and gently caressed the worried frown from the child's forehead. She looked up at Jones and, pushing back the colourless hair from her eyes, said something which he took to be an invitation to have coffee, a brackish, burnt liquid which he hated. He shook his head and shyly pushed the bread and corned beef into the woman's hand. She blushed and grasped his hand and the child looked up at Jones with an innocent expression of pride and gratitude.

He pulled the rabbit from his blouse and placed it on the tiles and again the child prattled excitedly to her mother who looked at the shivering animal and then up at Jones, and by the look in her eyes he knew that she was thanking him not for a pet but for the food it would eventually become. The rabbit hopped its way cautiously into the kitchen and the child took Jones' hand and led him upstairs to her bedroom, a small, blue-painted room where the floor and ceiling sloped away from each other and the grey, hard light of midday cut through the net curtains at the window. He knew what she wanted to show him. A photograph of her brother Willim, taken in slave labour to Germany a year ago, a picture of Mary which he had given her, both resting on the dressing-table beside a broken-toothed comb and a mirror. She picked up the picture of Mary and looked at it, her face tilted sideways with a look of satisfaction.

'Vrouw from my beste friend,' she said and put it down again.

She made a grotesque and disturbing figure against the pale blue paint of the walls. Her thin body and translucent cheeks, the brown eyes wide with satisfaction and the thin hair falling in straight spikes across her ears. She was an ugly child but he thought he had as great a love for her as he had for his own daughter. He knelt down beside her and without embarrassment kissed her on the cheek and she turned and hugged him to her.

'Dempsey will be all right, Nelly,' he said. It did not seem much to say but he knew that it carried the comfort that he wanted to offer her.

He walked slowly back to the butter factory. The wind was rising and coming in sharp thrusts from the river. The sky had turned livid and heavy, and a strange, thick dullness had fallen over the flat and desolate country. It was going to snow again, he thought.

In the cookhouse the air was noisy and hot. The detachment was gathered there, eating their dinner, leaning against the walls, holding their plates in their hands and pushing the food into their mouths. Some men were crouched on the floor, warming their hands about mugs of tea. Michaels and Hapgood were by the fire. From the open blouse of Hapgood's battledress there peeped the dirty white muzzle of the puppy, its eyes closed and the pink tip of its tongue protruding in a half-moon from its front teeth. Hapgood was angry. He was holding his tea in one hand, the mug thrust out from his body almost defensively. 'They've got no right to say he's gotta be killed. He'll get better. You see.'

Jordan carefully spread a piece of bread with treacle. 'It won't get better. It's a shame, Happy, carrying the poor little bastard about in trucks all the time. You don't even bath it.'

'Who doesn't? He gets a bath as often as you do.'

'That's not often enough,' said Pearce with a grin, and Jordan flushed.

'Just because I get all the dirty jobs . . .'

'Don't be so hard-necked, Busty,' said Michaels, 'We all know you have a rub-down in sump-oil every morning.'

Jordan went on spreading his treacle. 'You'd better put it out of its misery, Happy . . .'

Hapgood slammed the tea down on the table. 'You're telling me what?' he said. His fists came up across his body and the puppy withdrew its head with a whimper.

''*Kinell!* If you take them two stripes off your arm I'll dazzle you!'

'Oh, calm down, Happy,' said Jordan, 'It's not me, it's Baldy, he said you've got to kill it this afternoon.'

Hapgood's temper collapsed. His arms dropped to his side and he looked about the room helplessly. In the greasy half-darkness of the kitchen nobody returned his look. They stared down at their tea or their plates and said nothing. 'It's going to snow again,' said Jones at last.

'Why should the poor little bugger be killed?' said Hapgood. His mouth was twisted, his spotted face wrinkled and his short hair hanging over it in oily rings. 'He's mine ain't he?'

'He's pretty sick, Happy,' said Michaels who had no sympathy for the puppy now, and was almost ashamed of that which he felt for Hapgood.

'Turn it up, Joe,' said Hapgood desperately, 'He's mine, not Baldy's. You all left him behind to get run over. I picked him, and now just because that bow-legged twister wants him killed you all side with him.'

'He'll die anyway, Happy,' said Michaels, lighting a cigarette. 'Get it over quickly for him.'

Hapgood put one hand inside his blouse and stroked the animal's head; it felt hot and did not respond to his touch. He knew they were right, but as he looked about him for consolation he saw Jones staring at him, 'Go and see Claude for me, will you Ted? You speak to him, tell him Dempsey'll be OK.'

'It's no good, Happy.'

'You think he should be killed, Ted?'

'You know how it is, Happy.'

Hapgood stared at the floor and spat out a strand of tobacco. He nodded, and then shook his head. 'I can't do it, though.'

'I'll do it then,' said Jones, 'I'll do it after dinner.'

The cook, the only man who seemed in agreement with Hapgood said enigmatically, 'Some of these twisters would be better if they was taken out and shot themselves.'

It was beginning to snow when Jones and Michaels took the puppy round to the rear of the butter factory. The afternoon sky had a hard, unsympathetic glitter, like a strip of burnished metal. It was not quiet. The gun batteries were firing regularly and the air shook with a harsh impatience, and along the horizon, above the scrub of conifers that grew there, lay a long purple bank of smoke that bellied and erupted with sharp pricks of flame.

'This'll do,' said Michaels harshly and with quick movements of his boots kicked the earth free of snow. 'Shall I do it Ted?'

'No, I told Happy I'll do it.' Michaels knelt down on his knees in the snow with the animal in his hands, his fingers holding its body and his thumbs forcing its head down on to the snow. Jones swung Michaels' Sten from his shoulder and pressed the stud into 'Repetition'. He placed the muzzle of the gun on top of the puppy's head and curled his finger about the trigger. The animal whimpered and swung its head to one side.

'Hold the damn thing still, Joe,' said Jones angrily.

Michaels looked up at him. 'All right, Ted, don't get on to me,' he said easily, and his thumbs forced the animal's head on to the frozen earth. A sudden wild desire of life convulsed its body, it lost its lethargy and struggled furiously in Michaels' hands. 'Keep still, *keep still!*' he whispered to it.

Jones dropped the muzzle to the animal's head again and squeezed the trigger quickly. The puppy jerked once and the bullet spurted the earth into Michaels' face. He spat it out disgustedly and stood up, leaving the dead animal on the ground. Jones cleared the gun and looked across at Michaels. 'Nice way to spend Sunday, isn't it?' he said.

'Is it Sunday? I didn't know. We used to get Sunday off in

England,' said Michaels, 'I had my feet under a table in Winchester. Nice girl, her mother used to give me a smashing tea.' He smiled at the memory. 'What do you think Nelly's mother will do with Happy's rabbit?'

'Fatten it up for Christmas, I suppose.'

'Don't tell Happy, he's sentimental about animals. Where is he, anyway?'

'He probably went to the tent where Jimmy's cleaning the pig,' said Jones.

When they had buried the puppy they trod down the earth over the hole, and walked round to the factory. Crudely erected against the far wall was a tent, loosely pegged into the hard ground and flapping miserably in the wind. Half a dozen men were grinning and peering into the darkness. A thin cloud of blue smoke filtered through the opening, and as Michaels and Jones approached their nostrils winced at the acrid, fierce stench of burning flesh and hair.

'God!' said Michaels in disgust, 'Is Johnny cooking it already?'

They pushed their way into the tent. In the dusky air the scene was startling. The fleshy body of the pig hung by its hind legs from the centre strut, its head bloody and its eyes closed. The naked white bulk of its carcass was almost luminous in the dark. Kneeling before it like some wild creature the cook was burning the hair from its flesh with a blow-lamp. He passed the rustling blue flame of the lamp up and down the pig's body in careful, brush-like strokes, following its flickering passage with a carving-knife that scraped the burnt hair from the flesh. By his thigh was a chipped enamel bowl of water with steam rising from its blood-filmed surface.

The cook was a tall man with a narrow head set on wide shoulders, and his lank, dun-coloured hair dropped over his sweating face revealing a round, bald tonsure on the top of his skull that was blushing with the heat. His arms were bare to the elbows and marked with blue tattooings. He was intent on his work and paid no attention to the ribald comments of the men at the door, or the long whistle of disgust from Michaels. Behind the cook Hapgood watched morosely, now and then looking down at Pearce who was on the floor, leaning against the wall of the factory, and calmly pencilling on the slats of wood which he had nailed into a cross.

The cook stood up from the carcass, stepped back and regarded it critically. 'It'll do,' he said.

'It won't,' said Pearce, pushing his hat back from his black hair with one end of the cross, 'The best way, Johnny, is as I said. Put the pig in boiling water and scrape the hair off with a razor.' He spat. 'You wouldn't get this stink then.'

The cook looked at him darkly. 'Too many cooks in this mob,' he said, 'If you want any tea today I've got to do this quickly.'

'OK,' said Pearce with a grin, 'open it up.'

The cook turned to a pile of knives lying on a greasy cloth behind him. He selected one and tested it with his thumb, pursing up his lips with satisfaction. Grasping the pig's tail, he raised his knife and then looked at Pearce. 'If you don't like smells,' he said, 'you won't like the one that's coming now.'

'Don't let the knife slip, Slash,' said Pearce grinning, 'or it'll be worse.'

The cook began to whistle slowly, and gently he cut into the white fatty flesh. The sharp blade sank easily and the carcass gaped open bloodlessly. 'It's a good one, Ted!' said the cook over his shoulder, and Jones, who had been standing by the tent flap watching the scene with fascination, suddenly remembered his own part in this. The cook left the black-handled knife sticking from the pig's hide, rubbed his hands quickly together and spat on them. Then, grasping the handle in both hands and putting his weight on it, he guided the blade gently down the pig's body. The carcass opened up like the pages of a book as the blade moved slowly and without hesitation to the pig's throat.

'You should have cut the head off first,' said Pearce doubtfully.

'I've bled it, ain't I?' The cook was getting angry, but as he looked back at the pig his satisfaction conquered. With the opening of the carcass the discoloured intestines and stomach flowed slimily through the gap like great bunches of ugly blossoms bred in putrefaction and darkness.

'Here it comes!' said Pearce and tapped the wooden cross casually on his breeches. Jones looked across the smoky, grotesque atmosphere of the tent to where Hapgood stood at Pearce's shoulder. Hapgood's eyes were even more watery than usual and he was staring across to where the carcass hung, a white and red blotch from the roof, but Jones knew that Hapgood was hardly aware of what was happening in the tent.

Some of the men at the door spat in distaste and went into the factory, joined a moment later by Michaels who expressed his feelings with a contemptuous expression of disgust. But Jones found that, sickened although he was by the smell and sight, he could not move, the whole scene fascinated him too much. And Pearce remained where he was, still on the ground, still tapping the cross against his boots and whistling casually as he stared at the cook in curiosity and admiration.

The cook worked dexterously and quickly, with his arms deep inside the pig's body, bloody and wet to the elbows. Without faltering he swiftly cut out the stomach and intestines, whistling slowly to himself as he dropped them all in a hole at his feet. He cleaned out the body, placing heart, liver and kidneys on a plate beside him, pushing back the walls of the body with slats of wood. A cigarette, which Jones had hardly noticed, burnt close to his lips and now flickered like a patient spark against his sweating skin.

At last he had finished. The pig was cleaned, swinging gently from the centre of the tent. In the hole beneath it the head of the animal leered up with a bloody muzzle. The tension relaxed, Jones became aware of himself physically, the ache of his spine and the sting of his fingers where his hand had been gripping the tent-pole tightly. The cook pulled a cigarette from his pocket and lit it from the end of the other, wiping his forehead with his arm, the fingers drooping and the nails lined with blood.

'Congratulations, Johnny,' said Pearce, and got to his feet with a grimace. 'So that's how it's done.' He hitched up his trousers and thrust the cross at Hapgood. 'Here you are, Happy.'

'Eh,' said Hapgood with a start.

'Hooray?' said Pearce, grinning, 'Nothing to cheer about. Put that on Dempsey's grave,' and he went out.

Hapgood looked down at the cross in his hands. He read it slowly with a puzzled frown. '"Here lies General Dempsey, killed on active service, 19 December 1944." Where did you put him, Ted?'

'Back of the factory, Happy,' Jones was still staring at the pig, he did not hear Hapgood leave. The cook wiped his hands slowly on his apron, looked at his nails and yawned with weariness. He looked up at Jones. 'Some of these lazy...!' he said, 'They don't mind eating the pig, but we have to do the work, eh, Ted?'

Jones did not answer, he pushed aside the tent flap and stepped into the fresh air. The snow was falling, and riding fast before the quick wind it struck his face so sharply that he winced with the sting of it. He had not noticed that the guns had stopped and the silence surprised him suddenly. He looked towards the line. The snow had obscured the purple roll of smoke. The war was passing into one of its deceptive intervals of peace.

11. The Troop

The pig became their Christmas dinner. Christmas was a strange interlude of determined merriment. They had never been so cold. They awoke in the morning to find their blankets frozen, and as they sat up and briskly rubbed their thighs they wished each other a Merry Christmas.

But that Christmas was to be remembered for the day they cut down young, cheek-high Christmas trees within the sound of Bren-gun fire from the infantry. Jones and Michaels drove twenty-five miles to beg some coloured crepe paper for a children's party. On Christmas morning there was a ground mist and a fine, glittering frost, and the sun that appeared tardily after dinner made the surface of the earth shine within a brilliant paradox. And with the sun came the shells from the Germans, a short and furious burst of flame and black smoke that tore holes in the village and then left the rest of the day to peace and goodwill.

It was on that Christmas day, that a group of Dutchmen with the orange brassards of resistance on their right arms, and German rifles slung across their shoulders, passed the vehicle park. They were riding bicycles lazily behind a miserable train of petty collaborators who were pulling fresh-cut logs into the village. Only one of the collaborators looked at the British soldiers. While the others stared mutely at the ground between their feet he looked up with an odd, unembarrassed curiosity and nodded his head vigorously as if he were doing all this just for the amusement of the Englishmen. Some of them laughed back at him and shouted so that he became even more comic and bumptious, until one of the Resistance men cycled up to him casually and pushed him in the back with the butt of a rifle. Even then he kept turning back his head to grin delightedly.

All of the collaborators, men and women, had had their hair cut short, and on the crown of their heads was a tonsured cross that made them look more ludicrous than pitiable. They moved slowly, for the logs they were pulling were heavy, and their guards weaved and circled behind them on their cycles.

But whereas, for the soldiers, the little convoy was not much more than a broad joke, for the Dutch civilians, who crowded out of their cellars to watch it pass, it was as if a dam had broken and released their emotions in one great torrent of derision and abuse. The children ran up and down the column, pointing at the collaborators and screaming with laughter, and on the doorsteps men and women were shouting in fierce hostility. When the column passed through the village the Resistance men closed in about it and loosened their rifles on their shoulders.

It seemed the longest Christmas Day that the Troop had ever spent. At three o'clock in the afternoon a jet-propelled German bomber shot out of the iron-grey sky across the Maas, weaved in and out of the surprised shell-bursts and tracers, and dropped one bomb on the village. The soldiers watched it fall, a little silver pellet dropping so slowly, and they were so fascinated by the sight that they did not take cover. It fell on a house by the cross-roads and killed a family of five. The house seemed to open out in pain, its walls fell aside to permit the blossoming of a huge, poppy-like flame that withered almost immediately into an ugly black weed of smoke. And the bomber turned on one wing in the Christmas sunlight and flew back into Germany.

For the rest of the afternoon the bell in the church-tower tolled ceaselessly.

And at night the lights went into action towards Roermond, the long, icy beams pointing towards the line; and because of them, the ugly half-light that they filtered on the edge of darkness, the night was quiet. On both sides of the river men lay in their slit trenches and looked up at a sky diffused with the pale, artificial moonlight of the beams. To the Maas that night the Troop brought a fragmentary peace as the men stood freezing by the projectors, stupefied by the rum and the cold, and wishing that they were asleep, at home, or dead.

In the days that followed they watched the war as impersonally as their relations at home. They had newspapers and they listened to the radio and they knew that to the south of them the Germans had broken through the Ardennes, and as the weeks lengthened out into spring and the snow went the Troop learnt that it had been in a battle. But it had grown used to the guns, the endlessness of things, and the sun that came with the thawing of the snow was a mockery. The very changing of the weather seemed only to emphasize the changelessness of all things.

But there were changes. There was leave, leave for some to England and to Brussels. The men who went home came back with a curious elation. They had discovered that on their shoulders for a short while had rested a vicarious mantle of heroism. There were people in the world to whom the monotony, the dirt, discomfort, and obscenity of war was curiously exciting when related to them across a table marked with the wet circles of beer-tankards. And as each man of the Troop went home he wore that mantle for a while, postured in it, wore it casually and almost unknowingly, but in his heart hated it for its fundamental artificiality. There was no real heroism in it, no excitement, no fear now, more the momentary spasms that shot through him like pain, and were forgotten before they were felt.

They all knew that spring was coming quickly. They could almost feel the tremble of its impatience in the ground beneath their feet and see the flush of expectancy in the sky at dawn and dusk. But they knew too that not only the earth would thaw in the spring but the mighty machine of war that lay behind them. Spring would open the door to Germany, and as each man thought of that the enemy began to take on a new personality, not the uniformed, depersonalized shadow beyond in the darkness but a materialized being, who would shape in the very earth of his country, the bricks of his home, the faces of his women. And the Troop spoke of these things with a surprising unanimity of hatred and contempt, because hatred of the Germans seemed to be in the very earth of Europe. It was written in the lines of the faces about the Armies of Liberation. Revenge became an end in itself, an objective and a justification for what was to come.

There were other peculiar reliefs from that dark, stagnant life by the Maas. Sometimes little parties of soldiers went back, dressed in the cleanliness of new battledresses, with their hair cut and their bodies feeling uncomfortable and naked without a protective skin of grime. Back to the theatres and canteens of Helmond and Eindhoven, back to the noise and bustle which they had long since ceased to believe existed. Back to Brussels where they became drunk with liberty, licence, and hero-worship of the city, drunk with women, cognac, and a fear of having to go back when the three days were over.

Brussels became an experience. It was a base town, crowded with soldiers, noisy with sex, alcohol, and the wild music of cafés and symphony orchestras, the comforting sulphurous smell of trains at the Gare du Nord and the whine of trams down the Jardins Botaniques. It was unreal and dangerously intoxicating even through the distorting mirror which was brought down from the line.

But the dark days and nights by the Maas were the only reality. As some of the troops in the battery went north to Germany, manhandling their projectors with the Highland infantry across the water, they knew that the gateway to Germany was being opened and that soon they would be taken in with the flood that was to burst upon the Rhineland.

It was quiet now along the Maas, although all night long the guns in the north were thundering. The soldiers waited for the day to move. They stayed in the butter factory while about them the course of history was changing. The infantry went and the Airborne came, and their plum-coloured berets flowered like strange new spring flowers soon to be gathered. Then they went and the Americans came, a division from the Ardennes, tired, hollow-eyed, and bored with death. They chewed gum and sat on the running-board of the Troop's vehicles, exchanging packages of coffee for tea and listening to the British soldiers as they spoke of England.

The Troop had grown used to the butter factory. The village had dragged itself from the winter months like a dirty animal from a pool into which it had been flung and was now drying itself in the spring sun. A first lilac bloom flamed unseasonably, like an icicle against the church. The English were a little afraid of setting off again into the uncertainty of movement, but the thought of moving into Germany excited them.

They felt older, more grey, more sceptical. Had they known it they were perturbed by the knowledge that in the thirty or forty years they had yet to live there would never be anything to compare with these moments. They had no thought of the attention which the outside world was giving to their movements, yet they did not feel alone.

February had passed and they knew for certain that they were to leave Holland, that the next houses in which they lived would be German, the civilians in the street would be German, the children at the hubs of their vehicles and the women by the roadside, all would be German. During the next few weeks the soldiers were to touch the realities that lay behind the thoughts, the words, and the obscenities in which, for years, they had anticipated this day.

12. Waithman

Waithman finished his letter and re-read it carefully. It was to his wife. In his correspondence with her he maintained a jovial whimsicality that only just concealed his self-satisfaction. He wrote regularly twice a week, letters that were not much more than innocuous diaries; he spared her and himself the strain of critical essays. He sent her gossip, amusing, well-written anecdotes of the men he commanded and through his pen they became Dickensian creatures of sharp wit and humorous individuality. They were 'characters', a word he often used, and his wife got to know his Troop almost as well as if she lived with him and saw it through his eyes.

This last letter, however, had been something of a problem. With more application than he was accustomed to spend he had tried, not too expertly, to include words of comfort should he be killed during the next fortnight. It was the first time since he had landed that he had attempted such a letter and even now he did not know why he had done so. Something of his own experiences during the winter, a growing awareness of the impartiality of battle casualties, had disturbed his complacency. He liked to think that even after his death he could be of comfort to his wife, and at the same time, if he did survive the invasion of Germany and did go on writing those whimsical, chatty letters, he did not want this one to be too much of an anti-climax.

It had not been easy. Placed on his honour, with his letters uncensored, he could not inform his wife that the Troop was shortly to move into Germany; although he knew that every man in it had already said so in the green, uncensored envelopes granted them once a week for 'personal letters'. But by the insertion of one line, 'I hope I may soon be able to pick you up a watch or a Leica', he believed that he had given her an idea of what would be happening to him during the next week or so. He read it through again, placed it in an envelope and sealed it carefully.

Picking up his wife's photograph, half a dozen books and magazines, he turned to Jones who was strapping Waithman's bed and blankets into a roll. He did not know what to make of Jones. The man did not gossip, he did his work with a quiet thoroughness, and was level-headed at the wheel of the Jeep.

'Put these in too, will you Jones, old chap?' said Waithman and he tossed the books across, 'Got your own kit packed?'

'It's on the three-tonner, sir.'

'Good, we're moving at three. How do you feel about moving into Bocheland?'

'All right, sir,' Jones grinned a little, 'It'll be a change.'

'Be a change to see him getting some of his own medicine, eh?'

'It'll suit me, sir.'

'Eh?' said Waithman, 'Oh yes, of course.' He picked up his cap and pulled it down over one ear. The gold lace and red flannel of the grenade sewn there looked unusually bright to Jones, and he wondered if Waithman had bought himself a new cap badge for the occasion. 'I'm going down to Section. I'll take the Jeep myself, so you carry on here. Tell the sarn't-major I'll be back for the move-off. You and I'll lead the convoy in the Jeep.'

Waithman walked out of the house whistling, his brisk, confident step carrying his body forward with a hint of arrogance. Outside, in the yard surrounding the butter factory, the vehicles had been drawn up ready for departure. Their tail-boards bulged with kit and equipment, the vivid flashes of colour from mattresses and blankets, the dull, monotonous black and green of camouflaged canvas. His men were grouped about the lorries, still loading them, swearing and laughing. He noticed Hapgood and the cook, their broad shoulders beneath the greasy bottom of the kitchen stove, heaving it into one of the trucks. As he looked at them Waithman grinned slightly and almost without surprise he noticed the slight veiling of Hapgood's left eye as the dispatch rider looked back and returned his grin.

Waithman felt his satisfaction and contentment, as comforting as the glow of a warm fire. The morning was fine and bright. The sun lay in a golden band around the horizon and the sky was full of the steady throb of aircraft invisible above the misty clouds. He pulled on his gauntlets, slapped his hands on his Jeep coat and slipped easily into the seat of the vehicle. The engine started without complaint, and Waithman's mind, superficially agile, noted with approval how the Jeep had improved since Jones became its driver. Slowly he guided the car through the jumble of lorries and trucks, and he grinned cheerfully to Michaels who was standing by the wireless truck, his shirt open to the waist and the pale February sun shining on his hair. He flicked his fingers to Waithman who waved a gauntlet in reply, turned the Jeep on to the road, and pressed his foot on the accelerator.

It seemed to Waithman as he drove down the road that he had never felt a happiness so peculiarly satisfying as this. The long winter months had been monotonous and fruitless. Now he stood on the spring-board that was shortly to project him into Germany and the war of movement that must inevitably follow. The thrill of it made him boyishly excited, and the warmth of satisfaction he felt over his independence and competence was a feeling that never flagged.

He drove quickly and casually, leaning from the side of the Jeep, conscious of the figure he made. He noticed the American soldiers looking at him from the roadside, dark enigmatic faces staring from beneath the green buckets of their helmets. Their long legs sprawled out at startling angles and their idly-slung small arms gave them a dull appearance of spiritless efficiency.

He bent over the wheel and looked up from the canopy of his Jeep to the grey, dull-metal ceiling of the sky. It had a bleak, uncompromising look of foreboding. Except where the sun held its own on the horizon its dank colour merged into the tattered landscape and the earth churned by the wheels of vehicles and the scars of shells. He believed that winter was much kinder to war than summer. He remembered Normandy and how paradoxical the hot sun had seemed, the flaming scarlet shell-bursts among the green trees, the odd contradictions as the chatter of rifle-fire broke into the voices of the birds. Such things had appeared an unnecessary impropriety. It was better when it rained, for then the colours of the rolling Norman hills were washed into a general greyness, and the smoke and dust of the fighting became liquid mud.

As he drove down the marsh road to Smith's headquarters, he smiled condescendingly to think of the puerility and poverty of his life before the war. He felt that it had had no more significance than an hour's dreary stay in a railway waiting-room, where the pictures on the wall are unimportant, the emptiness of the fireplace a transient discomfort. He had been waiting for this, the liberty and opportunities which the Army offered him. He supposed that one day it would end, there would be civilian life again, the odd smoothness of civilian clothes, the day-to-day routine that would go on and on.

At Smith's headquarters the lieutenant came out to meet Waithman. He was in his shirtsleeves, his revolver holster open and his face sweating slightly with worry. Waithman did not bother to get out of the Jeep but leant over the side and tapped his hand gently on the running-board. 'Hullo, John,' he said, 'All ready?'

'Almost, Bob. I suppose I should let them have something to eat first?'

'Of course!' said Waithman irritably. He looked at Smith's worried face and he hoped there wasn't going to be trouble. 'You understand this is a big thing, John.' Smith nodded a little miserably, and Waithman went on briskly. 'You join the rest of us at the crossroad and then we go straight on, over the Bailey bridge at Gennep, through Cleves to the Hochwald. The Canadians are already going in to capture it and we should be in action tonight. Feel all right?'

Smith looked at him. I know what you're thinking, he thought, it's the same with the men here. They're frightened I'm going to make a mess of things again. I don't know whether I'm frightened, I think I'm past caring.

'Yes, yes,' he said impatiently, 'I'm all right.'

'If there's anything I can tell you ...' said Waithman, rubbing his moustache with a gloved finger.

'No thanks, old man, I've got all the gen,' said Smith, deliberately misunderstanding.

'OK John,' said Waithman and started his engine. 'Look after the blokes there, won't you?' He gestured vaguely over the river, slipped the Jeep into gear and grinned happily at Smith as he backed out of the yard.

He drove back to the butter factory whistling. No, he had never felt happier. He was within half a mile of the factory when he realized that the end of the war with Germany could not be more than two or three months away. The realization left him strangely subdued.

The men at the butter factory were ready when he returned. The lorries were strung out along the roadside with their engines running, and about them, ankle-deep in the melting snow, the men stood drinking tea. Mixed with them was a heterogeneous crowd of Dutch civilians and children whose faces were bright with excited smiles and whose voices rose above the noise of the engines in a high reiterative chatter.

At the head of the column, where he pulled up in his Jeep, he noticed Jones, Michaels, and Hapgood standing about a little girl. She was crying and staring up at their faces with a look of incredulous despair. The three men looked back at her uncomfortably. As Waithman switched off his engine he noticed Jones drop to his knees and hug the girl to him. Michaels strolled over to Waithman.

'All ready, sir?'

'Yes, OK. What's happening over there?'

Michaels looked back over his shoulder and smiled. 'Oh, it's Nelly van Huyk, sir, she doesn't want us to go.'

'Do you?'

'It is a bit rough on the kids, isn't it? If no other mob pulls in here they're going to find it a bit dull without fags and chocolate. Besides Nelly's a nice child.'

Waithman rubbed his gauntleted hands together. 'Well, this is it.

Tell Jones to hop in here and get the sarn't-major to start up, we're off to Berlin this time Michaels, me boy.'

Jones slipped into the driver's seat and pulled the Jeep coat tighter about his waist. The girl came and stood beside him, her hands pushed into her pockets and her face shining with tears as she smiled at Jones. Waithman stared at her curiously, and as he said, 'OK, let's go!' he noticed that before Jones put the Jeep into gear he leant over and gently placed the palm of his left hand on the girl's cheek. She caught it with her own hands and pressed it against her face. Jones released the clutch pedal and swung the Jeep into the centre of the road.

As the whole convoy slowly wound itself on to the road like a black, indolent serpent Waithman looked back to watch it, compressing his lips with satisfaction. Glancing at Jones he was surprised to see the girl running beside the vehicle, her feet stumbling on the ground, but her head held upright as if to force back the tears.

'OK Jones,' said Waithman, 'Open it up before she falls under the wheels.'

Jones ran his teeth along his lower lip and pressed his foot on the accelerator. The girl fell behind them. They could both hear her voice crying out until the roar of the following vehicles drowned it.

'Ted, you come back? *Come back!*'

13. Jones

He lay in a slit trench with his hands pressed tight against his head and the fingers locked behind his neck. His steel helmet bit into the frowning flesh of his forehead. With every belly-clutching crash of the falling shells he felt his body rocked by a terrible nausea. For half an hour the shells had been falling, an odd, unexpected barrage that had taken the detachment completely by surprise. It was midday. They had been standing about Johnny the cook as he ladled out the dinner, a battered silk hat on the back of his head and a German steel helmet full of hot water at his elbow. The sun was fierce for a March day and it burnt the skin of their necks and glinted on the hairs of their arms. The little valley was full of guns, vehicles and men who swarmed like insects over the green fields. The greasy smoke of their fires blotted the outlines of the budding trees, and to the east the smoke lay thick about Xanten, the sun painting fine pastel shades on the burning town.

Then, unexpectedly, came the vicious, red shell-bursts. Jones saw one truck split open with a thump of exploding petrol and beside it a man was lost with a flurry of arms and legs in the black smoke.

Jones flung himself into the nearest slit trench, falling into a little clay box of his own making, pressing his face against the wet earth and sucking in the damp fragrance hungrily as though it could give him immunity from the uncompromising impartiality of the shells.

The air was full of the rush and shuddering of a great commotion and it seemed to Jones that the noise alone could kill. His body had no time to adjust itself to one noise before that died away and was succeeded by another. The mortar shells moaned like grieving women. He had no conception of time. He had hardly slept since the troop entered Germany and the outlines of his experiences since then danced before his eyes like hideous nightmares, even while he was awake. He felt a great weariness, a prostration before noises that were far more horrible than anything he had ever imagined, and he believed there could be no end to it until his mind mercifully disintegrated.

A week ago they had entered Germany by the roundabout beyond Gennep and plunged into the green blanket of the Reichswald. The weather was dull, he remembered that, it was funny how one always remembered the weather. It was a reassuring, commonplace memory. The rain had been falling in heavy, spiritless showers, flecked occasionally by the brilliant contradiction of sunshine. They had been part of a long convoy pouring out of Holland, a wet, grey serpent twisting into the pine forest, with soldiers leaning from the backs of the lorries, shouting that this was Germany, growing drunker with a mad intoxication of spirits that had not yet sobered.

He remembered Hapgood and Pearce riding on either side of the forward Jeep, Hapgood seriously looking at the endless ruin of German villages with a peculiar amazement. But Pearce had been convulsed by mock hilarity, leaning forward over his handle-bars and slapping his thigh as he shouted sarcastically; 'Not a single bomb will fall on German soil!'

The roads had been littered with the bright, yellow cylinders of discarded shell-cases. At a crossroads a wayside crucifix rose uncertainly from a new Calvary of ammunition boxes and shells, the patient head of Christ dropping its eyes beneath a crown of signal wire.

He remembered the Hochwald, the kidney-shaped wood that lay before the Rhine and the town of Xanten. It was only a day or so since the Troop passed through it. Dusk had fallen before they went in, and the black trees seemed to open their arms to embrace the ugly, rolling lorries, and give up their secrets like complaisant women. Mortar shells had fallen, moaning in bereavement over the pine needles, and he had taken shelter like this, lying for an hour in an evil-smelling hole with a dead German beside him. As a lull came, one of those odd, inexplicable silences when each side draws breath quickly and impatiently, he lit a match, cupping it between trembling hands and looking at his odd companion. The man was dead but his eyes were wide and startled. His long hands (Jones remembered how the fair hair on them glowed in the light) were hanging between his knees as if to support the thick, vinous weight of his entrails that poured out of his open belly. And Jones could only stare and remember how the pig had looked so...

Seven days. It had not been long. The Army had taught him to be insensitive to the passing of time, to close one chamber of his mind that would normally have stored the hours and minutes with growing impatience. But these seven days had seemed like seven years. There was nothing left now but the ceaseless pounding of the earth four feet above him. Nothing now but the damp soil beneath his face and an eternity to be spent there, clutching the dirt, pressing his hot cheeks against it and breathing his nostalgia and bitterness into the ground.

With the others, Michaels, Hapgood, and Pearce, he had lived a madness that startled him by its intensity as he now thought of it. The endless thunder of battle, the paradox of sitting down to eat with the bright, sharp flicker of tracers whipping over his head into the dust and the green film of trees ahead. The miracle of sleep beneath the wheels of guns that never ceased firing. And then on again, deeper and deeper with no real halt, his clothes tightened to his body by filth, and his heart sweating as if it had pores like his stinking flesh.

The vehicles were piled with mattresses and beds from German houses. In mad, senseless, exhilarating humour they wore on their heads the top-hats that littered the ground at the foot of the looted houses.

They were men drunk with the realization that they were in Germany after years of cynical waiting. A madness empty of political consciousness but full of relief and pride that because of their relentless efforts a cloud was being lifted.

And, like shadows against the background, were the people of Germany, the people with whom speech was a crime; characterless, featureless people who peered palely from their cellars, and Jones remembered with bewilderment that these people whom he hated had as yet held no interest for them. They blew like seared leaves before the high, confident wind of the invading army.

Jones turned on his side and looked up to the top of the slit trench. He did not notice the flinching reflexes of his body now. The long rectangle above him gave a view of the sky only, a deep, delicate linen-blue with a single scud of white cloud tacking across it. Then there would be shells again, the whine, the fury and the fall of them, and across that rectangle swept the obliterating swirl of dust and smoke. It would never stop.

The memory of the past week lived in his mind in fragments only, as if the shells above shattered his own thoughts ...

There were no half-tones, no kind, soft colours, but a peculiar uncompromising vividness that was green and scarlet only. The green of the fields whose springtime struggle for life had begun again. The red blood on men's faces and chests, the scarlet slashes of slaughtered animals hanging from the backs of rolling Canadian lorries ...

The squeal of massacred pigs mingled with the noise of weapons. There was no peace from the slaughter of man or beast...

To Jones Germany was a great wood, and mud, mud, mud. It was a torn town, a boy in a black peaked cap. Graves like white flecks against a subtly-painted landscape. A shell-shocked old woman asking permission to cross the road, a girl offering strange money for coffee. It was a spring bed to sleep in, sheets to be taken from gutted houses, but no sleep, no sleep ever again.

There was no escaping the feeling that they were the proprietors of the land across which they were burning their way. They lived in an atmosphere of defeat and surrender. White flags hung limply from broken windows. They left them there. But it meant parting with years of life for every mile covered. None of them could ever be young again.

Jones looked down at his fingers. The mud, ingrained in every wrinkle, made them look like the hands of an old man. None of them could ever be young again. Yet over it all was a brilliant, youthful sun, and the dust rising up to it like bitter incense from a sacrifice ...

Someone fell into the slit trench beside him, and he felt the sharp, painful weight of ammunition boots landing on his calves. He twisted round in agony and found himself looking into Hapgood's scared eyes.

'Hello, Ted,' said Hapgood, 'You all right.'

Jones nodded. His mouth was dry and he could feel the grains of earth grating unpleasantly between his teeth. Were this a film, he thought, one of us would be saying something very funny now. He found himself staring at Hapgood's face curiously. It was white, with a greyish tinge about the eyes, and they were wide and bewildered. 'Where've you come from?' Jones asked hoarsely.

Hapgood opened his mouth to reply but the air was suddenly shredded by the whine of shells and the crash of their fall. The great cloud of dust billowed furiously across the lip of the trench and the air sang delightedly with the song of the splinters. Hapgood ducked his blunt head and buried it between Jones' thighs. Jones himself lay with his cheek against the damp earth and prayed in a peculiar giggling jargon. When Hapgood raised his head again his eyes caught the trace of an idiotic smile on Jones' face. 'Nothing to laugh at,' he said resentfully.

'Where've you come from?'

'I was under the Jeep,' said Hapgood. 'Christ, a shell got one of the twenty-five pounders and poured the crew over me! You gonna have a job getting the mess off them seats, and some little German bastard is machine-gunning down there. Who dug this?'

'I did. What's wrong with it, it's semi-detached.'

'You might've made it bigger, Slash. I don't want to get wounded.' He rubbed his face again, and in the momentary silence Jones heard the black stubble rasping against Hapgood's palm. There were other sounds too, thick, rustling echoes, and above them the bright, incongruous song of a bird. He looked up and saw the sweet blue of the sky so clear and pleasant again.

'I don't mind getting killed,' said Hapgood, 'but I don't want to get wounded.'

'What?'

"Ot? I'll say it's 'ot!' Hapgood grinned. 'Wounded. I don't want to be wounded. They pile you into ambulances and there you are. Too much traffic on the roads. In Normandy there was a big jam on the roads back to the beaches and the ambulances were stuck there for hours. Poor sods inside just bled to death.' He fished in his field-dressing pocket and pulled out the stub of a cigarette, sticking it in his mouth truculently. 'And that's no good to anybody, is it?'

But Jones was not listening. He was surprised by the silence. The whole valley, which he knew to be full of men, was deathly quiet, only the sharp, persistent whistling of the bird could be heard and that sounded a peculiarly obscene blasphemy.

'All right, Ted?' said Hapgood anxiously. The stub of the cigarette glowed against his cheek, the smoke curling in little whorls about his nostrils. He was leaning back against the side of the narrow trench, his knees beneath his chin and his hands thrust deep into his pockets. Jones rubbed his face roughly. 'All right,' he said. 'Bit tight on cigarettes, aren't you Happy?'

Hapgood dragged a hand from his pocket and tossed a bent yellow cigarette down the trench. Jones lit it and felt better as he drew the smoke down into his lungs. 'Quiet, isn't it, Happy?'

Hapgood did not reply at first and then he said, 'It's silly.' He paused and smoked a little and then, 'When I get out of this I won't even join a Slate Club.'

'What *are* you going to do, Happy?'

Hapgood looked at Jones as if the question was irrelevant, and Jones realized with peculiar regret that it *was* irrelevant. There would be no end to this, and if there was an end coming somewhere, he was strangely too frightened to consider it seriously. But Hapgood answered the question seriously enough.

'The foundry, I suppose. Or down in the docks. The wife'll decide that. I'd like a garden but I don't know a dandelion from a daisy. I know I'm going to get blind drunk as soon as I get out.'

The bird sang merrily, gaining courage from the silence, and far off Jones heard a man's voice shouting, and further still the short, sharp gossiping of a machine-gun. Other birds were singing now, and the sky seemed a deeper blue, the sun all the warmer for them.

'No more war for me, anyways!' said Hapgood.

Jones eased his body in the trench as he said, 'No more war at all I hope.'

'What do we get out of it?' said Hapgood, 'Anyway, you're the tosh for settling things like that. Stop the Jerries, yeh, but whose going to stop the bastards at home, I want to know? My old man lost a leg in the last lot. That's what he got out of it. He had no work for ten years, and then when he gets a job it's making little guns for son Happy to play with.' Hapgood grinned reflectively. 'He was a queer old bugger. When I was a nipper I used to lie in bed, it was something he knocked together out of boxes, and it was beside the big one he and the old lady slept in.' His eyes developed a salacious sparkle as he parenthesized, 'I heard some peculiar goings-on before I was old enough. But sometimes at night they used to spread out all the letters he wrote during the last lot, and read 'em aloud. Some was interesting too, but I've seen enough in this lot to know that most of it was bullshit.'

'Do you write letters like that?'

'Me?' said Hapgood in disgust, 'No, Lil would cry, she's a peculiar bit of stuff. Cries when she gets drunk too.'

'So do you.'

'Well,' said Hapgood defensively, 'There's plenty to cry about, isn't there?'

'Yes,' said Jones, and suddenly the earth erupted into flames, smoke, and noise again and they buried themselves deep in the darkness of their arms. Jones smelt the acrid fumes of the cigarette he had dropped as it burnt its way through his battle-dress, and he thought, inconsequentially, that it was hard enough to get clothing replacements in the ordinary way without burning those that were still good enough to wear. Across his buttocks Hapgood was lying and swearing with rich obscenity.

And so it went on. In that green valley where a thousand men lay in shelter, and some of them died despite it, each man locked in the lonely box of his fears, his sickness, his impatience, and his hatred. They lay and looked into themselves, and some of them were surprised by what they saw, and did not know that the memory of the revelation would be short-lived. When the bombardment was over they would get up from the ground and some extraordinary catalyst would knit them back into a corporate spirit and purpose. War has moments of such personal enlightenment, and, paradoxically, it is danger that produces them.

Hapgood eased his feet across Jones' body and swore gently, 'Oh the bastards, *the bastards*!'

It gave Jones some satisfaction to think that the earth which German shells were striking was German earth, although, close to Jones' nostrils, it smelt no different from the earth on the Downs behind Hove where he and Mary had lain the year before the war, digging their fingers into it and watching the colonies of excited insects that such ploughing disturbed.

It was hard to think she was dead. That her features would change and decay, that she was buried in a great crowded space, with tipping, sliding tombstones all about her.

As he moved his head on to his other hand, feeling the cool air strike his cheek, he realized that his body was quivering as if sprung to the vibrating air above.

He wondered whether, when he went back to London, to the grey streets and the peace with which his imagination had vested England, he would be able to live without the driving emotions and purpose that seemed to generate his thoughts and actions now. Life in the estate agent's office would seem dull, his imagination and his thoughts wanted a wider canvas. He realized, almost with horror, that this life was strangely satisfying, even in its discomfort. It had released something within him of which he had once been only dimly conscious, and which even now he did not understand.

Yet he remembered his last leave. He had gone to see his employer and he had come away from that interview strangely depressed, spiritually enervated, and conscious that this self-importance had been overshadowed by a greater feeling of impotence. Forbes, the estate agent, had greeted him effusively, had prattled the irritating commonplaces about civilian life and the war, the stale jokes, the grave reminder that civilians were 'taking it' too. And then he had begun to speak of the post-war years in a manner that had seemed to say 'Hurry up and get it over, it's been going on too long, you know.'

Jones had come out into Stockwell Road where the rain was falling onto the tops of trams and the flash of electric sparks was livid against the grey skies. He had felt that perhaps Forbes's hard perception was nearer the truth, that this was to be the real end to it all, a return to the essentials of life, the business of making money and the money-making business. Once dispersed Jones and his friends would be absorbed by that fever too. With contact lost they might soon sentimentalize their past and sink their memories and the fierceness of their hopes and passions into the inertia of ready-made compromise.

But, as he lay there in the slit trench and thought of it, it seemed more of a dream than anything else, because it was foolish to think that this war would ever end. It had reached a state of saturation, even here on German earth, and there was nothing else to do but go on, pushing forward, inviting death and apportioning it.

The shelling had stopped. The air was quiet now except that he could hear more and more men's voices, a laugh and the sound of engines starting. He heard Waithman shouting urgently, 'Stretcher-bearer, *stretcher-bearer!*'

'All change!' said Hapgood, rising, 'Someone's had it. Come on Slash, this is where we came in.' He vaulted lightly to the lip of the trench, stretching his body as he stood there, the sun glinting in irridescence on the hairs of his unshaven chin. 'Hey, Joe!' he shouted, grimaced, and began to kick out his legs as he sang, *Mr Whatchercallit, watcher doin' ter-night?*

Jones looked up at him and grinned. The warmth of the sun was somehow refreshing and the day seemed so clear, even where the blue smoke of the explosions hung in layers at head-height above the valley. He could see men emerging from holes in the ground, from beneath lorries, and the valley air suddenly filled with their laughter and shouting. Over by the Jeep, Waithman stood with his hands on his hips, his bare arms brown, and his head bent. At his feet Michaels and Pearce were rolling something into a blanket.

As Jones walked across Michaels looked up. His right arm was red to the elbow with a vivid slash of blood, but it was not his own. He did not seem to recognize Jones. His grey eyes stared and then suddenly dropped to the blanketed body between his knees.

Waithman turned his head and saw Jones. His eyes contracted into a little frown and then he smiled gently, 'Look, Jones, old chap,' he said, 'Help Corporal Michaels with a burial party, will you? I'm afraid this is a friend of yours, Tomsett.'

Jones looked down at the blanket. Because it seemed just a roll of cloth, darkening damply at one corner, he could not associate it with Tomsett, and his mind groped its way back to the foetid squalor of the cattle-trucks, the water bottle full of spirits, and the strong encouragement of Tomsett's undefeatable confidence. But all he could think was that Tomsett could not possibly be dead.

Behind them Johnny the cook shouted angrily from his kitchen, swearing because a shell had turned his pans into a beaten pile of blackened metal. High above his furious swearing rose the note of the defiant bird.

As Jones dropped on his knees beside Michaels, the latter recognized him. He smiled and wiped the blood from his arm with a corner of the blanket. 'Hello Ted,' he said in a peculiarly hard voice, 'You're safe anyway. I should've been annoyed if this had been me. I'm going on short-leave to Brussels next week.'

But Jones, who had hardly heard him and was not looking at his face, did not see the forced lines of Michaels' smile, nor did he notice the queer deliberateness of the words.

'It's over,' said Waithman's voice, 'We're up to the Rhine. I'm going into Xanten this afternoon, if anybody's interested in coming.'

Looking past him to the dusty road Jones saw a long, shambling crowd of men, German prisoners, coming towards him. There was dust on their clothes and on their faces. They walked with their heads bent and the clouds of dust were so thick about their feet that they seemed to be striding through a mist.

Behind them, lazily riding a farm-horse, with a tommy-gun hanging from his right arm, a French-Canadian chewed gum dispassionately. The war was over west of the Rhine.

14. The Three

Waithman drove his Jeep into Xanten that afternoon with the pleasant but somehow disconcerting feeling that he was a Scoutmaster taking an outing with particularly favoured boys of his troop. It was hardly the correct frame of mind in which to enter the last bastion the Nazis had held west of the Rhine. Essentially a sensual man he drew a primitive and satisfying pleasure from the rush of the sunlit air about the open sides of the Jeep, the lazy hang of his left hand over the side of the vehicle and the reassuring pressure of his revolver on his thigh. He knew now that the war was as good as over, and although this knowledge could still give him a peculiar feeling of regret he could not escape the excited feeling of pleasure its triumph gave him. These past days, the rush into Germany and the battle that was fought there so viciously, had given him an elation he never before believed possible, a feeling of unqualified self-satisfaction and confidence.

His eyes watched the roadside lazily. It was dusty, littered with debris and choked with vehicles. A long plume of purple black smoke that curled out of Xanten like a whiplash, hung over it and dropped a discreet shadow. As the road neared Xanten the ditches were still marked here and there with burning vehicles, grotesque bodies in grey uniforms. Behind him in the Jeep Michaels, Jones, and Hapgood stared curiously, jibing at occasional French-Canadian infantrymen who were escorting prisoners from the war. The Canadians were strange, piratical-looking creatures, riding looted bicycles and herding their grey-coated, indifferent captives as if they were so many animals. They stared back at the Jeep; Waithman felt uncomfortable, hoping that the three white pips on his shoulder exempted him from classification as a battlefield scavenger. He had no clear understanding of why he was going into Xanten, except that he felt he must. From the valley about Labbeck there was a general movement of vehicles into the stricken town, to extract from its chaotic ruins the last essence of triumph and excitement, to rob its bones of the last fragmentary flesh.

Waithman's material wants were short. He wanted a typewriter for himself and a watch for his wife. He had told Hapgood he would pay a good price for the latter, and behind him now in the Jeep, clinging with one hand to the cover-strut and the wind blowing his yellow scarf about his neck, Hapgood sang happily:

'Here we come gathering watches and rings!'

The town of Xanten sprang up at them suddenly from the earth, a mass of stunted, shattered debris that would have astounded the men in the Jeep had they not already seen its prototype in half a dozen other towns. They stared at it with the mildest curiosity. But Waithman, and Jones too, sensed even amid the ghastly ruin some of the beauty that had died there with the young German paratroopers.

The Jeep entered Xanten beneath the medieval gateway which still had the eagle and swastika hanging from its arch, and across it the stump of the old church threw a tortured shadow. The streets were strewn with rubble and the Jeep jolted its way across while Hapgood shouted his approval and encouragement. Men, dusty, sweating, grinning men with their blouses and arms, full of jars of preserved fruits, mattresses, bedding, wireless sets and clothes, were everywhere. Canadians, Scots infantrymen, and support troops who were moving methodically from house to house. Jones could hear the wrenching of wood, the cracking of glass, shouts and jeers.

There were no civilians anywhere.

To the east of the town, where it ended abruptly and looked from a slight rise to the Rhine, lay a bank of smoke, a thick, man-made fog protecting the town from the sullen scrutiny of the Germans on the east bank.

There was firing in the houses on the edge of the town, but the men in the streets hardly raised their heads at the sound.

'Hullo, hullo, hullo! What's that then?' said Hapgood sharply.

'Snipers,' said Waithman, 'You stay away from there, Happy.'

'Who me?' said Hapgood, 'This isn't my war, sir.'

'I know,' said Waithman, 'You've only a commercial interest.' He turned the Jeep into the square and stopped it beneath the bare skeleton of a tree, where a plain metal cross rose twenty feet into the air and caught the glint of the sun and flames from its brassy corners.

'Nice place for a war memorial,' said Michaels.

'None better,' said Waithman, and he climbed out of the Jeep, pulled off his gauntlets and stuck them into his belt. 'Get back here in an hour,' he said, 'And watch out for mines, snipers, and typewriters.'

'What no pigs?' said Hapgood and he swung his Sten on to his back, and rubbed his face with a shrill chuckle, 'Liberate 'em? We'll *paralyse* 'em!'

Already Xanten was giving up its material wealth. Its cultural wealth lay too deep beneath the rubble and was no longer of interest. The soldiers swarmed over the broken masonry, tugging, digging, breaking. Down the steps of the buildings the juice of broken preserve bottles ran in thick, blood-like streams, covered with a scum of fine silver dust. With Michaels and Hapgood, Jones entered the houses indiscriminately, pushing aside the splintered woodwork, precariously climbing broken stairways that led only to the open sky. The other two went carefully through the drawers of the cupboards, opened doors, emptied bookcases, and the rising dust settled in haggard lines on their faces and hair. They passed and repassed other groups of men as intent on such business as they. Jones made an effort to understand his own feelings, but he gave up the attempt almost as soon as he started.

Once he went outside a house and sat on the stones with a group of Scots infantrymen. Painstakingly they had dug a hole down into the cellar and from its narrow shaft passed up cool, long-necked bottles of wine which they broke on the masonry and emptied in a bubbling lemon stream down their throats. They gave a bottle to Jones good-humouredly and he drank some of it, found it dry, pungent, and distasteful, and he left it to dribble out of the neck of the bottle and sink into the dust.

Some of the houses were rancid with death, or the sharp, oppressive odour of burnt wood and cloth. The sight of the town itself appalled Jones. It was as if some infuriated giant had pounded and pounded each building in an agonized frenzy. The streets had disappeared beneath such anger, and over the mass of stones and woodwork climbed the patient soldiers. The smell of the town was impregnated with despair and dust.

Fluttering across the ruins a snowfall of little slips of paper expressed the town's private grief. Black-bordered, and bearing the pictures of German soldiers killed on the Eastern front, they blew from the windows and were trodden into the dust.

Here at last, Jones told himself, was Germany caught between inexorable millstones of its own manufacture, empty of everything but ruins and rapacity.

The civilians had disappeared into the earth, or to the vast tented camps that littered the fields at the foot of Cleve. But there had been one German, and he almost a caricature, whom Jones remembered. He had gone with Michaels to where one of the detachments was sited on a hill, by a German artillery observation tower built of green pine trees. Hanging from its girders by one leg was a heifer, its mouth open in a wet pink gash, its black lips curled back from yellow teeth. A man of the detachment was trying to cut its throat and the bloody work had left the black and white hide of the Friesian, the green grass below its foam-flecked nostrils, slashed with red. Then, from the darkness of the cow-byre had come the German. He was a squat, expressionless individual, his hair cropped short to his head and a thick tyre of flesh overhanging his collar. He had looked just like a cartoon and Jones had felt himself wondering why he was not wearing a ludicrous Tyrolean hat complete with shaving-brush.

The German went up to the heifer, took the kitchen knife from the slaughterer and neatly cut the cow's throat.

All he had asked for the service in killing one of his own cows was a few cigarettes, and having received them he supervised the flaying of the animal. He went away with a thick slice of the animal's flesh, thanking the soldiers without a flicker of emotion on his face. So characterless had he seemed that Jones had not known what to make of him.

So it was with Xanten. Its complete absence of character or subtlety evoked no feelings. Things happened, things just happened, that was all.

But Michaels was excited by the town. He was very much akin to Waithman. It brought out more acutely an awareness of his own strength and self-confidence, as if, by this peculiar, uncompromising route, his life had reached a climax, and half-understood he felt afraid of the inevitable bathos that lay in the future. He climbed over the ruins with the others, until their wandering brought them within sight of the church. It was unapproachable. The thunderous bombardment had broken all the houses about it, and they washed in a high, stationary wave of rubble about its roofless walls, forming an impenetrable barrier. The three men looked at it through a broken window-frame, and something in the wreckage of its beauty touched Jones at least. He stared at the grey, barkless trees in its graveyard, the sharp, splintered panes of glass, and the slipping screen of tiles about its tower.

Michaels looked at Jones' face curiously. He sat himself nonchalantly on the window-sill and kicked his heavy foot at a jar of scarlet cherries on the floor. The rolling glass described a parabola on the dusty boards, leaving a train of glistening fruit speckled with brick-dust. 'You don't like this much, do you Ted?'

'Do you?'

'I don't know, it doesn't matter much does it? It's Germany, I should think you'd be pleased.' He grinned. 'I'm sorry there isn't much left in it though. The infantry get the best, and they deserve it.'

Jones grinned back. 'Let's get on. Where's Happy got to?'

'He went down to the cellar with a Canuck who said he had a watch to flog.'

'Good old Happy, all this means is watches and rings.'

Michaels looked up sharply. 'What of it?' he said, 'How do you expect men like Happy to behave? They never had much in peacetime and when they took things they were whipped inside a bit sharpish. Deep down inside them, they've a hatred of those who have got everything without working ten per cent as hard as Happy and his like. Now he can take what he likes without anybody saying boo. What do you expect him to say, "No, that wouldn't be honest"? By God, I don't blame him! Good luck to him and all the others I say.' He got off the window-sill and with a vicious kick shattered the half-empty bottle of fruit against the wall. There it left a deep, dripping stain. He turned on Jones. 'Don't you be a bloody snob, Ted. Happy's good, really good inside. He's a mixture, soft-hearted and brutal. Don't you blame *him* because he doesn't behave like nice people are expected to behave, like the people who wouldn't lift a finger in peacetime to give him a decent education, or his father a permanent job.'

Jones flushed. 'I'm not blaming him!'

Michaels grinned. 'All right,' he said, 'Pardon my politics. Let's go on.'

As he passed the juice stain on the wall he dipped his finger in it and, with a sardonic grin, traced a hammer and sickle on the wall.

Jones was sick of Xanten. He no longer wanted to climb over its heartless ruins, but he followed Michaels. The Corporal took nothing from the houses, his quick, brown fingers went rapidly through drawers and cupboards with a hard, humourless amusement, kicking aside the emptied rubbish with his feet, his grin fixed and immobile on his face.

It seemed to Jones that the climax of the day was brought to him by a mirror. It hung on the pale, blue-washed walls of a house overlooking the platz. The ceiling had gone and one wall had been blown away. The floor dripped over in a stream of laths, plaster, and bricks to the dust below. Through the gap came the noise of men's voices, and a queer, untraceable murmur of a dead city that rises as much from an echo of its agony as the whispering, rustling fall of its debris. The slight wind blew thin clouds of fine dust that bit into his eyes and burnt his throat.

He saw the mirror as he entered the room and caught in it the reflection of a man, a man with a hard face, his eyes narrowed and a peculiar, fixed twist to his lips. There was a defiant arrogance in his carriage, the outward thrust of his chest below the half-opened blouse, the backward tilt of his cap. The rifle hung from his shoulder with an oblique slant of undisputed proprietorship. Jones did not like the face, there was something in its hardness that seemed unreal, too certain, too deliberate.

It was only by the scarlet scarf about the man's throat that he recognized himself. It was startling and he stood there staring, hardly able to believe either in the transformation or the sudden revelation of it. He walked across to the mirror, stumbling on the litter-strewn floor until he stood before it, still staring incredulously at his own reflection. The mirror was elliptical in shape, with a gross ormolu frame decorated at the top with faceless cherubs on whose bare buttocks earlier soldiers, or some German paratrooper lying in the room the day before death, had pencilled obscene additions. But these Jones did not notice. He realized that he had not seen his face for weeks, or his figure for months. Shaving in the mornings, in a scratched, metal hand-mirror, he had never seen his features as he saw them now.

It was not only that he was surprised, and a little frightened by what he saw, but he did not understand it. The grey dust that had settled on his hair made him look prematurely old, but beyond that he saw in the line of his face, the set of his mouth, and narrowing of his eyes, that he had in truth grown older. He searched vainly for some softness in the features, something that would remind him of the face he had seen every morning before the war. It was not here. The reflection was as much a challenge as a surprise, a challenge that he could not answer with anything more than a shrug of his shoulders.

He turned away from the mirror as Hapgood climbed up the flimsy stairs and swung himself into the room. He was dangling a watch in his hands and he thrust it into his pocket with a grunt of satisfaction when he saw the mirror. He went across to it and dragged it from the wall, the wire snapped with a sharp twang of protest. Hapgood laid the glass on the floor gently and then, raising his foot, broke it with his heel. The cracks spread starlike across the green glass and the mirror fell apart.

'Shaving mirrors,' said Hapgood in satisfaction. 'D'you want a piece, Ted? I'm browned off shaving blind every morning.'

Jones shook his head angrily, and, as Michaels came into the room, he said, 'Since when did Happy shave every morning, Joe?'

'Claude's down in the square,' said Michaels, 'He's niggly. Wants to get back.'

They climbed down the splintered stairs cautiously, and as they came out into the light the sun struck them with a fierce impatience. 'What a lovely day,' said Hapgood, 'Makes you feel good to be alive. It's going to be a good summer, you see.'

Waithman was waiting for them in the Jeep, a portable typewriter by his side. He grinned at them cheerfully, and as they left Xanten to its dust and the tall funeral column of black smoke, the Troop Commander began to whistle.

'The war'll be over in a month or two,' he said conversationally. But the others did not reply.

15. Hapgood

The small essentials of living were the most important, a mattress for one's back, a plate for food, and the hours for sleep that were always too short. And yet it was spring, the high, fine days of late March, and the Rhine was being crossed. So much was the mind riveted on the elementary necessities of life that it turned an indifferent blindness to the staggering significance of what was happening elsewhere. The battle is rarely real to the soldier, beyond the declivity of earth into which he presses his body. Only when the immediate passions and excitements die does the perspective appear and then its outlines are drawn by hearsay, by rumour, gossip, and presumption, fixed in proportions that are unfamiliar.

The Troop lay before the Rhine, drinking in the sunlit days and waiting, hidden in the forests. Then one night it moved up to the swift, broad river, raised its beams to the sky and let the Army cross beneath them. The Troop went back to Xanten, a city thick with dust, burning again and sending up its bitterness and smoke to the furious sun. Along the ditches the infantry lay, their faces white and the tartan flashes a sombre green on their shoulders. Their steel helmets left scarlet coronets on their foreheads.

The vehicles moved into darkness, a darkness not of night but an ugly, orange shadow that is thrown when the sun percolates through dust and the smoke of burning houses. At the crossroads a Military Policeman stood in his duffle-coat, beads of sweat tracing parallel lines like tears down his cheeks.

And the guns gave no rest; the Rhine was black with the movement of boats. The roadside signs shouted, *'Keep moving, keep moving! If you must stop pull over.'*

There was dust everywhere and behind the dust lay death. It seemed as if the whole world were burning. The ditches were littered with green smoke-canisters, with shell-cases, empty ration tins, longs belts of Spandau ammunition, steel helmets, and the startling freshness of wild daffodils.

The infantry walked to the boats, with life-belts puffed up on their Bren pouches, and they jeered amiably as the Troop dug in its projectors. Always, it seemed, the smallest man was pushing a perambulator loaded with bread and an anti-tank projector.

The village where headquarters deployed was small and destroyed. Shells or bombs had rolled the church stone by stone from the little hill where it had stood. A red cross had been brushed carelessly on the door of the garages, and the air was thick with the smell of antiseptic. The high, black sides of the amphibians nosed out of the Rhine and dripped their way to the doors of the garages. Blood was clotted on the Airborne berets that fell to the ditches.

At night the long, serpentine trails of the multiple machine-guns reached up to grasp the raiders that dived out of the dusk to the water's edge. White streaks of German tracer spun down at the earth and the bridge that was in the making. The sky was full of noise.

The prisoner-of-war cage by the bridge road had been an orchard, just shell-holes now, and the delicate blossom of an almond tree shooting up from the soft earth. Trampling its pure beauty, the jackboots of strange, grey, exhausted prisoners broke it down and trod it into the soil. By the gate, his face red and his voice a hoarse whisper, a Provost-sergeant stood with his hands on his hips. 'Look at 'em! Too bloody many of 'em. Nothing to give them but one cigarette apiece!'

Hapgood grinned cheerfully at the Provost-sergeant. He sat with both legs astride his machine, a cigarette hanging from his lips. There was nothing he liked better than this, to be part of an enormous movement, yet free of its immediate, nagging discipline. His machine, caked with mud, the yellow and black skull and crossbones fluttering from its front mudguard, granted him a relative freedom; the blue and white brassard of a dispatch rider on his arm gave him the right of the road, an unquestioned priority.

His round helmet was cocked jauntily on the side of his head, its leather straps dangling on either side of his dirty chin, and his eyeshields raised on the metal. His face was grimed with dirt except where the eyeshields had been, and there were two round patches of white that gave his face a look of incredulous astonishment. His blouse and shirt were open to the waist, and the Dutch rosary, with its scarlet beads and wooden cross, was entangled joyously with the sweat-caked cord of his identification discs. He smoked easily, with narrowed eyes, as he watched the traffic going over the river. To his right the Engineers were still working on the bridge, and at intervals he could hear the amplifier that directed their work playing snatches of fierce, rhythmic melodies that he loved. He tapped the studs of his ammunition boots on the earth and hummed an echo.

'Mr Whatchercallit, whatcher doin' ter-night?'

The air was full of noise. Beyond the avenue of trees that led to the old ferry, elms that were now splintered and dust-cowled, the guns were firing regularly. The air about him grinded with the noise of vehicles, the shouting of men. And above it all there screamed the reiterative query of the amplifier.

'Mr Whatchercallit, whatcher doin' ter-night?'

He looked across the broad water of the Rhine from the high dyke, to the ruined houses of Bislich, to the smoke, the men, and the amphibians clustered on the opposite bank, and his blood quickened. He grinned as a Red-cap on the bank, by the brown gap that had been cut in the dyke like a slice from a cake, beckoned to him imperiously. He kicked the starter of his machine and rode gracefully to the water's edge. The Red-cap grumbled fretfully at the request to ferry Hapgood's vehicle across, but the blue and white brassard silenced him.

To be first of the Troop across the Rhine meant five pounds in Hapgood's pockets. Waithman had promised that sum, almost knowing that Hapgood, by virtue of his duty, was sure to win it.

Hapgood looked at the two watches on his wrist. They did not read the same, and calculating a mean he decided it was twenty minutes to the hour. He could feel the sun beating on the back of his neck. At half-past he would be meeting Smith beyond Bislich, and between them they would reconnoitre a site for Smith's Section. Hapgood reflected that Smith always got these jobs, his Section had been first across at Nijmegen, and what had happened then had been, well, no good to anybody. He wondered who was for it this time.

As he rode up the east dyke of the Rhine his happiness felt no limits. It was, in essence, a sensual happiness, a pleasure derived from mere physical excitement, but into his blood throbbed something of the urgency of the day, an Army swarming across a river. Bislich was a ruin, but that was nothing new. Across its dusty roads lay the fading, wet stains of tank tracks. Three of its houses were burning still. In a mine-crater before a fourth lay three wounded men in Airborne jackets, eating green apples that were an incongruous blot of colour against the death-grey of their faces. Hapgood rode past them with a roar of the throttle and a loose flourish of his hand that they did not answer. Their eyes followed him down the road, the green apples poised before their open mouths, and the sun glinting on the beads of juice. Perhaps the vivid yellow gash of his scarf caught their eyes and held them, becoming a memory that would last longer than the confused, tangled incident in which they had been wounded by the cross-fire of two Spandaus.

Hapgood rode with a calmness that surprised him, for he had expected fear. But the sun was so splendid, the rush of air about his face so violent that it was as if between them they had driven out any apprehension. Even when he saw two amphibian tanks burning in a great black-scarlet stain of flame his curiosity was more childish than terrified. He knew his route. Last night, in the

Troop Commander's tent beneath the pine trees outside Walbeck, he had gone over it carefully with Smith and Waithman.

He remembered the scene as he rode. There was a stove in the tent, a tall, blue monstrosity of porcelain and iron. Its pipe projected through the back flap but a slight, downward breeze blew the smoke back into the tent and made the three men cough and swear. The thin grey whorls of the burning pitch-pine curled across the red and green splotches of the map. Waithman's finely-manicured forefinger had traced the line that the dispatch rider was to take, and Hapgood watched, chewing gum with smacking satisfaction. When Waithman said that once out of Bislich he must look out for mines and snipers he looked up at the officers with his blue, watery eyes open in mock amazement. "*Kinell!*" he said expressively.

Waithman smiled, and somehow in that moment Hapgood's shrewd discernment found the Troop Commander's friendliness more genuine than ever before. But Smith stood in the background, a little to one side of the smoke, wiping the sweat and dust from his forehead with a big handkerchief.

'It's easy, Happy,' said Waithman genially, 'Once you get out of Bislich keep on down the road until you come to the mill. It may be destroyed but you can't miss it. That's the rendezvous with Mr Smith.' He turned to the lieutenant as if the reassurance was as much for him as Hapgood, but he turned his eyes back to the latter and the laugh, slightly mocking and friendly, died out. 'I don't want any balls-up, Hapgood.'

'No sir.'

Smith moved across to the fire, opened its door and then clanged it to with a gesture of annoyance. Waithman looked up and frowned slightly. He looked back to the map where his long finger rested.

'Follow the road out through this village and you'll find yourself on a plain, it's pretty flat between here and the wood. The Boche should have been cleared out of the wood by this time, except for an occasional sniper. Wait at the mill for Mr Smith. And keep those eyes of yours open, and don't think you're on a liberating expedition!'

That had been all, but the map had not looked like this. It had been clean and white, with a pale green wash for the woods which now looked black and smoke-cowled. On the map the roads had traced a fine red fretwork of thin arteries.

There had been nothing on the smooth paper to indicate the dust, the blossoms of flame across the dry plain, the ceiling of smoke, and the sun shining bright jewels from the fuselages of the planes in the sky.

By the roadside there were prisoners, grey and undistinguished groups, splashed here and there with shoulder-straps or cap-bands of silver. The little Scotsmen guarding them winked at Hapgood as he passed and he thrust two derisive fingers in the air as a reply. The yellow scarf flickered behind his head in a last gay dance.

He saw the mill from a mile away. Its sails had been shot away and it looked like a red, upturned flower-pot, except that smoke trailed lazily in a black and yellow spume from its crown. All around it the fenceless fields were a counterpane of dull ochre and rich spring green. It all seemed unexpectedly quiet, and driving along the road that was free for a moment from any vehicles, Hapgood increased speed and shouted with the exhilaration, his mouth open and the wind gushing in through his yellow teeth with a force that made his cheeks vibrate.

He slackened speed as he approached the mill, staring at it carelessly. A German infantry-carrier was wrecked by its doors, the yellow metal twisted and the two front wheels raised in the air in supplication. There was a thick, sharp smell of cordite. As he stared at the mill he noted, with surprise almost, the sudden pricking of flame from its upper window, and as the air about him began to sigh with the high swift passage of bullets the sound of the firing itself reached him with a brutal, violent stutter. Unconsciously his hand twisted the throttle and the big machine leaped forward. As he rode past the mill he stared at it, his head slewed round over his shoulders, his eyes wide and his mouth open. It had been unexpected. The machine, unguided, swerved gently to the side of the road, fell over on its side and threw Hapgood into the ditch. More stunned by surprise than by the violence of the fall he stared incredulously at the spinning wheels of his machine. He had not been thrown from his bike for a long time, and for a second or two anger and resentment at the humiliation of it boiled up inside him.

Then, as he took his helmet from his head and rubbed the short, thick hairs there, he noticed the peculiar silence in the air about him. Only far off in the distance he could hear noise, the vehicles and the sharp fluting of shouting men down by the river, and, on towards the wood, the noise of rifle-fire and the thudding of mortars. The rosary, broken in his fall, dangled in a little pool of scarlet beads between his thighs, and his fingers scrabbled nervously between them.

After a while, unslinging his Sten-gun, he crawled to the lip of the road and stared at the mill. It was apparently empty. Its old wooden cap was still burning. He could see the smoke rising from it, a long, curling tail that seemed almost stationary against the clear blue sky, and, where it met the mill, there was a little crown of sharp-pointed yellow flames.

But its windows were eyeless and empty, until he noticed that little darting of red flame on the lower sill of the highest window. It was not directed at him this time, but down the road. His mouth was still open and sucking in the fine dust when his eyes followed the flash of the tracers. There, far down the road, was another motorcyclist, and without surprise he saw that it was Smith. The officer's fat figure was slumped on the seat and over the handle-bars of the vehicle with an obvious lack of grace that, even at that moment, aroused Hapgood's contempt. He saw the round, bowl-shaped helmet that rested on Smith's head, making him look like a caricature of a Japanese soldier, and Hapgood reflected that 'Tojo' was well-named.

But, with his eyes drawn back to that window in the mill, silent now and only a wisp of smoke drawn up like a thin hair to the rolling mane that flowed from the top of the building, the seriousness of the situation suddenly came to him. He thought of it a little stupidly, conscious that some responsibility rested on his shoulders, but what he could not decide. He looked down the road again and saw that Smith had stopped, drawn in beside the road, and stretched out across the tank of his machine were the fluttering white folds of a map. The fool thought he was lost, always looking at a map, even when he was within a few yards of the rendezvous. A certain self-pride cheered Hapgood, and then he realized that Smith had not heard the fire of the machine-gun above his engine, and that above, in the mill, shapeless creatures were waiting for him.

Smith was still by the roadside, his little legs stretched out on either side and his toes barely reaching the ground. He raised one foot to kick the starter. Almost without realizing what he was doing Hapgood climbed to his feet, stood by the roadside and swung his arms in great gestures across his body. He shouted futilely. Smith had already started his machine, had swung it into the centre of the road, and was moving down towards Hapgood. The dispatch rider swore at him in disgust, picked up his machine, and flicked its starter with his foot. He felt a thrill of satisfaction as the machine broke into a full-throated roar of life, he throttled it and it swung in a graceful curve on to the road, back towards Bislich.

Hapgood stood up on the foot-rests, waved one hand to Smith and shouted with utter futility as the officer's round, graceless figure moved erratically towards him.

Hapgood was abreast of the mill now. He stared at it curiously, his face a little tense beneath its helmet and the leather flaps beating a tattoo against his cheeks. He watched the upper window without emotion, saw the little tongue of flame shoot rapidly from its cell, but still it was not pointed at him but down towards the officer. Hapgood stood up again on his machine, shouted, and then dropped to his saddle, opening the throttle and leaning forward.

He saw Smith's machine slide sideways drunkenly. The roadway suddenly blossomed with a dozen grey puffs of dust that died almost as quickly and left a cloud in the air. Smith fell from his saddle and rolled into the ditch. Hapgood swung his head to one side and saw the sharp flutter of firing turn in his direction.

'*Oh, Lil!*' he shouted and lay flat upon the tank of his machine.

Down the road Smith raised himself in the ditch, stunned by the suddenness of the fall. His left arm hung loosely from his shoulder and turned at an ugly angle, but he was hardly conscious of the pain, or the blood which, coated with white dust, ran from his elbow to his wrist. He was staring at Hapgood, crouched over the handle-bars, his open mouth a black circle in his face and, in strange, hysterical incongruity, his curved legs thrust out from the side of the machine, pedalling the air as if it were a small bike.

Smith saw the line of bullets strike the road and traverse to meet the cyclist. He saw Hapgood's body straighten suddenly, the wildly gesticulating legs drop to the sides, and then the wheel struck a crater in the road, the machine bounded into the air as if it had suddenly found animal life. With the bound Hapgood's bizarre form rose from the saddle, his legs stretched out wide, his head flung back so that the white length of his throat showed like a pyramid above his yellow scarf. Then he fell back on the road, his knees jerked comically and were still.

Smith stared at the mill incredulously. The window was empty again, but slowly above it, like a smooth scarlet stream, the wooden cap sank inwards and the walls of the mill closed about the flames like hands clasped in prayer. The column of smoke spun upwards and against its black gauze a shower of sparks glittered like sequins.

16. Smith

Between the two officers, lying on the green tent-chair, were Hapgood's paybook, some photographs, a few letters, and his rings. They rested in a little heap that made a dip in the canvas seat. Waithman stared at them reflectively, running his forefinger across his moustache and digging his left heel at the earth. The determined thrust of his foot was the only sign of unusual emotion about Waithman as he sat watching the little green stool.

Suddenly he rubbed his mouth and chin briskly with his hand, felt in his pocket for his pipe, and looked up at Smith, 'Where'd you say you buried him?'

Smith was lying on the bed. His arm, bandaged and in a sling, was resting across his chest, and he was smoking a rare cigarette, staring up at the smoke as it curled and danced towards the canvas roof of the tent. As Waithman spoke he turned his head and smiled. He raised his eyebrows in question and Waithman was surprised, as he had been surprised when Thompson and Jones brought Smith back, by the calmness, the relaxation, and self-assurance in the round features. He repeated his question with a touch of asperity.

'Oh!' Smith looked grave and his eyes unconsciously wavered towards the little pile on the stool. 'By the mill,' he said, 'As I told you, by the mill. We marked it with some stones. We brought his bike back.'

Waithman dug his heel into the ground again and wiped his face with his hand. 'Michaels and Pearce want to go out with Jones again, and put a cross up,' he said.

'That'll be nice,' said Smith simply, 'I don't know why he drove down towards me like that. He must have been lying doggo in the ditch up there. He would have been all right if he'd stayed.'

'Yes,' said Waithman brutally, 'and we'd have been sending out a little cross for you. What is your religion anyway, John?'

But Smith did not flinch as Waithman had expected, his round features still looked grave and he nodded calmly. The lack of Smith's usual self-abnegation irritated Waithman. 'They'd've had to dig a bigger hole for you, John.'

Smith laughed. 'Yes,' he said, 'I was never one for ready-made clothing.' He pushed himself up on the bed with his right hand, and swung his legs over the side. Sitting there, with his wounded arm swinging across his body, he looked seriously at Waithman. 'When you think of it that was a pretty fine thing for Hapgood to do. I wonder if he *knew* what he was doing.'

'Probably,' said Waithman shortly, 'Happy was the sort of man who always took a dare. He was always dead sure he'd get away with it.' There was a touch of nostalgia in his voice. 'In England I believe he used to take French leave just to see if he could get away with it. When he did get sent to the glasshouse it was because he'd gone absent with a vengeance. His wife was ill.' He laughed shortly. 'It was a pleasure to give Hapgood jankers. He used to take it like a kid getting a scripture prize. All grins and thank-you-for-nothing.' He tapped out his pipe. 'How's the arm?'

'Pretty bloody,' said Smith calmly.

'How long have you got?'

Smith looked at his watch. 'About half an hour. If I get back to the dressing station at eight there'll be an ambulance there so the MO said. Pretty decent of him to let me come over for a bit like this.'

'And then?'

'Blighty!' Smith grinned like a schoolboy. 'I shan't be back. The war's over anyway. I'm going home.' He laughed. 'And wounded in a mentionable place too.' He saw Waithman's puzzled frown and he added, 'Just quoting.'

Waithman got up, took a bottle of whiskey from under the bed and poured a little in each of the enamel mugs that stood on the table. 'Well, here's to you anyway, John. You turned out to be a bloody hero after all. There's plenty of room on that cuff of yours for a gold wound stripe.'

Smith tipped the mug in the air and raised it to his lips. The burning spirits tasted of tea and there was a rich brown ring of tannin round the inside of the mug. But he did not notice that, he was looking over the rim to Waithman.

The Troop Commander stood in the middle of the tent, his shoulders bent and his head lowered so that it might not strike the tent strut. He held the mug clutched in his hand across his chest and he was looking at Smith with a peculiar grin of half-triumph and half-derision. But Smith did not notice this so much as the strain and weariness which had become evident in Waithman's features these past few days. His eyes were bloodshot, and sharp grey lines like the vein-work of a beech leaf marked their corners. Two sharp clefts cut deeply on either side of his nose and, Smith was surprised he had not noticed it before, the hair above Waithman's temples was flecked with grey.

'You look all in too, Bob,' said Smith, 'All right?'

Waithman tossed back the whiskey, pursed out his lips and wiped his moustache with a finger. 'I'm all right,' he said 'Tired, I suppose, but hell, who isn't? These three weeks have been bloody. It's been a lousy war.'

'I thought you liked it,' joked Smith.

Waithman grinned and poured another whiskey. He laughed, 'I do. That's the joke. Or can't you see it?'

Smith did not answer; he frowned and sipped the whiskey gently. Like a curate at a tea-party, thought Waithman roughly, it's about all he's good for. Hell, I'm getting hard, the man's all right. He raised his whiskey again. 'Here's to your wound stripe and the end of the war. You got them both, after all.'

Smith did not respond to the toast. He watched Waithman throw the whiskey down his throat and open his mouth to catch in a gulp of air as the hard spirits burnt his mouth. 'What do you mean by that, Bob?' asked Smith quietly.

Waithman sat down again and took out a cigarette, turning it round in his fingers as he looked at it. 'I don't know exactly, except that I've always thought that a nice wound in, what d'you call it? a mentionable place was just about what you needed. And the end of the war of course means that you can go home, back to your wife, back to your office, back to everything you left behind, and a hero into the bargain.'

Smith flushed. 'Never mind the hero business, Bob,' he said sharply, 'You talk as if I'm a fool.'

Waithman grinned, again that fixed, half-derisive, half-triumphant grin. He taunted Smith with it as he walked over to the door of the tent and stood there with his feet astride and his thumbs hooked into his belt, and then he turned. 'Well, aren't, you?' He saw Smith's incredulous face and then relented. 'I'm sorry, John, I'm a bit bomb-happy, I suppose. Even now I can't believe those blasted guns have stopped.'

'It's all right,' said Smith, 'I know how many men we've lost since Normandy.'

Waithman unhooked his thumbs and slipped his hands into his pockets. He looked down at his boots. 'Twenty including some wounded.' He looked up at Smith and grinned. 'Twenty out of a hundred and twenty, not much compared with an infantry mob, but there you'd expect it.' He turned on Smith viciously. 'You are a fool you know, John. You're best off back in England telling the London-cantakers all about the war.'

'I'll just be glad to get back,' said Smith, 'And so will you, you know, old chap. It won't be long. You must come up with your wife and stay with Ivy and me. We'd be glad to have you.'

'Oh be damned to all the old comrade nonsense!' said Waithman, 'I want no part of it. And if you think I'll be glad to get back you're barking up the wrong tree.'

'*Why?*' Smith stared at him in surprise.

'Don't mind me, John,' said Waithman, more tolerantly, 'You go on home. It's the best place for chaps like you, but mind you wear your medals on Armistice Day. There'll be lots of them after this lot, all pretty colours.'

Smith smiled. 'If I know you, Bob, you'll be the one for medals.'

'Course I will, what's the use of a battledress without ribbons? I'll take all they hand out, and the routine mentioned-in-dispatches I'll get for this job. I'll even take your wound stripe if you're prepared to flog it.'

'But you won't be in uniform long now.'

Waithman did not answer. Smith's words had brought his mind up with a halt, forcing him to admit that he had already decided not to go back, not to go out when the chance came. Unconsciously he gripped his cuff with the fingers of his right hand.

'What beats me', he said, turning on Smith again, 'is why you're so confoundedly chirpy now. Since Normandy you've been going round like two penn'orth of beeswax, and now when you get stonked and rightly should be gibbering all over a base hospital, you sit here large as life and as happy as a new lance-corporal.'

'You're drunk, Bob,' said Smith.

'Oh, for God's sake don't moralize. Why don't you complete the metamorphosis of mouse into man and get blind too?'

'I don't need it.'

'I suppose not,' said Waithman, 'And neither do I. I'm just browned off, that's all.'

'Why didn't you take your leave last February?'

'Why didn't you?'

'I didn't think it was right,' said Smith sincerely, 'You were short-handed.'

'Well,' said Waithman, 'I'd no high principles. I just didn't want to go home. Now why don't you clear off to the dressing station and let us get on with this war?'

Smith grinned and looked at his watch. 'I've got some time yet. I'm going to see Hapgood's wife when I get home, and young Hopkins' mother too.'

Waithman looked at him in astonishment. 'There you go again, another change. Couple of months ago you were so shut up in yourself you left your section-sergeant to write to Hopkins' people. Now you propose going on a comfort-jaunt. You *do* think you're a bloody hero, don't you now?'

He saw the flesh about Smith's eyes grow pale, and the smile harden a little. Thank God, he thought, at last I've made him angry.

Smith moved his arm across his body and placed the chipped mug on the floor. He spoke quietly and evenly. 'Yes, I feel changed. It's not a wonderful change, or very interesting really, except that I feel it . . .'

'That's right, tell me all about it,' said Waithman, turning his back and looking out of the tent again. But Smith went on.

'It's because I was wounded, yes. I've been scared all the time of getting killed and then I'm wounded . . .'

Waithman swung round. 'Jones told me that Hapgood was scared stiff of getting wounded, but he got killed,' he said dully.

But Smith had hardly heard. 'It's a silly wound,' he said, 'and almost impossible because we've seen enough not to believe that men get wounded in nice clean places. But *I* did, it's funny really, Bob. It hurts damnably but the pain's good and seems to clear my head. I'm going home and although I know it's fundamentally false reasoning I know that I can go home with an easy conscience because I'm going home wounded. Any other way I would still have been afraid of myself.' He looked down at his boots and seemed to be searching for words. Waithman poured himself another whiskey. He was hardly listening to Smith, he was looking out across the churned earth to the sunset. As a sudden chill seeped out of the ground with the mist he shrugged his shoulders quickly and tightened his blouse. With a cigarette gripped by his thin lips he narrowed his eyes as his breathing drew the smoke back into his face. He heard the quiet tones of Smith's voice, and, freed from the obligation to listen, or even to answer, he stared moodily at the great crimson blood-stain in the west. Against it the ruins of Xanten grew grey, then black, transformed themselves into an ugly wilderness of dark masonry.

'But it's more than that, Bob,' went on Smith, 'I learnt something else this morning . . .'

Waithman looked at his watch anxiously. 'Why aren't those beams exposing?' he said irritably, 'It's dusk. They should be testing station. Jerry'll be over as soon as the sun goes down.'

Smith looked up at Waithman's broad back and smiled. He knew that he no longer had a listener, but he went on speaking, as much to himself as Waithman. 'I discovered that my reputation wasn't as black as I had been painting it. If a man can get himself killed to save me, then I was *persona grata* somewhere.'

But Waithman had heard that. 'You're a hard-skinned man,' he said in surprise, 'Happy would have done that for anybody.'

'I know,' said Smith, 'but if he had thought of me as I believed everybody did, he would have lain there and let that Jerry get me.'

'You make me sick!' said Waithman and he turned back to the whiskey bottle. His voice was becoming thick. 'Where are those damned beams? They ought to be up by now.'

'I suppose it's the same with everyone,' said Smith slowly, and he looked down into the mug between his feet. An insect had climbed to its lip and was perched there with its feeble antennae flickering uneasily. He tipped it back on to the earth with his fingernail. 'Defeating Jerry, defeating the Nazis and all the evil that went with them is becoming history. We're beginning to talk about ourselves. Some of us have hardly been conscious that we have been part of a weapon that not only destroyed Germany but has destroyed a whole world, a whole way to thinking, as much for ourselves as Jerry. Pushed back an edge of a great darkness so that we can see things we never thought possible.'

'Christ, how you go on, John,' grinned Waithman across his mug. He glanced through the tent flap. 'Ah, there's one! I suppose I'll be duty officer every night now you're gone.' To the left a thin thread of lilac spun itself obliquely into the sky and rested on the low clouds in a little ball of incandescent light. Waithman looked at his watch. 'Jig Three,' he said, 'Your section's first up, Bob. Your section that was, anyway.'

Smith smiled again. 'I'll be going soon.'

Waithman stretched his legs. The appearance of the first searchlight had calmed his nerves and he grinned across at Smith. 'Go on, Smudger,' he said, 'What were you saying?'

'You weren't listening,' said Smith kindly, 'Anyway I was saying that this hasn't been one war, or words to that effect.'

'Oh, politics!' said Waithman with a studied yawn, 'That's your job when you get back, John. Stand for Parliament. You're bound to get in with your wound stripe but don't leave it too late. People will get bored with war-heroes after a while. Too much of a strain on the conscience.'

Smith did not bother to answer the good-humoured taunt. 'Two wars,' he said, 'Most of us weren't really conscious of the first, the really important one, because of all the fuss that was being made about it. We assumed it was so much exaggeration. Something unconscious in us, even in you Bob, you a moral hypocrite, rose up to stop the Nazis. I suppose that was the fine thing about it,' he said reflectively, 'except that its very weakness is its irrationalism. Had we thought about it there would have been no need for war.'

Waithman grunted. 'What's the other war?' he said without much interest. He was watching the other beams as they lightly fingered the sky, silently searching. 'I must be going to the Ops-room shortly, John.'

'I'm going soon,' said Smith again, 'It isn't really a second war. I said we were hardly conscious, really conscious of the first because most of us were so mixed up with ourselves finding out about ourselves. This edge of darkness ...' he grinned, 'Ivy always said I was too poetical.'

'Smart woman, your wife,' said Waithman.

'This edge of darkness we were also pushing back inside ourselves. What we found wasn't always pleasant, but we had to see it. I suppose it gave us strength somehow. The real heroes, Bob, were those men who didn't bother about themselves, not just in the moment like poor Hapgood, but all the time. They won't get the medals, they died in the wrong wars, in Spain and German concentration camps.' He stood up and neatly arranged his sling. 'But self-enlightenment comes in strange ways. I'm under no illusions about myself, I just see it, that's all. And I suppose that's something.'

He stood up and buckled on his belt with one hand. As his eyes looked down they rested on the little pile of Hapgood's rings and papers. 'I hope that'll be worth while,' he said.

Waithman swung himself off the bed cheerfully. 'What, still got doubts,' he said, 'after that pretty speech? Choose the right constituency, John. Labour'll get you in this time, that's a dead cert. But do a Vicar of Bray at the next election because Socialism's no place for professed idealists of your sort. Get in among the hardest, grasping realists of them all on the other side, and you'll find them all convinced that they're idealists.'

Smith grinned. 'You're not the fool you make yourself out to be, Bob.'

'And I'm not the fool you think I am, either,' replied Waithman. 'I know the side my bread's buttered. What used Hapgood to say? Number One first!' He took Smith's arm. 'Do you want a truck across to the dressing station?'

'No thanks, my kit's over there.'

'Sorry about the wound and all that, John.'

'What?' said Smith with a wry twist of his lips, 'It was the best thing that ever happened to us.'

The mist was thick, it lay between the dusky sky and the earth like a long roll of cotton-wool. The two officers shivered slightly and hunched their shoulders. They could hear the shrill piping of the wireless in the Operations Room, as they walked up the bulldozed track. There they passed Jones and Michaels who were looking up at the sky, staring at the crossing lanes of the beams. Their cigarettes were two points of scarlet against their faces.

Smith stopped. 'Just a sec, Bob.' And he walked across to Michaels. 'Good-bye, Corporal,' he said, 'I'm glad you got back from Brussels in time to see the last of me.'

Michaels looked at him curiously, took the cigarette from his mouth and gripped Smith's hand. He did not know whether the ambiguity of Smith's words had been intentional. 'Wound all right, sir?' he said.

'Fair enough, Michaels. Anything I can send you from England?'

He caught Michaels' grin in the pale light. 'You might send some duty-free fags, sir. When non-frat goes they'll be good to flog.'

They watched Smith walk away into the mist, his wounded arm making his gait seem all the more clumsy and ridiculous, and his trousers were stretched tight across his buttocks, the bottom of his blouse wrinkled and full.

'See the conquering hero goes!' said Michaels without much humour.

'Poor old Happy, it wasn't Tojo's fault,' said Jones, 'He's just dead unlucky.'

'No,' said Michaels, 'Nothing is anybody's fault any more.'

'What's the matter with you, Joe?' asked Jones. He flicked his cigarette into the air and it fell to the ground in a burst of sparks. 'You've been a miserable brute since you came back from Brussels.'

'Nice to come back and find your mate buried in a hole with that fat little caricature wandering off home with a nice wound.'

'It's not only that,' said Jones shrewdly. He stood away from the truck and put his hands in his pockets. 'You were like it yesterday, ever since you came back.'

'Jerry's late,' said Michaels, ignoring the question. He leant on the bonnet of his truck and pushed back his cap as he ran his hand through his thick hair. 'Queer thing, Ted. There are some people you never believe will die. They are just born to stay alive. A miserable sod like you I can imagine as a corpse, but not Happy. You feel as if someone had played a dirty trick on you.' He lit another cigarette. 'Happy used to make fun of Sunny Jim, remember? Well, there isn't much to choose between them now.'

Far out to the east, beyond the silver wake of the Rhine, they heard the bomber approaching. 'Ten minutes late,' said Michaels. 'I hope they're sober and properly-dressed.'

Jones joined him and leant on the bonnet too. They were both staring to the east, to where the noise of the plane was throbbing its warning. About them the searchlights began to waver nervously.

'It's being young,' said Jones, 'I always thought there was something wrong with the Army. We all seemed too young, and then I realized what it was. When my father used to tell me about the last war he was already old, his hair was grey and to me he looked as wise as a man could be. I got the impression that all the men in that war were middle-aged, with grey hair, never young like us, or Happy.'

Michaels swore. His words were lost as the noise of the plane roared above them and the air was cut with the cross of tracers. The dusk spun into life with furious fire, and then almost as suddenly the bomber turned on a wing and glided back to the east.

'A recce,' said Michaels briefly. 'The others'll be back.'

They stood there smoking, watching the east and the searchlights suspiciously stroking the low clouds. They heard Waithmans return, his quick, short laugh from the Operations Room in the lighted dug-out.

'It's always the Hapgoods,' said Michaels. 'They never had much before the war and look what happens to them during it, and unless they do something they'll be cheated out of everything afterwards. But they can't fool all of the people all of the time. What barrack-room lawyer said that?'

'Anything wrong, Joe?' said Jones again.

'Mind your own damn business, you snivelling little psalm-singer!' Michaels swung himself away from the vehicle, but before he had gone far he turned and saw Jones' face looking towards him, a white oval, expressionless. He came back and put his arm round Jones' shoulder.

'Don't mind me, Ted, but do me a favour, will you?'

'What is it, Joe?'

'I'm going sick in the morning, probably be away for a few days. Drive me down to the hospital, will you? I'd rather you did it, not anyone else.'

Jones looked at Michaels curiously, staring at his face, at the careless grin that seemed fixed there. 'All right,' he said, but he did not understand.

From the east the bombers finally came, and up into the sky, to where the searchlights spread their fictitious moonlight, the glorious rain of fire curled to meet the enemy.

17. Michaels

He lay on the bed smoking quietly. The three other men in the ward were asleep. Two of them lay curled on the bare, stained mattresses, their heads buried in their arms as he had seen babies lie. They were fully-dressed except for their boots and their toes peeped out of great holes in their socks. On the next bed the Pioneer lay with his mouth open, his thick brows drawn tightly together and his breath passing in and out of his yellow teeth with a peculiar singing noise. The air in the ward was quiet except for the deep noise of the breathing, and as Michaels blew smoke up to the cracked ceiling he could not believe that the silence was not artificial. It seemed to be a deceptive façade for some more devilish subtlety. His ears could not yet grasp that this was silence, a faithful silence that would not unexpectedly break into the crash of gunfire or the long throbbing of moving vehicles. He thought that since he landed in Normandy there had been no real silence for him, even the pauses, the fragmentary armistices of sound, had been sinister, full of evil promise. And in Brussels there had been no silence; the noise of dance bands, high laughter, and drunken shouting, of heels clicking a voluptuous tattoo on the pavements, the thudding of a heart stimulated by alcohol and fierce excitement. Even at night in Brussels there had been the noise of cars, the last drunken challenge of a voice.

These sounds, and others from far back in his life, struggled for supremacy over this unnatural silence. Michaels felt the muscles of his face aching in protest against the tension in which he had held them since he came to the Field Hospital. But when the silence was broken, by the bright clanging of the monastery bell, its discord seemed so great that he sat up on the bed sharply, and let his cigarette fall to the bare boards of the floor. There it burnt itself out in a sharp, unpleasant odour, the thin signal of its smoke rising like a cotton-thread to the high ceiling.

Michaels pushed his hands deep into his pockets as he lay there, his body stretched out and his blouse and shirt open. Behind him the spring sun filtered through the dusty windows to catch a golden glint from the hairs on his chest. He made no effort to direct his thoughts, but in an unusual, exhaustion of purpose he let them wander aimlessly from point to point. Now and again the monastery bell above the gate-tower chimed its meaningless notes, and once he heard a car changing gear. The firm, certain sound of it quickened his wits with an old nostalgia. If there was anything deliberate in his thoughts it was a defiant, a defensive bitterness against which he put the shoulder of his self-respect now and then. But in the arrogance of such a pose he could not seek out an opponent among the bewildering darkness of his reflective thoughts.

One thing seemed imperative. He must somehow drag from the confusion of unpleasant memories the picture of the girl's face. He did not know why this was so important, only that some impulse made it so. He could remember other things about her, the café where he had picked her up, the American soldiers fighting outside the Gare du Nord when she took him home, the round, bland-faced *madame* at the foot of the stairs; but the girl's face he could not remember. He remembered the cheap, tailored jacket that seemed too big for her shoulders, and the scarlet flash of her wedge-heeled shoes going up the stairs in front of him, the white over-fulness of her calves. But not her face. He could remember the cupboard in her room, with the American cigarettes and bars of candy on its shelves, but not her face.

He fumbled in his pockets for another cigarette, but before he found it he lost the desire to smoke again and he concluded that it was of no importance that he could not remember her face. Her face had not been important, and her body had now assumed an importance that far outdistanced anything he had believed possible that night. His fingers gripped the box of matches in his pocket and crushed it.

His mind switched abruptly to thoughts of his wife and he remembered her last instruction to bring her a present when he next came home. Well, he thought again, I have a present from Belgium now, but you won't want it. Who would?

Disgusted with his self-pity, his cynicism overriding that sensitive part of his nature, he bunched the pillow behind his head and looked about the ward. It was long and narrow, with high windows which on one side dropped long bars of dust-spangled sunlight to the dirty floor. From the others, opposite him, he could see the sky dappled with mackerel clouds, and silhouetted against it the high branches of a chestnut tree, heavy with green leaf. The sun shone on those brown, sticky buds yet unopened.

Beside him the big bulk of the sleeping Pioneer suddenly turned itself over with a convulsive jerk, and the broad, weather-beaten face buried itself in the pillow where the lips swore softly and muffled.

Michaels looked up to the ceiling and counted the cracks that splintered the yellow plaster, and before he had finished counting his eyes were caught and held by the fly-papers that hung from the centre beam. They turned gently in the air, twisting, winding and unwinding in a long ribbon of shining glue. The flies were clustered thick upon them and one, with the defiance and courage of all flies caught thus, buzzed incessantly.

On the far wall was a huge, black crucifix, and hanging from it the white figure of Christ. The pale, plaster flesh was stained with long streaks of discolouration which may have been intended as blood, or may have been merely rust from the nails. From the arms of the cross, looped casually over the nails, hung two more fly-papers, each with its thick cemetery of black flies.

As he listened Michaels realized that the silence was deceptive. There was the noise of the snoring, swearing Pioneer, the desperate fly, the bell clanging its futile tocsin, and far off down the tiled corridor that led away from the ward a broken cistern was leaking joyously. As he heard another car changing gear his feet ached for the pedals, and he could feel the wheel beneath his fingers.

But he could not remember *her* face. He could see the back of her head, the dry, crisp curls inexpertly combed. He smelt the harsh smell of her cheap perfume, but he could not see her face.

It did not matter. Had nothing happened as it had he would not have remembered her, any more than she probably remembered him. There would be other men, other customers, he thought, for the cool, confident orderlies at the prophylactic station beneath the green cross in the Jardins Botaniques.

He supposed that his wife was important now, but the link between them had always seemed so flimsy that even now he could not bring her into this as something substantial and vital. He had a sudden flash of pity for her, but whether it was because of the deception he had practised on her, or of the pain this would bring he did not know. He reflected a little grimly that the deception was artificial. Theirs had been a war-marriage, disturbingly commonplace in character.

He wondered too whether he could really bring her pain. There would be anger, indignation, a conventional and virtuous scorn. She had not the imagination to grapple with the problem on her own but would seek the ready-made answer. He could see her face, how she would raise one hand to pat the roll of hair behind her small face, a gesture which always gave her mind time to summon the words that did not come easily. She would reject him, he decided, not so much through sincerity, but through fear, distaste, impatience, and a refusal to face the issue squarely.

In any case he would not tell her, he would not give victory on such easy terms. He remembered that the Medical Officer had advised him to be silent. He remembered the interval after the examination when he had been told the truth of what he already suspected. The MO had been a thin, dry man whose wide blue eyes had looked at Michaels dispassionately from behind the thick pebbles of his glasses. Above his left breast-pocket, out of which sprouted a hedgerow of pencils and pens, there had been the stained white and purple ribbon of the Military Cross. He had talked to

Michaels without any partisanship, which somehow Michaels resented more than if the doctor had betrayed a bias. No man with such a task could be completely dispassionate, he must have feelings, but whether they were compassionate, tolerant, or indignant he gave no sign.

Neatly, dipping his pen carefully into a bottle of green ink, he had written on Michaels' papers. Without looking up he said 'Married? Well don't tell your wife, old chap. I shouldn't if I were you. It never works out, you know.' He looked up and something that might have been a smile twisted the end of his thin mouth and glistened behind his thick spectacles. 'Penicillin is a wonderful thing.'

In the hands of the orderly, a fat, bucolic man with a rolling rich voice that seemed to slip happily from his thick lips, the syringe of penicillin was no more wonderful than a walking-stick in the hands of a circus clown. Every four hours he visited the ward on what he called 'his errand of mercy, you've had the lady with the lamp'.

Michaels looked down at his long body lying there on the stained mattress. It looked no different, and yet to him now the grace of it, its muscular symmetry, seemed particularly artificial. His mind, which he realized without emotion was growing increasingly macabre, flew back to the sun-drenched fields that opened out to them once the Hochwald had been passed. He and Pearce had come across a German in a trench. A mortar-shell had torn away one wall and flung the man back against it, and he lay there with his arms behind him, his body relaxed, as if he were taking full advantage of the deep warmth of the early sun. His face stared up at them impassively, the eyes open and the lips parted slightly. He seemed untouched, alive, and particularly handsome with his fair hair.

Then, as Pearce leaped lightly to the other side of the trench, the earth gave way, and slowly, as if turning in the sensual enjoyment of repose, the German's body rolled sideways and they had seen the great cavity in the back of the skull and the unbelievable things that crawled there.

Michaels felt now that there was not much to choose between them. A night, a girl in red shoes, or his own stupidity and recklessness, had sapped his own self-pride, not so much by the incident itself, which he regarded quite cynically, but by its uncompromising result. In a life where he had used that self-pride as the foundation of his whole philosophy, a buttress to his emotions and ambitions, he had built nothing else that could support him now. He thought of Jones with some respect, the queer tortured impulses that had brought the Londoner to Europe, the seemingly detached determination that motivated him. Michaels saw in his own actions only a reflection of his conceit in the perfection of his body. He now saw himself aligned with all the things that had once disturbed him and aroused his irritable scorn; with Smith in his cowardice and obesity, with cripples, his pity for whom had been mostly impatience, with the grim, physical façade of a German soldier in a slit trench.

Impatiently he swung his long body from the bed and in his stockinged feet he stood by the window, looking down. Below, between the wings of the monastery, was a little garden, bisected by a narrow path of fine yellow sand. On one side there grew a profusion of young vegetables, the rich, pale green of their young shoots shining as if illuminated against the black earth. On the other side the dark leaves of rose shrubs stood straight beside the steadying support of thin canes. On some of them, like dark stains of blood against the leaves, were a few early blossoms. But he hardly noticed them, and barely considered the fact that roses were blooming so early that spring.

He was looking at the nun that stood among them, a long wicker basket on the ground beside her and a pair of shears in her hand. She was cutting the rose-blooms carefully, and laying them in the basket, the long stalks straight and the blossoms themselves grouped in a deep red glow at one end. Her head was covered by an enormous starched coif of dazzling whiteness, with wings that stood out on either side like the staysails of a fine ship, and they trembled gently as she moved her head over the flowers. Her dress was of pale blue dungaree and swinging across its skirts was a heavy crucifix on a bead-strung rosary.

Michaels watched her dispassionately. He knew that there must still be people in the monastery, even though the British had taken it for a hospital, but he had never expected women, rather the brown-clad, tonsured monks he had seen so often in Holland. He wondered what she thought of it all, whether she was worried about being a German these days, as all of them seemed to be, or whether being married to Christ was sufficient nationality in itself. With a wave of self-pitying bitterness he reflected that marriage with Christ ran no risks at any rate.

His hands fumbled for the catch and he swung up the heavy sash of the window and leant over the sill. The sun seemed even warmer, and as it fell on his face he welcomed it gratefully. He wanted to go down into the garden but he knew that it was out of bounds, and that he was imprisoned in the ward. But at the noise of the window the nun looked up, her white headdress forming a translucent sunshade for her head and lighting her face with a faint incandescence. She stared up at him, the shears shining in one hand and a cut bloom held across her blue dress. He looked back into her face. It was round and colourless, with that peculiar bloodless pallor of the cloisters. It was a young face, a very young face, and this surprised him, and embarrassed him too, and he would have drawn back into the room had not a sudden scorn for his own weakness prevented him. He looked down into the girl's face and caught something of a smile there before she dropped her eyes to the flowers again.

'Close the window, Mac, there's a good bloke.' The Pioneer was awake, stretching himself slowly and looking up at Michaels' face. 'How long have you got?'

'Until tomorrow,' said Michaels, pulling the sash down slowly and sitting on his bed. 'Have a fag?'

The Pioneer moistened the end of the cigarette with his lips and then lit it. 'This is dog-rough,' he said, 'I don't like waiting.' They did not speak of why they were there, and across the room the two infantrymen breathed heavily. The sun had fallen and the long bars of sunlight had moved across the room to catch the vivid scarlet from the infantrymen's shoulder-flashes. The Pioneer jerked his thumb at them. 'Kid over there's only twenty,' he said. 'Seems a shame, don't it. We were smokies for his mob before they crossed the Rhine. He was out of that do, anyway.' He spat out a strand of tobacco. 'I suppose it's better here than digging in under the eighty-eights. Poor bloody infantry, eh? Poor bloody all of us, I say!' He looked round the room and his eye seemed held by the fly that was still buzzing ineffectually on the twisting paper. 'There's more'n one way of getting wounded. Do we get a gold stripe for this, cocker?'

Without waiting for a reply he lay back on his bed, pulled a copy of *Lilliput* from his pocket and thumbed through its pages indifferently. He stared at its graceful nudes, posed discreetly in artificial chiaroscuro, and he pursed his lips with the cynical disbelief of experience. Then he dropped the book on the floor and closed his eyes again. 'Nothing like kip,' he murmured.

Michaels returned to the window and stared through its dusty panes at the garden. The nun was moving gracefully down the path, her blue skirts swaying about her black shoes and the white headdress nodding stiffly. He watched her enter the monastery, the dip of her basket gave him a last glimpse of the crimson roses, and then she was gone. He recalled her face and wondered if she reminded him of the girl in Brussels, but he did not know. He thought that perhaps he would go on thinking that, whatever woman's face he looked into, and there did not seem so great a gulf between the girl in that high-ceilinged Brussels room and the nun in the garden, a difference only in himself.

He supposed he should feel angry, direct his bitterness against the girl but he could not. He felt a pity, but a spark of his old intolerance burned against such weakness until his own experience extinguished it. 'There is more than one way of being wounded.' The war was a jig-saw of major suffering, cross-cut with minor problems that went on repeating themselves, driving the mind to greater introspection until the major plan was forgotten. When you begin by regarding it all as fundamentally exciting, a liberation from commonplace things, how easy it is to ignore the causes, the inevitabilities that fling one half of the world against the other's throat. He remembered those hours in the darkness before dawn, with the beams lying along the horizon, the sharp, brief chatter of gunfire protesting against the unnatural silence. Sitting with him in the Jeep he would listen to Jones talking softly. Casual, silly conversations they seemed now. The war had picked Jones from a life where, in common with thousands of others, he had learnt its first and only important principle, that one mounts on another's shoulders. But whereas Michaels had found the Army a release from this competitive struggle, Jones had paradoxically grown more deeply aware of it. Behind all of Jones' bitterness, his condemnation of the ugliness which war had revealed in men as much as nations, Michaels knew there burnt this hatred of the Germans, a strange, unwieldy emotion which Michaels almost envied for the natural volition it provided. For himself he had no real feelings one way or the other. He supposed he disliked the Nazis, he hated obvious, vindictive cruelty, but he freely admitted that but for the war he would probably have thought neither one way nor the other. But Jones, Jones was a little Bolshie.

None of these thoughts, as he looked down at the empty gardens, was of any comfort. For the first time in his life he failed to draw any strength from within himself, and he was shrewd enough to know why. Because he had betrayed the very source of his self-respect, that pride in his own physical cleanliness, he felt lost, peculiarly angry with himself. At least, he thought, I'm still a damn good driver. With a half-smile he realized that he was learning something about himself as if the revelation of weakness was the first foundation stone of a new strength. But that thought, no matter how adroit, was cold comfort.

He walked slowly down the length of the room, his hands in his pockets and his shoulders hunched slightly, his spirits rebelling against the narrow, drab imprisonment of the ward. He had a wild, impatient longing for Hapgood's company and he grew angry with the clumsiness of a life that could suddenly extinguish so crude and brilliant a flame as the little Tynesider.

There had been surprises. Thompson most of all. The sergeant-major, rubbing his bald head and looking at Michaels with unfeeling eyes across a mug of tea, had said that it would be all right, *he* knew something about these things. And Waithman had looked at Michaels as if he had asked for weekend leave and said, 'Well, look after yourself Michaels, you'll be back soon. Don't worry about it, old chap!'

Don't worry about it. There was no real worry, but a curious, empty feeling, a dispirited sensation of something gone, like the memory of the girl's face. An unapproachable thing like the white, dispassionate features of the nun, neatly clipping roses among the dark green leaves. An ugly revelation of artificiality like the unmentionable skull of the German in the slit trench.

From along the corridor the orderly's rich voice was shouting, a high, challenging voice, 'Char up!' It was tea-time. On the beds across the room the young infantrymen stirred. One of them bent down and dragged a mug from beneath the bed and looked into it, thoughtfully, swilling the cold, scum-laden tea around. He looked up and caught Michaels staring at him. He smiled back and pushed the hair from his face.

Together, drawing comfort from the unity of their mutual experience, the four men went down the tiled corridor to the mess-hall. None of them would have thought of going alone.

18. Jones

Leaving Michaels at the door of the hospital Jones swung the Jeep back on to the road, passing beneath the red arch where the lilac fronds and the fresh green leaves dropped idle fingers to the earth. He drove quickly to the east, his eyes watching the land as he passed, his lips pursed in a whistle of which he was hardly conscious. His long fingers moved confidently on the wheel and the gear lever; his body had long since acquired a suppleness and strength.

    He found the land, this German land, strangely disturbing, emptied of troops, with few civilians as yet in the villages, only the slipping, drunken signs that pointed on towards the Rhine crossing. Now and then he did see a little group of children in bright scarlet pinafores and heavy shoes, playing by the roadside, swinging on the signal wire. As his Jeep roared towards them they would stand up by the trunks of the trees silently staring at him until he had passed. There would be old men by the roadside, touching their peaked caps in a greeting he did not return, and he did not know whether to marvel at their tolerance or to despise their obsequiousness. It was hard to avoid the pleasant sensation of absolute power that membership of a conquering army gave him, the knowledge that nobody, whatever his previous station or importance, could now claim superiority over him. That in this ravaged country there was nothing of more importance than his stained battledress, his dusty, shaking vehicle. His whistle grew louder and as he caught the notes of it above the noise of his engine he pursed out his lips and lifted the tune into a jaunty rant of arrogance. It was in such moments as this that he missed Hapgood.

    The unseasonable heat of spring drew beads of sweat from his forehead, and he pushed back his cap, sat nonchalantly in the seat with one hand hanging over the open side of the Jeep.

His thoughts were drifting, he was hardly thinking at all, but drinking in the moments of deep, unaffected sensual pleasure that come rarely to a soldier. Yet as he drove on something in the uncontrolled destruction about him sapped the good humour from him as easily as the heat might have evaporated a film of rain on the road's surface. The reaction was complete. He felt tired, deflated, and exhausted, and he realized with surprise that he had slept little for days. But it was only weariness. It was as if the thick dust that hung over every Rhineland town was impregnated with a foul toxin rising from the decay of the buildings and the putrefaction of the bodies beneath them. Long ago he had tried to imagine moments like this, these days when he would drive his Jeep on German soil, when he would see German houses broken, German faces as mutely twisted with suffering as he had seen the faces of other peoples'. But now, once seen, they left him with the same sensation of disgust, the same disturbing despair.

He appreciated that much of what he was now feeling was surprise, surprise that destruction could be so complete; that no claim for neutrality, even from the wild growths of the fields, was observed. There had been no mercy in the Rhineland. The first tanks and flame-throwers drove their tracks imperturbably over the earth, the buildings, the face of the land. He did not regret it, it was just that the violation of it all surprised him by its immensity. He remembered the tank he had seen one late dusk in March, resting drunkenly by the roadside, slowly and carefully placing its shells into the surrounding farmhouses until the flames of their burning roofs painted the rich scarlet of the sunset across all of the evening sky. Waithman, in the seat beside Jones, had watched too, and had cursed the wanton destruction, and had added the peculiar rider 'that it served the Boche right'.

The Jeep rolled easily down the long avenues and the drowsy hum of its engine soothed the ragged edges of Jones' thoughts. There had been moments when it did not seem very important that he was in Germany. The character of war had not changed because of it, nor its intensity because the flood of its advance had carried it across yet another border. The faces of dead men, the details of physical destruction wore the same inhuman mark, except that here in Germany it had been deeper, more comprehensive. The odd, half-conscious reservations of his comrades, which had been observed in the liberated countries, had now been broken down, choked with the dust of German roads. Licence, excess, and near-brutality had replaced them. There was little talk of anything but loot, and German houses stood amid the welter of their own entrails. He accepted it, he did not condemn, and he could feel no pity. It was as if a skin had grown over his heart in self-defence, and his eyes no longer held communication with his brain.

Yet there had been incidents that shook him from his indifference. Below the single-span Bailey bridge which the Engineers had flung across the little river in Cleve, he had seen a woman lying in the water. He had been driving quickly over the bridge in the late afternoon, bumping into the dust of the river road, his face hot and tired. But he had not been too weary to see her there, lying naked on her face, and the pull of the stream, the obscene fingering of the water, had stretched out her limbs until they seemed to be clutching the shallow bed of the river. This startling white body had lain there for two days, and when he passed again, he noticed that someone had tumbled the debris over it and given it an unconsecrated burial. It did not seem important then that she was a German, but when the significance of the memory tapped its urgent message to his brain he answered 'They asked for it.' All along the length of the Rhineland the sentence ran, 'They asked for it!' He thought of Mary, perhaps the flying bomb had stripped her of decency before it tumbled the building over her head. He almost believed that now, and then the war had driven on and blotted the memory from his mind until it returned this afternoon with its irritating, unspoken question, and its insistent reminder of Mary.

He drew in the Jeep beneath the fruit trees, switched off the engine, and lit a cigarette. He looked over the fields towards the river. He could not see it and despite the broken trees, the fractured roofs of the isolated farmhouses, the scene seemed remarkably quiet, and the road deserted. He was glad to be alone and he wondered whether he might sleep awhile. He did not wish to go back to the Rhine yet, to the tents and the trenches grouped in the muddy earth about the pontoon bridge, deafened by the roar of crossing vehicles and the endless, intolerant braying of the throaty load-speaker, for all the world as if the greatest battle in the world were but a hucksters' fair. He looked up through the young leaves of the pear trees, the half-born blossoms, and he watched a small cloud scudding against the blue. He smiled contentedly; laced his feet on the wing of the car and enjoyed the quiet and unusual solitude.

The children's voices surprised him, for he had not noticed them. He twisted his head round and saw them standing behind his Jeep. There were two young girls in blue pinafores, with their fair hair braided about their heads. With them was a small boy in a peaked cloth cap, his hands thrust down into his pockets and an angry frown on his face. Jones stared back at them curiously, without smiling, and although there was no welcome in his face they walked up to him and stood nervously to one side of the Jeep. The smaller girl chewed her lower lip with thoughtful concentration and the small boy carried his angry frown more truculently until Jones grinned at his furious face. In sudden irritation the boy kicked the near wheel of the Jeep. Jones leant out to box the boy's ears but the children jumped back quickly with shrill jeers of derision. The boy stuck out his tongue and the frown dropped over his eyes again like a mask.

Feeling that he was playing with three wild animals Jones flicked his cigarette-end down the road and the boy ran after it delightedly, picking it up quickly and dusting out its end with his thumb. He stored it away in a little tin which he dragged from his pocket.

The elder girl spoke to Jones suddenly, in a high, toneless voice, but with a bright smile. 'Uncle, you got cigarettes chocolate?'

'Oh God,' said Jones, 'You've got a hard neck, haven't you?'

The girl looked at him suspiciously. *'Bitte?'* she said, *'Was haben Sie gesagt?'*

Jones stared back. 'Nix verstand!' he said, 'Now hop it all of you. Go and ask Hitler for cigarettes.' He switched on the engine and pressed the starter. The engine growled and then died away.

'Hitler no good!' said the girl happily, and although the boy frowned and stuck his tongue deeper into his cheek the other girl nodded. 'Not Nazis,' she said, 'Poppa Polski.'

Jones leant out of the Jeep and placed his hand on her shoulder. A flicker of fear passed across her eyes and he felt her shoulder draw back as she looked down at her brown fingers. 'Now look,' he said, 'You don't have to tell whoppers like that. Go home and tell your poppa to think up a better one. There's a good girl!'

The girl looked back at him doubtfully. 'Cigarettes for poppa?' she said cautiously.

'I've given 'em all to Nelly van Huyk!' he shouted at her angrily, 'Now go on home, all of you!' The children leaped back with a scream of laughter as he waved his fist at them, and the engine of the Jeep coughed and growled its way to life. He steered it back on to the road and pressed his foot on the accelerator. As he changed gear he heard a stone bounce from the rear mudguard and he looked back over his shoulder at the children. They were standing in the middle of the road, growing smaller and smaller until they were only flecks of colour against the grey dust and the green of the pear trees.

He drove on, unpleasantly dissatisfied with the incident. He wished, with more passion than he had ever felt, that Mary were here beside him, and the thought of her, like a nostalgic fragrance amid all this aridness, brought tears to his eyes, and he left them there although the roadway before him grew misty and distorted. He sobbed unrestrainedly in bitterness, anger, and despair. For a year almost he had fought down some of his grief by his determination to reach Germany and witness some of the retribution he felt it had deserved, or to exact it himself.

He opened his mouth and let the air gush in to cool the hot saliva, and as he pressed his foot on the throttle he shouted against the rising note of the engine, '*Oh you bastards, you murdering bastards!* I hope it's like this all over. You kill Mary, you kill hundreds of Marys that never meant anything to you and you send your children to *me* for cigarettes!' He swore, incoherently, passionately, and the infection of his bitterness poured out in obscenity, like poison from a lanced wound.

One thing remained in the scar, a fierce and unrestrained delight in the destruction he saw about him. As he drove past further groups of children, past men and women moving to the roadside to let him pass, he leant out of the Jeep and shouted incoherent taunts at them, looking back over his shoulder with flushed cheeks and wet eyes to laugh at the bewilderment in their staring faces.

The land dipped down in a gentle decline to the Rhine. He could not see the river yet but he could see the thin signals of smoke from its banks and far away to the east where the Ruhr lay and the German army was still fighting, he could see the smoke lying in one thick segment on the horizon. In fire he recognized an ally, something purifying, cleansing, and revengeful. Fire was the only blossom that could grow from the seeds of battle, a short-lived flower that bloomed quickly, and died as soon as its hot life had devoured what had taken men years to build. It was a cynical ally, changing sides continuously, but always satisfying its own unquenchable hunger. Jones had always found its bright petals repellent, and the black weeds it left repugnant, but now, as he saw it flowering from the Dutch border to the Rhine, he drew a fierce, angry pleasure from the sight. In his bitterness he wanted it to bloom in one great garden of smoke-rimmed scarlet across the length and breadth of Germany.

Where the road reached the crossroad and parted to drive south and north, there stood a cottage. Jones had noticed it before and had been surprised by the fact that it had escaped destruction. It lay back from the road behind three sentinels of beech trees. It was empty. Armies, in green and khaki, had passed through its rooms, cynically stripping them, throwing the debris to the ground below the windows until it lay like a broken earthwork about the house. It was deserted, but behind its black, broken windows there seemed to lurk a sullen and silent defiance.

Jones remembered it as it had been the last time he saw it, with a rifle section resting among the vegetables of its garden. The white faces of the infantrymen, with steel helmets pushed back from their foreheads and their dusty hair screening their eyes, were splintered with strange grins when the Troop convoy went past. They stuck derisive fingers in the air and catcalled Smith as he rode gracelessly by on his motorcycle. But now the house was deserted and Jones pulled over to the side of the road, switched off his engine and looked at it curiously. The more he stared at it the more some indefinable characteristic about it irritated him. Perhaps it was that, despite the rubbish of its rooms, it still remained firm and undamaged. Even the gate, as he leant out and kicked it idly with his feet, swung efficiently on its hinges.

An inconsistency in the scheme of things struck him forcibly. Somewhere at home in London, in a sea of wretched gravestones, lay Mary, her body broken and her life extinguished quickly and sharply in a quarrel that had not been of her own choosing. She had been taken from him by men he had never seen. The same men had starved little Nelly, had snuffed out the bright, happy ignorance of Hapgood in one second, and so on and on until Jones' mind was numbed by the catalogue.

Yet despite all that this house still stood. Retribution had burst in upon Germany but this house still stood, and in a few days, or a week or so, its owners would return, would clean out its rooms, put back the furniture, and restore the ravaged garden. A fire would burn in the grate, and the Germans would rest comfortably before it. The peat on the hearth would burn up the memory of five years.

Jones got out of the Jeep suddenly, and pushed open the gate with anger. He strode down the little path into the house. The rooms were thick with a queer, musty odour of damp plaster, stale food, and rain-damp wood. Beneath his feet as he walked the glass crunched, and his heavy boots kicked aside the crockery, the cartridge cases, the fragments of books that lay there. Leaning against the wall, with a smear of mud across its face, was a great china doll in a scarlet pinafore and blue dress. He picked it up and looked at it slowly, ran his fingers gently through its straw-coloured hair and then, on an impulse, he tucked it beneath his arm.

He went outside again and stared up at the house, puckering up his face with a look of childish incredulity. The doll hung downward from his arm-pit, its pink fingers stretched towards the soil and its eyes rolled back until the whites showed.

Suddenly, consumed by a fierce and almost unprecedented anger, he turned and stumbled back to his Jeep, flinging the doll into the rear seat. He dragged a full jerrycan of petrol from the floor of the vehicle and carried it unsteadily to the house. With his heel he kicked open its cap and lifting the can beneath his arm he walked through the ground floor, the living room, the kitchen and the hall. The pink fluid spurted and gulped from the neck of the can, staining the floor, the rubble, and the dusty textiles, and the thick odour of it rose up and made his eyes and nostrils smart. Then he went outside and threw the jerrycan into the weeds, standing back and breathing heavily. So intense were his emotions that he could not control his hands and he thrust them into his pocket angrily.

When his temper subsided he picked up an old newspaper, twisted it in his hands, and lit it with a match. He held his arm straight from his body, with the paper pointing down, and he saw with satisfaction how the yellow flames curled sensuously up the dry paper. Then, inclining his body backwards, he flung the torch through the open door.

The thump of exploding air struck his face and took his breath away. From every window on the ground floor an exultant tongue of flame leapt out and curled impertinently at the sky, almost immediately withdrawing to gorge itself with the rich fuel of the little house. The heat was intense, as if someone had just opened the door of an enormous furnace.

Jones stepped back slowly, holding the palm of his hand before his face, his lips fixed in an ugly grin, his eyes hard.

For ten minutes he waited and watched the house burning. The fire spread quickly from room to room and from the upper windows grey, dirty smoke twisted up to raise an enormous column in the still air. At last he had seen enough, his anger and gratification were burnt away in the fire itself, and as he turned heavily towards the Jeep he did not at first notice the little group of people standing by the gate, just a little to the left of one of the beeches. When he did see them he stared back at them curiously, as if they too were made of some highly inflammable material that had not yet caught fire.

The little group, huddled together more in embarrassment than apprehension, consisted of a woman and two children, a boy and a girl. The woman was quite young, her plaited hair wound in a coronet about her head and her body wrapped in a fur-collared coat much too large for her. The children clung to her hands and the leaping flames of the burning house caught and exaggerated the curious stupefaction of their expressions. The woman looked at Jones dully, her body relaxed in the coat in an attitude of resignation and despair. When the girl, taking her eyes from Jones' face, turned and looked at the Jeep, she caught sight of the doll. Her mouth opened with surprise, and she tugged at her mother's coat, but the woman paid her no attention; she was staring at Jones and he was staring back at her, realizing that it was her house that was burning.

The building was now completely aflame, a ball of flame with ribs and roof crackling furiously. A sharp cloud of smoke and sparks began to dip and eddy about the soldier and the three Germans. None of them spoke.

Jones was surprised by the appearance of the woman's face. In the moment of realizing that he had burnt her house he had expected some expression of her grief and anger, but she was watching the consuming flames almost with apathy. The dull, immobile outline of her features was turned towards him, carefully watching him but betraying nothing. Yet in her eyes there was a fulness of experience, as if what happened to her now could be only more physical pain driving inwards only.

Jones was the first to move. He turned quickly, and with an odd, ridiculous forcefulness he strode up the path, past the Germans to the Jeep. The children cowered away from him behind their mother's legs but the woman moved nothing but her head as her eyes remorselessly followed him. As he reached the rear of the vehicle his stomach revolted in bile and his limbs felt weak. Unashamedly he dropped to his knees and vomited on the dusty soil. When he got to his feet his face was hot and his forehead damp with clammy perspiration. He was not surprised to find that the woman and the children had followed him, that they had stood there watching him as he retched on the grass. The expression on the woman's face had not changed, but the children were frowning in bewilderment, and the girl, seeing her doll again in the Jeep, began to cry.

Jones got into the Jeep and drove away quickly. His stomach felt weak and his battledress was heavy with the smell of smoke, a smell which he thought he could never lose. He drove quickly, hardly slackening pace at the craters, delighting in the hard punishment which the broken road gave his body. One of these sudden, bone-wrenching jolts flung something against his right thigh. It was the china doll, its yellow hair blown back from its face and the blue eyes wide in startled amazement. He picked it up angrily and was about to throw it from the Jeep when the paradoxical thought of damaging it stopped him.

Three miles later he drew up beside another group of children who were swinging on the signal wire. They ran screaming from the screech of his brakes and the hard, set look of his face. But as he beckoned them a girl came back slowly, her hands behind her back and her body swaying self-consciously. She looked at him suspiciously and seemed ready at any second to turn and flee. He held out the doll towards her impatiently and her eyes smiled at him in astonishment. She took it from his hands and opened her mouth, but he drove off without waiting for her thanks.

He did not look back lest he should see far back and between the avenue of beeches, the high, rising column of smoke from the burning house.

Part Two: 1945

1. Jones

In all of that dark, shattered street there was one building only that still held within its four walls the floors, staircases, doors, and ceilings that are the ribs of a house. Bombs had broken its windows and lacerated its façade with long, deep scars like the marks of malicious claws, but for all these it was whole, substantial and inhabitable. As such it seemed almost to be in bad taste, devoid of feeling and tact. It wore its security with the air of a man determined to detract from the gravity of a funeral with meaningless smiles and inward complacency. For the rest of Hamburg was in mourning, and this street, black and inhospitable, lamented the loss of its past vitality with the low keening of the wind through its open walls. In the dark the fragments of the houses stood high and supplicatory in the night sky, their windows hollow and their gables sharp, but behind the faces of them there was nothing but mountains of rubble; the twisted agony of rusting girders, the damp, dripping ugliness of naked bricks. When the moon passed from behind the clouds it was possible to look up at the top windows of the houses and see the thin wafer of the planet, motionless and inscrutable in the sky, as if it had stopped in its course to stare with cold horror at what it saw below. None of the houses had a roof. None of the houses had floors, doors, or ceilings. They had gone with their inhabitants on the night of the catastrophe two years before. Decay had followed destruction with dialectical inevitability, and now it sat securely behind the false fronts of sham granite, the hypocrisy of buildings that pretended to live at night.

But the house on the corner had no need for pretence, its hoydenish vitality flooded from the windows of its first floor in a blaze of light that laid thin parallelograms of shadow across the road. The strident indecency of dance music flowed with it and mocked the sombre sepulchre of the street. The noise of laughter and singing had a fine edge of unsympathy that cut sharply.

There had been no reason for this house in particular to be preserved from the major disaster that stretched across Hamburg like an evil disease, consuming fifty per cent of its buildings and regurgitating an unending spew of broken masonry and brick. The quixotic impartiality of high-level bombing had granted it a fortuitous survival. But it was no accident that it now housed men of a British military unit, whose red, white, and blue sign was screwed firmly to its wide, front door. The soldiers lived on the first floor, while below and above them, sandwiching them between thick, impenetrable slices like black German bread, the civilian flats were quiet and dark.

The music of the dance band swept through the windows and into the night. It was autumn and the leaves of the dying trees drifted over the broken ruins and rustled the sympathy of their mutual grief to the stones of the houses. The pavements shone with the bright jewels of an early frost, marked here and there with wavering footprints. Night was the time when shadows came to life and danced a silent, mournful pavane. Along the main roads that cut ruined Hamburg into neat slices, and were well marked with road signs, the lights were still burning so brightly that from the air they must have looked like long lanes of fire. Along these roads army vehicles rushed joyously with proprietorial abandon, and in the enclaves, the dark, fathomless blocks of endless rubble, the shudder of their passing brought tears of dust falling from the face of the ruins.

High over the city rose the weird note of the air-raid siren, in itself as much a horrible ghost as any of the buildings. There could be no forgetting. But it no longer brought anxious eyes to the dark bowl of the sky, it turned them instead to the pavements, to feet that moved the more quickly and urgently. Yet its curfew was a reminder that there could be no end to grief yet, no early moratorium on memories.

But in this street it could not compete with the noise of the music or the laughing, as if they deliberately rose in volume to shut out the ghastly persistence of its message, and the Germans, moving furtively homewards, stopped outside the house to crane their ears and then hurry onward.

The Provost Jeep moved slowly down the street, its white bumper rising and falling, and it stopped outside the house while the driver turned an eyeless face up to the lighted windows of the first floor, the peak of his cap dropping a deep visor over his nose. His white belt and cross-braces gleamed lividly in the half-darkness, and beside him a Sten-gun rattled sharply as his comrade moved as if to dismount. But with an indifferent curse the man drew his legs back into the vehicle and the Jeep drew away, the sound of its engine rising firmly and confidently.

In the large room on the first floor, where the folding walls had been turned back to make more room for the dancers, Jones turned away from the window through which he had been looking apprehensively at the Military Police below. He stood with his back to the wall, his shoulders pressed against the peeling paper, and a glass of beer slopping over on his fingers as the wild circles of figures brushed against him. It was very hot in the room, the tubular stove in one corner was crowned with a circlet of red-hot metal, and he wished that someone would open the window and let in the fresh air from the street, however impregnated it might be with the fine dust that seemed inseparable from it.

For most of the evening he had stood there like this, drinking the weak beer which little Jock Buchan brought him from the barrel behind the bar, and watching the atmosphere of the room change. In the cold sobriety of early evening it had been strained and stilted, a peculiar, self-conscious embarrassment as the German girls arrived and stood in a group about the table, eating sandwiches quickly and giggling. The soldiers had been over-nonchalant. But now those barriers had worn away and the two groups, Germans and British, had merged into a peculiar, frenzied homogeneity. There were seven German women there, most of them dancing now, and by the bar three Germans stood eating, and talking quickly to Buchan whose face, red and excited, was shining with a high-spirited good feeling. Before him on the white cloth of the table stood a parapet of glasses, some broken and others lying wearily on their sides. Buchan was waving a glass of beer across his body with every word and the amber liquid leaped up its sides in little waves. Even above the noise of the band, the excited babble of voices and the singing, Jones thought he could hear the Scotsman's voice.

'Aye, but ye must admit he didna do right by you ...'

And Jones knew that 'he' was Hitler, the ghost that always seemed to be walking behind Schroeder, as if the interpreter must always be discussing him in order to disclaim any fidelity to his memory. Schroeder was standing against the bar, a tall figure in an immaculately-pressed blue suit, his white shirt gleaming (where does Mrs Schroeder get the soap, Jones thought) and his long head of white hair nodding slowly.

Jones looked at the room again. It was lit by two standard-lamps; one stood by the bar, tilting drunkenly over the barrel, and the other by the band. There the pianist, the violinist, and the accordionist, with sweat beading their foreheads, were rushing furiously through the tango rhythm of 'Die Rote Laterne von St Pauli'.

The tune had a peculiar effect on the Germans present. The women flung back their heads exultantly in nostalgic happiness, their long hair dropping from the crown of their heads and their bodies swaying back from khaki arms. Sitting on top of the piano, his thin legs doubled beneath him, young Ulrich, the architect from upstairs, was shouting the refrain drunkenly, his handsome head lolling on his shoulders and his face set in a peculiar expression of indifferent despair. He waved his glass as he sang:

> 'Unter der roten Laterne von St Pauli
> sang mir der Wind heut' zum Abschied ein Lied,
> Ay-ay, ay-ay, ay-ay!'

St Pauli, smiled Jones a little cynically. Nothing there now to catch the memories of a song. The bombs had flattened its streets, levelled its high buildings, and driven its cafés to dank cellars underground. He wondered if the German women had forgotten that they were dancing with British soldiers, 'the barbarians', and as he looked at Ulrich's face, at the maudlin tears that began to trickle down the pale cheeks, he wondered what the boy was thinking. He wondered too whether it was true that Ulrich had been a conscientious objector, living underground in the St Pauli area for most of the war. It was hard to decide what was true in this country, and he looked across to the large poster which Michaels had pinned to the wall earlier that evening.

It was the usual outline of the puckish, bald-headed man overlooking a wall, his knuckled fingers grasping the bricks over which dropped the solemn length of his heavy nose. Beneath the ironic incredulity of his expression was scrawled '*Wot, no Nazis?*' Jones noticed that since the dance someone had pencilled a black swastika on the nose.

The music stopped, the musicians put down the instruments, their mouths grinning beneath their expressionless eyes, and on top of the piano Ulrich leant back against the wall and held his face in his hands. Jones felt suddenly sorry for Ulrich, for the tortured, incomprehensible confusion of thoughts that must be burning behind those thin cheeks. He smiled again; it was a change to feel sorry for a German.

He felt a push on the shoulder and turned to find Michaels there. Michaels was a little drunk and his face shone with exaggerated good humour. 'Hi-ya, Ted, old Tosh! How's it going, son?'

Jones grinned and supported Michaels with one hand. 'I wish someone would open the bloody window. I'd enjoy Anglo-German friendship a bit better then. Some of the foul air would get out.'

Michaels swayed and stared at Jones a little uncertainly. With a sudden and rare demonstration of affection Jones put his arm about Michaels' shoulders. 'Wot, no Nazis?' said Michaels with a giggle, 'The place is full of 'em. Look at old Schroeder, Ted. He's trying to sell Jock some black market schnapps. I've tried it. You could run a Sherman tank on it.' He leant against Jones and his voice dropped a little. 'Schroeder's a Nazi, Ted, a *Nazi!* They're all Nazis. You watch 'em, Ted old Tosh. You keep Joe out of trouble.'

Jones grinned and put the glass of beer down on the floor behind him. 'There was a Red-cap Jeep outside just now,' he said, 'Lucky they didn't come up and find these Jerries here.'

Michaels swore. 'When they lifted non-frat they ought to've expected us to invite the frauleins in. What do they expect us to do in this perishing town anyway? Look at it!' He waved his arm in a gesture that took in all Germany. 'It's like a cemetery.' He pushed his face close to Jones' ear. 'Do you know how many people were killed in that big raid on Hamburg. Eighty-five thousand, forty-five thousand in one night. That's what I call pin-point bombing. It's been a bloody humane war all right.'

'Who told you that?' asked Jones, 'Irma Grese?'

'That's right,' said Michaels, straightening his body, 'My SS baby over there.'

Jones looked across to the bar where 'Irma Grese' stood, a tall girl, sensuously attractive, with her thin hair pulled up to the crown of her head, and her well-proportioned body swaying unsteadily. She was drunk, but her face was flushed with a deeper excitement that was almost arrogantly challenging. She held two sandwiches in one hand, biting hungrily at each, and a glass of beer in the other. Her body was so voluptuous that Jones found it suddenly repellent; even her face, which carried no cosmetics, flamed with an uncomfortable indecency. She was laughing at Schroeder and her high-pitched giggle rose above the confused noise in the room. He saw Schroeder's fine brows contract in an expression of disgust as he turned his shoulder on her contemptuously. She laughed again and thrust her glass towards Jock behind the bar, but the Scotsman pretended not to notice it. Thus ignored, the hard, brittle arrogance splintered from her face and she looked no more than her childish eighteen years.

'Silly bitch!' said Michaels tolerantly, 'But what a body! She wants me to give her a baby.'

'What did you invite her for?' said Jones angrily. 'We don't want people like her!'

'Now don't get on to me, Ted!' said Michaels sorrowfully. 'At least she's honest, all the rest of them pretend they didn't touch the Nazis with a barge pole. She doesn't mind saying she still is one. She's only a kid, doesn't know a thing. She was arguing the other night, saying that Churchill is a Jew.'

'That's all right, but she expects us to give her medals for honesty.'

'All she wants is a spanking,' said Michaels sorrowfully. 'I'll give her one tonight.'

The band started playing again and Michaels went across to the girl, pulling her away from the bar with both his hands.

Jones lit himself a cigarette and leant against the wall again. It was three months since the Troop had been disbanded, and the men dispersed throughout the British Zone, yet he was still lonely for their company, and lonely too, he realized a little inconsequentially, for the war itself which had ended so peculiarly long ago. The war had been a catalyst that had united them all, the peace had brought a moral and physical disintegration from which, spiritually, he had not yet recovered. Where the others had gone he did not know, but he and Michaels had been posted to this unit in Hamburg, a quasi-military welfare organization where he was a driver, and Michaels, with the strange, unpredictable logic of Army reasoning, had become a clerk. It was an easy life. They were billeted far away from the two officers who lived in the grand isolation of the Atlantic hotel.

He walked across to the bar and asked Buchan for another drink. The Scotsman winked slowly, turned his back, and almost by magic twisted round with a glass of whiskey in his hands. As Jones drank it slowly he became conscious of Schroeder staring at him from the other end of the table. He returned the stare with some truculence, for he did not like the interpreter. Without looking into the man's deep-set quizzical eyes, he studied him closely. Schroeder was about fifty-five, but his hair was brilliantly white, fine, and neatly-parted, sweeping back like a mane. The neatness of his clothes was almost blasphemous, and a great ring gleamed on the little finger of his right hand. As Jones noticed it he thought of Hapgood with a sudden touch of painful humour.

Schroeder stepped closer to Jones and began to nod his head regularly. It was a signal that he was about to speak and he reminded Jones of the little porcelain figure with the sprung head that stood on his mother's mantelpiece at home. There was something compelling in the slow, calculated movement of Schroeder's white head, something that automatically fastened one's attention upon it and the words that came from the thick pink lips. Schroeder was obviously, so obviously continental in appearance and manners that it always came as a shock to Jones to hear the strong American accent adulterating the interpreter's fluent English.

'Well, Mr Jones,' said Schroeder deliberately, 'Are you having a fine time now?' And as Jones shrugged his shoulders non-committally the interpreter went on. 'I always reckon it's good for folks to enjoy themselves. During the Great War we had plenty of dances, but this time that guy Hitler wouldn't let the boys have their dances.'

Hitler, thought Jones, and he wondered if that was true. He noticed how all of Schroeder's carefully-chosen sentences seemed designed to disassociate himself from the ghostly apparition of a comically-terrible figure. For want of a better answer he pulled out his cigarette-case and offered it to Schroeder.

'Now, that's mighty swell of you, Mr Jones. I'll take it home to the wife.'

There was even something artificial in Schroeder's American accent, it was a decade or more out of fashion; as if he had learnt it from an old film and had never brought it up to date. He took the cigarette from Jones' tin and placed it carefully in a cigar case, already full of other cigarettes. He noticed that Jones was looking at the case curiously and he smiled tolerantly, 'Mrs Schroeder will be right glad to get these cigarettes, Mr Jones. She likes, what do you call it, a "fag"?'

Jones nodded apathetically and turned his face to the dancers again. The room was thick with cigarette smoke and the dancers turned and whirled amid it, stamping their feet, their red, laughing faces flung back from their shoulders. Behind them, sitting in the circle of light from the standard lamp, the musicians worked furiously at their instruments, the sweat beading on their foreheads, cigarettes gripped firmly between their lips. At the feet of each of them was a glass of beer, a plate of sandwiches, and a little saucer of jealously-preserved cigarette-ends. They, as much as any of the Germans there, were fanatics in the cult of the cigarette, the new currency of Germany, the humble white cylinder which had been the physical manifestation of the liberation and occupation of Europe.

Jones looked at his watch. It was eleven o'clock. The dance would go on for another two or three hours yet before Michaels and Sergeant Wilson bundled the Germans into the trucks, lacing up the covers so that none in the street would see the illegal load. Then he and Buchan would drive them back to their homes, to the cellars, the air-raid shelters, the old barges on the putrid canals, back to the darkness of reality. He would drive with Michaels in the first truck. He hated those night drives through Hamburg, where the ruined houses ran mile after mile in a desert of brick and dust. Night relieved the Germans of the pretence of living and took the smile from the face of the corpse that was the city itself.

Standing there, feeling almost that he was the only substantial person in the room, that the others were all part of some hideous nightmare, Jones felt suddenly lonely. He could not yet bring himself to participate fully in the abandon of affairs like this. But such was the exhaustion of spirit he felt these days that he accepted their welcome relief from the tedium of duty, the enervating drives to the outskirts of the city where the wide breadth of the autobahn was like a medieval wall separating the houses from the ugly, flat plain, the Germany that was still an unexpected dream to the world beyond.

He knew, indeed it was no secret to anybody there, that there was nothing deeper in these dances than a mutual desire to escape from the ghastly physical impotence about them. Germans and British, driven by the growing and appalling realization of the ruin, lived for things like this, clinging to each other for cheap spiritual and sensual support, clinging to the oblivion of alcohol fumes, to a wild, transient, sexual excitement. And the crumbs from British tables, freely given with both hands, the sandwiches, the crusts, and the cigarette-ends which the band would collect in payment before they left early in the morning, would be rich payment indeed.

Yet everybody was not dancing. Over against the opposite wall; as far away from the band as the tight confines of the room would allow, sat Macleish and his girl. They had hardly danced all that evening, Jones realized, but had sat there holding hands in the fixed, spiritless pose of a conventional portrait, now and then talking to each other, but more often just sitting there and following the dancers with their eyes. They seemed perfectly happy and Jones wondered to notice how young Macleish seemed. Jones liked him. He was an infantryman who had been badly shell-shocked at Overloon and he had a quiet, reserved manner behind which one could sense the tight strain of his nerves, the mind feeding upon itself.

Of the girl Jones knew only a little. She was much older than Macleish and sat beside him more like an elder sister than anything else. She was thin and nondescript, a nurse in a hospital on the far side of the town, a dark gaunt building surfeit with patients but starved of supplies. She was, inevitably, the wife of a German officer killed long ago at Dieppe. She wore her husband's polished jackboots even here in the dance-room, and an old fur coat was flung across her narrow shoulders. She watched the room with a fixed smile, a tolerant forward inclination of her head, but the smile was as if she had long ago forgotten it was there. All sincerity had gone from it and left it strangely ludicrous. Memory seemed to have deserted her in the untouched glass of gin held listlessly between her fingers, the cigarette-holder with a cigarette burning away into a bent finger of grey ash.

He knew a little about her, that she had been the first of the German nurses who volunteered to go to Belsen and tend the sick. He had often wondered why she had gone. He remembered that Macleish had told him that he had met her there, and Macleish had been abrupt and queerly defensive as if he had expected Jones to attack his association with the woman.

Apart from the little group laughing and singing about the bar there was only one other woman not dancing. She sat at the other end of the sofa to Macleish and his partner, and Jones remembered that she seemed to have been sitting there all evening. He looked at her and wondered who could have brought her, since all seemed to be ignoring her. Then he remembered that somebody, it had been Michaels, had mentioned her name earlier in the evening. 'That's Kaethe Lenz,' and Michaels had spelt out the Christian name carefully, 'Friend of Schroeder's. This used to be her flat, you know. Don't mind her, she comes for the food and liquor. Her husband was a Wehrmacht colonel and she hasn't forgotten it, the cow!' Jones had intuitively realized that Michaels' amorous experiments with the woman had not progressed beyond that information.

The remembrance made him look for Michaels in the crowd. He was there by the band, very drunk by now, leaning happily over the generous body of 'Irma Grese' and whispering in her ear. The girl's face was flushed with excitement, her mouth open and her fine white teeth gleaming in the light. Michaels was pressing her close to him and swinging her body, for all his intoxication, very gracefully across the floor. A little sadly Jones wondered why Michaels was always drunk now, why everything was changing so irremediably.

He looked back to the figure of Kaethe Lenz and was struck by her calm aloofness which, as he studied her, seemed a particularly transparent defence.

Even sitting down she seemed tall, her long legs crossed and the high heel of one shoe pointing sharply at the floor. Her hair was fair, but it was heavily peroxided and fell in a large roll to her shoulders that caricatured the more or less obvious gentility of the rest of her features. Looking at her unusual face Jones was surprised by such an obvious attempt to grasp at the ephemeral attraction of a younger girl. Her face was round, with a plumpness below the eyes that did not seem healthy, but her blue eyes were wide-spaced and her nose straight. Her lips were well-cut and parted slightly, as if in constant anticipation of the cigarette she rarely raised to them.

As he watched her she ground out the cigarette beneath her heel with a trace of anger, picked up her bag and handkerchief and then looked at them in surprise and put them down again beside her. There was a nervous urgency in all of her pointless movements. She uncrossed her legs and leant forward, with her elbows resting on her knees and her fists thrust beneath her chin. A slight, impatient frown drew her brows together. There was a queer deliberateness in the pose that puzzled Jones, until he realized that she too was a little drunk and trying hard to disguise it, even from herself.

On a sudden impulse he turned to the bar, picked up two sandwiches, put them on a plate, and carried them across to her. As he did so, remembering Michaels's sarcastic reference to the woman, he was conscious that the action was more of an insult than anything else. He stood before her defensively and thrust the plate rudely in front of her face. She pushed her head back sharply, startled, and then smiled her thanks. Without a word she took the sandwiches and began to eat them, and as he sat down beside her he wondered if she could speak English. He was surprised when she turned her head slightly, not looking at him, but speaking obliquely. 'You do not dance?'

'Yes,' he said, 'But I don't feel like it tonight.'

'You don't like to dance with German girls?'

He did not answer her. 'You speak English well.'

'I learnt it before the barbarians came.' He felt the mockery instantly. 'It was as well to learn their language.'

He sat beside her staring curiously at her profile, while, on the floor before them, the dancers quickened the maddening movements. The inchoate thoughts of his mind were caught by the ceaseless beat of the music and were dissipated before he could grasp their direction. High on the piano Ulrich was leaning back against the wall, his long hair forming a halo for his head and his eyes closed. His face looked pale. As Michaels danced past the sofa, with 'Irma Grese' hanging on his arm lazily, he glanced at Jones and then at the woman beside him. 'Get stuck in, Ted, old son!' he said encouragingly, and whirled the girl away. Her screams of excited protest struck Jones sharply. He frowned and was surprised to see that Kaethe Lenz was staring at Michaels and frowning too.

'Don't you dance?' he said tentatively. She shrugged her shoulders and did not answer him, and then turned, smilingly, as if conversation was something she could control like a tap. Her hand, he noticed how slender and finely-jointed were the fingers, waved towards the stove in the corner. 'We have no coal like you,' she said simply, and although he was nettled by the obvious implication of the words he did not answer. She half-turned her head towards him, the smile still twisting her lips, but as she spoke he got the impression that she was afraid to look him in the eyes. Instead she ran her glance quickly over the dancers, her intelligent eyes moving quickly from one object to another. She spoke casually, with a defensive, mocking tone.

'In England you have open fires, yes?' He nodded. 'That is not very civilized, we think,' she said.

Anger and resentment burnt suddenly at the back of his head. 'In England we don't think it's very civilized to have gas chambers and concentration camps!' he said hoarsely.

But she did not move, the smile became a little fixed on her lips and died from her eyes. Her head nodded slightly. He could have guessed what she was going to say and he was surprised that anything so trite should be said by her.

'We did not know of those things.' It was the forbidden subject, the nightmare, the German schizophrenia to be forgotten.

'Funny,' he said sarcastically, 'None of you did!' and he got up and walked away. Looking back at her from the bar he noticed that she had not changed her position, she was still staring at the dancers, the same peculiar defensive smile on her face. She stood in strange contrast to the brazen excitement of the other women, the wraith-like depersonalized character of Macleish's girl. He felt half-sorry for what he had said, but he realized angrily that he had meant the thrust.

He felt Schroeder at his elbow and turned to see the white head nodding wisely. With his increasing drunkenness the interpreter became more sententious. 'A very nice dame that, Mr Jones,' he said, and somehow Jones immediately thought of him as a pimp, and was disgusted by the picture. 'Frau Lenz's husband was a very important Nazi, of course, but she is a very nice girl, a protejee of mine.' In sudden alarm Jones thought that Schroeder might be procuring, but the thought died quickly as he looked back at the inscrutable face of the woman on the couch.

Schroeder hiccupped gently, but seemed unaware of it, for he went on with a gravity that seemed unusually ridiculous. 'Mr Jones will you be going back to the old country soon?'

For a moment Jones did not understand him. 'Oh, you mean demob? Not for a while yet, I suppose. Got to stay here and keep the Germans down, you know.'

'Now that's mighty smart of you,' said Schroeder owlishly, and his head began to nod, 'But I guess you know, and I know that the British are only here to fight the Russians when they come, eh?' His shoulders shook with silent laughter that was not betrayed in his serious face. 'But I've got a proposition that might interest you, Mr Jones.'

'I don't want to buy any schnapps, if that's what you mean,' said Jones tersely, 'Your stuff makes 'em blind.'

'You're wrong there, Mr Jones, it's pretty good liquor. I'll let you have a bottle some time. But that's not my business with you. The proposition is this: Before the war when that guy Hitler upset things ...' *Again*, thought Jones impatiently. '... I represented a few overseas merchants here in Hamburg. When business relations between Germany and the outside world get settled I guess I'd like to pick up the loose ends, d'you see?'

'Yes?' said Jones in disinterest. He was staring at Kaethe Lenz again, to where she sat on the sofa, and he did not know whether it was the thick air of the room, the fumes of the alcohol he had drunk, or whether it was some more genuine passion that fired his emotions as he stared at her. He heard Schroeder's voice droning on with its musical-comedy American drawl.

'I'd like you to take a letter back to England, so if some time anybody asks you whether you know anybody over this side who would represent them, in a commercial way, you see, you can tell them about me.' Jones smiled inwardly at the impossibility of him ever receiving such a request; and the dank, grey streets of Stockwell, the matter-of-fact office of Howard Forbes, Estate Agent, appeared before his eyes in startling clarity. He felt Schroeder's fingers tapping imperatively on his arm.

'OK Schroeder,' he said impatiently, 'Perhaps I will.' And he walked back to Frau Lenz. 'I'm sorry,' he said, half against his will, 'That was bad-mannered of me.'

She did not look up at him, but inclined her head sideways and smiled, as if she were only half-interested in the apology, but nevertheless had expected it. He wondered why she never looked him in the face.

'It does not matter,' she said, 'Perhaps you were right. We Germans are children now.' It was not so much the unimpassioned defeatism of the sentence that disturbed Jones, but the feeling that it was not sincere. 'Will you dance with me?' he asked.

They danced. He was not surprised to discover that she could dance beautifully. Her body was light in his arms and he realized, oddly, that it was months since he had held a woman thus. The wild longing with which it filled him was disturbing and he could feel his eyes burning. The tension of months, the heavy, dragging pain of the days in Holland returned unsteadily. In response to their urgent appeal he wanted to hold this woman tight in his arms and to cry on her shoulder. If she sensed any of these feelings, in the nervous tightening of his arms, or the flushed colour of his face, she did not show it. She did not look him in the face, and again he wondered at the way she kept her head turned to stare at the other dancers, at the band, anywhere but at him. He could not understand it at first, and then he began to realize the probable reason. Close to his her face showed its age, the thickening of the skin, the heavy pull on the cheek-bones beneath the mask of powder, and he was struck by the strange pathos of her attempts to keep this from him. He was sure of this conclusion when, with a gentle but determined persuasion, she guided him away from the brightness of the standard lamps.

He was not surprised to realize that he felt sorry for her. It was a simple emotion after all, and the effect of the colossal destruction about them in Germany drove the mind and feelings to the simple, the commonplace emotions, seeking refuge in their simplicity.

Yet as he danced the old nostalgias came back. This was the first dance since Mary's death, and he thought of *her* now and tried to recapture the memory of her presence, the touch of her body close to his as they had danced. But her face was indistinct, the years lay between and a great darkness. Inside his thoughts he called to her and heard her answer, but their hands could not touch. He realized that Mary, like everything they had shared in those days, had become 'pre-war'.

'You are very quiet.' Frau Lenz had turned her head so that she was looking over his shoulder and her hair was brushing against his face. Her voice was low.

'It's hard to be happy all the time,' he said dully.

'You should get drunk,' she said with a peculiar hardness in her voice, 'It is much easier when you are drunk. All Germany would get drunk if they could, to forget what has happened to them.'

His thoughts drove his words before them brutally. 'It isn't you who's got to forget,' he said, 'It's us, the rest of the world. You've done things it's hard to forget.'

'It is true,' she said again, without feeling, 'Germany is hated everywhere. There is nothing and nobody for us now.'

'Bit too late to worry about that now, isn't it?' he said, and he stepped away from her as the music stopped. She did not look at him, but turned her face away from the light, smiling that slight, artificial smile, and he felt that she was ashamed for having danced with him. They sat on the sofa again as the band, refreshed by the beer at its feet, began to play 'Lili Marlene'. Immediately everybody in the room, German and British, picked up the refrain and sang with a peculiar gentleness, and when the music stopped there was an odd, embarrassed silence. Over by the bar Jones saw Schroeder's white mane of hair nodding tendentiously at Michaels and the blonde girl clinging to his arm.

'Your husband was a soldier?' asked Jones.

'He was a German officer,' she said, slowly, 'I am not ashamed. He was a brave man.'

'Schroeder says he was a big Nazi.'

'He is bad that man,' said Kaethe Lenz with a sudden twist of her head that made her hair fall across her shoulders, 'My husband was a doctor, not a politician. But he was proud to serve in the German Army, just like Frau Weber's husband.' And Jones realized she was referring to Macleish's friend. 'Of course he was a Nazi, I am not ashamed to say it. I do not know whether it was right. I cannot tell nowadays. He was much older than I am, and we did not understand each other too well, but he was brave, my husband.' She turned to him suddenly and he caught a rare glimpse of her face, the wide eyes and firm mouth. 'You hate me because of that.'

Jones laughed, and she turned her face away from him without expression. Then she said 'You are married?'

'My wife was killed by a flying-bomb.'

She nodded slowly. 'It is cruel. In the shelters here during the raids it was horrible. Your airmen came over so often that it seemed the sky was never empty. On the night of the Catastrophe the people ran into the Alster and were drowned, they were so frightened. We did not know what to do. It was frightful. Air-raids are inhuman.'

'A German flying-bomb,' persisted Jones bluntly.

'You hate me for that?' She turned and faced him, holding his eyes with her own for the length of the sentence only.

'I don't know,' he said. 'Perhaps it is too soon, for all this.' And he waved his arm about the room.

'You hate me,' she said, and her voice rose a little, 'You hate all the Germans. We were made for hatred. To be hated and feared, but never loved.'

'Well, *we* won't put you in a concentration camp for my wife.' He was staring at her angrily, his fingers trembling on his knees.

She smiled back at him tolerantly, and he felt then that she was much older than he. 'All Germany is a concentration camp now,' she said.

He lit a cigarette to stop the trembling of his hands. 'You Germans never understand. Why should I feel sorry for you?'

She turned on him angrily, her cheeks flushed. 'You think I am asking for your sympathy? You forget I am the wife of a German officer!'

'And you forget I'm a British soldier!'

They were silent for a long time, and the silence between them lay heavily on their thoughts. When she spoke it was so softly that at first he hardly heard her voice. 'It is true. That is true too. Some of us want your sympathy. Your Churchill said that we Germans would be either at your throat or your feet. It is true for some of us. But I don't want your sympathy. I want my Germany, not the Nazis, not the politicians you give us, but my Germany.'

'Why do you come here, then?'

'Your friend Corporal Michaels has perhaps told you? To eat your food and drink, perhaps to make a British soldier fall in love with me and to hurt him. Yes, that will be my little revenge for what has been done to Germany.'

He laughed again. 'You're a little drunk,' he said, 'You shouldn't tell me these things, let me guess.' But by her frown he knew that she had not understood him. They drifted apart.

He stayed by the bar after that, talking to Jock Buchan whose Glasgow brogue, under the influence of his secret store of whiskey, had become even more incomprehensible. Jones cold-shouldered Schroeder, whose efforts to importune him were becoming increasingly more irritating. At two o'clock Sergeant Wilson, a bandy-legged Londoner with steel-rimmed spectacles, told the band to finish. The three men nodded vigorously and after a hurried consultation between themselves they began to play 'God save the King'. The dancers and the drinkers stood to their feet self-consciously. Beside him, as he stood resentful and strangely irritable, Jones was conscious of Schroeder's figure, rigid and austere, the mane of white hair flung back and the arms stiff at the sides of the well-made suit.

The British soldiers, who had not expected this sudden honour, stared at the band cautiously, as if suspecting some subtle ridicule. Against the wall Michaels was grinning feebly at the ceiling and Jones wondered whether he would have to put the Corporal to bed again tonight. Macleish stood by the sofa and his girl was leaning affectionately on his arm, still smiling insipidly. Jones noticed the infantryman's fingers twitching nervously at his cuffs, the artery in his neck pulsing furiously. It must have been hell at Overloon, Jones thought, and he remembered, as if it were something from a particularly horrible nightmare, the little Dutch town itself, as the Troop rolled into it one night and bivouacked in the churchyard.

Suddenly, from the wall where Michaels was standing, 'Irma Grese' broke away from his hand and flung her body sensuously to the centre of the floor. Once there she seemed embarrassed, with sudden fear in her eyes. Then she thrust her hand into the air in an arrogant salute and shouted high above the music 'Sieg Heil! *Heil Hitler!*' Even when her voice had stopped her mouth remained open, her body thrust out from her hips. Michaels stared at her incongruously, his mouth open too.

The band stopped playing, and in the uncomfortable silence the girl's body wilted, the rigidity left it and her face stared at the rest of the room in sudden alarm.

From the darkness of the corner Jones saw Kaethe Lenz step out towards the drunken girl. He heard the sharp report of her hand striking the girl's cheek, and then 'Irma Grese', weeping bitterly, dropped to the floor and buried her face in her lap. Her body shook with sobbing screams. Michaels came towards her and stood looking down at her with a mixture of incredulity and disgust in his face.

'She's a silly sonofabitch!' said Schroeder to Jones with conversational brightness, his head nodding quickly, 'I'm mighty glad Frau Lenz did that.' And Jones wondered why he did not agree with the interpreter.

He drove one of the trucks that took the Germans home. Michaels sat in the other seat, while Frau Lenz was perched on the battery-box between them. He remembered how Hapgood had sat thus, long ago in Holland, with the seven-pound hammer between his knees, and his heels beating a rhythmical tattoo on the floor of the cab. But there was a great difference between the dispatch rider's rugged form and this peculiar creature who sat there now. He thought of

Hapgood and again there was the old nostalgia, the longing to hear the high Tyneside voice, to see the dirty muzzle of Dempsey poking from Hapgood's blouse. He thought of Nelly van Huyk and wondered what the child would think. Things had changed so.

The road was frosted, and the marks of vehicles had traced fantastic lines down its length. Above them, fixed to the opaque sky it seemed, the blue lamps glowed frostily above the centre of the road. The truck skidded frequently on the tramlines. With every jerking bump Michaels groaned painfully, but although Jones felt the woman sway against him and steady herself with her hand on his shoulder, she said nothing. Michaels began to sing defiantly.

> 'Orders came for sailing, somewhere over there
> All confined to barracks was more than I could bear.
> I knew you were waiting in the street,
> I heard your feet, but could not meet
> My lily of the lamp-light, my own Lili Marlene.'

'Shut up Joe!' said Jones tensely, 'We don't want a Red-cap on us with this load.'

'Bless 'em all!' said Michaels and his voice drifted lazily into sleep.

Jones was aware of the girl holding his arm again. At her request he turned off the main road and bumped down a strange street where the jungle of half-ruined houses rose up about him and clutched frantically at the black sky. Now the grip of the girl's hand tightened. 'If you will stop here,' she said, 'I will get out.'

Behind them in the back of the truck there was a giggling, a screaming, and a catcalling that Jones inwardly cursed. He pulled up the car and Michaels fell forward against the wind-screen, swore gently, and slipped to the floor. They heard him muttering to himself, 'Who cares? Who cares? It's been a lousy war!' Jones was ashamed that Michaels should behave so before the German, but she did not seem to have noticed it.

He got out and helped her down to the frosty pavement. Beneath their shoes the frozen leaves cracked and splintered with a noise that sounded uncannily loud. They stood there silently, and he was hardly conscious that he was still holding her hand. He could see the outline of her head, the thin scarf she had tied under her chin which was raised almost challengingly. He wondered if she expected him to kiss her, whether he wanted to. Her hand lay listlessly in his until suddenly it pressed his fingers gently and heard her say:

'If you care . . . come to tea with me on Sunday, my brother will be with me. It is a small room. Come to tea.' He heard a laugh strangely forced. 'We have food. Did I tell you, I am very important in the Black Market, as important as Herr Schroeder? My brother does not like me to go with the English soldiers. But I would like you to meet him. You will come?'

'I'll come,' he said, 'Thank you.' He wondered why she did not ask his name.

'Then you will get your little revenge for Belsen, and eat my food.' The voice came clearly and deliberately from the obscure outlines of her face but did not seem to be part of her.

'Oh, hell!' said Jones dispiritedly.

'Wha's goin' on here?' said Michaels as he suddenly leant across the wheel towards them. The light of his torch, held unsteadily in his hand, flooded over the woman's face so that it stood out like a mask from which the eyes shone black and hard. She said something sharply in German, swung her head away quickly and threw up her hands before her face. Jones turned and angrily knocked the torch from Michaels' hands, and as he did so he heard her feet tapping on the pavement as she ran into the dark, ragged outline of the house. A door banged. In the back of the truck a babble of voices, English and German, arose in confused complaint.

'Wot, no Nazis?' queried Michaels happily from the dark cab.

'No, no Nazis, Joe,' said Jones deliberately, 'Get off that gear lever you drunken cow!'

2. Jones

During the week that followed Jones wondered at the invitation. It had been unexpected, there had been little between them, little intimacy, little sympathy. A conversation during which each had fenced bitterly with the other's thoughts, a waltz where each had partnered the ghost of old memories. Jones realized that the woman had hardly touched his consciousness, and he reflected bitterly that perhaps Michaels had been right. It was better to speak to the honest Nazi, the unashamed, the arrogant and incorrigible who left no doubts in one's mind and did not cloud the air with bitterness, an underlying fog of opportunism. It would be easier, he thought, to take things as they came, to reject this sensitive, searching inquisition. Of what use was a persistent demand for explanations and understanding? How much easier had it been when the Germans were only a depersonalized mass, separated from him by the Maas, eighty million people without features or characters, just 'the enemy'.

It had been easier to hate them then.

Even after the entry into Germany it had been easy. The Germans had been self-effacing and obsequious, anxious to disclaim any allegiance to the Nazis, anxious even to disown their German blood. The obvious terror which drove them to call themselves Dutch, or even Poles, was something that sickened Jones even as it surprised him. The war was still on then, driving flame-edged and inexorable. It had been easier to think of the enemy; but peace had brought subtle legions that had never been employed in war, and they were now winning silent victories, though for which side he could not yet decide.

Living among them it was impossible to forget the Germans,

and the destruction and suffering in Germany was far greater than Jones had ever seen or believed possible. It could not be shrugged from his shoulders however much he tried.

In the streets, in the cafés, and in the newspapers the story was growing. Two million Germans would die that winter from starvation. It was impossible to think of numbers like that, but Jones was compelled by some inner force to watch the Germans about him, wondering who would see the spring alive. Would one of them be the old tailor who came to sew and patch the British uniforms, an old man with his grey hair parted in the middle, a bushy Bismarck moustache bisecting his features? Would it be young Karlheinz, the waiter in the mess, with his bright eyes and terrible, simple ignorance? Or perhaps his mother who sat fat and happy in her empty café, rocking to the music played on an accordion by a drunken girl:

> 'Deine Liebe, meine Liebe
> Die sind bei mir gleich.
> Jeder Mann hat nur ein Herz ...'

Man has one heart only. It hardly seemed enough.

The guns had stopped and the silence was frightening for it held the echo of a greater explosion far away to the east, across continents and seas, where two cities, their names strange and unfamiliar, had been obliterated and their populations massacred. Although at first there had been only relief brought by the end of the war, now had come a gnawing doubt, a fear, and a strange unquenchable unrest.

The guns had stopped and in their place had come the clamour of voices, incoherent, raceless, a babel of confusion obscuring the clear cut, uncompromising outlines of the war. The mind fled back before them, back to the old days, to Normandy and the Maas, to familiar, almost comforting horrors; the smell at Falaise, the desolation at Villers Bocage. The Dakotas, those beautiful Dakotas high in the spring sun above the Rhine. They were the realities, the days when the mind was free.

And the Election, standing in a muddy field to mark a piece of paper, while at the gate a ragged, rain-washed group of German civilians watched curiously. He remembered how he and the others had raised their voices, spun an extra swagger into their walk that day, just to impress that stoical, featureless group of Germans. They paraded their democracy and freedom with intent to hurt. He had got drunk when the election results were announced, and in the tent, that night, while the rain dripped steady approval on the taut canvas, they had talked of the new happiness to come, the future of promise, even those who had been disappointed by the election result. It had seemed that at last something had happened, as if the suffering and hardships of the war had been carefully annotated, the final punctuation made, and now the record was to be set before history and action taken for the betterment of mankind.

Looking back upon them the emotions of that night seemed almost sad now.

Yet Jones saw some things clearly enough. He was one of the men still young, the young and healthy men of Europe who would not starve that winter, nor be cold and homeless. There would be more watches and rings and cameras for them, more fur coats and willing women, and the numbers of them available would be an index of suffering.

He was puzzled that for all the hours of daylight he had spent in the country he could think only of its night-darkness; of all the laughter and jokes he had shared he could feel only the sadness, the maudlin sentimentality of old songs. He wondered why it was that he remembered, of all things in the sepulchre of Dusseldorf, only the pool of mellow light that flooded from the doors of the Opera House, staining the wet pavements as he stood there, his mind still intoxicated by rich music. Or the wind and the rain whipping at his hair and coattails as he stood queuing for an ENSA show. Or the thick, smoky atmosphere of canteens housed in old German beer cellars. And about all these memories the mountains of rubble, the jagged stalagmites of shattered buildings over which the weeds climbed in a thick and tenacious jungle.

In May, Jones had wanted nothing but to sit down and savour his relief at the war's end. Yet it was not really over, for there around him, and even inside him at times, was the turmoil of Germany in defeat. There was something in the omnipresence of social and physical ruin that absorbed him and strove to readjust his thoughts. It was not surprising that when he returned to England on his last leave he had felt lonely and lost. He remembered the days on the shore at Hove, when he had walked to the water's edge with little Mary and sat there watching her as she paddled in the water, lifting her small pink legs from the inhospitality of the shingle and laughing back at him over the noise of the sea. He had felt frightened, ostracized by the peculiar bustle of England, the forward thrust it seemed to have made away from the atmosphere of the war years, and he had felt that he was an anachronism. Unjustly he hated England during those days, and he returned to Germany with a peculiar relief.

A few days before the Troop was finally disintegrated he and Michaels took one last drive together to collect rations. In Osnabrock the rain was slanting down like fine wires from the grey ceiling of the sky, made fast to the wet tarmac of the roads and cutting the smoke of the tar-boiler where Polish soldiers were energetically re-surfacing the roads. 'Jerry weather!' Michaels had nicknamed the perversity of the rain.

Riding through it, in a cold and dripping cab, they had watched the German Army on its homeward march, watched it dispassionately, hardly remembering the arrogant might that had marched towards them on countless cinema screens before the war.

Jones could not remember the faces of those German soldiers they saw in twos and threes along the roadside. It was as if they all had but one face between them as they stood motionless beneath the trees and let the truck pass. Their features differed, young and old, fat and thin, brutal and strangely sensitive, but a face is not a matter of flesh and bone structure alone, it is the canvas on which a man paints his thoughts and emotions. And because of that it seemed to Jones that all these men had but one face between them, and that drawn to a sharp, hungry apex by the jutting peaks of their Wehrmacht caps, their dusty grey skins immobile in its shadow. Occasionally they grinned at the truck, but to Jones the grin did not alter the face or the empty eyes.

And in the towns, in Ahaus, Bocholt, Rheine, Osnabruck, the living were awaiting the dead. Little knots of women and children, in brightly-coloured pinafores and with ash-blonde hair, were waiting in the summer rain to greet the Wehrmacht back from the wars, the conquerors of the world. They stood by the sodden rubble of their homes to clutch at a grey sleeve and ask quick questions.

'I'll bet this shakes them!' said Michaels as he watched the women waving to the trucks that crawled past, filled with green ghosts in decaying uniforms. But although Jones could appreciate the dramatic irony of the scene, he could not jeer.

Now it seemed that all things had passed beyond a controversial point, beyond the time for jeering, to a moment of grave and bitter urgency, just as the Germans themselves had changed from a depersonalized mass, from being 'the enemy' to human beings, characters, personal and intimate things about whom one could not generalize. And closer to Jones, nearer to the realities he kept locked within himself, had stepped one of them uninvited, Kaethe Lenz. He felt afraid of her because she was forcing him into a position where he would be unable to compromise with his conscience ...

As he walked across the city to her home that Sunday afternoon he was conscious of this fear. He felt that he was deliberately doing something that challenged all of his past convictions, betrayed his hatreds and his longings. It *had* been easy to generalize so long as the war and the newspapers kept one from the Germans, but having once met them, having made those first, cautious overtures that followed the end of the war, there was no going back to the old ideas, the old platitudes, the old, comfortable pictures in black and white.

By the Alster, the artificial lake with its ugly fringe of broken trees and houses that dipped into desultory ruins, he stopped to lean on the terrace and stare at the water. It was dirty and scum-laden, and moving uneasily as if conscious of the ghastly human and material debris that littered its bed. The city lay about it in a festering scar, rearing gaunt monoliths of broken stone, strange totems of destruction. But here and there, where the autumn sun caught the lip of a ripple, the surface of the lake gleamed with deceptive brightness.

Jones smoked restlessly, half-inclined to go back to the billet to the warm fire, the derelict, requisitioned furniture, the comforting small-talk of the rest of the men. He had never wished to know the Germans. Since Mary's death he had never tried to picture them beyond a monochromed outline which he hated and on which he wanted an obscure revenge. He had never considered how they might feel about him, or what his ill-fitting uniform represented. As he thought of it now he realized that he had always pictured them as a fierce, exulting, uncompromising mass, rejoicing in his personal sorrow.

It had been surprising to find them with their hatreds, their bitternesses, even their desires for revenge too, a nation looking inward and never beyond the limits of their personal suffering. He knew, before Kaethe Lenz had mentioned it, that he was one of 'the barbarians', and without any attempt to justify the accusation he was surprised by the obvious fact that reactions could be so mutual. A great wall of bitterness was being built between Germany and the outside world, each side methodically placing its bricks and building higher and higher until the whole edifice threatened to topple over and engulf them both. But it was not easy to feel sympathy.

He looked down into the black water, tracing in its whorls and hidden currents the deep and hidden bitterness of the brooding city, and he knew that for a while he dared not look up, or turn his face about and see the enormity of the destruction about him, and that destruction which he could not see with his eyes but which lay far away in Nagasaki and Hiroshima. He realized that most of the British Army were feeling this peculiar unrest. In the earlier days the destruction they saw had been peculiarly inspiring, it brought to them evidence of their own strength and power, and unconsciously they taunted the Germans with it. While the war lasted the more they saw of Germany in ruin the more they had exulted in their own invincibility. Now, as the dust settled, the passions cooled, there was left only an unanswerable doubt. At home he knew, he had heard it too often on his leave in the bars and unshattered houses, voices were saying that it was wrong to be 'soft' with the Germans, and he hated the half-truth of the assertion.

He had lived with hatred for so long that he was bewildered to find himself hated just as fiercely. It shook his self-respect. In an effort to defend himself against the injustice of it he had turned to the Germans almost unwillingly to find the reasons for it, and what he saw stunned him. He wanted to explain, to tell the Germans of the enormity of their crimes, but while they were resilient they were unconvinced, and he had realized that it was because they did not think he was himself immune from the accusations he made. He wanted to exonerate himself, to proclaim his inviolability and his innocence, and his mind was brought up with an unpleasant jerk when he realized that he was doing precisely the same as every German.

Roughly he shook the thoughts from his mind and walked quickly towards the Church Army Canteen where it overlooked the inner harbour of the Binnenalster. About its swinging doors grouped a score or more young children, stridently begging for bread or cigarettes. Their white faces stared up at him challengingly from the scarves that muffled their heads. Their bodies were hunched on the pavements like shapeless bundles of rags.

He sat in one of the upholstered seats by the window, drinking his tea apathetically from the chipped mug. The canteen, one of Hamburg's better restaurants, was warm and cosy, full of a busy hum of pleasant conversation, and the khaki uniforms flamed with the colours of divisional signs and medal ribbons. He watched the crowds below as they moved along the streets, as aimlessly as drifting leaves. The wind was becoming colder and to the north across the grey, metallic sheet of water, dark clouds moved up and obscured the face of the sun. The sight depressed him, for, dressed in sunlight, Hamburg could still smile a little through its scars, but once the sun died the lacerations, the miles of deserted, ruined streets became distorted by a dreadful and enervating ugliness. As Jones sat there, toying with an unlit cigarette, he was almost ready to go back to the billet, to find Michaels if he was not with 'Irma Grese', even to get drunk for once. But contempt for his own cowardice would not let him change his mind. At the door of the canteen he pushed a handful of cakes into the clutching hands of the children. A policeman in a green shako smiled at him and saluted.

He took a tram-car across the city, standing on the platform carelessly, while about him the press of the crowded civilians seemed to draw away from him. The peculiarity of living amid an atmosphere of despair and latent hatred was something he could not easily accept. And then, wryly, he realized that the Germans in the tram were staring at him less for his nationality than for the unlit cigarette between his fingers. The realization made him start and the cigarette dropped between his feet. He did not pick it up and it remained there rolling a little with the movement of the vehicle, until a soldier in a grey Wehrmacht overcoat bent down and picked it up carefully. He returned it to Jones with a click of his heels and a slight forward drop of his head, but, as Jones shook his head angrily, the German soldier carefully put the cigarette in his own pocket.

The tram moved cautiously through the Gänsemarkt, where the drab Waterloo cinema flamed with highly-coloured posters advertising *Rembrandt*, and Jones looked up at them to remember how he had seen the film with Mary, years before, and the same posters had shone with the reflection of the neon lighting outside the cinema in Clapham. Now they glowered over the Germans who stood in apathetic queues outside this cinema.

He stood there, swaying with the roll of the car, hardly conscious now of the Germans until, impatiently, he dropped from its running-board, deciding that it would be better to walk, to liberate himself from the cold and curious stare of the soldier to whom he had given the cigarette. He was surprised to find that he was almost near the road in which Kaethe Lenz lived.

It had once been a fine residential district, rows of high, grey buildings whose façades were ornamented with the twisted faces of mythical creatures and the heavy fronds of impossible, exotic plants frozen into stone. The roads were lined with trees, most of them now only stumps, showing raw and yellow wounds to the grey autumn sky. The earth about them was scattered with chips of wood which the gleaners who came nightly from the cold cellars had yet to garner.

The battered appearance of the street was heightened by an immense conical air-raid shelter that rose eighty feet into the air and towered over the houses, its brick-work chipped, and its sombre, windowless bulk squatting like a sullen animal.

The street was deserted as he walked along it, and he was startled by the sharp fall of his boots on the pavement. Those houses which were still inhabitable were closed and silent behind their patched windows. The ugly tin stove-pipes that were thrust through the walls exhaled a thin whorl of yellow smoke. He shivered suddenly.

As he put his hand on the fragment of the iron gate that led to her house he knew that he would have been happier had he gone back to the billet, but he went in nevertheless.

3. Kaethe

She was afraid that he would not come, and yet paradoxically alarmed because he might. She remembered the sceptical grin on Frau Meyer's hard features when Kaethe told her of the expected visitor. It had been necessary to tell her because the only entrance to Kaethe's room lay through Frau Meyer's. The woman had said nothing, but she had looked indignant and scornful, and yet proud of her own complacent virtue. But later in the morning she had knocked at the door to ask if Frau Lenz did happen to acquire some English cigarettes, or perhaps even a loaf of white bread, then Herr Meyer would be only too pleased to give her more than the rate that was being paid along the kerbstones of St Pauli. When Kaethe slammed the door without answering she heard Frau Meyer's laugh triumphant and humourless, echoing in the next room. No matter what was said to her Frau Meyer was always able to win a cheap victory by the strident derision of that unhealthy laugh.

Bitterly Kaethe felt that the end of the war had been worse than the bombing. It had brutalized and degenerated everybody. During the war she had spent many evenings in the shelter with Frau Meyer, while Herr Meyer was away with the Volksturm, and they had been a great comfort to each other. But now there was only suspicion and latent hatred between them. Frau Meyer despised her because she accepted invitations from the British, claiming, what was indeed half-true, that Kaethe went only for the food and the drink. But at night Herr Meyer went down to the darkness by the Dammtor station, obsequiously accosting British soldiers and offering them money for chocolates and cigarettes, not for himself, but for Schroeder who paid him a meagre wage for the dangerous work.

She no longer cared what Frau Meyer or anybody thought of her. She wondered whether she cared for the opinions of the British soldier, whether she really wanted him to come. Nowadays she had no clear idea of her motives or desires and was afraid to inquire too deeply into the darkness beyond her superficial thoughts and actions. In her most bitter moments of introspection she likened herself to the women who lurked in the shadows of the ruined houses, hiding their faces from the glare of passing headlamps. Women whose husbands disappeared long ago in the war or who have never returned from the prisoner-of-war camps. Women whose bodies and souls were so hungry that they ached only for the sound of a male voice, the touch of male hands, whose anguish had numbed them past feeling and released only greed and a cynical expediency.

She remembered the jeers of the Wehrmacht men when they came home, back to a nation of women without men. She thrust the ugly thoughts quickly from her mind.

She sat alone in her little room awaiting him, and she reflected that she was lucky to have that room to herself when many Germans in the city were living two families in a room of this size. But she knew that perhaps Schroeder had managed it for her with that clever subtlety and smartness that never failed him, even with people who detested him. She thought of Schroeder's own apartment in Fuhlsbuttel, five rooms all to himself, his wife, and his son. It had been very clever of Schroeder to keep out of the Party, it was standing him in such good stead now.

The room was cold. Winter came so quickly to Hamburg, and although a few seared leaves were still clinging to the branches outside the window and beating a brittle tocsin on the panes, there was a sharp breath of frost in the air again. She was afraid of the winter that was to come. She was afraid of everything that lay in the future. It had been a stupid impulse that made her invite him, and yet there had been reasons for her depression beyond that, reasons which she was afraid to disturb lest she should discover the full depth of her loneliness.

She looked about the room regretfully as she sat on the sofa, her legs close together and her elbows resting on her knees with the fists clenched tightly beneath her chin. It was a small room with a high ceiling where the paper hung in tired yellow rolls, and the ornate rose of the electric light was blotched with unsightly stains. The narrow window was thickly veiled with two lace curtains through which the failing light came thinly to catch a pale gleam from the brass headrail of the iron bed, to make the white coverlet gleam strangely.

She was not afraid of the meagre light, she welcomed its veiling sympathy, its kindness to her features, the gentle shadows it cast across the emotions she unwittingly betrayed in the lines of her mouth and eyes.

She coughed in the smoke that twisted in oily whirls from the intransigent stove in the corner. Herr Meyer had brought her the coal, he was more tolerant than his wife, a little more conscious of his own humiliation and less inclined to censure others. Apart from this he was afraid of Schroeder and was anxious to please any whom Schroeder favoured. He had brought Kaethe the coal in the string bag which she used for shopping. He did not say where he had obtained it but she knew that he must have been down by the railway sidings at Altona that morning, collecting the lumps which the engine-drivers threw from the passing trains. But it was poor coal, it burnt uncertainly and with a great deal of smoke.

She hated the English. Because of them the Germans would have no coal that winter, but the soldiers would have their fires, their cigarettes, their food, their essential happinesses. For the Germans there would be only 'Montgomery's bread', the turnips stewed endlessly in soup, the garbage gathered from the swill bins of the occupying troops, or the Black Market.

She hated the English. She hoped that he would come now, so that she might torture him, so that she might tell him what she thought of his country, his war, of how proud she was that it had taken the whole world to defeat Germany and only then when it was crumbled in dust.

She hated the small room for its wretched poverty, the humiliation of its narrow imprisonment, and her memories retreated, to the fine days before the war, the holidays she had spent along the rolling Baltic coast in East Prussia. Then there had been the stern, implacable figure of her husband on whom she could lean, who could take upon himself all responsibility for her conscience and emotions. She flung up her head so that her long hair swept in a coil about the base of her neck. What could the democracies offer to Germany that was as good as anything that Hitler had given? She thought of the men in brown shirts, and the memory brought another, of a phrase that was rapidly seeping in cynicism through Hamburg. 'The hot sun of democracy,' they were saying, 'will soon burn every German brown.'

But she did not want the Nazis back. She hated them for their betrayal of Germany.

She dropped her head on her knees and began to cry, unashamedly, moaning and beating her fists on her knees. It seemed that with each sobbing intake of breath she could soften the sharp edge of her bitterness. Next door there was the noise of Frau Meyer's chair scraping along the floor, and her hard, bony knuckles knocking on the wall. She could almost see Frau Meyer's face, with its curiously sharp eyes lit by an indecent excitement as she craned her ear close to the wall and cried 'Frau Lenz, Frau Lenz, what is it?'

'It is nothing, nothing at all. Do not bother with me!'

She knew that Frau Meyer was moved more by curiosity than sympathy. Even so she wanted no one to pity her, no one to sympathize. She clung to the thin support of her pride with a fanatical determination although she knew that her heart ached for kindness. She moved forward on the red plush sofa, and as she did so a broken spring, poking through the rough sacking and the scarlet cloth, twanged a protest with such a paradoxically comic sound that with the tears on her cheeks she began to giggle. How like Germany was that wretched sofa, down-at-heel, a shabby remnant of artificial grandeur, its only voice a discordant pathetic twang, and that from something which should normally be silent.

She got up and went over to the little mirror that rested on her dressing-table and carefully powdered her face, flapping the old pad of swansdown hard against the flesh in tense concentration. She stared at her face curiously and with anxiety, and then, reaching across to the curtain behind her, drew it further across the window so that the kindly half-light of the room was deepened. While she was there by the window she saw Jones entering the gate, and she stared down at him, surprised that she felt no emotion at all.

But she looked back at the room hurriedly, anxiously seeking for something that might betray its general poverty. Everything was neat and in order, including the little table with its four empty cups and plate of black bread, unopened beside that was a tin of pilchards. Beneath the stove the little grate began to blush rosily. She smiled at it, almost ready to cry again with gratification.

There was a knock on the door and Frau Meyer's head, the hair drawn up to a tragicomic knot on the crown, and her face alive with an agitated excitement, poked itself round the jamb. 'It is your barbarian,' she smiled, and then frowned. 'It's so difficult when your visitors have to pass through my room. Herr Meyer doesn't like it. He is going to the Esplanade to ask the Military Government to do something about it.'

Kaethe Lenz waved her hand impatiently. 'I'm sorry Frau Meyer,' she said, 'But we really should have won the war, and then none of this would have happened.'

'I don't suppose the English would have invited our lads in like this!' said Frau Meyer waspishly as she stood there, still with her head projecting into the room like some extraordinary caricature. 'Shall I ask him to come through?'

Kaethe nodded and the head disappeared. She heard voices in the next room and the heavy fall of Jones' boots on the carpetless floor. Frau Meyer was talking quickly in German, asking Jones if he had cigarettes or perhaps chocolate to sell, and as Kaethe opened her mouth to call out in indignant protest the door was pushed open again and Jones stood there with his cap in his hand, facing her sheepishly. Frau Meyer darted her head round his shoulders like an agile bird and nodded quickly.

'Frau Lenz, please don't forget. If your friend has any bread or cigarettes...' but she had no time to finish for Kaethe grasped Jones by the arm and pulled him into the room, pushing the door shut in Frau Meyer's face.

Once there they stood and looked at each other gravely. Jones watched her intently, one hand in his pocket and the other twirling his cap. He was self-conscious, but he felt from the way she avoided his eyes, or, by taking his coat, evaded shaking his hand, that he was the more self-possessed. He was surprised. He had come prepared to be on the defensive, and he had expected her to be harder, more challenging, just as she had been on the evening of the dance. But now she seemed essentially feminine, and as he noticed the flushed shadows beneath her eyes he wondered why she had been crying.

She smoothed her dress down over her hips with a nervous palming of her hands, and then pushed the hair back from her face, turning it away from him so that its profile was lost in the shadows. 'It is very cold,' she said, 'But in Hamburg it will be colder this winter yet. We have no coal.' While he sat wondering whether that was innuendo or mere comment she looked round at him over her shoulder, almost archly he thought. 'I am foolish, I do not know your name.'

'It's Ted. Edward Jones. Not a very unusual name.'

She nodded seriously and pushed a chair towards him, nearer the fire. He sat down cautiously and wondered why there were four cups on the table. She noticed his glance and said. 'There will be four of us. Mr Schroeder is bringing my brother.'

'Schroeder?' He frowned, and not realizing that he was surprised by the word 'bringing' she answered with a touch of irritation and defiance, 'Yes, I told you. I am big like Herr Schroeder in the Black Market.'

He laughed easily, but she went on, 'Oh yes, it is true. I live very well but I cannot do it without the Black Market. See?' She held up the pilchards. 'I have these from a soldier and the coal on the fire which Herr Meyer brought is out of the law too. Under Hitler there was no Black Market, but we learn quickly, from our democratic conquerors.' She seemed to be taunting him with the information. 'Or did you expect me to be a poor, honest girl? We Germans are not honest are we? We are all like little Goebbels.'

'I shouldn't think you needed a Black Market,' said Jones indignantly, 'You were starving the rest of Europe to feed yourselves. Why don't you stop talking about being German? You don't hear me calling myself English every other sentence, do you? What difference does it make now? People matter, not nations.'

'Now you are quoting from something,' she laughed, 'but we have to remind ourselves that we are German. What else have you left us? Not you. You do not have to think of being English. You won the war.'

'We've been thinking Uncle Joe did that,' he smiled, 'The Russians.'

'Oh, the Russians! *Schrecklich!*'

'Was it so bad to lose the war?' he asked, leaning forward suddenly serious. And as she flushed angrily he went on quickly, 'No, I mean is it all that important in the long run?'

'You don't understand us,' she said dully. 'It would have been better for us if we had won.'

'If the Nazis had won?'

She looked back at him. 'The Nazis. All you English speak of is the Nazis.'

'They're gone. Sooner or later the rest of you have got to be friends with us.'

She laughed and he was surprised by the cynical bitterness of it. 'Do the English want to be friends with us? They hate us. You hate us . . .'

'No!' he said quickly.

'Yes, we killed your wife. You told me at the dance. It hurt. A German killed your wife. You hate us.'

'I used to,' he said slowly, and he remembered the black plume of smoke that had hung in the air above a farmhouse across the Rhine, 'But hatred makes you sick after a while. It frightens you.'

She stood up suddenly and the sofa spring twanged its irritation at the sudden movement, but she did not notice it. Her face was flushed with a peculiar triumph and arrogance that he hated. 'So your Churchill was right?' she said, 'Only it is you who want to be at our feet. No German would ask to be friends with the people he conquers.'

'Oh shut up!' he said in embarrassment, and fumbled for his cigarettes, 'Anyway, it's one lesson we can teach you. Have one?' And as she stood there, silently jeering at him, pathetically childish in her defiance, he burst out angrily, 'Don't your people realize that some of us want to give you a chance? I ought to hate you, every one of you. It was lucky for you that you never invaded England, it left you one likely friend. You and your rotten superior civilization. Do you know even while we were fighting it we were laughing at it. Now we've come here and seen how terrible it was we can't laugh any more. You've got your pretty feet ankle-deep in bones and suffering and horror and you're too high and mighty or afraid to look down and see them.' He stood up, as if to go. 'I knew it was no good coming. What right have you got to jeer at me?'

'You must not talk to me like this,' she said furiously, 'I am not a common woman. You forget I am the wife of a German officer!'

'And you forget I'm a British soldier!' Only he realized that they had said these things before.

They stood staring at each other, and then suddenly she turned away. 'It is not good to talk like this,' she said, 'Germany is hated by everyone. It is not good that we should hate each other too.' He was surprised to see that she was crying and the tears rested on her cheeks without shame. She held out her foot to him. It was small and neatly formed, and wore a well-built high-heeled shoe. 'The shoes came from Paris,' she said, 'My husband sent them to me. He was killed by partisans at Kiev.'

While he was wondering at this inconsequential remark he heard a chair scraping in Frau Meyer's room. He looked up at Kaethe and she smiled ruefully. 'It is Frau Meyer,' she said, 'She hates you barbarians, unless you give her cigarettes.'

He smiled, for cigarettes were a joke, a particularly coarse and tragic joke, but one which Germans and British mutually enjoyed.

As he sat down again she said 'You would like some music?' and without waiting for his answer she wound up the gramophone and gently placed the needle on the record. As the sweet music began to fill the dusky room with sudden sunlight he looked up at her and found her face radiant.

'Mendelssohn,' she said, lifting her head, 'He was a Jew, and forbidden. But I have kept it since I was a little girl.'

'But Hitler drove him out,' said Jones relentlessly.

'They were not all bad, the Nazis,' she said.

He shook his head. 'You can't say that. They may have been nice to you, but didn't you ever ask yourself questions, if they could ban music like that?' He felt that she was not listening to him, she had turned to the cupboard by her dressing-table and her long fingers were tugging at a book and a big bundle of postcards. He was strangely moved by the carriage of her head, so much so that he almost suspected it for a clever device to win his sympathy. She turned back to him and smiled, and in a flush of emotion he returned the smile, finding the atmosphere between them warm suddenly. She brought the book and the cards to the table and showed him the title. He could not read it but he recognized the author's name, it was Thomas Mann.

'He was forbidden too, but I kept him.' She pointed to the date at the foot of the title-page, 1933. 'I was young then.' She looked up at him challengingly. 'How old am I, Ted?'

'Twenty-nine?' She seemed satisfied by his answer, for she said nothing more but spread out the cards on the sofa before him. They were brilliant and crowded the dull room with a flame of hot colour that spilled across the dingy plush and strangely excited him. He looked at the titles, and although he could not understand them he recognized some of the painters' names, Picasso, Gauguin, Van Gogh. He remembered how he and Mary had seen such paintings in the windows of a print shop years ago, and had wondered whether they would ever have the courage to hang such wildly exciting things on the walls of their own flat.

'They were forbidden too,' said Kaethe, repeating a phrase that was now assuming a monotonous note of challenge. 'But in a little shop in Berlin you could always get them out of the law...'

'Illegally.'

'Thank you,' she smiled. 'Illegally. I wanted them. They are so happy.' He looked at the cards again and found happiness too in the colours. Mixed with the prints were photographs of Germany itself, its big, steepled cathedrals, its gabled streets, and the deep fir slopes of river banks. 'Germany!' she said slowly, and then looked up at him brightly. 'And once out of the law ... illegally, I saw that Charles Chaplin film, you call it *The Great Dictator?*' he nodded, and she clasped her hands delightedly at the memory. 'Oh, how we laughed at it, it was so like Goering! We used to say our Hermann went to bed with his medals on.'

'He'll hang at Nuremberg.' He felt he wanted to bring this curiously erratic conversation into perspective. 'You are sorry because of that?'

She shrugged her shoulders coldly. 'If he is guilty of those things they say. But people will feel sorry because it is Germany now.'

He laughed incredulously and she went on, 'We will quarrel again. It is not good.' She gathered up the cards and packed them neatly in her hands, holding them up before his face. 'You see,' she said with a spurious brightness, 'Now you know I have always been an anti-Nazi. You will get me work with your Military Government. It will be put on my *Fragebogen*. "She is proved an anti-Nazi because she collected post-cards and read forbidden books"!'

Without answering he looked up at her. One card on top of the pack was a rosy mass of colour that glowed against her dark green dress. It caught and held his eyes away from her face so that he did not see the strange sparkle of new tears in her eyes. Then, when he did see them, he stood up on a sudden impulse and, hardly conscious of the action, put his arm about her waist. It was slim, and for the moment he thought that it responded to the pressure of his hand. Looking into her face he saw it soften, and then she turned from him, twisted her body from his arm and went across to one of the table-lamps, switching it on, pulling the heavy curtains across the window.

'Where *do* you work?' he asked.

'You know the little shop in Grossebleichen? It has paintings in the window and glass?'

'I shouldn't think Germans would be buying paintings now.'

She smiled at him pityingly. 'You are very simple. I think you are a boy. They do not buy paintings but cigarettes and ...' She picked up the tin of fish from the table.

'You mean the Black Market?' he said, and laughed shortly. 'What a hard neck. It's a practical form of German culture anyway.'

She rubbed her arms with her hands in a strange sensuous manner, hunching up her shoulders and looking sideways at the floor. 'It is getting late,' she said, 'My brother and Mr Schroeder should be here soon.' She turned on him suddenly with a hint of ferocity. 'Please do not talk to my brother like this. Please do not hurt him, he was a soldier.'

Downstairs in the hallway he heard the door-bell ringing, and as if reacting to a signal she became suddenly younger, glancing hurriedly about the room with an ineffectual alarm, holding her cheeks with both hands, her mouth opening slightly. As she passed him on her way to the door he caught her hand in his and held it. She looked back over her shoulder and smiled slightly, and he felt the gentle pressure returned.

The door was opened before she reached it and the extraordinarily bizarre head of Frau Meyer thrust itself into the room again, and although her voice spoke rapidly to Kaethe her eyes were fastened curiously on Jones.

'*Bitte, bitte, Frau Meyer!*' said Kaethe quickly, and the head disappeared abruptly. 'It is so difficult to live like this,' she said with a mock despair. 'But there are no houses ...'

'We're in your flat?' said Jones.

'Yes, it was mine. It was so lovely a flat,' she sighed, 'But you are there, and perhaps I come to your dances just to see it again.'

The door opened and at first he saw nothing but the tall, nodding figure of Schroeder, the light in Frau Meyer's room framing his leonine head with a halo of white hair, and his face strangely lugubrious in the shadows. The white of his shirt gleamed translucently, and Jones had the strange feeling that if he went closer he would be able to see through Schroeder, to see the chairs and table in the next room. As Schroeder walked into the room, shaking hands with Kaethe and bowing condescendingly, he seemed to fill that tiny place, not only physically but with some odd circumambient aura of premonition. Struck by this Jones did not at first notice the man who followed.

It was the tap-tapping of a stick on the floor that took his eyes from Schroeder's nodding head. In the doorway Kaethe was being lifted from the floor like a child in the arms of a big man whose broad shoulders, in an old Wehrmacht overcoat, stood out beyond her slim figure like the span of a bridge. Jones could not see his face, it was hidden by the hard roll of her hair. But pointing into the room from one of his hands where he grasped her waist, was a white walking-stick, like a long, accusatory finger. Sewn to the right arm of his coat was a yellow brassard with three black balls stamped on it.

Jones recognized the armband, and knew that it meant that Kaethe's brother was blind.

The big man placed her on the floor and dropped his arms from her waist. She turned to Jones and Schroeder with her face shining in an unusual transfiguration, and behind them both Frau Meyer, her sharp, inquisitive eyes travelling over them all in a last, calculating scrutiny, slowly closed the door.

Jones was aware that the blind man was speaking, a deep booming voice that fitted his enormous figure but seemed bizarre matched with his sightless eyes. He was staring directly in front, and although he was smiling his body was rigid with a strange tension that told Jones that he had not yet grown used to his blindness. Kaethe drew him into the room and taking his hand in hers she placed it in Jones'. It was a firm and confident grip.

'This is my brother Josef Weber,' she said and spoke to the blind man in a manner that made him smile.

'How are you,' he said, 'English I speak is bad. Please forgive.'

She took him to the fireside where he sat tensely upright, the walking-stick between his knees, his neck straight and his wide, blue eyes staring with a strange fixity at the dirty chimney-pipe, as if he were amazed that anything so wretched could be so effectual. His hair was thin, and bald on the crown. Kaethe rubbed it affectionately.

She looked up suddenly to Jones and, frowning slightly in question, raised two fingers to her lips and drew them away again in the action of smoking. He took a cigarette from his tin and gave it to her and she lit it, placing it between her brother's lips. He nodded once, inhaled slowly and then turned towards the middle of the room. 'English,' he said, 'Good cigarettes. Thank you.' He inclined his head forward sharply in a gesture that made Jones think that he was not altogether pleased with the gift.

In Jones' mind was the persistent memory of the three Germans that they had captured in the trench at Guderijn. He could not, no matter how much he tried, associate them with this blind man, with Michaels' confident arrogance on the lip of the trench, Hapgood's boyish bravado. A world stood between the two pictures, a veil had dropped away.

He was conscious of Schroeder's hand fumbling for his own and he turned to see the white head nodding regularly.

'Glad to see you here with my little protejee, Mr Jones,' said the interpreter affably. 'There isn't much hospitality we can offer you British in return for what you give us, but what we can do, we do.'

The unctuous hypocrisy, and the easy manner in which Schroeder assumed the role of host irritated Jones, and as he looked quickly across to the girl, where she knelt at her brother's feet, he noticed that she was smiling at Schroeder. Her graceful femininity seemed to be flowering quickly, and the hard cynicism that had been the tight calyces for this unexpected blossom, dropped away unnoticed. Her face had grown softer, and her mouth, which she normally kept tight-lipped and defiant, had grown kinder. She seemed to have discarded her resolute self-reliance as her body curled like a young girl's at the foot of her brother's dusty jackboots. Behind her the fire, which was glowing in sympathy with this strange metamorphosis, shone in her hair and softened its ugly, artificial tint.

'Well!' said Schroeder, rubbing his hands in good humour and walking across to the fire where he towered almost threateningly above the blind man and his sister. 'This sure is a family gathering. Young Josef here isn't long out of hospital. I'm helping him along a bit, nothing much you know, but I like to do it for Frau Lenz's sake.'

Looking at Kaethe again Jones saw her cheeks touched with an angry red and he thought that he suddenly recognized the truth. The link, the obscene and ugly link between her and this absurdly irritating man, stood out nakedly in its coarseness. He wondered why he had not guessed it before, and yet half-wondered whether he was not wrong even now.

The blind man laughed, a particularly brittle laugh in which Jones did not think there was much humour. 'I understand!' was all he said, and Jones thought that for a moment Schroeder looked down at him in alarm.

They had tea. Kaethe boiled the water in a saucepan, and from his pocket, with a broad wink at Jones, Schroeder produced an envelope of sugar, a slab of butter and a pot of jam. From his overcoat he took a bottle of schnapps. 'Now this is good stuff, Mr Jones,' he said, 'For the other things, no names no pack drill, eh?' Jones reflected that it would not take long before Schroeder discarded his American accent for the vernacular of the occupying army.

Throughout the meal the blind man sat at the table opposite to Jones, eating with a queer, fumbling uncertainty. Several times Kaethe guided his hand to the cup or fork, and although she looked tearful the bright, determined smile never left her face. Jones shifted uneasily beneath her brother's steady, brilliant stare.

The conversation was mostly in German. Schroeder took little part in it, but sat back in his chair with a long, black cigar unlit between his fingers, his thick lips smiling generously. Jones found it significant that the interpreter, in this company, did not mention Hitler's name. He felt strangely ostracized by the voices in German, and they bred in him a rankling resentment. He had slipped into a background where he was of no importance, where he became embarrassingly conscious of his uniform, and more than at any time that evening he wished that he had not come. He pulled his cigarettes from his pocket and flung them roughly to the table, pleased to see the hardness and anger start into the woman's eyes.

Then, as the conversation lagged and they sat there, staring through the cigarette smoke, and now and then smiling at some inner thought, Jones suddenly asked the blind man where he had served during the war. There was a queer silence. Schroeder looked down between his knees and brushed his trousers with both hands. Kaethe looked at Jones with apprehension, but from behind the brightness of the blind man's smile the answer came easily. He said that he had served in Russia and Holland, that he had been in the artillery.

'Eighty-eights?' asked Jones, and the man nodded and smiled as Jones said that they were an unpleasant gun. There was a touch of pride in the smile which he suddenly seemed anxious to counteract. 'Your artillery was terrible,' he said, 'Cleve . . .' And he spread out his hands in a gesture of despair.

'Were you at Venlo?' asked Jones curiously, and with the name of the town the old memories came rushing back, as if anxious to intrude themselves once more upon his imagination and bring this narrow, dusky room into its correct perspective. He remembered the flat marshes, the bitter cold, and the broken Dutch farmhouses slipping sideways into ruin, the infantry in the ditches and the sunlit days of snow when the black figures of his friends stood out like fine etchings. He remembered Nelly van Huyk, the last anguished expression on her face as she ran beside his Jeep, and he looked up at Kaethe and did not realize that she frowned because he was scowling at her angrily.

'We were there,' he said, 'Do you remember the searchlights, the lights at night?'

The blind man frowned, his thoughts receded behind his smile as he too struggled with unbelievable memories. 'The lights. . .' he said slowly, and then the smile widened, quickened this time by a flicker of excitement. He raised his hands in the air. 'In the sky ... the lights. Yes I remember.' And the hands dropped to his thighs with a peculiar double-flap of sound.

Struck by sudden suspicion Jones said, 'On Christmas Day some eighty-eights fired into a little village at the crossroads outside Venlo, on the Roermond road. Were they yours?'

The blind man searched the room vainly with his eyes, as if trying to pierce the darkness, not to see what lay within those four walls but what lay in the greater darkness of memories he was trying to forget. 'Christmas Day ... four guns. Yes, yes. They were we.' He turned his head slowly in Jones' direction. 'We shoot you ...?'

'Not us,' said Jones, 'But you hit the café and killed...' He stopped suddenly.

'Yes,' said the blind man simply, and he held his cup in the air. As Kaethe took it her face was turned to Jones and he saw the anger, the bitterness there again.

Schroeder cleared his throat again, ostentatiously stretching out his legs as he lit his cigar, puffing out little balls of blue smoke with his words. 'That was a mighty fine party you had the other night, Mr Jones, eh Frau Lenz?' He raised his eyebrows in Kaethe's direction but she did not reply, and he spoke quickly to her brother. The blind man did not reply immediately, and when he did it was in English. 'I do not like these parties,' he said shortly. He gripped the stick firmly with his hands and tapped it lightly on the floor. He was not smiling now. 'We Germans are not like that!' His eyes stared brightly at Jones. 'I do not like these parties.'

Jones looked at Kaethe for her support, but her face was as cold as her brother's. He wished that the man was not blind. Angrily he hated him for taking refuge behind the infirmity.

Kaethe spoke quickly to her brother, laying her hand on his wrist and gripping it tightly as she spoke. Schroeder glanced slyly at Jones and winked, but the latter felt that the interpreter's remark had not been uncalculated.

He got to his feet, looking at his watch. 'I'd better be going,' he said.

'Well, now look here ...' began Schroeder.

'It's all right, Schroeder!' snapped Jones abruptly. 'An old soldier like you knows how it is.' But the sarcasm did not seem to penetrate the older man. He grinned cheerfully as if he had appreciated some hidden jest and nodded vigorously. He was obviously content that Jones should go. The blue cigar smoke rose about his hair in thin twisting fronds.

Kaethe saw Jones to the street door, passing through Frau Meyer's room with her head held high in arrogance. At the door, where the cold night air was sharp and unkind, Jones took her hand and said 'I shouldn't have come, you know.' In the darkness he thought he saw her shake her head. 'It was unfair to your brother and me.'

'You mean he had no right to talk to the English conquerors so?' Her voice was brittle with the intent to pain, but he laughed tolerantly.

'Here we go on rights again,' he said. 'He can talk how he likes, that's our democracy. But personally I should think it's better to wait before you say some things. That's plain commonsense, not democracy. Even Germans qualify for that, don't they?'

'*Democracy!*' she almost spat the word at him from the darkness, although their hands were still linked. 'It is all we hear, your democracy. We eat it in Montgomery's bread. The hot sun of democracy will soon burn every German brown.'

'What?' he said curiously.

'It is no matter,' she said, 'Perhaps you are right, but you hurt me to agree with you.' They stood in the darkness, with the cold air of the street seeping in about them and chilling their emotions. 'It is wrong, you should not have come.'

'I'm sorry,' he said sincerely. 'It was good of you to ask me, even if I don't like Schroeder, and I shouldn't take offence at your brother.' He pulled his cigarettes from his pocket and pushed them between her hands. 'Please give him these.' Because she took them without a word he did not realize the insult of his action until later.

At the moment he thought of nothing, for as their hands touched he instinctively drew her closer to him and kissed her on the lips, resting his face against her soft cheek and then breaking away from her abruptly to walk quickly into the street. When he heard the door close behind him he put his fingers gently to his cheek and found it wet with her tears.

He did not want to go back to the billet but walked instead through Hamburg's silent streets, watching the oily surface of the Alster moving sullenly, staring up at the sky where the ruins broke the dark blue with black, probing fingers.

It was late when he finally went home, and it did not please him to find Michaels there with his feet resting on top of the stove. Stretched out beside him on the couch, like some brooding, passionate animal, was the loose-limbed figure of 'Irma Grese'.

Jones stood in the doorway looking at them while Michaels grinned back with cheerful impudence. In the corner the radio brayed noisily, breaking suddenly into the sentimental nostalgic signal tune of Hamburg station. He recognized it, he knew the words, and it pleased him to see their effect on 'Irma Grese', whose sullen underlip was thrust out petulantly.

> 'I have surrendered myself
> With hand and heart,
> To you, my German Fatherland.'

4. Jones

He deliberately avoided her during the following weeks. He did not know why, except that when he thought of her, or when Michaels or Schroeder mentioned her name, he felt a peculiar embarrassment and a desire to exonerate himself before some unspoken accusation. Twice during that time she telephoned the billet asking for him. On the first occasion he answered the telephone himself and when he heard her voice he replied gruffly that Jones was not in, that it was not known when he would return. He replaced the receiver feeling that the action had been ridiculously childish. She phoned again a few days later when he was out, on the evening he was duty driver. He had returned at midnight from Kiel, dirty, tired, and irritable, and Jock Buchan had met him cheerfully with a cup of tea and the information that 'Your bit of frat phoned you Jonesy.'

He had replied surlily and the rest of the room had laughed and discussed her for a few minutes with a blunt frankness that turned the edge of his tongue upon them. Then the conversation had drifted mercifully, to the price of cigarettes, the old nagging thought of demobilization, the grumbling, cynical humour that laps at the walls of all barrack-rooms before sleep subdues it.

As if to escape from the memory of her and the essentially feminine reflection she cast in his thoughts, he deliberately sought out the company of others, drinking with them, standing in the eddying queues outside the Garrison Theatre, accepting the post of duty driver before his turn just to fill in his time. In the evenings he began to make an elaborate doll's house for his daughter, and as the work progressed he warmed to it, gratefully forgetting everything in the attention it demanded. The memory of Kaethe Lenz grew fainter.

In the office Schroeder no longer spoke to him of her, but he often felt the interpreter's eyes on his back. When they were alone in the driver's room together Jones would deliberately bury himself in an old and yellow copy of *Lilliput* or *Picture Post*. He felt choked by an irrepressible disgust at the sound of Schroeder's voice.

Winter came to Hamburg suddenly, bustling in like a man arriving from a late train, anxious to announce his arrival as quickly and as forcefully as possible. The skies became sluggish beneath their burden of snow. The earth between the broken paving-stones, the fragmentary buildings, and the dead and twisted bushes in the deserted gardens, acquired an uncommon brittleness that threatened to splinter beneath the weight of the dark sky. The faces of the civilians grew paler in that seared light, drawn to a sharp urgency by their permanent scar of querulousness. Along the side-streets that had once been beautiful, more trees were felled each morning and taken away on crude two-wheeled carts drawn by oxen or horses. In the gutters ragged urchins fought and scuffled for the bright yellow chips that looked like blots of bright and dazzling colour dropped from a careless palette. About the butchers' shops the queues grew longer, fixed into an apparent immobility and indifference. The long, black loaves that hung from the string bags thrust futile and accusatory fingers into the air.

The sun had left Hamburg.

The soldiers lived with hunger, hunger mute and stupid in the faces of the Germans they passed in the streets, or with whom they worked. The stamp of hunger, monotonously stereotyped, was mocked by the replete and satisfied figures of some Germans; women in fur coats and knee-boots and silk stockings, men whose faces glowed behind astrakhan collars over which upthrust cigars signalized an arrogant triumph over adversity. Not all Germans were starving. The soldiers had long ago grown used to the fact that in the countries they had liberated or occupied extreme hardship was counter-balanced by the comfort of a few. The conversation was always of the Black Market, sometimes triumphantly, sometimes with bitter, burning envy. But never with guilt. The Germans knew that they had one ally at least who would support them through the battle of the coming winter, the black marketeer. And his agents were the thin, characterless youths who clung to the darkness about the Dammtor importuning the passing British.

As the days shortened, and the November winds cut keenly from the plain of Schleswig or the white-scored face of the Baltic, the unctuous confidence of Schroeder became almost tangible. Jones felt as if it surrounded him like some impenetrable, elastic film. He seemed always to be deep in whispered conversation with one or other of the men, his white head nodding and his long fingers clasped in satisfaction before his neatly-buttoned jacket. The British despised him, but were ready to turn to him for assistance, for there was nothing that Schroeder did not know or was unable to obtain.

And the other Germans, the five men who worked in the garage and the two women who were clerks in the office, seemed to despise Schroeder too, but Jones could never understand whether it was with envy or contempt. If Schroeder was aware of these feelings he did not seem to notice them. He was always in the office early, carrying a little black attaché case. Its contents were a constant mystery and subject for speculation. It was called Schroeder's 'flog-bag'.

Schroeder went home daily for lunch. Not for him was the beggarly, surreptitious meal that the other Germans took at half past twelve. They brought out their packets of sandwiches, black bread smeared with sugarless jam, eaten with a thin soup of turnips brought from the canteen. Schroeder's face glowed with a paradoxical health and vitality that made the faces of the others seem all the greener. In the evenings, sometimes, Jones and Michaels would see Schroeder and his fat wife in the Café Faun by the Gänsemarkt, his dark suit and white hair glowing above the plates of highly-coloured delicacies and his long head nodding in didactic conversation.

Relations between the German workmen and the British drivers were good and of a rough, tolerant nature. It was a threadbare relationship supported by a flimsy knowledge of each other's language, by the cigarette-ends which were gathered from the office ash-trays and shared among the Germans, by mutual, however opposite, experience of the battlefields.

The Germans' foreman was a man called Bronstedt. He had been a mechanic in one of Guderian's armoured divisions. His passion for the unit's cars was something that amused the indifferent, cynical driver-mechanics, but they admired his ability and skill, and spoke frankly of them, as if they demonstrated a point which they had always maintained: that the German Army had been far more efficient, far more capable, far more like an army than anything that Britain had produced. That, in their opinion, was why it had been defeated, for they believed that their own laissez-faire and undercurrent of contempt for soldiering had been contributory factors to victory.

Although they thought Bronstedt was a fool they admired him for his refusal to buy cigarettes or food from them. He spoke no English, and they would have found it hard to explain just how they had discovered what they did know about him. Bronstedt had been a Social-Democrat. When Hitler came he had been left alone. He had never joined the Nazis and had been penalized in a negative, inoffensive manner. He had turned in upon himself, comforting his conscience with the faith that some day, somehow, the Nazis would be destroyed. And in this vacuum he had lived until he was called up, until during the disintegration of the German Armies of the East he had deserted and made his way back to Hamburg.

At times, as if to justify his claim to this long-passive Socialism, he would arrive in the garage with a bundle of crudely-printed pink leaflets which he waved at the British soldiers excitedly, pointing a broken and dirty fingernail at the shouting phrases, and grinning with a peculiar, self-conscious triumph.

In the office the clerks, led by Michaels, joked good-humouredly with the women of whom the most remarkable was Marie, a round, volatile woman of indeterminate age. She had served with the Luftwaffe as a nurse, and had been shot down in a hospital plane, over Normandy. The Americans had interned her near Oxford. She taunted the English with the good food that the Americans had given her, and they in return called her a 'GI Bride'. They laughed at her when she called them barbarians, and wore her admiration for Hitler with a childish frankness. They threatened to denounce her to the Criminal Police, slapped her on the behind or pinched her calves just for the pleasure of hearing her giggling scream. 'What is it that you do with me?'

But with the second girl, Lisa, a child of seventeen, they were polite and conventionally gentle. Her parents had been killed during the great fire raid on Hamburg, and although grief had now passed over her, in her presence the soldiers muted their voices and spoke with a reserve and politeness which irritated more than pleased her.

It was through these people, the workmen in the garages and the women in the office, that Jones and the others learnt something of the temper and realities that lay beneath Hamburg's ruins. It was not much but it allowed an undemanding intimacy, a degree of mutual forgetfulness agreeable to each. The soldiers' open and critical contempt for their officers, for Military Government, and all authority, shocked the Germans at first by its abandoned anarchy. But eventually it destroyed that initial animosity and suspicion which the Germans felt. In the end they came almost to regard the soldiers as companions in a general misfortune for which neither one nor the other was to blame but which could be laid at the door of a depersonalized authority generally referred to as 'they'. The soldiers, after six years of military life, were familiar with this scapegoat. Unconsciously it had borne the bitterness of their indignation and anger, the fury of their hatred, and the sharp sting of their acid humour since the day of their attestation.

In initiating the Germans into the shibboleth they betrayed nothing but their own inability for rationalization.

Having once discovered that the Germans too suffered from the idiocies and unfeeling brutalities of 'they', the soldiers readily felt the warmth of sympathy and understanding. They became verbal champions of the Germans, without ever losing their own fine consciousness of their nationality and justice. It expressed itself in odd ways.

One day Michaels arrived in the office with a shapeless bundle beneath his arm, wrapped in sacking. He gave Marie her customary smack and when she leaped giggling from his desk he told her to fetch Bronstedt. As he did so he emptied the sack on the desk and stared approvingly at the three loaves and six tins of corned beef that rolled there in an untidy heap. The smell of the crusty bread filled the room with an unusual, pleasant smell. Lisa stood up from her typewriter and stared at the loaves with a peculiar fascination. 'They're white!' she said slowly.

'That's right,' said Michaels, 'But I'll spare you one and all the Sermon on the Mount.'

In the background Schroeder gave a throaty unamused chuckle. 'What do you want for those, Mr Michaels, eh?'

Michaels looked at him coldly. 'I'm not flogging these, Schroeder. Today I'm going to demonstrate the forgiving nature of the English. On this table you see England turning its other cheek. And no puns, please.'

Jones wondered why Michaels always spoilt a good action by a hard, banal sarcasm, and Michaels, as if he sensed what Jones was thinking, turned to him with a wry smile. 'We might as well give them these, Ted, if only to stop the cook from flogging them.'

The door opened as Bronstedt came in, his ugly face creased by a particularly twisted smile of greeting. The thick, leathery flesh of his cheeks seemed to resist the attempt to mould them into anything else but the hard, scoring bitterness of age. He nodded his head vigorously and thrust his greasy fingers through his hair with a nervous gesture. 'Here you are Branny,' said Michaels, and he tossed across one of the loaves, following it with two tins of the corned beef.

The foreman caught the loaf between his hands, almost unconsciously, and the meat tins thudded on the floor at his feet. He gazed at the bread as it lay there across his arms, its brown crust glowing darkly. And as he stared the heavy skin of his face drooped listlessly on his cheek-bones and his lower lip hung open.

For a moment Jones thought that he would burst out into tears, but Bronstedt made no sound, he was staring at the loaf as if he could not believe in its existence.

Schroeder chuckled briskly, stepping into the middle of the room and rubbing his hands together. He did not look at Jones or Michaels, but sideways at their feet. 'You've just given him four hundred marks, Mr Michaels. It would take him ten weeks to earn that in the garage.' He palmed his white hair as he spoke to Bronstedt, and he seemed to be saying the same thing to him, for the foreman looked up and scowled angrily. His upper lip curled viciously. He spat out a word which neither Jones nor Michaels could understand, but at which Schroeder flushed and Marie giggled. Schroeder chuckled again as he looked at Michaels.

'An ordinary sort of character this Bronstedt,' he said, 'Not the best type of workman Germany can produce. He has no discipline.'

'Let him alone, Schroeder,' said Michaels easily, 'He's all right.' He threw the rest of the loaves and the meat across to Lisa and Marie. 'Here you are, Marie,' he said, 'This is what I do to you, you silly old bitch.'

'Mr Michaels, that is not a nice word.'

'That's what the Yanks called you, wasn't it? *You* said so.'

The woman raised her hands in the air and they looked like two lifeless pink fish. 'The Americans give me bread like this, and candy. They didn't take our turnips and telephones for themselves, like you barbarians.'

Michaels grinned. 'If you don't want it give it back, and I'll flog it to Schroeder for four hundred marks, and he can flog it to the Café Faun for six. That's the drill isn't it Schroeder?'

They had forgotten Bronstedt, and his harsh voice, coming suddenly from the doorway, startled them. It was Jones who first, noticed that the foreman was crying now. His narrow dirt-rimmed eyes were brimming with a peculiar translucence, and it was as if the whole of his face was trembling with a great emotion generated behind his leathery features. He said something halting, and the sobbing reduced his husky voice to a senile, stuttering gibber. He weighed the loaf up and down rhythmically.

Jones and Michaels looked at Schroeder who said, with evident ill-humour, 'He thanks you for the bread, and says that together British and German democrats will conquer hunger as they conquered Fascism.' Schroeder got rid of the words with obvious distaste.

Michaels hooted, walked across to Bronstedt and banged his hand on the foreman's back. 'Good old Bronny!' he said, 'Fine sentiments, except that you're a bit late with them.' He guided the man through the door gently.

It was not until later in the day that they saw Bronstedt again, just before the duty truck took them back to the billet for tea. He was standing by a work-table at the door of the garage. He had opened the tins of corned beef and the fresh, pink meat had been cut into ten equal slices. He was busy slicing the bread with a long knife. As they watched him he handed a piece of bread and two slices of meat to each of the men who stood about him, the peaks of their Wehrmacht caps jutting over their faces like the beaks of predatory birds.

'Well, of all the stupid. . .' began Michaels.

'Better that than flog it like Schroeder would do,' said Jones, and he flicked his fingers at Bronstedt as the foreman looked up and smiled sheepishly.

The incident clung tenaciously to Jones' memory, and remained a tireless challenge to his thoughts. It was another factor that helped to soften the sharp differences of the war years, mocking a hatred that struggled to live on, to perpetuate its prejudices, its hard, uncompromising dogmas. He wished that he were away from Germany, from its compromising actualities, its contradictions, and harsh, unsympathetic challenge. He knew that he was afraid to see Kaethe Lenz again because such a meeting would add yet another doubt, another confusion.

But he was not allowed such relief.

It was Sunday evening late in November when she called for him at the billet. He was alone there except for Jock Buchan, and he, with his blouse discarded, his braces stripped down over his hips, and his fly-buttons loosened over his distended stomach, was snoring strangely on his bed, disturbing the silence. Jones sat before the fire, carving the window-sills for Mary's doll's house. By now it was almost completed, and in the work he discovered a deep and satisfying escape from his thoughts. The house was elaborate, painted white with red tiles of fine metal made for him by Bronstedt, and real glass in its tiny windows. Three of its four walls opened out like the pages of a book and exposed its two storeys, the little rooms, and the tiny furniture that had been turned on a lathe under Bronstedt's direction.

Working on the thin matchwood and coloured cloth his fingers had come to life with a skill and ingenuity that surprised him. When he had begun the house he had been aware of a strange irony in the work. He remembered the house across the Rhine, with its tall ladder of smoke climbing up into the blue March sky. A doll with flaxen hair and wide, incredulous eyes, staring up at him from the floor of his Jeep. But the bitterness of that memory was dying now. Sometimes it did not seem that he had really burnt the house on that bright day when the Second Army was flooding into Westphalia, rather had the whole incident been merely a dream, pictured against the damp earth of a slit trench as he lay there in sickly fear.

His mind seemed to have lost any faculty for rationalization that it might once have possessed. It had become instead a screen upon which events projected indelible pictures, frozen into a startling immobility.

There were the damp, grey streets of the festering ruins; young girls hiding their faces from the passing glare of headlamps as they waited for British soldiers. There were the queues waiting listlessly and hopelessly outside the butchers' shops. There was the lasting picture of the day he had waited on the platform of the Hauptbahnhof.

He had been sent to collect the unit's officers who were returning from a conference in Kiel, and while he waited he watched a refugee train arriving from Berlin and eastern Germany. It crawled into the station like some lice-infested animal, crowded with a crawling mass of human beings whose violent, struggling activity welded them into one ugly body that writhed, screamed, and fought with itself. The dead had been left at Berlin, but the living, except for the young men who clung to the buffers and the truck-tops like wild animals, seemed to be no more than dying.

Above the sulphurous smell of the engine the rotting stench of that tram triumphed quickly. The buckets of ordure at each end of the trucks had slopped over and the liquid ran in evil, dripping streams down the sides. Men, women, and children lay about it unheedingly.

Slowly the train was unloaded. Some of the aged were lifted off and lowered to the platform where they sat or lay unconscious of anything but the deep and impenetrable mystery of their thoughts. Red Cross workers hurried up and down the train with soup and the refugees ate like animals.

Jones stared at them with a shocked amazement, a conventional and worthless indignation. As he leant against a pillar his fingers gripped his cigarette in shame and crushed it. To his right a young girl sat on a small attaché case, her body listless and apathetic beneath her dress, her hair hanging about her face. She stared at him without emotion. He took a bar of chocolate from his pocket and held it out to her, feeling ludicrously self-conscious, but she did not take the chocolate, nor did she seem to notice him. The fingers of her right hand began to scratch at the sores on her legs in an action that seemed curiously detached from her mind or the rest of her body. He turned away and thrust the chocolate into the hands of a small child who sat wide-eyed and pale on top of a pile of bedding.

The train and its passengers were a world on its own into which they would not even admit the consciousness of outsiders. The refugees did not seem to be aware of the soldiers that stared at them curiously, or the civilians who looked across from the other platforms in cold hostility. The old men, the children, the parents, and the girls from whom all bloom and vitality had strangely ebbed, did not move far from the trucks. They seemed unwilling to risk themselves away from its reality, however horrible. They had ebbed from it in a black ripple, and now, as the whistle blew and the engine puffed its disgust, the wave flowed back on to the woodwork, back into the smell and the confusion.

The noise was the most horrible feature of the refugee train. It was a sustained, high-pitched clamour, strident and ugly, into which all voices, old and young, male and female, merged into a cacophony that was sexless and ageless. It was itself the greatest indictment of its own obscenity.

When the train had gone it seemed to leave a black and puslike stain on the rails, that was not entirely due to the trickling trail of the ordure that had dribbled from the trucks. Down the platform a Sapper walked, lazily spraying disinfectant on the stones ...

The memory had already blotted out the sight of the doll's house beneath Jones' fingers when he heard the doorbell ringing.

Kaethe Lenz was standing there when he opened the door, smiling slightly, her hands thrust into her pockets and her body inclined away from the door as if she were ready to turn and leave before he spoke. He stared at her, unaware that he was frowning angrily and that the frown frightened and embarrassed her.

'Hullo!' he said, without much enthusiasm, and then bluntly, 'Have you come to see me?'

She flushed in anger and her head went up sharply. For once she stared back at him. 'No!' she said abruptly and turned from him, but he leant forward and caught her arm.

'I'm sorry,' he said, 'I wasn't expecting you. Please come in.'

5. Kaethe

After that evening he did not try to resist her. Almost fatalistically he capitulated before her urgent demand for his company. They did not meet again at the billet. He did not invite her there as the others brought their women, nor was she anxious to come back to her old home under such circumstances. He met her always in her own room, within the narrow walls where the fire puffed an indignant and surly welcome. There she seemed most resilient and feminine. Elsewhere she was harder, more defiant, pulling on a brittle arrogance as easily as she drew on a coat in the face of Hamburg's sharp and bitter winds.

But in her room, sitting on the old sofa, still jealous of strong light, she was softer and more gentle, and she no longer seemed afraid of him. He discovered her laugh, not the harsh, challenging derision he had already heard, but something less bitter and with a subtle spontaneity that was infectious. They sat next to each other on the sofa where the broken spring twanged unnoticed, their arms interlocked, and leant forward to watch the fire for which he brought wood and coal from the billet. But although their conversations now became more intimate, more sympathetic, they glittered now and then with the sharp edge of old antagonisms.

She began to teach him German, and he cooperated more or less to humour her. Sometimes she would suddenly interrupt her reading, break away from him and place a record on the gramophone, moving about the room alone in the steps of a dance, the lines of her face set with a peculiar hardness.

There was an uncontrolled nervousness in some of her actions. She would turn on the radio, change the stations rapidly, switch it off, comb her hair, lift up books apathetically, and place them down unopened, and when, on these occasions, he pulled her down beside him she would keep her head turned from him until she burst into tears.

He grew used to her tears. At first he had been strangely embarrassed, a little angry. He tried to suppress them with an exaggerated, rough humour, belittling her fears. Then she would speak angrily and bitterly of Germany as if it had betrayed her, repeating again and again that she wanted to leave it, to go to the Argentine, and never speak German again. She felt the hatred that hung about Germany like a thick and suffocating curtain and she beat herself against it ineffectually like a moth. On these occasions Jones was surprised to find that he did not feel sorry for her, only angry. His sympathy and affection was anchored to a sandy bottom.

Sometimes her brother was there when Jones came, and the first initial shock of the man's blindness and the automatic sympathy it provoked rarely returned. Jones began to discover that Weber too was bitter, nursing a stubborn and angry pride behind the darkness of his eyes. He would sit by the fire, brooding on the deep and impenetrable wall of his blindness. He would greet Jones politely enough, but with a coldness and indifferent attitude.

Occasionally he was drawn into their conversations and Jones discovered that there was a blindness too in Weber's thoughts. He would not talk about the small difficulties, the petty hardships of occupation. The vast tapestry of his imagination abounded with highly-coloured dreams and dark prejudices. On one evening he sat by the fire, staring sightlessly at its warm glow, his hands clasped tightly over his white stick, his head drooped in brooding. Haltingly he drew back a corner of the dark curtain of his mind and revealed something which startled Jones by its unexpectedness.

Weber raised one hand from his stick as he spoke, holding it in the air like an ancient patriarch. His English was fuller and more competent than on their first meeting and Jones wondered if Kaethe had been teaching him.

'The world is bad,' her brother said, 'The good, pure races are few. The white peoples, Germany and England should ... *sich vereinigen?*'

'Unite,' said Kaethe gently.

He nodded. '*Ja*, should unite against the coloured people. Or they will conquer us. The Slavs and the black people.' He turned his head towards Jones and his eyes shone with a glasslike translucence. 'You do not know the Russians ... *dreckig!*'

Jones stared at him in horror, shocked by the hate and spite that lay behind the impassive face, and he felt Kaethe's fingers tightening about his wrist.

He was glad when Weber was not there, when the air was free of his brooding hatred. Because of Weber, Jones talked to his sister of many things that had long lain dormant in his mind, and she listened patiently and calmly with an air that sometimes seemed to Jones to be tolerance only. He talked not only of himself, his wife, and daughter, but of wider, less tangible things. He wrestled tolerantly with her impatience and bitterness, and as he spoke he stared in wonder at her still face, the imperceptible, sceptical smile on her lips.

Sometimes they would walk by the Alster, where the oily waters moved uneasily, and on occasions, in civilian clothes borrowed from her brother, he went to the cinema with her.

He knew that German cinemas were out of bounds in Hamburg, but he seized at the chance to go. He would sit there silently with her hand in his, conscious of the mass of oddly resentful people about him, as if they were ready to close in and crush him. Even there, when there was no uniform to strike a hard and uncompromising difference between them, he felt no closer to them.

They saw films he had seen long ago in English theatres and garrison cinemas, but the picture of them now came before him in a strange significance. For the most part the Germans watched the English films apathetically, but sometimes the flickering screen drew sharp and sudden reactions from the audience, bald and harsh derision, whistling and bitter laughter. It angered him without apparent cause, and because of that he quarrelled with Kaethe.

As they walked home by the water's edge he talked glumly,

feeling uncomfortable and ostentatious in her brother's ill-fitting clothes. The sardonic, sceptical laughter of the cinema had been directed at him he felt, and he wanted to answer it, if not to them, to her.

'They're fools!' he said bluntly, aware that he still derived pleasure from attacking Germany before her, 'Don't they realize that's how we feel about the Nazis? Are they all still blind?'

She did not reply. 'You're afraid to answer me!' he said.

'Always you want me to turn on my own people.' There was no emotion in her voice. 'I am still a German. You don't know how bad I am to be with you.'

He released his arm. 'You pretend to agree with me when I talk, but you don't really.' He stared disagreeably at the great black mass of the surface air-raid shelter that rose up above them like a medieval fortress. 'Sometimes I think you all might as well be shut up in there for what little you learn of life.'

'I have been . . . shut up in there,' she said simply, and she looked up at the massive concrete bulk and frowned slightly.

'All right,' he said surlily, 'Germans weren't the only ones who had to go into air-raid shelters. Only I don't think they had any in Warsaw.' He walked a pace ahead of her, staring angrily at the pavement, until he heard her voice, calmly and evenly, behind him.

'You think I agree with you only because I love you?'

He stopped and turned, wanting to laugh. 'I've never thought of it. Do you?'

'It does not matter. I ask to tell you not to think that.' She walked along beside him. 'Young people can love. It is freedom for them, but for others it is a shelter like that,' she waved her hand at the glowering fortress. 'We are happy to go into it.' Her voice flushed with an old defiance. 'Why should I love you? I tell you, you don't treat me like a gentleman.'

He grinned. 'Don't be silly, Kaethe. You can't have dignity in this place any more. Be real.'

But they walked on in silence, and as they passed under the railway bridge by the Dammtor station, where the trams clanged a hollow alarum, they passed two Belgian Military Policemen who stared curiously at Jones in his civilian clothes. He stumbled and jerked his head nervously in his embarrassment. She must have noticed it, for she began to talk to him quickly and excitedly in German, and when they were out of earshot of the Red-caps they laughed delightedly like children and ran a few yards arm in arm. As they walked thus across Loigny-platz the grass and dry earth, hardened by the frost, crunched pleasantly beneath their feet.

But at the gate of her house she turned and faced him resolutely, as if there were something she had to say. 'Ted, you must know why we laugh. But you think we should feel sorry because we see films of your hospitals bombed and ships sunk by us? We have seen films like that made by the Nazis, and if we saw them now we would laugh too. We like your *Henry V* and *Quiet Wedding*. They are comforting. But in our newspapers you show us only Nuremberg pictures. Why do you not tell us about Eva Braun?'

He looked at her incredulously. 'It's not my pigeon, but I should think you ought to know more about the Fuhrer's concentration camps than his mistresses.'

She shook her head slowly smiling, and he went on angrily. 'All right, perhaps we shouldn't show films at all, just make a free issue of coloured prints and books by Thomas Mann.'

He knew that he had hurt her by the way she did not respond when he kissed her good night, and he did not see her again for a week until, with the doll's house finished, he telephoned her in remorse.

Sometimes, driven by a peculiar vindictiveness which he did not attempt to justify, he searched brutally behind the changing masks she held before her face. Long ago there had been an unspoken agreement between them that they should not talk of Belsen and Buchenwald. Now the thought of them was always with him, as if summoned up to stiffen his resistance to a new legion of emotions flooding his mind. He felt hard and implacable as he beat down her spontaneous protest that she had not known of those things, and he flung himself away from her angrily when she cried. She would not reply, but rose and brought him his hat and coat, thrusting them before his face until he too stood up, brushed the clothes aside to the floor and held her in his arms until she stopped crying. Yet it was when she was in tears that she felt most foreign and his spirit hardened.

They sat together by the fire, while the logs burnt up into warming flames. She was the first to speak. 'I must say,' she said, 'If I do not say you will hate me, and there is too much hate.'

'You don't have to say anything,' he said dully, 'It's just me, don't mind me.'

'No,' she said gently, placing her hand tenderly on his and smiling. Then she leant forward stiffly, with her fists thrust beneath her chin so that her head was veiled by her hair, and he thought that perhaps she intended that he should not see her face. 'Perhaps Germans should say these things now,' she said.

'What things?' he said, glad that it had come.

'Here,' she said, placing her fingers on her temple, 'We know what was done by our people and our soldiers. We know it in our minds because all the time with the Nazis we knew what they could do. But it is hard to admit in our hearts.'

'Why?' he said, 'Why Kaethe?'

'Why?' Her voice was suddenly shrill. 'Look around you, you conquering English soldiers. What is there for us? You have destroyed our cities, our people are dead, and our stomachs are empty. Our universities are closed, there are no books for the children and our men cannot work at anything that is a ...?'

'A career?'

'Yes,' she said, 'There is nothing for us in the future, and perhaps nothing for our children. We are humiliated and that is bad for German pride. You say it is good for us, perhaps it is. But we cannot escape the future except by death, and we are still frightened of that.'

'But if you realize...'

'You speak like a priest,' she sneered, 'You will give me absolution after my penance? Punish the Germans you say. But what more punishment can you give us? Perhaps you could sell us to the Russians.'

'Oh Christ!' he said, lighting a cigarette furiously, 'Leave the Russians out of it, please.'

'You do not know them. They are like the Nazis.'

'Is that good or bad?' he asked sarcastically.

'You treat me badly,' she said with an incongruous dignity, 'You should offer me a cigarette when you smoke.'

He pushed the packet towards her with a grin, but she did not take one. 'I do not want one. But it is polite to offer me one.'

He smiled again, and it was on the tip of his tongue to mimic, 'You forget I am the wife of a German officer!' but he touched her hand and said, 'Please go on Kaethe, don't let's quarrel again.'

'There is too much quarrelling,' she said dispiritedly, 'They are all quarrelling for Germany now. The Nazis are gone, but now are the priests and the little politicos, they quarrel like people in a queue by the ... *Fleischer?*'

'Butcher's shop?' he said.

'But there is no meat,' she nodded, 'There is nothing.' She stared down at her feet and pushed the toe of her shoe at the ashes that had gathered in little drifts about the stove. The leather of the shoe was peeling, and in sudden anger she bent down and tore a strip from her heel, holding it up as if it were a trophy. 'See?' she said.

Quickly he bent down, took her foot in his hand and kissed it. As he bent over she put her hand on his hair and ruffled it tenderly, and he looked up to see how distant her eyes seemed. 'You are wrong,' she said, 'I should be at your feet. That is right, is it?'

He sat up beside her. 'Go on,' he said, evenly.

She continued, rubbing her hands together softly and speaking slowly as if to pick up the threads that the incident had broken. 'We keep alive because we must. We keep alive by our self-respect. It is nothing to you. You have won a war and your self-respect comes ... how do you say it, Ted?'

'Automatically?'

'That is it,' she said, 'But it is hard for us. We must feed our self-respect on a Black Market. It is a queer thing this self-respect, you would say, but it helps us. If we say like Pastor Niemoller.' Her face darkened. 'He is a bad German that! If we say we are all responsible for the *Konzentrationslager* we would kill that self-respect and we would die.'

'I don't believe it,' said Jones stubbornly, 'You won't admit it because you don't really believe it. Why didn't you stop it any of you? Look Kaethe,' he leant forward tensely. 'I've been in Germany nine months and I've only seen three Jews. Where are all the thousands of others there were? *Didn't you ask yourself where?*'

'*Ach, die Juden!*' she said sorrowfully. 'There are so many. They will never forgive.'

'Hell's bells!' he exploded with clumsy incredulity.

'You are too simple,' she said, 'Ted?' She caught him by the shoulders and turned him so that he looked her in the eyes, and although he hated the thought, he knew that she was not afraid of him doing so because the light was kind where she sat. 'In three nights your bombers came to Hamburg and it was terrible. Eighty-five thousand people were killed. I saw them and it was so terrible we did not want to live. They ran into the Alster with fear.' Her eyes began to dilate. 'Each street burnt and the road was like an oven. The air ran like rivers and carried the pieces of the houses and the bodies. And in the days afterwards the ash kept falling on us as we walked, and we knew that it was perhaps the ash of our friends.'

'Yes?' he said tonelessly.

'You think it was good for that to happen?'

'My wife was shopping,' he countered, 'She was happy, she didn't hate anybody. I don't think she really understood what the war was about. And then she went under one of your flying-bombs.'

'And you do not forgive us for it. You do not think that perhaps we will not forgive.'

'Yes,' he said, 'but it was a war ...'

She broke in upon him. 'It is never good to kill children and women. I hate them both, the Nazis and your airmen. And your atom bomb killed so many thousands so quickly. You think that was good?' She was thrusting the questions at him, but although he was being required to answer he knew that she was still on the defensive. Yet her questions disturbed latent doubts and fears. They stared at each other across a gulf that had suddenly widened, something that was almost tangible for they had drawn apart from each other and the warm air of the room had grown suddenly bleak and comfortless.

'So many people killed,' she said slowly, 'but their death is a little thing if you are far away from it, and it means nothing. But we remember your atom bomb and perhaps we laugh when you tell us how horrible we are.'

'For all the laughs you get,' he said, half-smiling and rubbing his lower lips, 'you look a surprisingly miserable people.'

She shrugged her shoulders and her face was emotionless and cold. 'It is not good to talk of these things.'

'I suppose it wasn't good to talk of them when the Nazi boys were getting Jews to clean the pavement,' he said, but she might not have heard him, she poked her toe petulantly at the ashes.

But they continued to talk of them, driven by some inner emotion they shared but which caused conflict between them. It was at times like this that he thought of Nelly van Huyk, the thin, translucent cheeks and the crooked forefinger drawn quickly across a childish throat. He told Kaethe of that, watching her face closely to see if it would betray some emotion which her pride would not let her express.

'Josef was in Holland,' she said evenly, 'He had a little friend just like that.'

'A collaborator's kid,' he said bluntly, 'We watched them in the snow, marching along and pulling logs, with their heads shaven.'

She smiled at him thinly. 'It was bad of them to start that custom. There are people here who would shave my head. I collaborate with the enemy. I share my room with a British soldier.' Then suddenly she clasped her hands together and her laugh, however derisive, was sudden music in the cold room. 'Oh Ted! How easy it is to make you a German. You make the wrong arguments.'

He stared back at her suspiciously, lighting a cigarette with nervous fingers and then, smiling, offering her the packet. He felt that the ground was giving way beneath him. He was not making her see things as he saw them. He knew intuitively that he was right, but he sensed the sincerity of her delusion. She seemed to be aware of his thoughts for, suddenly gentle and affectionate, she leant across to him and kissed his cheek. 'Do not be angry, Ted. It is better that they are gone, the Nazis.'

'Oh, we're glad to liberate you!' he said sarcastically.

'No, we are still German and the Nazis were German. I believed in them. I say it and am proud. We would believe anybody now, or perhaps nobody. That is why I believe you.' She caught his suspicious stare and laughed again, standing up and pressing her dress against her hips with a voluptuousness that suddenly alarmed him. 'We are not all bad. You see I am a German but I can love an English soldier.' He caught the challenge in her eyes and foolishly answered it. 'You don't love me.'

She clasped her hands together, playing with him. 'I did not say it. Oh, your conceit!'

'You meant me,' he said stubbornly. 'You were wrong and you were right. I know what it is.' He drove his thoughts into words. 'You're grateful because I don't hate you, because I'm not like you expected us to be.'

She was angry now. 'And so are you! You are sorry for what you have done to Germany. You are kind to me because you think that will build houses or give Josef back his eyes?'

'Oh, hell!' said Jones despairingly, 'Here we go again!' He stood up beside her and shook her shoulders, and then kissed her angrily. 'I'm going back. We do nothing but quarrel.'

'You should not be serious, Ted,' she said, not moving in his arms. 'You should be drunk, like your friend with that girl you call "Irma Grese". Oh, I know! Would you like me to be like her, would that not be better? My friends say I am.'

'What do you know of her?' he asked, releasing her arms.

'She is many,' Kaethe said with a shrug of her shoulders. 'She is despised and our soldiers when they come home whistle and shout at her. But they do not understand, nor your friend Mr Michaels. It is hard for these girls. They have nothing. There are many ways of forgetting, and they are unhappy.'

'I'm beginning to understand the Germans,' he said.

'Then you must write a book and sell it to all the English so they can see how terrible we are. The world should be grateful to Germany for so many interesting books.' She swung suddenly from the subject with an abruptness that did not startle him for he knew she was close to tears again. 'You are going home soon. To England, your little daughter with whom you will be happy and can forget Germany?'

'In a month, perhaps, I don't know. I'm making her a doll's house, Kaethe. It's a beautiful thing, though I made it myself.' And she smiled at his sudden enthusiasm.

'You will not tell me when? Not until the day. You promise?'

'All right,' he said, and held her hand in his.

6. Michaels

For most of the time that Michaels had been sitting in the café he had been watching the lamp that hung from the ceiling like some sickly, hypertrophied planet. As the atmosphere grew thicker with the smoke of cigarettes and coarse black cigars the bowl of the lamp, a hemisphere of blotched porcelain, seemed to cast itself loose from the dusty chain that moored it to the ceiling and set out alone on an unwavering voyage through the blue tide of the smoke.

Michaels watched its course with a child-like curiosity. He sprawled forward across the table, resting the weight of his shoulders on elbows that were thrust resolutely into the beer stains and the damp oases of cigarette ash. He had inclined his head upward to see the lamp and his face had remained fixed in a stupid grin which the girl sitting at the table with him found increasingly irritating. She reached out a hand and touched his forearm, but he did not respond to the touch, and she withdrew it sulkily. She did not know what he was thinking, nor perhaps would she have understood if she had known.

Michaels was waiting for the lamp to move. When it took wild and uninhibited life, and bounded into the thickening smoke, twisting, curling, and rocking like a paper carton caught in a gutter stream, he would know that he was drunk. Hapgood had assured him of that. For Hapgood such a moment had been as good as the absolution he sometimes sought from the many padres who had wrestled with his inarticulate recital of sins. 'When it begins to move, Joe,' Hapgood had said, 'I know I'm pissed. And if I dazzle anybody after that it's not my fault.'

Although, beside his elbow, an overturned and empty gin bottle rolled gently on the unsteady table, Michaels did not feel drunk. The lamp remained steady in all the confused convulsion of the thick smoke. He looked away from it at last and his red-rimmed eyes stared instead at the girl, with no intelligence in them beyond an impotent curiosity. She seemed to be swaying in the thick air, but he knew that it was because *she* was drunk. Intoxication gave to her vibrant animal features a peculiar urgency of desire; the red mouth was a startling gash below her straight nose as she smiled at him, grateful for the fact that he had noticed her again. But he nodded amiably and dropped his head to stare at the beer stains, at the sordid rings of ash.

He was hardly aware that the girl was with him. He had almost forgotten that he had brought her here, forgotten too that this café was out of bounds. He raised his head again, surprised by the strenuous effort it took, as if it were clumsily weighted with lead shot. His eyes protested against the strain and he closed them, feeling sharp needles of fire burning the pupils. His hands groped for his forehead and be rested his head upon them gratefully. He heard the girl calling his name petulantly, but he did not answer.

Something of the wildness of the evening came back to him. It had begun when he called for the girl in his truck. He had already been drinking then, and in a stupid foolhardiness he had driven the truck along the electric railway, with the hubs of the wheels resting on the lines. He had arrogantly stopped an approaching train and ordered the passengers to lift the truck from the rails.

The girl had then dared him to take her to the Reeperbahn, where troops were banned and even Military Police were reported to patrol in twos with magazines fixed to their Stenguns. Yet it had not been so exciting as the mad drive along the railway track. Two, three, or perhaps four cramped little cafés like this, burrowed beneath the ruins that still raised agonized arms in one last caricature of the Nazi salute. And in each of them there had been only more smoke, lamps that refused to move, unsteady tables spilled with weak beer, bands that played incessantly, and strange, half-sexed men and women who sang with a bizarre joviality.

He hated the Germans he found there. When he entered the cafés they stared up at him, squinting uneasily through the smoke, surprised to find a British soldier among themselves. Then they ignored him, ignored too the girl who was with him. He belched his dislike and contempt for them and he cursed his boredom. His exhausted spirit craved excitement of some kind, excitement which he could no longer find in drunkenness, no longer in a wild animal desire for the girl. He was bored with her, and as he looked up at her, at the pleading of her full mouth and the young body pressed tightly into an old suit, he felt nothing but disgust.

He wished Hapgood were there, and then perhaps between them they might see the lamp moving and in the inevitable brawl set the world into tidiness.

But Hapgood had bought it somewhere in Westphalia ... Now he was becoming sentimental, Michaels thought. That was a good sign. Soon the lamp would move.

The girl was tugging at his sleeve again and he looked up at her angrily. 'I know you,' he said thickly, 'I met you in Brussels. Go away!' He swung his arm towards her and the gin bottle rolled off the table and crashed on the floor. At the noise the band stopped abruptly, and, grinning, he watched the civilians staring curiously. He stared back with a truculent lift of his head until they returned to their glasses and their side-long conversations. He did not see the girl get up from the table and leave him, for he had dropped his head between his hands again and was staring unhappily at the beer stains.

So many things had changed. He regretted the passing of the war. He did not seem so close to Jones as they had once been when Hapgood was alive. And now, in two days, Jones was going back to England. He would be home for Christmas. Michaels did not envy him, but it was the sort of silly thing that pleased Jones. Still he had a little girl there. For Michaels life was complete enough as it was and yet strangely empty. The ruins, the confusion, and the desperate bitterness caught a reflection within him that was paradoxically satisfying. No one could feel too disgusted with oneself if the environment was even more appalling. That was the philosophy and in these days every soldier carried a philosophy in his knapsack.

During these days he never thought of his wife, and he wondered why she suddenly occurred to him now. Hardly a compliment to be summoned up like a genie from a bottle of Schroeder's schnapps. He remembered how impatiently he had once awaited his wife's letters. Now her face angered him with its complacency, its self-righteous conviction of what was right and what was wrong. He looked up and found the other chair empty. He realized that the girl had left him.

His pride was suddenly pricked, and he sat upright, gripping the sides of the table until the metal bit into his hands, his eyes blinking through the smoke. His face was flushed as he stared arrogantly about the room, and the Germans looked at him apprehensively as they might at a dog roughly disturbed from sleep. His body was poised on the edge of the chair expectantly, and then the outlines of the room stood out in sudden clarity.

It was small and the slender iron tables were grouped in an untidy circle about the little dais where the three men of the band were playing. A single waiter, yellow and fragmentary behind his short white jacket, drifted from table to table apathetically. At the tables the Germans watched the band disinterestedly. There were men in querulous peaked Wehrmacht caps, and women with their hair braided or falling in hard waves across their faces, like Jones' girl, Michaels thought reflectively.

Sitting by the band, alone at a table Michaels noticed, was a huge cartoon of a man in a German naval officer's uniform. He was fat and bloated and he seemed to grow larger as the smoke became thicker. His body was distended within the tight limits of his uniform. His thick wrists stuck out from his cuffs and his round, boneless fingers were coiled effortlessly about his beer-glass like rolls of rubber. Thrust up from his teeth to the braided peak of his cap was a long, black cigar. It was like a dark bar across his scabeous cheeks and its scarlet tip winked and flashed sardonically at Michaels.

Conscious that the sailor was watching him intently Michaels tried to focus his own eyes on the watery-blue flecks of stone deep-set above the German's suppurating cheeks, but he could not. The German, like the lamp above, seemed to be floating above the ground in the smoke, something ponderous and unpleasant.

It seemed to Michaels that everybody in the room was now staring at him, secretly laughing because the girl had left him. He stood unsteadily to his feet, picked his cap from the table and thrust it beneath his shoulder-strap. He tightened the belt of his battledress blouse, and flexed his shoulder muscles aggressively.

He saw the girl at last. She was sitting against the wall with two Germans, a tall, thin-cheeked man in an old Wehrmacht overcoat, and a round, red-faced boy whose head was glowing with fair curls. He was laughing furiously and banging a rough, wooden crutch on the floor in time with the music. Michaels looked at him curiously, from the circlet of gold hair to the stump of the right leg that was thrust out over the edge of the chair, ending just above the knee where the blue trouser was pinned back neatly.

As Michaels then looked at the girl his anger and impatient desire for her returned. Her head was thrown back showing the long white column of her neck and her breasts were pressed against the green blouse beneath her jacket. Her eyes, black shadows in her white face, seemed to be staring at him as she laughed, reminding him that he had renounced all property rights to her. He swore slowly and, releasing his grip on the table, walked slowly across to the group. He rejoiced to see the smile drop from her face, and her mouth, open and emotionless, become somehow stupid and forlorn. The fine, exciting tension of her body relaxed. He grinned at her in foolish pleasure.

Reaching the table he pulled up a chair and sat down unsteadily. He was hardly conscious of the man in the Wehrmacht overcoat who seemed to be carried away by the dusky light and absorbed in its general greyness. Michaels watched the girl and the cripple cunningly, waiting for them to say something. The boy smiled suspiciously and nodded over the glass of beer that was poised before his lips. Through its pale fluid his features became contorted into an expression of diabolical triumph, and Michaels, although he appreciated the false illusion, was infuriated by it. He tugged a packet of cigarettes from his pocket and flung it on the table. 'Have one!' he said roughly.

The boy nodded, put the glass on the table, and took a cigarette. Once the glass was removed Michaels felt a sudden and illogical affection for him. But the girl did not take a cigarette. She pressed her body back against the wall and stared at Michaels in alarm. 'Have one, I said!' he shouted, pushing the packet towards her until she took one, twisting it between her fingers.

Michaels was conscious of a long, thin arm that culminated in a claw of prying fingers reaching across his body as the man in the Wehrmacht overcoat leant forward and took a cigarette for himself. Michaels looked at him in disgust and put the cigarettes in his pocket. 'You're the type of bloke I usually sell them to, Tosh,' he said, 'I only give them to my friends.' And he grinned stupidly at the legless boy.

They sat there silently for a few minutes, smoking, and the girl began to flirt with the boy, while Michaels stared at her in solemn disappointment. Moved by a sudden curiosity he tapped the stump of the boy's right leg and said sympathetically *'Verloren in the Krieg, ja?'*

The boy nodded calmly and answered in a clear, unhesitating English, 'Yes, I was in the *Luftwaffe*.'

'Pilot?' asked Michaels conversationally.

'No,' the boy frowned as he tried to explain, but he could not find the words and he gesticulated wildly with his fingers. He crooked them about his eyes, squinting down at the floor. As he bent over before Michaels the latter was surprised by the strength and breadth of his shoulders. Then the boy took his hands from his face, whistled slowly in imitation of the lazy fall of a bomb until he threw up his arms in a mock explosion.

'Ah!' said Michaels sagaciously, 'A bomb-aimer?'

The cripple nodded and then began to laugh, throwing back his head on his thick brown neck until the girl, catching the infection of his laughter, giggled and leant across the table towards him, pressing her breasts against its edge and stroking the boy's hand tenderly. Michaels frowned at her and wondered why it was that he did not feel angry. He shook his head with a ludicrous solemnity and gripped her arm, tightening his fingers until she winced and pulled it from him with a hiss of pain. He smiled a distant, meaningless smile. It had pleased him to feel her soft flesh crumpling beneath his grip.

He forgot her quickly and turning to the cripple again he tapped the neat stump with his forefinger. 'Lose it in Russia?' he asked.

The boy shook his head doubtfully.

'France? Holland?'

The boy continued to shake his head in a slow, regular movement. The noise of the café seemed to swell up about Michaels in a sudden clap of sound. He grinned and banged his fist on the table. 'England then!'

The cripple glanced quickly at the girl, his eyebrows meeting across the high bridge of his nose in a questioning frown. She smiled back at him simply, and taking his hand again began to caress it, crooning gently. He snatched it away and looked back at Michaels. 'Yes, England!' he said.

'That's all right, Slash,' said Michaels in conciliation, 'The war's over now. It's been a lousy war and who cares who bombed who? We've blown some corners off this place. And how!' He became suddenly solemn again. 'What town was it?'

'Bristol,' said the boy simply. He looked apprehensive.

The atmosphere lay thick about Michaels' brain, its tendrils threaded their way through his thoughts and snared their normal agility. 'Bristol!' he said in sudden illumination. 'That's my home!' He slapped the stump of the boy's leg. 'That'll teach you to go mucking about where you weren't wanted.' He sat back, very pleased with himself, and he did not see the boy's arrogant frown and stiffened neck.

'It was a big fire. It burnt all over.' The cripple spread his arms wide across the table until his fingers brushed the girl's cheeks. She caught them and pressed them to her lips theatrically. 'Bristol is kaput.'

The room seemed to be closing about Michaels. He fought

desperately for breath. In the distance, moving slowly up and down in the fog like a fat and bulbous buoy, the face of the naval officer was still turned in Michaels' direction, watching him glassily.

'Was it hell!' said Michaels resentfully, 'You fellows couldn't hit a barn door with a brick.'

'It was destroyed,' said the boy stubbornly. 'I see my bombs burst.' He flung up his hands as if he were opening a yellow, blossoming explosion. 'Bristol is kaput!'

'Now look,' said Michaels, and he leant across kindly, 'You're ...' But the boy brushed the hand aside and rubbed his stump nervously.

'We saw them burst,' he said and his face flushed with an unexpected enthusiasm. 'It was like a great garden of red flowers. We wished that it was daylight so that we could see the walls falling and the people running. Up there,' he waved his hand towards the ceiling, 'there was so much power. There was nothing that could stop us ...'

'Well, try this!' said Michaels and he picked up a half-empty glass and flung the contents in the cripple's face. Even as he did so he wanted to laugh at himself, because he had never really liked Bristol. He stood to his feet and shouted ironically, 'Good old Bristol! Up the Rovers!'

After that he had no clear idea of what followed. He heard the girl screaming beside him, and he caught a glimpse of her standing against the wall, pressing the palms of her hands flat against it, her mouth a black cavern of sound. He pressed one hand against the cripple's chest, forcing him back into the chair while the boy struggled to strike him about the head with his crutch. On Michaels' left the shadowy figure in the Wehrmacht overcoat was clawing ineffectually at his blouse. Michaels struggled to release his heavy webbing belt so that he might swing its metal buckle in the faces of the crowd which, he sensed, was closing in about him. But he could not release the catch, and he wished he had not been such a fool as to leave his Luger in the billet. He had a mad thought that all this was nothing more than melodrama, and he wished that the girl would stop screaming.

In the noise and the struggle he realized how Hapgood must have felt. In a brawl all gnawing doubts, the consuming frustration and bitterness vanished in the excitement. The faces and figures before his glazed eyes personalized the indistinct things he hated about himself and others. The cripple, struggling with exasperated tears beneath Michaels' hand, became distasteful and horrible. Michaels released his hand, and as the crutch swung viciously at his head he struck his fist heavily at the round, red face, five inches below that gleaming coronet of hair.

There was not much more that he remembered, but before the darkness burst into red flame inside his head he saw three things clearly and accurately. Standing at the door of the café, immobile and frozen into a mock heroic pose, were two Military Policemen, their blancoed cross-belts shining luminously, the gleaming black barrels of their Sten-guns hanging by their hips, and the sharp visors of their caps cutting all expression from their dark faces. As the light glittered on the brass lion in their caps Michaels thought, 'It would have to be Belgian Red caps!'

And then the lamp. As his eyes swept over it he saw that it was moving now, rushing through a wild, impassioned dance, tossed storm-swept on a surfaceless sea of smoke. He knew that nobody could really blame him for what was happening because that was how Hapgood had always seen it.

Last of all before the café, the screaming cripple, the grasping wretch in the military overcoat, and the hysterical girl, passed into darkness, he saw the German naval officer coming towards him through the noise and smoke. The sailor's enormous shape grew with every step, his huge, imponderable body swaying and rolling like an unwieldy barge. The sharp, flint-like eyes and blotchy sores grew and grew until they dominated the whole of Michaels's vision.

Raised above them to strike, gripped firmly in the officer's fat hand, was the empty beer mug.

7. Jones

As he sat in the canteen with Michaels, Jones was aware of a peculiar incongruity in the development of events. It irritated him and left him with an uneasy suspicion that it was a deliberate trick, designed to discountenance him. It was not only that Michaels, slumped ill-humouredly in the ornate chair by the window, looked unnatural with his sleeves stripped of their corporal's stripes, the stray threads hanging forlornly from the obvious pock-marks in the khaki cloth. Nor was it only the pink strip of plaster that clung to Michaels' forehead and transformed his self-confident features to a fixed frown of malice.

It was the realization that by the rule of things he should not be sitting there with Michaels at all, but should be cramped in a seat on the demobilization train crawling south to Hanover. The Channel storm that had cancelled his departure this morning and left him in an emotionless state of suspension, had thrust upon him this gratuitous day in Hamburg, in Michaels' surly and uncommunicative company. The irritation he felt was out of joint. His mind and spirit had stopped short, a heartbeat held on the stroke, as he waited for the next day and the train which would quicken them into conscious and sensitive life.

The climax had been passed, the good-byes had been said last night, the memories recalled, and this peculiar bathos had been the greater for them. Having exhausted their emotions in farewell his comrades had acted this morning as if he had in truth departed. Time hung heavily, yet he knew that the enforced delay had given him time to think, to coordinate and reorient his thoughts if he wished. But he did not wish. He sat there idly, staring out of the window at the wintry aspect of the frozen Binnenalster, and the cold pavements of the Jungfernstieg. The lowering threat of more snow had wrapped the buildings in a dirty yellow mist that seemed to lift them from their insecure foundations and leave them in the air, detached and motionless. The Jungfernstieg was blotted with the hunched figures of civilians driving black furrows into the cold.

Beneath his fingers he crumbled a bun until it lay across the table in round, dirty balls that he pressed methodically with his thumb.

In the shop-windows along the Jungfernstieg a faint touch of Christmas warmed the empty shelves with the deep green of paper holly and the bright scarlet of wax berries. Their pathetic fronds surrounded rows of Christmas cards, stamped with ungrammatical and ill-spelt greetings in English. In the designs the artists had attempted to reconstruct Hamburg as it had been before the catastrophe. In bright, happy colours of an impossible summer sun they had painted the churches, squares, and buildings which the English soldiers, blowing indifferently on their woollen gloves, knew only as gaunt and ghastly ruins crowned with snow. As he stared at them on his way to the canteen that morning Jones had been struck by the harsh dramatic irony of those Christmas cards.

Between him and Hamburg at this moment the windows of the canteen, smeared with steam into which earlier customers had lazily fingered their initials or grotesque designs, stood as thick and impenetrable as a wall. Buttressing it was Michaels' surly anger. The bitter thoughts that pulsed so obviously behind Michaels' black features were ridiculed by the ludicrous strip of plaster. Jones suddenly laughed and Michaels looked up at him with deeper anger until he smiled ruefully.

'Nothing to laugh about,' he said, 'I'd like a few minutes alone with that fat-gutted Jerry who hit me.' He looked down at the table as if he expected to find the obese German naval officer waiting there behind his cup. 'Fancy him hitting me with a beer glass! What would Happy've said?'

'He would've cried,' said Jones.

'It was no crying matter!' said Michaels indignantly. 'And that silly bitch! I'm sure she was kicking my ankles all the time.'

'You were lucky to get off with a stripping,' Jones grinned, 'Think if it'd been me. I'd be in the glasshouse now.'

'I can't see you in a brawl. Anyway, you bloody civilians never understand the squadees.'

'I'm no civvy yet. There'll probably be another cancellation tonight.'

'That'll give you time to go and say good-bye to Kaethe again,' said Michaels, lighting his pipe. 'Oh, my head . . .! What did she do, cry her eyes out?'

Jones shook his head and stared out at the ice on the lake. It was growing darker as the sky overhead thickened into an unpleasant grey. The ice on the Binnenalster was scored by white furrows that shone lividly in that strange fog. The strange, dancing figures of skating children spun on its surface like unseasonable insects.

She had not cried. That had surprised him, for he had grown used to her tears, and at first his conceit had been pricked by her refusal to cry on this occasion when they were to part. When he arrived, ushered into her room by Frau Meyer, over whom winter had drawn a sharp and bitter mask, he had told Kaethe bluntly that it was his last evening with her. She stared at him slowly, and he noticed that nowadays she no longer bothered to hide her face from him when the light was strong. She stared at him coolly, and then nodded, and they did not discuss the matter further until he raised it again later. There was no fuel for the fire and they sat together on the sofa in their coats, with their arms about each other, saying little. When he said again that it was his last evening with her her reply surprised him.

'Ted, you are so rich!'

He misunderstood her. 'Rich? I'll be lucky if I get my job back, and I don't know whether I want it back. I haven't a house, my gratuity will buy me a suit of clothes and not much more. And there's little Mary to feed and educate. . .' He stopped, thinking suddenly of his dead wife, and it was one of those rare occasions when her face appeared in his memory, clear and undistorted as he had once known it. 'Rich, Kaethe? I'm not rich.'

'You are rich,' she said slowly and dispassionately, 'You are free to go home. You are young and you have faith in yourself. You have a little daughter, so sweet. And there is England you talk about as if it were heaven. And the great things you believe ordinary people can do.' She looked up at him and there was no irony in her faint smile. 'And perhaps you will marry. You are strong inside here.' She placed her hand over his heart. 'You are rich.'

He did not know how to answer, and what he did say he found lame and bitterly futile. He put his hand beneath her chin and lifted her face. 'Keep it up Kaethe. You're rich too. Germany wasn't only the Nazis. There are other things, fine things here, that can outlast people's memories. But you're still ill. This country's like a man who's just come through a terrible operation. The doctors don't know whether he'll live or die. It all depends on him, whether he wants to.'

She shook her head and her long hair brushed across his face. He saw that its bright, harsh colour was stronger than usual, and the pathos of her attempt to keep its wasting beauty by bleaching it filled him with a pity he hated. 'Is that all you think it is? But if the doctors don't want us to live, or the other people in the hospital, the people outside. Everybody wants us to die, everybody is glad and laughing because we are ill.'

'This is silly, Kaethe, let's cheer up.'

'You don't know me, Ted,' she said evenly, 'If there should be another war and Germany wins, I should cheer, I should be happy, because the shame was gone.'

'You don't mean it,' he said increduluously, 'You say that now, but you don't mean it.'

'You don't know me, Ted,' she repeated softly, 'Germany is like that. We pretend that we don't care what others think. But we do. We would like them afraid of us, because we would know we were powerful. You don't know, Ted. You don't know what it is like when all around there are enemies, hating and rejoicing because Germany suffers. It makes us want to run away.' She turned her head sharply. 'I want to go. I must go. I would marry anyone to go. I hate Germany!'

'Because it's betrayed you?' said Jones sadly.

She sat there silently, holding his hand for a long time before she spoke again. 'You have been kind to me Ted. You have been kind because you are sorry, and it hurts you to see people in pain. A lot of things you have taught me, but never have I forgotten that I am German. I have tried to forget sometimes that you were kind just because you were sorry. A woman does not like to be pitied. You have never said I was beautiful?' she challenged.

He gestured speechlessly and she went on bitterly. 'I would like you to say that, better than hear that you think it fine of me to read Thomas Mann and collect the forbidden prints. I am still young. It is the time to be beautiful and for men to say that I am beautiful.'

'Stockings and perfume from Paris, food from Russia and Holland,' said Jones coldly, 'It cost Europe quite a bit to keep German women beautiful.'

She pulled herself from him angrily, pulled up her skirt and wrenched off her stockings and shoes, flinging them across the room. 'There! Am I still beautiful? I hate them!'

'Can you still feel them on your legs?' he said pointedly.

She ignored the question. 'I know sometimes you have thought I was only nice to you because of the food and the coal you brought me...' She smiled, suddenly gentle. 'Even that it is true too, sometimes. But you have never tried to buy me with them, or with the cigarettes for Josef.'

'Like Schroeder, eh?' he said, and as she tightened her lips, he went on, deliberately changing the subject, 'How is your brother?'

'He has left Hamburg. He has gone to my mother in Münster, where he can be warm and safe.'

'And Schroeder?' he asked, swinging back on his thoughts perversely.

'Ach, Gott sei Dank!' she said ironically, 'In Germany we are thankful for these Schroeders, and sometimes,' she added, touching his hand, 'for the English.'

At last he left. At the doorway the bitter wind blew the brittle leaves about their feet and rustled them irritably across the stone flags in the hallway. They held each other tightly, hardly conscious of what they were doing, the thoughts of each busy with the future, until suddenly she shivered and pushed him away from her.

'You will write?' she asked.

'Of course, I'll get a letter to you somehow.' He saw only the pale oval of her face, and her hair, black now in the dusk, broke across it in a deep shadow.

'No!' she said, 'I ask that to hear you say you will, but you must not write. Go back home where you are rich. I have not been bad, I have done nothing wrong with you. I have not asked you to marry me and take me away from Germany...'

'Will you?' he asked on a sudden impulse that was as sincere as it was irrational.

She was silent, and as he reached out his hand to her she said, 'No, you hurt me to ask that. Good-bye, Ted.' And the door closed in his face as a fresh wave of dry leaves, swept up by the wind, washed against it and quarrelled sibilantly on the ground...

'That's funny.' Michaels' voice recalled him suddenly to the hot, steaming atmosphere of the canteen. 'I should have thought she'd have cried all over you. That silly bitch of mine will, if ever I go.'

'What do you mean by "if"?' said Jones, looking down at his hands, where they were spread out on the table-cloth among the crumbs.

'Oh, I think I'll sign on,' said Michaels easily.

'You?' said Jones in amazement, 'Stay on in the Army? You're due out in a month. I thought you wanted to get home.'

'What for?' said Michaels with a grin, 'What would I do? Can you see me sitting before a ledger, touching my forelock to some little bugger who clung tight to his stool during the war? I like it here. It suits me.'

'It sickens me.'

'You don't fit in here, that's why,' Michaels tapped out his pipe and grinned up at Jones. 'I don't believe you've ever flogged ten cigarettes over here.'

'Don't give me the old abdab,' said Jones with a grin, 'How about your wife?'

'She'll be all right. Probably be relieved,' said Michaels. 'That wouldn't work out anyway. You don't know women, Jonesy. Never give them a chance of forgiving you, they'll make life hell ever after if you do.'

'What's she got to forgive you for,' said Jones, grinning again, 'Getting brained in a beer cellar.'

'No,' said Michaels abruptly. He seemed to have lost interest in the conversation. 'I'll sign on for two years if I can stay over here while you blokes sort out England. I'm dead easy.' He looked out of the window. 'It's going to snow at last,' he said inconsequentially, 'Are you going to see Kaethe again now you've got the chance?'

'I hadn't thought about it,' said Jones. There had been such a finality about their parting last night that to go through it again would be an anti-climax. Yet all day the desire to see her again had been latent inside him, and he clutched at its offer of a few more minutes of bitter happiness.

'Anyway,' said Michaels suddenly, 'I'm going to get a divorce.' He smiled at Jones' look of surprise. 'Oh it never worked anyway. Marry in haste, divorce at leisure. Joke.'

'Well,' said Jones banally, 'Don't marry that silly Nazi bitch.'

'Not Pygmalion likely,' said Michaels with deep sincerity, '*Look who's here!*'

He was looking over Jones' shoulder with an expression of sudden surprise and welcome. Jones swung himself round in his seat and was just as surprised as Michaels to see Waithman approaching them. The officer's smartly-creased battledress and clean medal-ribbons shone unnaturally in the clammy atmosphere. He held out a hand which Michaels gripped enthusiastically.

'Only got a minute,' said Waithman, in that peculiar, staccato manner he always adopted when talking to other ranks. 'We're passing through and check-halted for tea. Nice to see you both again. Thought you'd be home by now.'

'Jones goes tomorrow,' said Michaels with a grin. His happiness at seeing Waithman again was patently obvious. 'What racket are you in now, sir? You should've been out too.'

'Not me!' said Waithman, slapping his driving gauntlets on his hip, 'I know a good thing when I see it. I've got deferment for two years.' On his shoulders they saw the red and blue embroidered cross, stamped with the yellow initials of Military Government.

'That's what I call smart,' said Michaels approvingly, 'Like some char, sir?'

'No, I've got to go,' said Waithman, pulling on his gloves, 'I've decided to stay on over here. It's a good life, plenty to do, and a bit better than England.'

Michaels grinned. 'You always said you'd sign on if we threw Churchill out.'

'You'll wish you hadn't done it, my boy, you'll see,' said Waithman, 'Anyway, the job over here's got to be done by somebody. Might as well be done by us as a lot of civil servants from Whitehall. I'm bringing Mrs Waithman over when it's possible. They're clearing the Jerries out of the houses to make married quarters. Plenty of room, furniture, and so on. Why go home?'

'Too true!' said Michaels, 'Seen any of the others since we split up?'

'No, you're the first. Mr Smith's out, you know, settling down nicely,' and he reciprocated Michaels' faint smile of mockery, 'He'll do well in civvy street. How about you?'

'Thinking of deferring myself if I can scrounge a good job like you.'

'Good show!' Waithman grinned and shook hands with them briskly. 'Well, I'll see you again some time. Not like old times, is it? They were the days. Cheerio, Jones, all the best in civvy street, but rather you than me!'

Jones felt he had been dismissed with a slight touch of contempt. They watched Waithman leave the canteen, walking quickly and confidently past the tables, slapping his thigh with one glove and swinging his Jeep coat across his shoulder lazily.

'See what I mean?' asked Michaels, rising and stretching his arms lazily. 'You'll be back too, Ted. The Army of today is the last refuge for scroungers. Remember the pig you killed in Holland? That qualifies you. Let's go!'

That night the wind grew angry. It swept down the deserted streets of the dock area, whipped away its winding-sheet of snow, and caught up the dust of the ruins. It carried fine particles into the centre of the city and stung the buildings yet standing with a bitter resentment. In the sky the snow clouds huddled together before the wind and slipped away to the south.

On the pavements the few civilians abroad clung close to the walls, bent and prematurely aged. In the Gänsemarkt the wind clattered furiously at the lids of the garbage tins and whisked up the clothes of the weird scavengers who dug into the cans with long, probing hands. Where the lights of the Naafi canteen and the cinema flung pools of cold cheer to the roadway, queues of soldiers eddied and shivered, stamping their feet and catcalling apathetically.

Jones, standing outside the empty walls of the Opera House, turned up the collar of his overcoat and pulled his scarf across his mouth. He took the route to Kaethe's house almost unconsciously. An hour ago he had given up a half-hearted search for reasons against his going; the emptiness of the evening drove him to her.

He left the lights, the harsh music of the yellow trams, and the sad arias of the wind through the roofless girders of the Opera House, and turned into the dark streets to the west of the Binnenalster as if into a cave. In his pocket, where his fingers were clenched in the dust of old strands of tobacco, was a tiny wooden chair. He had taken it from the doll's house and he intended to give it to Kaethe. It was an odd gift, and he had no clear understanding of why he was making it, except that he wanted to leave something with her. He fingered it gently and the touch of it seemed to comfort him. He quickened his step and began to whistle.

As he turned into the road where she lived he was surprised by the light which lay in two broad beams along its cratered length. They lit the houses with an artificial pallor that reduced them to a cheap, theatrical backcloth of no real substance. Where the beams of light joined the bonnet of a car Jones noticed a small crowd of people, their hunched and wind-beaten figures sharply silhouetted and the light flickering like icy jets of flame on their moving faces. He stared at them curiously as he approached, noticing how their shadows were twisted into long, writhing shapes that curled about his feet. The noise of voices had a desultory, hopeless ring and echoed queerly in the air. When he saw that the crowd was gathered outside Kaethe's house he stopped irresolutely, and then went on.

The crowd was smaller than it had first seemed, as if the figures had suddenly contracted in size, reduced from their nightmarish contortion to a woman or two talking volubly and indignantly, and a few silent, reflective men hunched in the inevitable Wehrmacht coats and jackboots. On either side of the gate stood a green-uniformed German policeman, their faces stolidly unexpressive beneath the peaks of their shakoes.

Beside them stood two Military Policemen, their white revolver holsters hanging heavily on their duffle coats, and their stamping feet quivering the flesh on their cheeks. Jones stopped by them, hardly conscious that he was beating his hands together, going through an almost mock demonstration of extreme cold.

He did not attempt to piece together an explanation for the crowd, or the car which he now saw to be an ambulance. 'What's up?' he said curiously.

The policeman looked at Jones curiously, pursing out his lips and sucking a deep cleft in the lower one before he replied casually, 'Just another one. The gas pressure went up again today.'

'I don't get it?' said Jones.

The Red-cap looked at his companion and they grinned quietly at each other. The second Red-cap said, 'Every time they put the gas pressure up a bit one of the Jerries decides to buy it. Most of 'em make a mess of it, or there isn't enough gas. This one was lucky. She's had her lot.'

'A woman?' said Jones dully.

'Frawleen on the first floor,' said the policeman, 'Blonde bit of frat. You know her?'

Jones did not answer. He was staring up at the window of the first floor, where the light fell in an orange rectangle to the tangled mass of leafless bushes in the garden and broke upon them in an intricate network of shadows. At the window he saw the dark shadow of Frau Meyer, her untidy hair and forward thrust of her inquisitive head. She was looking down at the crowd about the gate.

'You can't blame 'em, I suppose,' said the policeman evenly, 'Cigarettes being the price they are.' He seemed to be talking of a species apart from himself, a form of life deserving of sympathy but outside the pale of human relationships. By his words he drew Jones into this circle with him, and Jones felt disgusted by it.

The civilians broke into an excited whisper, that was whipped up from them suddenly by the wind. They shuffled their feet on the paving-stones and peered round the shoulders of the German policemen. From the doorway of the house four men emerged slowly. Half-obscured by the dusk they seemed to be quarrelling silently among themselves as they wrestled with a long, unwieldy object. Behind them Jones caught the white flash of a nurse's apron.

The stretcher-bearers came down the pathway quickly, as if in a hurry to reach the ambulance before the wind picked them up in its furious arms, and on the stretcher the body rolled uncertainly. The German police stood aside to let it pass, and the civilians were suddenly silent, locked in an immobile miming, their faces grey and tired and their eyes black shadows of curiosity.

As it passed him Jones saw the stretcher and he noticed, almost casually, how the blanket was not long enough to cover Kaethe's head. A wave of her hard, bright hair dropped from beneath it and swung above the ground like a triangle of brass.

'Peroxide,' said the Military Policeman nearest Jones. 'Seems a shame, don't it?' He did not indicate whether he meant the familiar recurrence of death or the artificial yellow gleam of Kaethe's hair. 'You know her, mate?'

'She wanted to go to the Argentine,' said Jones foolishly.

'Who doesn't?' said the Red-cap sympathetically, pulling at his duffle coat. 'Well, she took the wrong train this time.'

As the ambulance pulled slowly away from the kerb Jones' fingers closed over the tiny wooden chair in his pocket, his feelings gratified by its flimsy resistance.

8. Jones

In its sluggish caution, the bewilderment with which it hesitated for long and hollow minutes of eternity, the impulsive jerks of misplaced enthusiasm that shuddered every part of its structure, and the despairing immobility that inevitably followed, the train seemed to epitomize the weariness and disillusion of the country it traversed. It fumbled its way along the line like a man gently fingering an unfamiliar darkness. The night hung about it in thick, unsympathetic folds, touched with a faint rime of snow that brushed ineffectually against the windows and melted there in hysterical tears.

The engine was a black stain of dispirited impotence, and in the carriages that trailed wretchedly behind it the windows were only a grubby illumination, or stared at the night, black and sightless. Inside the soldiers crowded together on the wooden seats, with a froth of kit, cigarette-ends, crusts of bread, and torn paper clinging to their feet. For twelve hours they had sat there in that confusion and added to it, resisting sleep with the short-lived stimulant of cigarettes, or patiently courting it with closed eyes and listless bodies. The air became heavy with their breath and they slowly leant against one another like willing lovers, snatching at oblivion with open mouths. In sleep they caricatured their own masculinity.

Jones had been surprised by the spirits of his companions. He had expected that among the hundreds of men entraining at Hamburg for demobilization there would have been a light-heartedness and an indifference to discomfort on this their last journey in uniform. But there had been nothing to distinguish it from a hundred other troop trains thrusting their passengers into the Army, rather than away from it. Nothing except a sprig of paper holly which had originally been pinned to the doorway and had now been knocked to the floor and broken beneath passing feet. A voice that had risen in a defiant, sarcastic carol had been strangled by indignant and unanimous protest.

It was as if the anticipation of past years had left the soldiers with no further enthusiasm for freedom. Their suspicion and doubt lay upon them like a blanket. Sharing this feeling it seemed to Jones that he understood one cause of it. The corporate spirit which had sustained them for so long was in process of disintegration. These men were now irrevocably committed to separation, to sudden isolation in the cities and villages from which they had once come, in the narrow streets and narrower rooms of civilian life. During that rocking, procrastinating journey towards a nebulous freedom the thoughts of the men in the train were darkly turning the leaves of their memories, preoccupied with what they were losing rather than what was to be gained.

The new fears and new doubts were disturbing, and their impress was not smoothed by the high, defensive wave of joy that they provoked. Among some of the men there was a certain steady equanimity, but in most the doubt and fear, the uncertainty and apprehension had expressed themselves earlier in the journey by loud braggadocio and deep obscenity.

And now, with night and the inevitable enervation of the long journey, there was only a surface apathy beneath the blessed cloak of silence.

Jones had welcomed the silence and the physical idleness, for in them his thoughts could be heard, and he enjoyed a strange armistice for the first time since he had stood outside Kaethe Lenz's house with the Military Policemen.

He eased his body painfully on the hard seat, pulled up his coat collar about his ears, and thrust his hands deeper into his pockets. His legs rested across the thighs of the man opposite, and he, as if by some mutual agreement reached in sleep, had stretched his across the calves of the man beside him. Throughout the train men lay thus, their bodies entwined, their thoughts free.

From the broken window above Jones' head the wind entered the carriage with a peculiar, high-fluted whistle, fluttering nervously at the corner of his collar and passing a cold finger across his brow. He stared at the black rectangle of the window as if it were a darkened screen on which would be projected at any moment some familiar face or picture. But it remained opaque and fathomless, occasionally flecked with a bright constellation of whirling sparks, that danced furiously across the night, blinking one by one into extinction.

In the silence, for the train had stopped again, only its wheels giving an occasional squeal, the breathing of the soldiers was a confused and surly grumble.

Jones eased his body to one side, supporting its weight dexterously on his hip-bone as he dragged a bar of chocolate from his pocket, eating it indifferently, thankful only that it filled in a few minutes of dragging time.

In that black window, the box which held the outside world in a limitless darkness, Jones felt that he could touch the past. He knew that he was tired, for he felt no emotions, yet exhaustion had sharpened his thoughts paradoxically and given them a fine cutting edge.

This was the culmination, the close of a life. This was the moment often anticipated by other moments of frustrated despair. This was the theme of song and coarse jest, the dream-sought moment of emancipation. It was the time when restriction, persecution, pain, disillusion were all to become a memory. This was the day when threats, promises, and ambitions could reach fruition. This was the moment which marked the boundary between actuality and memory, the second of metamorphosis.

But it did not seem like it. The process of demobilization had become too long and it was humanly impossible to sustain excitement over it. Nothing in the Army had ever been as it was expected to be. Mixed inseparably with the things the soldier ached to leave behind were the things he wanted to perpetuate. He was discovering slowly that in submitting himself to this machine he had abandoned volition and direction within himself. He was beginning to grope. The physical juxtaposition of the men in the train, locked limb in limb, the head resting on a companion's shoulder, was an unconscious demonstration of their spiritual interdependence.

The train jerked and moved slowly forward again. Its wheels began to beat a happy tattoo on the rails, and, far ahead, the engine gave a faint whistle of unjustified triumph. Past the window curled a long tail of delighted sparks.

And in the carriage a man stirred, swore, and retched a yawning sigh. Movement was an anti-toxin. Movement in any direction now was welcome.

The rhythmic and soporific beat of the wheels coaxed Jones gently towards uncertain sleep, but his mind struggled against the influence. He tried hard to determine the extent of his relief and happiness, to steady his thoughts. He sought for grief at Kaethe's death, and found only an emptiness and sense of horror. He knew that were he still in Hamburg his feelings would have followed conventionally, but now Germany was becoming a dream. The division between his life in Germany and the life that was to come in England was being cut sharply, and the razor-edge passed through emotion and thought impartially.

The cities of England were substantially whole, the countryside green and not pitted with the spoor of war, the people were once again comfortably concerned with the importance of little things. He realized uneasily that he would be disturbed by their apparent complacence, the stability of their houses. He felt that he could never see a house again without seeing a jagged ruin superimposed on it. There was only a hair's breadth between the two. This much he had learned.

Yet there had been moments that had lifted his emotions to elation. He would never forget the faces of the slave labour that flooded across Westphalia after the defeat of the Wehrmacht. They had not been filled with the wild jubilation of the liberated countries, but something more terrible in which hatred predominated. He remembered how their dirty hands had clutched at the sides of his

Jeep, fondling it and exulting over the tangible substance of liberation.

And then that picture was inseparable from the German women who haunted the camp, who sidled past him and Michaels in Düsseldorf, muttering, *Mann kaput.* I live alone!' The ugly, distasteful subservience of the Germans during those days had surprised everybody.

He would carry these memories into the future. Yet they were not the theme of tea-table talk, a saloon-bar anecdote. He must be careful not to be a bore, not to think too much of the Army, not to forget that peace was a thing in which England believed, half-ashamedly. That peace which had appeared unexpectedly in unpleasant nakedness from the edge of darkness. The train was full of incipient problems that peace was to bring, germinating with the mind and soul of each man.

He felt only a void where the memory of Kaethe should have been, her suicide had robbed him of the warmth that should have been there, contracted the recollection of her face to a wave of harsh hair swinging above the ground. She had passed out of his life abruptly, and he felt ashamed of himself for having intruded upon the privacy of her death. By her suicide she had rejoined the grey mass of her countrymen and stolen from him a memory he wanted.

To her belonged a few months that would develop its proper perspective in the years to come. He could grieve for her with part of his mind only.

He was leaving other things: Michaels, strangely unfamiliar in his shoddy self-dependence; Waithman amorally confident and self-contained like the busy civil servant he despised; Schroeder, that busy scavenger among the stones and broken towns of Germany; and Hapgood's grave at the end of the wheel tracks that curled from Normandy to the Rhine.

It was strange to think of Hapgood as a personality more alive in death than Kaethe Lenz, a warmer, more vital character that did not need the conventional emotionalism of tragedy.

Coincidental with Hapgood Jones thought of Bronstedt, and the connection between the two did not seem unnatural. Bronstedt's leathery face smiling confidently above the sliced bread and corned beef, or Bronstedt waving his pink pamphlets so certain of the new life that lay beneath the tumbled masonry. The thought of them both reassured Jones.

Yet for the first time in his life he felt conscious of his own impotence and insignificance. He was realizing that the war had given him and the others a spurious notoriety only. He felt angry that the future should now belong to men like Forbes, who could spread his fat fingers over it as smugly and easily as he rested them on his desk in Stockwell. It seemed surprising to Jones that Forbes had even bothered to include Jones in his plans for the future.

The future was to become a reality at last, but in common with the rest of the men in that laggard train he was unwilling to part with the past. His nodding thoughts went back over it carefully, clutching at old intimacies and searching for old reassurances. Mockingly they came to the front, obscuring the frustration and the miseries from which they had once been inseparable. In a last bid the Army made an appeal to him against the unknown. He saw what he was leaving, the friendships full of casual intimacy, the humour, the past, even the past dreams of the future. The old urgencies were now thread-bare, there was nothing to laugh at or grumble at. He felt a sudden sympathy for the thoughts that must have lain behind his father's frequent comment on the first war: 'I enjoyed every minute of it, son!'

Even these last hours were comforting. He could sit there in the train, dirty, untidy, yawning with red-rimmed eyes, sinking himself into that mass of khaki, experiencing a conditional freedom, comforted by the knowledge that the man next to him, lolling against his shoulder, or a man five or six carriages away knew and felt every thought and pain, every frustrated emotion.

Had it been worth it? He did not know, he did not care any more.

The train was stopping again, jerking spasmodically on the rails with a shrill whine of steel. In the carriage the men woke abruptly from sleep, and the sound of their voices burst suddenly with the movement of their bodies. They grumbled fitfully above the scraping of matches, the deep, satisfied inhalations, the hawking, coughing, spitting, laughing, and swearing. Another period of wakefulness had begun.

'Where are we? Hanover?'

'Naow! Duisberg.'

'Aren't we out of this bleeding country yet?'

'Those bloody Jerry drivers do this on purpose!'

Windows were lowered and as the blast of fresh air cut joyously through the thick smoke a soldier began to shout furiously into the night. 'Get a move on! We're Group twenty-four not thirty-four. Put some more coal on you Nazi bastard!'

Jones rubbed the steam from the window and stared into the darkness. At first he could see nothing but the oily blackness, and then dimly against it he made out the inevitable, shadowy jungle of ruins. They had stopped in a town of some sort, but it did not matter which town. As the men continued to shout from the windows until the whole train became alive with their strident voices, other voices began to answer them from the embankment below.

Jones heard the quick, stumbling rustle of feet on the loose shale, and then suddenly there appeared on the other side of his window a round, white circle of a child's face, its mouth open, and a small fist beating furiously on the glass. A ripple of children's voices curled up aggressively from the ditch.

'*Habt ihr Brot?*'

Jones stared back at the child's face, where it was caught by the light of the carriage and seemingly suspended in the air by the scarf which was knotted about its throat. It was a sharp, truculent face, and from the open mouth beneath the blue eyes came the repeated demand:

'Have you bread? *Habt ihr Brot?*'

For some time the soldiers listened apathetically to the children, and then they began to swear slowly.

'What time is it?'

'Six o'clock. These kids get up early, don't they?'

'So would you if you had to collect your breakfast this way.'

'What you talking about? I been in the Army, ain't I?'

'Give the little bastards some of them haversack rations, Yorker!'

Scuffling in the dirty mess of paper for the crusty, half-eaten sandwiches the soldiers opened the windows and shouted back at the children below. Immediately the clamour increased. The frantic face disappeared suddenly from Jones' window. He stood up, clutching his parcel of sandwiches, and dropped it out into the night. As he stared down into that nightmarish pit he saw the white faces flashing up at him, unchildlike, unhuman.

The train began to move slowly, and for a while the children kept pace with it, running close to the wheels, or scuffling and floundering down there in the darkness. It was bitterly cold. As the train moved it continued to shed its manna of stale cake and bread, until finally it gathered speed with deep, panting sighs of relief, glad to leave this human debris behind. The noise of its beating wheels grew louder until they overcame the children's cries and left them behind, floating incoherently on the empty air.

'It's all laid on with the driver. He always stops there. Same in every town. He pulls up so's we can feed the kids and the fireman can lob off some coal for the Jerries.'

'You wouldn't give anything away if you could eat it yourself.'

'No, I'd flog it, and so would you!'

Jones pulled his overcoat about his ears again and eased his body as he pushed his hands into his pockets. The movement of his feet disturbed the man opposite. He was a long, lank infantryman, with a curious lower lip that protruded from his face like the spout of a jug. He yawned so prodigiously that his open mouth seemed to engulf his face, and as he closed his lips he licked them like a cat. He returned Jones' stare and grinned, nodding his head in an expression of tolerant disgust that summed up not only his opinion of this journey but of the whole of life. It was a philosophy in a gesture.

Jones grinned back, comforted by the quick intimacy of the incident, and he closed his eyes. His thoughts began to beat in rhythm with the wheels, returning and ebbing with mechanical regularity. In that tightly-sealed carriage he and the others had passed untouched through hunger and desolation. The railway line was a slender thread that crossed a desert of uncertainty and despair, but it was anchored to security somewhere in England.

Or was it? Jones was not sure any more. The future was hard to assess, and of late it had become something beyond the control of his hands or the grasp of his mind. He had lived so long with little groups of men, each dependent upon their collective skill and ingenuity, that he had come to accept their natural intelligence and compassion as a microcosm of humanity. Now he was no longer sure that their tolerance was typical.

The films and the newspapers had shown him less familiar faces. In the world beyond this railway carriage, where great things were happening, he was conscious of the sombre men who were entering trains, opening portfolios, making speeches, pouring out reassurances. All of them were busy with a furious energy that frightened him. Their faces seemed cold, they lacked the spontaneous intimacy he had come to expect, like the infantryman opposite. He looked into their faces expecting to find an expression that would remind him of Hapgood, of Nelly van Huyk, of Tomsett, Pearce, Jordon, or Michaels. Even of Waithman. But they were strangers to him.

Now he was returning to them, returning to Brixton Road, to the french-polished counter and Mr Forbes' calculated good humour. It was no longer of any importance that he had seen a nation rotting. It would be of no interest that his heart had once found happiness in a bent cigarette shared in a slit trench. No more would be required of him than the dutiful docility of six years ago. Those years would be the dead years for Mr Forbes, it would not matter to him what Jones had done with them. His cold, dispassionate eyes would suggest that it was a presumption for Jones even to think of them.

Yet they had been *lived*. He wanted more from them, more repayment than just an intangible victory. It seemed incongruous that these chill-souled men, leaning confidently across the microphones, or stepping briskly from their aeroplanes, were really to carry the world upon their shoulders. Within himself he felt a new hatred stirring, a hatred of those who in their hearts had always stayed at home. He knew it was an unjust and childish prejudice, and he sensed, somewhat obscurely, that such feelings were only a new defensive wall.

The end of the war had not been as he had expected it. That had not really surprised him, but he wondered now why he felt a stranger in the world, now after the intimacy he had shared with joy, with suffering, and despair.

He wondered whether Michaels had been right. 'You'll be back too, Ted!' Or Waithman. Was England going to be as bad as that? Would it have been wiser to hibernate here in Germany, unconscious that it was a storm-centre? He could not agree, he felt closer to Hapgood, and he remembered Tomsett's philosophy on change. 'It always browns me off, Ted, to go to a new unit. But then I tell myself there's good friends to be made everywhere.'

The infantryman was awake, cramped in his narrow seat as if he were compressed by the weight of his feelings. The lines of his long face were immobile and his head nodded ridiculously with the rocking of the train. As though he had been waiting for Jones to open his eyes the infantryman pulled his hand from his side and thrust his cigarette-tin before Jones' face. He did not ask any conversational repayment, it was enough to have offered the cigarette, and he leant back and smoked, with his eyes closed and his lip jutting forward. As he nodded slowly into sleep, grunting fitfully, the cigarette fell from his fingers to his knees, and Jones leant forward quickly, nipped out the end with a smile, and placed the cigarette on the window-ledge.

The train was moving faster now, with a peculiar enthusiasm that rattled and banged and shuddered. The carriage had grown quiet, sleep had come again to most of the men there, except those who sat wide-eyed and thoughtful, staring at their companions or the black face of the windows.

Slowly Jones stood up, shivering his body beneath his overcoat, and yawning lazily. He stepped over the legs that barred his way, and pushed the doll's house more securely on to the rack. Then he walked unsteadily down the carriage, past the lavatory, and into the guard's van.

The floor was covered with bodies, wrapped silently in their blankets and rocking gently with the sustained motion of the train. But at the end, beneath the yellow light, three soldiers sat by the guard. He was an old and morose figure in a blue and red uniform that hung about him in loose folds. He was holding an enamel mug in his hands, and into it one of the soldiers was pouring a twisted, amber stream of cognac. The guard was drunk already and Jones saw the tears like gelatinous beads clinging to the grey, stubbly beard on the old man's chin. His waistcoat and trouser leg were spattered with crumbs of bread and corned beef. He was crying without much emotion.

'What's the matter with him?' said Jones to the soldier with the cognac bottle.

'He's all right,' said the man laconically, 'I don't think he's had anything to eat before today. He's tried to throw himself off the train twice, and he's been kissing my mate here and shouting "Germany kaput"! We'll get him really piddled so's he can go to sleep.'

'How about the train?'

The man grinned. 'That's all right. They know the way up front. Turn sharp right once we get into Belgium.'

The old man stared up from his knees apathetically, and the tears welled out of his eyes and ran down his cheeks to fall like broad, spattering jewels among the crumbs on his waistcoat. He raised the quivering mug to his lips and shuddered as the fierce spirits burnt him. His body shook with a horrible, soundless cough. The soldiers laughed. *'Prima!* Eh, Dad?'

He looked up at them and nodded sagely as if he had heard a great truth.

Jones left the guard's van and went out to the vestibule where two men lay together in a crude bed of their own making above the noisy wheels. Their heads were under their overcoats and their bodies curled embryo-like beneath the blankets. He stepped over them in the darkness and opened the window of the door. He leant out, exhilarating in the quick rush of air past his face, looking upward to where the sky was a black arras embroidered with faint silver stars. Below the train the darkness moved swiftly, a black river changing shape in twisting, endless convolutions.

He was going home. There was an odd, artificial roundness in the symmetry of events. It had all begun on a train, in a cattle-truck smelling vilely of dung and lime. It had begun in darkness, this peculiar country, a darkness beyond Cleve, torn by flame and full of ugly death. And now for him it was ending the same way, abruptly, uncompromisingly. It was becoming an incident.

He suddenly knew that despite these doubts he was glad to be going home, and it was not just the joy of escape. He had lost his old intransigence and yet he realized that these years had perhaps been the most compromising of all his life. They had meant more than the convenient division of his memories into three water-tight compartments: before the war, during the war, since the war, just as his parents had once divided their lives. He wondered if that was all it had meant to them.

He felt a peculiar impatience, a desire to get things done, to see them done. He could not understand why he felt the pressure of a great urgency, only that it was there. He wondered why he felt like this, whether it was because he was now thirty, or whether it was because to him delay in human happiness now meant the stagnant desolation he was leaving.

As the wind beat with a refreshing coolness on his face he knew that he must now fight his own cynicism. He wanted to live, and he found that he wanted it most of all because he wanted others to live. Again the faces of Hapgood and Bronstedt drifted into his mind without sadness, and although they comforted him he fought against them by trying to clutch at the cold, spiritless thought of Kaethe Lenz. He felt angered by the sharp and sudden termination of her life, the gesture of bitter finality. It moved him, but he could not sympathize with it.

He stayed by the window until the train began to hesitate again, jerking and finally relaxing into an agonizing crawl. The darkness might have become so thick that even the panting energy of the engine could not penetrate it, but as he looked up from the ground he saw that the night was over. To the west, ahead of the train, the sky had grown grey, a warmthless, chilling colour that was a mere dilution of the night. Silhouetted against it were the inevitable ruins of another town.

As the train stopped the untidy clamour of children's voices swirled about it again. There must have been scores of them down there in the darkness, scrambling and fighting on the loose earth. The shrill insistence of their voices had one theme only.

'Habt ihr Brot?'

He could not see them, he could hear only their odd voices, and as he looked along the lighted train he saw the heads of his companions projecting uncomfortably. Here and there an arm joined the heads, tossing a white bundle in a parabola which the darkness swallowed before it was completed. He was suddenly aware of the nature of the things he was leaving behind.

A voice from behind startled him. One of the sleepers was sitting up, rubbing his hair furiously. 'I'd rather give these little sods bread than give the Belgians ten francs for the water they'll be flogging us once we cross the border. Oh Christ, what a mucking journey!'

Jones looked to the west again and saw that the dawn was coming quickly. The air was sharper as if it too had awoken. Already the grey ribbon along the horizon had widened and crept higher in the sky, and at its lowest fringe it was flushed with crimson. The clouds were visible now, a wide shore of sand rippled by the night ebb, and each corrugation caught the fire and glory of a sun not yet risen.

The darkness drew back from the sky and revealed a grandeur that transfixed Jones with a peculiar happiness and excitement. It gave to the day a significance beyond all others, a greeting not only to himself but to all the others on the train. He rubbed his hands, straightened his body, and stamped his feet. He lit a cigarette and felt the comfortable tug of hunger in his stomach.

The light grew quickly until it seeped down into the ditch below the train and drained the pale shadows from the children moving there. The grey ruins on either side of the track lost their gauntness as the sun suffused them with life. All night they had stood sleepless, mourning their own death. Now they were warm and alive, however grotesque. In the early daylight the train contracted in size, shrinking beneath the vast bowl of the sky. Even the wind was stilled by the magnificence above it.

Jones still gazed at the clouds as they moved out of the darkness and gathered in welcome about the rising sun. Along the train he heard the voices swelling, mixed with laughter and the music of a mouth organ which, for once, was not sad or nostalgic. He smiled slowly to himself. He did not look down to the ditch again, to the darkness and ugliness that were moving there. The new day held his attention.

But, sensing an enemy in the fine, glowing optimism of the dawn, the children swarmed up the embankment into its light, standing there blinking, screwing up their mouths with a pathetic truculence. Their voices rose higher in a shrill, desperate treble:

'*Habt ihr Brot?* Have you bread?'

www.panmacmillan.co.uk/bello

Lightning Source UK Ltd.
Milton Keynes UK
UKHW010258270721
387830UK00002B/74